D0972075

Other Avon Books by
Nancy Kress

AN ALIEN LIGHT

BRAINROSE

NANCY KRESS

AVON BOOKS · NEW YORK

For Marcos, with my love

AVON BOOKS
A division of
The Hearst Corporation
1350 Avenue of the Americas
New York, New York 10019

Copyright © 1990 by Nancy Kress
Cover art by Dorian Vallejo
Published by arrangement with the author
Library of Congress Catalog Card Number: 89-38126
ISBN: 0-380-71015-3

Published in hardcover by William Morrow and Company, Inc.; for information address Permissions Department, William Morrow and Company, Inc., 1350 Avenue of the Americas, New York, New York 10019.

First Avon Books Printing: July 1991

AVON TRADEMARK REG. U.S. PAT. OFF. AND IN OTHER COUNTRIES, MARCA REGISTRADA, HECHO EN U.S.A.

Printed in the U.S.A.

RA   10 9 8 7 6 5 4 3 2 1

"The thing that hath been, it is that which shall be; and that which is done is that which shall be done: and there is no new thing under the sun.

"Is there any thing whereof it may be said, See, this is new? it hath been already of old time, which was before us."

—ECCLESIASTES 1:9–10

PROLOGUE: ROBBIE

JUNE, 2022

The front gate of the Institute was blocked by a Gaeist demonstration that the cabbie wouldn't, or couldn't, drive through. Robbie Brekke, carrying his old blue duffel in one hand and a new real-leather travel case in the other, paid the driver and climbed out to watch.

It looked like fun. Stodge fun, but fun. Men and women in short white robes, vaguely Oriental in cut, formed three ragged circles. Each figure twirled slowly, one hand shielding a lit white candle. It was still an hour before twilight; the candle flames could hardly be seen. This bothered no one. In the center of each circle a woman—always a woman—knelt to play a music box set to draw out each note in an eerie wail. Everyone smiled.

A girl from the fringe of the closest circle walked over to Robbie and held out a blue-green rose, its variegated petals familiar from a thousand electronic billboards.

"The world is a living rose, Brother."

"And so are you," Robbie said, smiling at her. Her expression shifted from professional beatitude to a sparkly, slick flirtatiousness. She had thick black lashes above bright violet eyes, a wickedly expensive-looking job. Young Gaeists were often rich. So were old ones, but old ones didn't interest Robbie.

"You are part of the world, Brother, part of the rose. Nothing you can do is foreign to Mother Gaea."

"We could try," Robbie said softly.

"Are you familiar with Mother Gaea, Brother?"

"Not as familiar as I'd like to be."

She dimpled. The dimples looked expensive, too. Expensive—and obvious. Robbie decided to push. "For instance, there's something I've always wondered about Gaeists . . ."

"Yes?" When he didn't answer, only went on smiling, she took a step closer. "Yes?"

"Is it true that you're all required to be naked under your robes?"

The girl gave a delighted little gasp of laughter. Turning away from him, she flounced back to her circle. Robbie grinned, waiting. Halfway, the girl paused, threw a glance over her shoulder, and flipped the back of her kimono to her waist. On her smooth pink ass shone a holographic rose.

Robbie laughed. The girl disappeared into the dancers. Too bad, he thought, that he had such an important appointment— but he did.

And no, it *wasn't* too bad. This was his big chance. It was, in fact, fucking *wonderful*.

Another cab pulled up to the Institute gate. A man in his thirties got out, carrying a briefcase. He limped. The cab pulled away, leaving the man scowling at the Gaeists as if at shit on his shoes.

Robbie shrugged. Some people had no sense of fun. Or of adventure. Holding the blue-green rose, Robbie waded into the joyous twirling Gaeists, flashing his smile at everybody. They all smiled back. The sea of white robes parted for him, and he reached the electrified and barbed-wire gate of the Rochester, New York, franchised Previous Life Access Surgery Institute.

1 CAROLINE

Someone had put a vase of yellow dahlias on the featureless institutional dresser, and beside it a blank name tag, white glossy face bordered in blue. A name tag! Caroline felt the hysterical laughter well up inside as she dropped her purse on the bed and walked to the dresser, trailed by a fat and too solemn "hostess."

"Is the room all right, Ms. Bohentin?"

"It's a *name tag*."

The woman glanced without interest at the dresser. "Yes. For the reception tonight. Dinner this first night will be brought to your room, and then Dr. Armstrong wants to see all the surgical clients at eight o'clock in the Rose Room. That's on the second floor off the—Ms. Bohentin?"

"A name tag," Caroline said.

"Well, yes, but I don't see what—"

"A *name* tag!"

"Please—try to control yourself!"

"I am," Caroline gasped, between whoops of laughter. "I'm . . . sorry. It's just that I had this sudden picture of all of us writing frantically, crouched over our desks . . . late to the reception . . . because we're trying to fit on a two-by-three square all the names we'll have in a few days—every one.

'Hello—who are you?' 'Third from the bottom, left column—can't you read?' "

She was off again, whooping like a kid. This had to stop. The hostess—nurse, bellboy, whatever she was—stood stiffly, hands by her sides, white uniform straining across a decidedly sloppy bust, poor thing. Caroline focused on the nurse's left earring: gold-colored helix enclosing a chip of blue plastic. An old trick, but it worked; you couldn't have hysterics while concentrating fiercely on an earring; it was too boring. The manic laughter stopped. Caroline held out her hand to the hostess, who took it reluctantly.

"I *am* sorry. Please forgive me. I'm not crazy, really. The name tag just struck me as funny."

"Well, I . . . if you need anything else, the terminal screen folds out from the wall like this . . . you can position it over the desk or the bed. Only the PLAS programs are voice-operated—standard banks key in manually. The list of Institute call codes is right here. Or you can use the phone. Room service closes at eleven o'clock, but I'm sure that for you the concierge—"

"I promise not to make any extra work," Caroline said, smiling. She could feel herself putting everything into it, working for a response. *Nada*. The woman let go of her hand as if it had been a cadaver.

"Then if you want to settle in . . ."

"You *can* tell me I'm crazy, if you like. Or just nervous. Oh, go ahead—you'll feel much better."

"I'm sure your preliminary psychological evaluation is in order, Ms. Bohentin," the hostess said primly.

"I doubt you're sure of any such thing," Caroline said, still smiling warmly, still trying. The woman didn't answer. She closed the door with pointed calm.

Bitch. Well, no, probably not. To be fair. Probably just jaded by too many weird people passing through. Through this room, through the Institute, through time. Through the looking glass.

Just the same—it had too been funny. A name tag. "You Tarzan—me Jane/Messalina/Nagako/Maria/Bootsie and Og."

Still grinning, Caroline began to unpack the suitcases the staff had piled on the bed. Like all the hospital rooms Caroline had ever seen—and this *was* a hospital, no matter what it chose to call its nurses, no matter that there was supposed to be a cozy little bar on the top floor—this one was pretending ignorance of the advanced technology for which it existed. Antique bed, dresser, sleek Japanese desk, two comfortable chairs, mediocre framed prints, and standard-issue screen. But if the room was smaller than she had expected, the closet was much larger. What had the old building been before it was remodeled into the Institute For Previous Life Access Surgery? Or maybe one needed an extensive wardrobe for this desperate adventure. Did one need more clothes for past lives? Did one need past lives? Did one need?

"Like mushrooms need bees/Like goldfish need knees/Like binaries need threes/—I neeeeeeeed you." God, what terrible music Jeremy had written for that show. And she had sung it just as terribly. No wonder they'd closed in three days. Could it really have been fifteen years ago?

In a few more days, fifteen years would seem like only a minute fraction of her memories, instead of nearly one half.

How small a fraction? Intrigued, Caroline dropped the blue leather dress she had been unpacking and flipped on the screen. If she eventually remembered, say, back to 2000 B.C.—just to pick an arbitrary date—then that was 4,022 years, divided into fifteen years equals .0037294 percent. Only thirty-seven ten-thousandths of her life would have occurred since she sang Jeremy's stupid lyrics, divorced him, married Charles, had Catherine, and all the rest of it. An insignificant percentage. Hardly worth noticing. The last fifteen years would hardly count at all.

Caroline stared at the numbers on the screen. Then she punched it off, strode to the window, and yanked open the curtains.

Dazzling blue light flooded the room from water and sky. Lake Ontario stretched unbroken to the horizon, a gently rocking mirror for June sunshine. Sunshine in Rochester, New York: an omen. The average, she remembered, was only 103 days a year. Where had she read that? No way to remember; bits of essentially useless information stuck to her like lint. "You have that sort of mind," Charles had told her in the melodious voice he used for cruelty. "Built for either the theatrical or the trivial."

It was true. But that didn't mean she had to forgive Charles. For anything.

A discreet knock sounded. Not turning from the window, Caroline called, "Come in." A young, white-uniformed waiter with the full name of the Institute on his headband entered with a steaming tray. He set up a small table and laid out the dishes with meticulous ceremony. Caroline recognized the imitation of the Japanese service currently popular in the New York dining clubs. Amused, Caroline smiled at him. The boy bowed stiffly, blond head botching Oriental nuances.

The dinner smelled surprisingly good: lamb in a thyme sauce, she guessed. But she knew she was not going to be able to eat. She poured herself a cup of coffee from the antique silver pot fitted with optic-controlled warmer and returned to the window.

Her room was on the highest floor, the fifth. Between the Institute and Lake Ontario to the north sloped a stretch of green lawn dotted with the tops of maple trees and stone benches. Woods bordered the east. To the west lay a jumble of rooftops cut off from the Institute by a very high fence. And, Caroline guessed, by an unseen electronic shield as well. The

Institute was apparently a well-protected enclave. Rochester, she suddenly remembered, had been home to the first municipal cemetery in the entire United States.

She stayed by the window, watching first the sun set at the west end of the lake and then the slate-blue evening gather over the horizon, until it was time to put on her glossy name tag and go down to the reception for clients for Previous Life Access Surgery.

In the Rose Room of the Institute three dozen people stood holding glasses. French doors opened onto a terrace overlooking the lake, where more people leaned against a wrought-iron railing in the June twilight. Caroline thought that the room looked schizophrenic: on the north wall straight heavy velvet curtains, carved molding on the French doors, and the terrace; on the south wall a huge high-resolution display screen with an unabashedly bleak console like an airline cockpit. Fake nineteenth-century elegance outstared by real contemporary blankness. She felt instantly cheered.

"Dead TV wins," she said to the bartender who handed her a glass of wine. He looked startled.

"Pardon?"

"Have I got my name tag on straight?"

"Yes, ma'am."

"Good." She smiled at him. He turned away and continued to slice lemons.

Someone on the terrace laughed loudly. Caroline sipped her drink and eyed the people. She had a good eye; it was the attribute her father had liked best about her, the source of their best times together. "DBase that one, Princess." And even as young as thirteen or fourteen she could do it, sizing up character, extrapolating details, playing up the drama or the ridicule or the weirdness, until they were both wrapped in the delicious intoxicating laughter of their own private ongoing frenetic party. After the party was over—

after Jeremy, after Charles, after Catherine—she had kept the eye. A legacy.

The man and woman at the far end of the room were both doctors: They stood with home-turf ease, exuding uninvolved courtesy like delicate scent.

The fat woman with terrified eyes was of course a surgical candidate. She wore a ruffled red dress with a red headband, too rich and too frowsy. She wanted desperately to not be here—so why was she? Possibly she had one of the nerve disorders, Alzheimer's or MS, that getting plazzed cured merely as a side effect.

The man in the shabby jacket and plain headband was an academic—outside chance, a poet—spending the savings of a lifetime on some romantic conception of his own past.

The gorgeous woman holding court in the corner— obviously an actress. Older than she looked, less recognizable than she wished. Caroline shrugged and looked away. She had grown up with actors.

But the teenage boy in the expensive Japanese-cut suit and silk headband—him she couldn't place. Getting plazzed was not for children. Wasn't it even illegal? The boy had smooth dark features. Indian? Arab? As she watched, he crossed the room to talk with the doctors, interrupting their conversation with an imperious, faintly foreign gesture which made both turn toward him respectfully. Better and better!

Another burst of laughter exploded on the terrace. Caroline walked through the French doors. Four people stood at the far end of the railing, silhouetted against the darkening sky. The younger of the two men was talking. ". . . and then of course Liberian security couldn't be left out, so *they* showed up the next night at the marina," and both women laughed. The young man looked past them, caught Caroline's eye, and made a join-us gesture.

She found herself smiling back, although what he was couldn't have been more obvious, or less interesting. Tall, blond, dressed in a good-but-shabby jacket and gaudy head-band tied—not clipped—at a raffish angle. From the way he leaned on the railing, the tilt of his head, and the easy way he appraised *her*, Caroline could dBase his whole history. Petty con man, social climber, charm enough but not grit enough to attract the money he undoubtedly wanted. A flashy pilot fish, endlessly diverting, endlessly circling. Who had paid for him to come here?

His handshake lingered just a second too long. "Robbie Brekke."

"Caroline Bohentin."

"So I see," Robbie said, touching the name tag over her left breast. His blue eyes sparkled. His own name tag said TO BE ANNOUNCED. "This is Jane Fexler, Sandy Ochs, Joe McLaren."

"I'm not really here," Jane Fexler said in a high, breathy voice. "I mean, I'm not getting plazzed. I'm just here to say good-bye to my husband over . . . um, there." She waved vaguely toward the other end of the terrace and snuggled her arm through Robbie's. Sandy Ochs, a dumpy, flat-featured young woman in dark blue canvas jumpsuit, looked suddenly glum.

Amused, Caroline said, "Your husband is having the operation."

"Yes," Jane said. And then, with sudden savagery, "Maybe it will make him somebody better."

"Maybe it will make us all somebody better," Caroline said.

"Not me," Robbie said with such mock solemnity that Caroline laughed. "What will it make you, Caroline Bohentin?"

"Who knows?" she said, turning away the light challenge, still smiling. But a little silence followed her words.

Sandy Ochs broke it. She said suddenly, with unnecessary force, "I know what *I'll* be. I already know. I was a queen of Egypt, and all I need this operation for is to convince the rest of my stupid relatives that I have the powers I say I have."

Oh, God, Caroline thought. There would of course have to be one, there always was. But why did it have to be the second person she talked to? Robbie said silkily, " 'Powers'?"

"To save mankind!"

"Mankind can certainly use a savior." His voice was respectful, interested: He was baiting her.

"See, *you* understand," Sandy Ochs said plaintively. "Why can't my parents and sister?"

"Perhaps we knew each other in a past life," Robbie said gravely. He tried to catch Caroline's eye; she evaded the glance.

"Oh, we did," Sandy Ochs said eagerly. "I knew it as soon as you walked into the room."

"Ah," Robbie said.

"A queen of *Egypt*," Sandy Ochs said fiercely, and glared at each of them in turn. Caroline was startled by her eyes. They were a flat and shiny black, blank as pebbles.

"Did you have your own temple, Queen Sandy?" Robbie asked.

"Queen Ptahsut!"

"Yes. Of course. Did you have a temple like the sun? With . . . oh, dancing girls and human sacrifices?"

Sandy Ochs ducked her head and gave them all a wolfish grin. The terrace lights, tiny white beads on overhead strings, slid over her blank eyes like flecks of foam.

Joe McLaren said quietly, "Do your parents know you're here, Ms. Ochs?" Caroline looked at him for the first time. He was her height, no taller, and stood leaning heavily on the terrace railing, just beyond the rectangle of light from the French doors. In the gloom she couldn't see his features or coloring clearly, only the sharp thrust of one cheekbone turned away from her and toward Sandy Ochs.

I'm over twenty-one," she said with the same ferocious energy. "And I know what you're thinking. But you're wrong.

Do you hear me—you're *wrong*. I got through all the psychological tests here."

"Yes," McLaren said gently. "I believe you. How long were you hospitalized before, Ms. Ochs?"

The woman's flat eyes suddenly blazed. Caroline took a step backward. Sandy Ochs raised both hands toward McLaren in a weird gesture—one fist clenched, one palm open—and froze, holding the pose an eerily long time. No one said anything. Then she turned and stalked regally through the French doors.

"Brains fried as eggs," Robbie said.

"You were baiting her." No trace of gentleness remained in McLaren's voice. "Don't."

He walked away. Caroline noticed that his left foot dragged slightly.

"Oh, God,"Robbie said, sighing theatrically. "Twenty minutes into a place and I've already made two enemies. What do you think, Caroline—do I need a bodyguard?"

"You *were* baiting her."

"Was I? I genuinely didn't mean to." He looked suddenly bewildered, and much younger.

Caroline resisted the impulse to touch his arm. The terrace lights blinked three times, strobing them all with shadow.

"Your meeting's beginning," Jane Flexner said stiffly. Caroline had forgotten she was there. "I guess I'd better leave. Bye, Robbie darling. Give me a call when you get out. We're on the net." She stood on tiptoe to give Robbie a light kiss. Her eyes darted sideways, presumably in search of her husband. Robbie's eyes watched Caroline's until he felt the movement of Jane's; Caroline saw the moment he too looked for the absent Mr. Flexner. Amused—he wasn't nearly as good at this as he wanted to be—she left them there and walked back inside.

The bartender placed the last of three dozen chairs in rows facing the huge wall screen. One of the doctors, a slim black woman in a crisp white dress and headband, waited by the console. The other doctor stood listening intently to Joe McLaren in a far corner of the room. Caroline saw both glance at Sandy Ochs, crouched in an aisle chair at the other side of the front row. Caroline took a seat in the last row. A moment later, Robbie Brekke slid in beside her.

"Time for the medical boot up."

She smiled. "I bet everyone in this room already knows every single thing they'll tell us."

"I don't."

"You didn't read everything you could find on plazzing before you came here?"

"I didn't read anything." Caroline twisted in her seat to look at him. His blue eyes sparkled. "Have you ever been in Liberia?"

"I'm not that reckless."

"Don't believe everything you see on the news. Not everybody in Africa is shooting or starving. About half of them are smuggling. Some friends and I chartered a boat in River Cess and—"

"Why would you tell me this? A total stranger? How do you know I'm not with the Zurich heat?"

He looked her over slowly, from the forehead down, with such exaggerated disbelief, such frank yet self-mocking pleasure, that she had to smile. It was a charade, and an invitation to join in the charade, and an amused superiority to the charade, all at once. And he was good at it, better than she would have thought from his performance on the terrace. Deliberate outrageousness, by itself, got tiresome. This was something else.

"You're a natural, aren't you, Robbie Brekke?"

"At what?"

She shook her head, smiling. At the console the slim black doctor cleared her throat. The room quieted.

"Welcome to the Institute For Previous Life Access Surgery. I am Dr. Maxine Armstrong, Chief of Staff, and I want to thank you all for coming here tonight to our presurgical reception. Some of you are not scheduled for surgery for a few weeks yet, but talking to all of you at once permits us, the medical staff, to be as thorough as possible. You will, of course, also have conferences with your individual doctors. Meanwhile, we at the Institute For Previous Life Access Surgery are aware that some of you have traveled long distances to come to us, and we wish to thank you for adapting yourself to our scheduling needs."

"Canned speech," Robbie murmured to Caroline. She nodded slightly. Dr. Armstrong stood on the floor as if it had obligingly molded itself to her graceful feet. Caroline had seen doctors like this before: completely controlled, completely sure of themselves. Too many doctors.

"I'd like to start with a presentation on the basics of reincarnation, although I'm sure you're all familiar with this material already. Please bear with me." She smiled with practiced charm and spoke to the console.

The room darkened. On the screen a stylized graphic of a huge three-dimensional brain glowed, turning slowly. After ten seconds the brain suddenly shot outward and throbbed around and throughout the audience: a holographic projection. A few people jumped, then laughed nervously. The narrative began in a deep, rich voice.

"For at least eighty years, neurologists have known that a given specific piece of information is not stored in one specific place in the brain. What we know—and how we know it—is more complex than that. The information in our brain—whether it concerns remembering what we ate for breakfast this morning or how to calculate trajectories for the lunar shuttle—is stored in a sort of ever-moving net of neutral connections affecting the entire brain. *All* of it."

Orange dots, thousands of them, began to pulse through the holographic brain filling the room. Caroline saw orange dots whip past her at eye level, race over the head and shoulders of the man sitting in front of her, arc up from the floor to disappear into the ceiling. It was like sitting in the middle of an orange blizzard. Just as she was starting to feel dizzy, the dots vanished.

"But the idea of a moving net doesn't *really* explain memory," the rich voice went on. "A better model may be a hologram, like the one surrounding you now. In a hologram, *all* the information to create it is stored throughout the entire surface. If one piece of a hologram is removed, the whole image can be reconstructed from that one piece—although it may not be quite as sharp and clear."

The holographic brain disappeared, replaced by a shot of a rat—a very white, clean, sanitized rat, Caroline noticed—running a maze.

"This is why scientists can remove up to fifty percent of a rat's brain and the rat will still remember how to run specific mazes. That happens no matter *which* fifty percent is cut away. The cortex of a brain—any brain—functions like a hologram. Memory is stored not in one single place but in neural patterns, like images on a holographic plate.

"But what does all this mean to *you*, who have used *your* brain to choose previous life access surgery?"

The nonthreatening rat vanished. The screen displayed a three-dimensional computer simulation, incredibly complex, of hundreds of tiny brains forming the solid shape of a single, giant brain. Caroline thought she had never seen better advertising-style graphics, not even on Broadway.

"Twenty-five years ago, a brain research team led by the brilliant Nobel-winner Robert Carl Untermeyer made a startling discovery. Not only is memory stored holographically *within* the individual brain, but holography is also a working model for a human 'over-memory' formed of *all* human minds. This over-memory exists independently of any one of us. Sometimes it is called 'racial memory.' Just as the memory of what you ate for breakfast this morning exists independently of any

one specific site in your brain. Cut into this over-memory—
which is what happens when one person dies—and the holographic storage of information is still there. Still *whole*."

On the screen, one tiny brain among the thousands suddenly glowed bright orange, then disappeared. The surrounding brains projected a hologram into the vacated space—
and the pattern remained the same. The chocolaty voice continued.

"Cut away fifty percent of the human over-memory, as
people throughout centuries and millennia come to their time
to die, and the whole can still be reconstructed."

Half the giant brain disappeared; immediately it projected
itself again.

"There is yet another parallel between holography and the
human over-memory. With all holograms, the smaller the
piece from which you try to reconstruct the whole, the fuzzier
the image. This is true of the over-memory as well. When the
human population of earth numbered only in the hundred
thousands, the over-memory had fewer pieces. Those early
over-memories are fuzzy.

"But today the earth's population numbers in the *billions*."
Caroline noticed that he didn't give a specific integer. Either
the Institute didn't want its expensive presentation to be dated
too fast, or—more likely—it was designed to avoid reminders
of the huge death toll AIDS had taken in the Third World,
where even now the cure was not always available.

"The over-memory is sharp and clear—waiting for humans
to access it.

"How does that happen? And why can't you access your
share of it throughout the centuries without previous life access
surgery?"

The giant over-brain was wiped off the screen, replaced by
a montage of decades-old news clips of Robert Carl Untermeyer's laboratories. Despite the clumsiness of the antiquated,
two-dimensional clips and the quaint look of the labs, some-

thing of the scientists' passion came through. Caroline leaned forward.

"Accessing the over-memory was the inestimable contribution of Untermeyer's team. They discovered the presence of 'inhibitors' on the limbic system, a part of the brain deep in the cortex, which prevented access to the over-memory. He also discovered how to remove those inhibitors."

The twentieth-century labs were replaced by shots of the Institute's modern hospital wing.

"Removing previous life access inhibitors requires a delicate and meticulous combination of computer-directed wave manipulation, drug control of neurotransmitter fluids, and modern surgical techniques. But *why?* Why are these inhibitors on our brains in the first place?"

The brief shots of operating rooms vanished; Caroline grinned. Don't let the audience dwell on the fact that their skulls were going to be pierced by laser. Keep to the theoretical.

Preferably the *startling* theoretical. A huge Cro-Magnon man snarled from the screen. Smell filled the room, the first time the scent synths had been turned on: dirt, sweat, and the hot dusty smell of animal pelts. The Cro-Magnon carried a spear and a dead lynx. The camera pulled back and the Cro-Magnon lumbered toward a distant cave, snorting a little.

Caroline smiled. She knew actors: How disgruntled had this one been with such a part? No lines.

The voice-over lightened just a little, enough to carry a hint of professional laughter. "Picture Og. He will live in his fierce wilderness maybe sixteen years—if he's fast enough. Not much time to learn everything needed for survival in that world. But if Og can *remember* what he knew in his previous lives, his learning curve is substantially shortened. If he can look at his dead lynx—"

—close-up of the carcass, as sanitized as the rat had been—

"—and have evoked in his brain by the object itself exactly

what he should do to skin and preserve it, he can eliminate trial and error. He can learn faster. The over-memory, even fuzzy as it was at that time of few minds, will give him an evolutionary advantage over the lynx. So that *he* can eat *it*—and not vice versa."

Og, now eating lynx, dissolved to fashionably dressed men and women eating hors d'oeuvres in an expensive restaurant. Caroline recognized Fifth Garden, and maitre d' Lingh Tuc hovering in the background. She grinned; Tuc loved publicity.

"But for twenty-first-century humanity—or even for our sixth-century B.C. ancestors—so much access to so much memory became a distraction. To see a crystal goblet"—quick flash of antique Baccarat crystal in a woman's hand—"and have evoked for you every goblet you had ever seen in every other life—that would be overwhelming. It would be so distracting that evolution would be hindered, not helped. So at some point in our development as a species, limbic inhibitors evolved.

"Today, however, previous access life surgery makes available to you the best of *both* worlds. Untermeyer's pioneering techniques, much refined, help men and women reclaim their true birth heritage—their *complete* selves. And modern, safe medication keeps us from being overwhelmed. The medical staff of the Institute For Previous Life Access Surgery of Rochester, New York, is proud to be able to assist you in your quest to become your whole being, undivided by time."

The descent from science to salesmanship was a little dizzying. Caroline glanced around. The woman in the red dress, who had looked so terrified earlier, leaned far forward, her hands twisting together on her knees. The academic in the shabby jacket sat like stone. The foreign teenage prince lounged carelessly, smiling faintly in the light from the screen.

Something more interesting was happening on the other side of the room. Dr. Armstrong and the other doctor both squatted beside Sandy Ochs's chair at the far end of the first row. The three whispered; Sandy Ochs shook her head. Then all three rose and walked toward the door, Sandy Ochs between the doctors. Caroline watched them go; what was that all about?

The presentation went on to explain in glowing terms the unexpected side effects of the surgery: it had been found to cure or arrest several neurological diseases that medicine had once considered discrete disorders but which had turned out to be linked to the all-pervading nerve patterns of memory. Alzheimer's. Parkinson's disease. Multiple sclerosis. Happy, cured patients waved from the screen.

Next came explanations of the global data bank for reincarnation information, available to all who belonged to the "international brotherhood of those who have found themselves." The stylized graphics for the global net were dazzling. The presentation finished with interviews, softly lit, with those who had accessed their previous lives. They spoke movingly of the spiritual benefits they had gained. All the benefits were high-minded and middle-class; all the interviewees were young and well-dressed.

Robbie leaned close to whisper. "You'd never know they refer to themselves as 'carnies,' would you?"

"And where are all the old carnies?"

"Bad PR. You still can't take it with you."

"From this thing, you'd never know that sixty percent of all carnies are over sixty."

"Show-off. You just remember that because the numbers match."

She grinned. The presentation ended in a burst of music, the lights came up, and Dr. Armstrong, returned from wherever she had escorted Sandy Ochs, stepped in front of the screen.

"It's now my great pleasure to present to you Dr. Graham Park, our distinguished Chief of Surgery. Dr. Park will personally oversee each of your surgery. He is here tonight to answer any questions you might have."

Park had recently been on the cover of *Time*. Caroline

recognized the fierce dark eyes—she thought of Og, with his lynx—the stocky build, the faint Oriental cast several generations old.

"I'm glad to be with you tonight," Park rumbled in a voice incapable of sounding glad. Caroline saw that Armstrong was PR, Park was technical power, and that the former did not trust the latter. Armstrong hovered gracefully behind the great surgeon, smiling steadily.

"Previous life access surgery is new to this century, but it is already well past its beginnings. The rate of complication is the lowest of any elective head surgery. You are safer having your memories accessed than having your eyes permanently glittered for night vision."

The audience tittered politely. Robbie murmured, "Not to mention having your ass made curvier."

Somewhere beyond the room, a door slammed very hard. Caroline twisted in her seat, but there was nothing to see.

Park said, "Does anyone have any questions?"

The fat woman in red ruffles said timorously, "Will the operation hurt?"

"I'm sure your own doctor has discussed that with you. During the surgery itself you will, of course, be under anesthesia. Afterward there will be a slight headache, but the surgery is performed at a site of few pain-nerve endings. Medication easily controls the discomfort."

A man said, "Then why do we have to stay at the Institute a full month?"

Robbie murmured, "Insurance money," at the same time that Dr. Armstrong moved deftly forward. A PR question, Caroline realized.

"Oh—the question itself shows how many horizons surgery will open that are closed to you now! Your month's stay is partly, of course, to allow time for complete recovery from the surgery. But mostly—*mostly*—to provide you with the best possible orientation we can to your expanded self. Trained researchers will help you learn how to access your memories—I know you all know from your presurgical conferences that the process is not automatic. Psychologists will help you interpret what you learn; computer experts will teach you the PLAS datanet; historians will locate your new memories in time and place for you. The Institute stands ready to aid you in every way possible."

More PR; anyone not living in a hermetically-sealed Safehouse knew all this from endless television broadcasts, endless datanet presentations. Memories of previous lives did not come crashing in on carnies all at once; each had to be evoked in response to an object, a smell, a sound, an experience in this life. No way in to the past, Caroline thought sardonically, except through the present. Too bad.

Dr. Armstrong went on explaining what everyone already knew. Dr. Park stood stolidly, his face impassive. "You take a walk on our beautiful Institute grounds and you see a rose. Suddenly you remember picking roses in Vallois, a nineteenth-century French resort renowned for its masses and masses of gorgeous roses. The year is 1868, and you are an Italian lady traveling abroad with her husband and children. You can see their faces, feel the warm French sunshine on your hand, smell the pink rose. Bits of that life suddenly come back to you—but not all of that life. Bits."

The doctor smiled as if offering them all a gift. Her voice grew slow and soft. "*And*—you will remember the bits in English, not in Italian or French. There's a very good reason for that. The limbic system, the 'gate' to the over-memory, is preverbal. It has no words. But memories coming from the limbic reach your consciousness through the cortex. And for most of you, *your* cortex thinks in English. So whatever words you remember from that other life, you will 'remember' in English.

"But there will not be many words. The over-memory, except in moments of extreme stress, works mostly in images, emotions, and sensations. You will remember the rustle of your

Italian silk dress, the freshness of the clean air, the beauty of that long-ago garden of pink and red roses."

The woman in red nodded several times. In the row ahead of Caroline, a man and woman reached for each other's hands, smiling mistily. Robbie Brekke leaned forward to murmur something to Caroline, but before she could hear it, a man's voice cut across the room like dry ice.

"Roses are all very fine, Dr. Armstrong. But isn't it true that as many as five percent of all carnies can't handle their own evoked memories and suffer nervous collapse? That your psychological prescreening is in fact woefully inadequate, merely a sop to public relations?"

Dr. Park's head swung up like a great beast. Dr. Armstrong said swiftly, "Are you a journalist, sir?"

"Isn't it true that this Institute and the others like it would never have been allowed to exist in the United States if the way hadn't been cleared by the castrating of the FDA—in order to test every possible avenue to a cure for the plague?"

"This is a closed meeting for surgical candidates," Dr. Armstrong said icily. "You will have to leave."

The bartender—who, Caroline noticed for the first time, had not left the room when the bar closed—strode toward the disruptive man, who stood up. His face and gray hair looked about fifty, his suit as if he had slept in it. Turning to half face the bartender, he said to Armstrong, "I *am* a surgical candidate. Also a journalist. Bill Prokop, *Philadelphia Globe-Net.*"

The skin around Dr. Armstrong's dark eyes tightened. Dr. Park, however, stood impassive; evidently the great surgeon was sure enough of the surgery he performed to not be rattled by a minor journalist. Caroline realized she liked that.

"Mr. Prokop, we're of course glad to have you with us," Dr. Armstrong said. "But you seem to have confused two different occasions. This is a reception to welcome the newest members to the international reincarnation fraternity. The next press conference at the Institute is scheduled for—"

Another door slammed in the corridor, followed by a scream of pure rage. Caroline started; Armstrong jerked her chin upward. Feet pounded in the hall. Then Sandy Ochs ran into the room, stumbling to a halt halfway between the door and the last row of gilt chairs. She held a gun. Caroline had never seen one before, except in museums; she stared at the slim barrel, the gray plastic stock wavering in the woman's fingers.

"I will have this operation—I will! I will!" Sandy Och's voice rose to a shriek.

Dr. Armstrong said, "Ms. Ochs, I—we—understand your feelings completely. I'm sure we can work something out. Please put down the gun."

"I was a divine queen of ancient Egypt! All of you are dirt under my feet—you hear me? I will *not* be denied!"

"Of course not," Armstrong said soothingly. She did not move forward. Park said nothing, watching keenly. Caroline wondered why she wasn't afraid.

"I want the operation tonight! Tonight—do you hear me. Tonight!"

"You can have it just as soon as we make arrangements," Dr. Armstrong said. "I don't know if it can exactly be tonight but—"

Sandy Ochs fired. A beam of light sliced from the barrel— laser? Caroline wondered—along with an artificial-sounding rasp. The fat woman in red in the front row began to scream, a wordless syllable wavering in pitch, monotonous and shrill as a siren. Sandy Ochs took a step forward and swung the gun barrel toward the fat woman, then back to Armstrong, who leaned against the screen console, shaken but apparently uninjured.

"Make her stop that! Make her stop that now!"

The fat woman in red continued to scream. The gun in Sandy Ochs's hand shook violently. Caroline watched, fascinated, as people began to slip quietly under the insubstantial protection of the upholstered gilt chairs, tortoises in rose plush shells.

"Make her stop that, do you hear me!"

"Of course, Your Majesty." Robbie Brekke, his voice respectful and firm, stood up beside Caroline. He walked toward the front row of seats, grabbed the screaming woman, and clamped his hand over her mouth, looking all the while at Sandy Ochs with alert deference. The woman in red slumped against him like a marshmallow. Too quickly for anyone to object, he dragged her off her chair toward Sandy Ochs. The gun barrel trembled on them both.

"Apologize for disturbing the Queen!" Robbie said loudly. He dragged the terrified woman to within an arm's length of Sandy Ochs. Caroline caught a glimpse of his face just before he turned; the blue eyes sparkled. "Go ahead, woman— apologize for disturbing the Queen!"

The woman stayed mute with terror. Sandy Ochs herself looked confused. Her gaze darted around the room; she dropped it to stare at her suddenly cringing subject. In that moment Robbie reached over and took the gun from her hand.

Sandy Ochs screamed in anger. Her face folded in on itself, distorted and horrible. She grabbed for her gun but Robbie had dropped the woman in red and stepped backward. He was grinning. "Now, now—this wasn't even invented in ancient Egypt!"

She threw herself at him across the woman on the floor, clawing at his eyes. Robbie threw his other arm up across his face. Sandy Ochs stumbled over the woman in red, scrambled sobbing to her feet, and began to kick at the cowering mass until the bartender, springing away from Bill Prokop, grabbed her in a full nelson from behind. People began to yell and wave their arms.

Robbie slid into the empty chair beside Caroline. "There seems to be some commotion in here," he said gravely. "Would you care for a stroll on the terrace?"

Caroline studied him. He wasn't even breathing hard. Mutely she shook her head. Robbie shrugged, his eyes still dancing. He was obviously having a wonderful time.

The bartender and two other uniformed men dragged Sandy Ochs out the door. She screamed obscenities and curses. In the hall a door opened, slammed, and her voice died away. The fat woman in red, helped to her feet by the assistant doctor, filled the sudden silence.

"No operation! No operation! I won't have the operation. I changed my mind—"

Dr. Park himself strode toward her from the front of the room. "Ms. Selby—" The distraught woman slapped him across the face.

The great surgeon hardly seemed to notice. "Ms. Selby— calm yourself. I know that what has happened is upsetting. But, I assure you—listen to me—the operation is worth it. I have had it myself." That had not been in the *Time* article, but Caroline found she believed it. Park did not admit of disbelief. "I have had it myself, and it is worth it. It will change your life." He turned and strode from the room.

"I won't," the fat woman whispered. But either the slap or Park's utter conviction seemed to have calmed her. She covered her face with both plump hands and let the assistant doctor lead her away. One torn red ruffle lay on the floor.

"Please," Dr. Armstrong said shakily from the front. "Please . . . all of you . . . stay where you are. Please. I want to say that nothing like this has ever happened at the Institute before. Never—*never*—have I ever seen . . . For you to take this unfortunate woman's personal mental problems as any way connected with the Institute would be a gross distortion of truth."

Armstrong straightened; her voice grew stronger. "Let me be completely frank with all of you. *Anyone* who chooses to unlock his or her entire past must be in some way a creative and adventurous person. Creative and adventurous people are of necessity more unusual than the common run of humanity—but that does *not* have to mean instability as in that unfortunate woman. There are all stages of what we call instability, some of them useful . . . The Institute offers its most profound apologies that this incident should have happened, and our most fervent reassurances that it never will happen again to such a committed and wonderful group of mental adventurers—"

"I will take that walk on the terrace after all," Caroline said to Robbie.

The night air beyond the French doors smelled of grass and water. "She's never had it herself," Robbie said. "The operation. Park has, but not her. 'All stages of instability, some of them useful'—I'll bet you anything the good doctor's not a carnie." He laughed.

Caroline turned to look at him. She hadn't expected him to catch Armstrong's distaste—so carefully hidden until she was shot at—for the surgery she oversaw. Robbie leaned against the terrace railing, his powerful young body completely at ease. Leaving the meeting, he had stopped to scoop up the torn red ruffle from the fat woman's dress. Now he tied it to his headband. The ruffle hung down jauntily over his left ear. If he was giving a performance, it was the best she had ever seen.

"Are you really as calm as you look, Robbie? Or do you go about disarming crazy people every day?"

"Not usually, no."

"Were you afraid?"

"I'm never afraid. You mean you've never tussled with someone who wasn't feeling socially correct toward you?"

"Not physically."

"What a stunted life. All the more reason you should let me fascinate you with my brief career as a smuggler."

"Is that what you were trying to do?"

"You know it."

He put his hand over hers on the terrace railing and began to play with her fingers. She pulled them away. He was much less interesting in this role, and much more juvenile.

"You're not fascinated," he said lightly.

"Sorry."

"Well, in the interests of the global datanet, you could tell me why. Purely in the name of research, you understand."

The lake had gone completely black, shimmering flatly under a low moon. Caroline suddenly felt very tired. She had left New York before noon, flown to Albany to visit Catherine, and then flown to Rochester. Catherine had a cold. The flight had been late. Sandy Ochs had tried to shoot a doctor.

"Come on," Robbie said, "be honest."

"When people say that, honesty is usually the last thing they want."

"I do."

"No, you don't."

"Sure I do. Let me have it. Why couldn't I fascinate you, on a strictly temporary basis? Don't be coy."

The pathetic red ruffle drooped beside his ear. Caroline flexed her arms; the muscles in her shoulders ached. "I have an immunity to your type. You are a type, you know. Charming, funny, adventurous, selfish, bird-brained. Hook up with one once and you're immune for life. Like chicken pox."

"How do you know I'm selfish?" He didn't seem offended.

"From the way you baited that poor sick woman when we were on the terrace before. And from the way you *enjoyed* that stupid scene in there."

"Cortical stimulation is always nice. Didn't you listen to the presentation in there? Who vaccinated you against my type?"

"My first ex-husband."

"Ah. Sounds like a sad story. But how do you know I'm bird-brained? I could in fact be an eminent boy mathematician. Or a top Congressional aide. Or a razor-minded lawyer. They all smuggle now and then. I could be anybody. You don't even know who you're refusing."

He was smiling, enjoying his own flow of words, with no trace of anger at hers. She said wearily, "You're an actor, aren't you?"

"No. But your first ex-husband is, isn't he?"

"Good guess." She waited for him to mention her father. When he didn't, she had a moment of doubt; perhaps he *wasn't* an actor, didn't know the theater world at all. Or perhaps he was just shrewder than most. Perhaps he had the patience to bide his time before angling for the introduction, the audition. *If you could just mention my name to him, anything at all from Colin Cadavy might help*—Usually she could tell instantly. Maybe she was losing her eye after all.

Robbie said, "How many ex-husbands are there?"

She was tired of fencing with him. She was tired. Gripping the terrace railing with both hands, she leaned out to smell the soft night air and said, "Why are you here, Robbie? Why this operation? What do you hope to get from unlocking your other lives?"

He didn't hesitate. "Money."

" 'Money'?"

"That's why I do most things. Although not all. How many ex-husbands are there, Caroline?"

"I never heard anyone say that plazzing yielded money. Only cost it."

"Ah, but it's a good investment. Especially if you're doing it with someone else's money."

"And are you?"

"You know it. It's a great story. But unfortunately I can't tell it to you. There are people who might object." He said this last with a mixture of amusement and self-satisfaction that Caroline recognized immediately. Colin Cadavy, leaking tidbits about his new role, the new resort he would take her to, his new drug deal. Herself, younger and more credulous, teasing him for more thrilling details. A game, like all the games she'd played with Colin, with Jeremy—with Charles? No. Charles did not play games.

"I'm getting cold. I'm going in."

"In a minute," he said. "Now you have to tell me—why are *you* having the operation? What do you hope to get from your pasts?"

She hadn't expected him to ask. "Oh, not much."

"Then why do it?"

"I ask myself the same thing."

"Come on, Caroline. I gave you one pithy succinct word."

Caroline laughed, startling herself. Impulsively she placed both hands on his shoulders, brought her face close to his, and matched his self-satisfied tone. "If I could answer that in one pithy succinct word, I wouldn't need to get plazzed at all. It's a great story, but unfortunately I can't tell it to you."

Robbie tried to put his arms around her. She pulled away, smiling, shaking her head, and turned to open the French doors. He caught her shoulder. "Don't go in yet."

"I'm cold."

"Take my jacket."

"No, thanks."

"Well, at least let me leave you with a good joke." She paused, one hand on the door, tolerant. "What do you get when you cross a plague victim with a Gaeist?"

Caroline froze.

Robbie said, "A guy who pollutes daily in the same spot."

With one smooth moment she opened the French doors, closed them behind her, and turned the lock. "Hey!" came muffled through the glass. Caroline yanked the rose-colored velvet curtains across the window. She was trembling.

Stop it, she told herself angrily. He didn't know, couldn't know. He is just a stupid young man, making stupid jokes.

The meeting was over. Three or four people stood in a knot at the far end of the room, talking. In the first row of seats Dr.

Armstrong sat, stony, listening to Bill Prokop, the Philadelphia journalist. Caroline saw Joe McLaren limp from the room. She caught up to him easily.

"Mr. McLaren. What will happen to Sandy Ochs?"

He looked surprised. "I don't know. I don't work for the hospital, Ms. Bohentin."

"Caroline. But it was you who convinced the doctors to have her removed from the meeting in the first place. I saw you talking to Dr. Armstrong."

McLaren studied her. They were almost the same height. His hair was brown, a light brown the same color as his eyes. He had an impressive face, neither handsome nor plain. "Are you a journalist? Like Prokop?"

"No." When he didn't seem to believe her, she said, "I'm a sometime dealer in antique doll houses, when I'm anything at all. Are you a doctor?"

"A lawyer."

"Then when you decided Sandy Ochs was too unstable for plazzing from what she said on the terrace, you were protecting the Institute?"

He said, a little stiffly, "I have no interest in protecting the Institute."

"In protecting Sandy? Did you know her before?"

"No. Why all the questions, Ms.—Caroline?"

"No reason. Just curiosity. A childhood flaw." She could still feel the anger in her from Robbie's "joke," cold and hard. "What kind of law do you practice?"

For a moment he didn't answer. "I represent plague victims."

She hadn't been prepared for that, not twice in ninety seconds. Whatever her face showed, it made Joe McLaren's eyes sharpen. He said, "Do you have the plague, Caroline?"

"My daughter Catherine does." She shook her head. "And that's not something I blurt out like that. I'm sorry. Good night."

What was wrong with her? Furious at herself, she walked away before McLaren could answer, before Robbie Brekke could get someone to open the French doors to let him in. And why was she furious? Because it was painful to mention Catherine? Yes.

No. She was angry with herself because she had started by firing personal questions at McLaren, and ended by answering one herself. Her anger was that self-centered, and that petty. God, she was sick of herself.

In a week she would have other selves.

The other selves—some of them—one of them—would have to be better. Would have to.

"You're an escapist. A weakling," she said aloud, into the quiet of her room. After the fresh air on the terrace, the room felt stuffy. Caroline keyed the air-conditioning up three degrees, changed her mind, turned it off, and knelt by the window. It was not supposed to open, but the building remodeling had not included sealed windows. When she braced herself against the bed and pushed with the force of her whole body, the window swung outward. Sweet cool air drifted in.

It all depended on what you were escaping. Was a prisoner a weakling? Was a political refugee from someplace like Liberia, where there was no order or sustenance left? Was someone running from a mob?

Kneeling on the floor, she saw that the long sleeves of her blue leather dress had ridden up, exposing the thick white vertical ridges along her wrists. Had the sleeves ridden up when she pushed at the window, or when she gripped the terrace railing? Had Joe McLaren seen the scars? Had Robbie Brekke?

It didn't matter. She could have had the scars removed, of course, and never had. There was no reason for it to matter; neither McLaren nor Brekke were anything to her. And in two days she would be plazzed, linked—as the tabloids invariably said—with her "long-lost selves." They made it sound like star-crossed lovers. A whole fucking *platoon* of star-crossed lovers.

Now *there* was a thought.

"It seems they hang upon the cheek of night
Like a whole damn jewel collection in Armstrong's ear.
They speak, and yet they all say nothing.
Thus with a kiss, the whole bunch of us die!"

Smiling, Caroline sat on the floor, hugging her knees by the window, breathing in the June night air and listening to the lap of small, unseen waves at the edge of the great lake in the darkness beyond the window. Her operation was scheduled for Thursday, three days away. Figure a day or so doped-up afterward. Then she would have a month at the Institute, learning to explore her own long past. She would have other memories besides Colin, besides Jeremy and Charles, besides Catherine, a small diminished prisoner at a Home in Albany. She would have a wealth of new experiences gained without experiencing them, a treasure chest of novel diversions, a library of new ways to live that were actually old ways, *her* ways. Other Carolines. Better than this one. A customized internal data bank of options and possibilities and exciting new solutions . . .

She wished it were over.

2 JOE

His foot was too bad for the stairs. Joe dragged himself to the elevators, waited, rode up alone to his room on the fifth floor. The screen flashed multiple messages, but before he looked at them, he lay across the bed, closed his eyes, and began to breathe deeply. Concentration came hard: too uncongenial a situation. His hind brain knew how much he hated being at the Institute. But at last he caught the biofeedback rhythm, all at once, like music switching on in his head. Lungs and heart responded, then muscles. Not nerves. But he didn't expect that. Damaged nerves did not respond to biorhythms.

Sister Margaret had seen immediately that he had MS.

On the way to the Institute, he had had the cabbie detour to the Sisters of Mercy Home for the Afflicted, site of the latest hate bombing. The place had been ancient: 1970s, 1960s. Too old to be comfortable, too new to be interesting. Perfect for housing people nobody wanted.

"The patients were not in these two rooms," Sister Margaret had said. It was the first time she had spoken to him. Now Joe heard why: Her voice crawled with rage, like something cold and scaly on a tight leash. "This third room was occupied by a single plague victim. He was asleep."

The walls of the third room were splattered with reddish

brown. Joe looked closer, to avoid looking at Sister Margaret. Embedded in the splatters were hard white bits.

"The police have given permission to start repairs, haven't they, Sister? They're done with their forensic work?"

"The Order has no money for repairs," she said; her voice did not change. "You must already know that, Mr. McLaren. I assumed it's why you're here."

"No," Joe said, startled. "Why did you assume that, Sister?"

"Aren't you a lawyer from the government? The Plague Victims Relief Agency?"

He felt the familiar sinking feeling. "No. From the government, yes. Not from the PVRA."

Sister Margaret stared at him steadily, her brown eyes flat. From her headband draped a sort of drawstring bag of white cloth that hid all of her hair except the center-parted crown. Compared to the brief blue wimples of Joe's youth, this looked deliberately ugly. Two plagues—AIDS before the turn of the century, MFRD after it—had once more turned the American Catholic Church conservative.

"Then what part of the government *are* you from, Mr. McLaren?"

"The Presidential Blue-Ribbon Commission On Plague Control." He knew he was giving the full, grandiose name out of irritated shame: They had controlled nothing. Commissioned everything, yes—studies, population tracking, contingency plans, clinics, centers. This time—after the horrible mishandling of AIDS thirty years earlier—no one had wanted to be caught with his lasers down. Five million Americans had plague; another fifteen million were projected to get it in the next seven years. In some countries, estimates ran as high as ten percent of the population already afflicted. Money had flowed like water. And none of it had mattered.

The factionalism had happened anyway, the red tape had happened, the political double-speak and pork-barreling and hysteria and, finally and inevitably, the public economic burden and its plasti-explosive backlash in rooms like this one. The special handpicked politically balanced Blue-Ribbon Commission On Plague Control, with its model legal and medical and educational arms liberally funded in an election year, had controlled nothing. People still had their brains attacked by a slow virus no med team could isolate. People still lost their ability to form new memories. People still lived in one room, physically and mentally, over and over, until they died or the money ran out or someone blew them to bits.

And this woman knew it. She read the papers.

Joe said, "I'll key a report to the PVRA that you request emergency assistance."

"We've already done that." Sister Margaret turned and began to pick her way over the debris toward the door. Flakes of paint and synthfoam clung to the cuffs of her jeans. "The PVRA will take two months to process the application, another three to decide whether this particular Catholic institution meets the Church/State Exemption Act requirements, and one more month to transfer the credit to our banknet. Meanwhile, the police will not catch the bomber. And your Commission will not find a cure for the plague. Or even isolate the slow virus."

Joe said nothing. He had nothing to say.

But the nun found something. Silent all the way along the dingy corridors, through the lobby with its bare floor and sagging ceiling, right up to the steel-reinforced front door with its manual double bolts, she finally turned to face him. Joe braced himself. Even understanding that the rage had to go somewhere—even that didn't really help.

"Why did you come here, Mr. McLaren? From Washington, wasn't it? All that way?"

"Yes."

"Why? You have no help to offer us. Washington has its own bombings—there are resentful and stupid people everywhere. Why come all the way to Rochester?"

"Good-bye, Sister. Thank you for your cooperation."

"What's wrong with your foot?"

It stopped him. He hadn't even felt much aware of the foot today, of any of the symptoms. Sister Margaret's eyes remained flat, unwarmed by her own rudeness.

Joe said shortly—wondering why he answered at all—"Multiple sclerosis."

"Ah. And that's why you're in Rochester. For the Institute. Visiting a bombed plague home lets you make the trip at government expense."

He fought to keep his temper. The white bits in the bedroom wall had been human bone. "Not true, Sister."

"Isn't it?"

"No!"

His anger seemed to neither upset nor deter her. She looked at him steadily, and he was surprised, through everything else, to find himself noticing how firm and pink her mouth looked. She was younger than he had thought.

She said, her voice suddenly very quiet, "Your immortal soul is in danger if you go to that place, Mr. McLaren."

Joe reached for the top door bolt.

"You're a Catholic," Sister Margaret added, "or were. I can always tell. It's a gift."

Oh, Christ. He slid open the bolt.

"You don't believe me, I know. And I'm saying it badly. *Baldly.* But don't go to the Institute to have your MS corrected, Mr. McLaren. You must have some doubts or you would have gone whenever you had your first gene print—isn't MS one of the early identification tests? But you had doubts. You were baptized a Catholic. Curing your disease is not worth the price of your immortal soul."

"Good-bye, Sister." He escaped to the street. Behind him the door had shivered a moment, undecided; then he had heard the dead bolts slide across.

Not a good memory. There were no good memories connected with his job. Joe gave up on the biorhythms and hobbled off his bed to activate the wall screen and check his messages.

There were three. Angel Whittaker, his secretary at the Washington office from which he conducted a private practice separate from the Plague Commission, had accessed early in the afternoon on routine legal business. Then Angel had accessed again, a few hours later, to leave a PLEASE CALL. Joe frowned; the only messages Angel wouldn't leave on the shielded office datanet were ones he didn't understand himself. And Angel rarely admitted he didn't understand something. When Joe had explained why he would have to be away from his practice for several weeks, Angel had grinned and rubbed his hands together. "Hot data! I get to be the gringo lawyer while you get plazzed!"

"*You* go get plazzed while *I* be the gringo lawyer," Joe had said sourly. Angel had laughed.

The other message was a PLEASE CALL from Jeff Pirelli, old friend and fellow member of the Plague Commission. Joe eased himself into one of the small room's Japanese chairs and dialed the Washington number. He had spoken with Pirelli this morning; there was no reason for him to be calling now, either professional or personal.

He phoned Angel first, at his city apartment. A blast of slow, intense music, heavy on the drums, and over it Angel's voice at a shout, "Hello? *Hola?*"

"Angel, it's Joe."

"What?"

"Joe!" he screamed. After a moment the music died.

"Angel Whittaker."

"It's Joe. You left a message."

"Just a minute." A muffled rattle of Spanish, then Angel's voice, oddly high and strained. "Yeah. I did. A message."

"What's wrong?"

"Nothing's wrong. You just got an incoming from California, and she said to pass it on to you personally, so I'm doing that."

California. Robin. Joe said, "Yeah, but what's wrong with *you*? You sound weird."

"I'm fine," Angel said shrilly.

"Angel—you sound like something terrible has happened. What is it? Can I—"

"I said I'm all right! Give it a hard break, man, all right?"

Joe was silent, baffled. Angel had been his secretary for a year and a half; he was by turns brash, cool, secretive, outrageous, and always phenomenally efficient: a chameleon in bright green suits and Chinese moonsynth headbands. But Joe had never before heard him sound frightened.

"Sorry," Angel said sullenly. "You want your message?"

"Go ahead," Joe said. He didn't know what else to say. His relationship with Angel took place strictly during business hours. Angel had seemed to want it that way, and Joe realized now that he didn't know enough about Angel's personal life, beyond the fact that he was single and lived in a trendy, young section of Washington, to even formulate a question about what could be wrong.

He closed his eyes, right hand gripping the phone, and waited to hear Robin's latest message. They had been coming for a month now, all the same: "Please call." Angel had passed on each repetition without comment; he had come to work for Joe after Robin had divorced him. Angel had never met her. Joe liked that. Angel could say, "Oh, a please-call from Robin Nguyen," and Joe could say, "Thanks," and that was that. No mess. None of the awkwardness her name still caused between him and Pirelli. No anger, no pain. He had not called.

"She says to tell you," Angel said, still in that strained, jagged voice, "she says, 'Purple martins flying.' "

Somewhere behind Angel the drum music started again, lower this time.

"Boss? You there?"

"Yeah," Joe said. "Thanks, Angel." There was an awkward pause. Joe sensed that Angel wanted to say something; he wanted to as well, but didn't know what. Finally Angel said something lost in the music—it might have been no more than "Bye"—and hung up. Joe sat in the Japanese chair holding the phone.

Purple martins flying. He hadn't even known Robin remembered. Or that she would be sentimental enough—manipulative enough, stupid enough—to use the phrase if she had.

It had been their secret code, the three of them. Pirelli had been the one who had formed it, of course, slouched in front of his cheap Apple, a Cortland so ancient it ran without parallel processors, even then. They had been twelve years old, all of them, playing after-school war games against another grimy middle school team four miles away by modem, drinking Cokes in Pirelli's bedroom with the gaping patches in the drywall and the view out the window of the interstate overpass whizzing with Japanese cars. Pittsburgh in 2002. Joe McLaren, Jeff Pirelli, Robin Nguyen. The trio. Inseparable.

Pirelli invented the game. Pirelli at twelve, obese and greasy-skinned in an obscene T-shirt and Coptic cross on a brass chain. Already brilliant on the outmoded equipment his faded and deserted mother bought him in grudging, angry hope that she could somehow compensate for the father dead of AIDS from a contaminated needle. She had been trying, Joe saw now, to make a rotten pattern into a better one with cables and keyboards she didn't understand and didn't trust. And she had succeeded—Pirelli had become one of the country's best professional data scanners, that curious hybrid of analyst and gambler, hatching hunches on patterns of data too unexpected to be caught by programmed odds.

" 'Vultures gathering'—what a stupid password," Pirelli had said, peering at his streaky screen. "*Of course* vultures are gathering, it's a war council, isn't it? Minniti has the subtlety of a cabbage." The pudgy fingers flew over the keyboard; in ninety seconds he had pulled up the other team's entire game plan.

"This is as good as won," Robin said in her formal, faintly accented English. Her family was Vietnamese, late immigrants to a country hungry for labor to support an AIDS population not quite finished dying, despite the discovery of the cure years earlier. So long as the immigrants were clean, of course. Robin was clean. She leaned over the back of Pirelli's chair, her dark hair swinging forward; Joe felt his chest tighten.

"Stupid, yeah," he said, to say something. "Vultures. They could have at least picked another bird."

Robin said, "Eagles gathering."

"Nah," Pirelli said. "Too historical. Bible. Nazis."

"Ostriches gathering," Joe said. He had stopped reading the Bible a year ago, had barely heard of the Nazis. Did Robin mind that Pirelli knew so much more than anybody?

"Hiding in the sand. Messages you don't want anyone to see."

"Cowbirds gathering."

"They lay eggs in other birds' nests. Messages piggy-backing on another program."

"Robins gathering!" She smiled at him; he felt his groin swell.

"Sign of spring."

"Well, damn it, Jeff," Joe burst out, "all birds mean something. Everything means something!"

Pirelli only smiled; it was one of those afternoons when there was unnamed tension in the friendship, coming and going like errant smoke. It was Robin who twisted her body to face him, saying in her soft voice, "Purple martins. They are beautiful without meaning."

"Yeah," Jeff said with unexpected seriousness. "Absolutely meaningless. That can be *our* message, whenever one of us has something completely urgent to communicate. 'Purple martins flying.' And the others *have* to answer. No matter what."

"You're crazy," Joe said automatically: It was one of their touchstones.

"I'm a genius."

"I like it," Robin had said with her pretty accent. "Finish the game, Jeff, and give the bastards hell."

Purple martins flying.

Joe grimaced and replaced the phone. His window faced south; lights from Rochester made a pink glow against the sky, fading whatever stars might have been visible. Rochester, he suddenly remembered irrelevantly, had been the first city to adopt the voting machine. He phoned Jeff Pirelli.

"Pirelli. McLaren here."

"Christ on a ramchip, where have you been? I left word for you to call more than an hour ago."

Joe sat up straighter. "Why? What's the matter?"

"Nothing's the matter. What would be the best possible news I could be bringing you, old buddy?"

For a second the room swirled, then Pirelli's voice cut in again, apologetic. "No, no, I'm sorry, not a cure—I'm such an ass. But a breakthrough. Someone on the medical team isolated the plague virus for sure out of the probables. We have it, we can study the structure, we can splice it for variations if we have to, and maybe now we stand a chance at finding out how the bloody fucker has been getting itself transmitted all this time!"

"*Tell me,*" Joe said.

Pirelli launched into a long, complicated explanation of the slow virus's structure; Joe lost the sense after a few sentences. He was a lawyer, not a doctor. Pirelli, member of the President's Blue-Ribbon Commission On Plague Control—it was he who had brought McLaren aboard—wasn't a doctor either, and within thirty seconds he switched from medical jargon to data jargon. Joe didn't follow that any better. But he heard the jubilation in Pirelli's voice, and tried not to clutch the phone too hard.

"It could be another dead end, Jeff. And even if it's not— isolating a slow virus is still a long way from curing it. Even from finding out how it's transmitted."

"Same old go-slow Joe. Never mind—we got it. We fucking *got it*."

"What do you want me to do?"

"Nothing. You're on vacation. Esparza and Eastley can handle the legal end till you get back—there had to be *some* reason Caswell stuck three lawyers on the Commission. Quick—what's the fastest way to slow down a fiber optics link?"

"Don't know. What?"

"Take the configuration from a lawyer's brain."

"Cute. Keep me posted on the medical team's progress."

"This could really be it," Pirelli said. His voice was full of wonder, radiated wonder, was rotten with wonder. "You know? This could really be it. Finally."

"Yes."

"You could sound a little more excited, old buddy."

"I will when you're sure."

"How you feeling? Is the operation scheduled yet?"

Muscles tightened in Joe's shoulders. "Next Tuesday."

"Vision okay?"

"Fine. Just the foot's dragging again."

"Not for long. Who's handling the office? The Puerto Rican Crown Prince?"

Joe had to grin. "Angel's got it all on fast forward."

"I'll bet. One of these days that temperamental pseudo-lawyer's going to actually try one of your cases in court. Try to try anyway."

"With my clientele, would it make a difference?"

Pirelli laughed. An old joke—Joe's career as a civil liberties lawyer, defending plague victims against a government that wanted to ditch the responsibility of housing them, versus Pirelli's high-powered career as a probabilities data scanner. "You pays your money and I takes your choice." Like that. Dumb jokes, old jokes. Good jokes.

"We got it," Pirelli said. "We son-of-a-bitchin' *got* it."

After Pirelli hung up, Joe sat still, wondering what he felt. Why he didn't feel more. It was the scope, he decided; it was hard to grasp. The plague had always been there, as immutable a fact of nature as sex. Awareness of both had grown at the same time, just before his twelfth birthday, and in some perverse way they had become forever linked in his mind: the newspaper headlines CDC ADMITS MEMORY PLAGUE COULD TOP AIDS and the quick hard stirrings in his groin every day, every night. There had been a popular song everywhere that year, "Lotus Machine," and it too had become tangled up in his mind with the headlines and the painful, delicious swelling between his legs, so that for years afterward any tune even vaguely close—da da da DA da—could summon up tangled memories of panicky adult conversations, cinematic TV riots, locking the bathroom door behind him, and the sweet smell of Robin Nguyen's hair. That this plague, unlike the one in his parents' generation, had nothing to do with sex made no difference. For Joe it did. And for all those who had come of age at the turn of the century the memory plague—Memory Formation and Retrieval Disorder—had hung over the high-school dances and hologram concerts and datanet wars with the same selective inevitability as rain; sometimes it happened, sometimes it didn't.

It might never happen again.

The doctors had known from the beginning that it must be a slow virus. It took years to develop, fully as long an incubation period as AIDS had had. In the beginning the symptoms looked like Alzheimer's disease: confusion, memory loss. Then they looked a little like agoraphobia. The patient become reluctant to leave his house, to engage in any new activity. Joe could remember his mother's voice, high-pitched with unspoken fear: "Why don't you go outside and play baseball? Don't you *want* to go outside?" All the mothers, all the fear.

By the time the symptoms were done looking like twenty other diseases, the slow virus had spread throughout the brain, destroying all capacity to form new memories. The plague patient lived in a limited past, sometimes as large as one day, sometimes only as large as a single repeated action. Making a bed. Taking a bath. Writing a letter. Over and over and over and over . . .

And now the med team had it. The slow virus identified and isolated. Maybe soon, the transmission mechanism identified. Maybe soon, an end to the suspicion and hatred, people with plague shunned, relatives harassed, group homes like the one this morning bombed—Joe couldn't take it in. Sitting on the edge of his bed, watching his foot once more begin to tremble, he wondered whether he believed the cure would ever really be found, and chided himself for his disbelief. What the hell was he doing on a Presidential Commission, Joe McLaren from inner city Pittsburgh, if he didn't believe the Commission would do what it had been formed to do?

He did believe it. They had the first step. They had—in Pirelli's words—son-of-a-bitching done it. It would just take time to realize, time to grasp . . .

He eased off the bed and switched on his box. The *Brandenburg Concertos* filled the room with forceful sound, almost drowning out the chime from the terminal.

He called up the message without thinking. There were only six words. JOE—PLEASE CALL. PURPLE MARTINS FLYING.

Anger flooded him. How had she gotten this access number? Not from Angel. No matter what unknown problem Angel was struggling with, he had relayed Robin's message through channels. The only other people who knew Joe was at this Institute were those on the Commission, and the only Commission member who knew his ex-wife was Pirelli.

PURPLE MARTINS FLYING.

Robin had left him five years after their marriage, running off to California with a handsome young Gaeist who told her she was a living rose. Joe had never told her anything so embarrassing; he had not told her much of anything. He stared at the computer screen. Bach surged through the air, triumphant and complex sound. When he finally heard the knocking at the door, he jabbed at the OFF button so hard the box slid across the dresser.

He was surprised to see the young blond man from the terrace leaning against the doorjamb, a stupid red ruffle dangling from his headband. Brekke. Disarmer of hysterical women. Porous-headed hero.

"Yes?"

"Hello again," Brekke said, smiled, waited for a response. Joe didn't give him one. It didn't seem to make any difference; Brekke plunged ahead. "Are you a lawyer?"

"Why?"

"Someone downstairs said you were."

Caroline Bohentin? She hadn't seemed especially taken with Brekke's mock heroics, but that didn't necessarily mean anything. You never could tell with women. She could have talked to Brekke again after Joe came upstairs. He waited, doing nothing to help. Brekke smiled again; he seemed amused.

"Because if you're a lawyer, I'd like to ask for some legal advice. As a fee-paying client, of course."

"I'm not here to take on clients."

"Well, no, of course not. I'm not here to be one."

"Then we're agreed. Good night," Joe said. He started to shut the door, but Brekke said, "It involves a legal question about memory."

"So?"

"So memory interests you. It must."

"Why?"

"Because you're here. Just tell me this, really fast if you want to—what happens if someone signs something, a confession or business deal or something, while under the influence of a previous life? Is it binding?"

Brekke spoke with sudden earnestness, a shift so unexpected that Joe mistrusted it immediately. It wasn't that the earnestness seemed contrived, but that under it simmered a kind of excitement, an overheated confidence that already knew what it believed. It was evident in the taut line of Brekke's wrist along the doorjamb, the excited tilt of his head. It was the look of junior defense lawyers contemptuous of routine police reports, of hotshot politicians whose every constituency need was a national crisis. Joe knew the stance well and disliked it intensely: its self-absorption, its lack of proportion. Because he knew he did, and that his dislike was apt to be unfair, he made himself answer Brekke.

"I don't know what you mean by 'under the influence of a previous life.' "

"Yes, you do, damn it!" The flash of anger disappeared as fast as it had come; Brekke's smile was reconciliatory. "Look, I don't mean all the complete legal ramifications, all the loopholes. I mean in general. If, say, I signed something while I thought I was someone else, someone from a previous life who might want different things than I do now, would that be legally binding?"

"You just saw an entire holovid explaining that memories of a past life are just that: memories. Plazzing doesn't make you think you *are* that person. It isn't supposed to work that way."

"Fuck *supposed to*. Are there legal precedents? You're the lawyer!"

Joe looked at him. After a moment Brekke said, "I'm sorry. And I *can* pay you."

"I doubt it."

Brekke brightened. Apparently this was what he wanted: thrust and parry, conversational adversity. With great distinctness Joe said, "There are very few legal precedents in reincarnation law. I don't know what information you're after, and it's not my field anyway. But if what you're asking is whether you can sign an otherwise legal contract and then later repudiate such a contract on grounds of mental or emotional extremity arising from reincarnation surgery, the answer is no. The courts are clear on that. Increased memory is not a legally incapacitating state."

Brekke nodded. "I see."

"Good for you."

"And now get the hell out, right?" The grin flashed. "Are you always so stodge about the letter of the law, Joe? And do you always take such instant dislikes?"

"Pseudo-outrageousness is less interesting than you think it is."

Brekke laughed, acknowledging a hit; reluctantly Joe saw what Jane Flexner and Sandy Ochs and Caroline Bohentin had found so appealing. It didn't make him like Brekke any better.

"I'm going. Thanks for the data. And good luck on your surgery tomorrow."

Joe refused to ask how Brekke had known the date. The younger man stepped back from the door, blue eyes vivid. Joe's foot throbbed. His stomach felt sour.

"Did you notice," Brekke said, "that they never mentioned the sexual side effects of getting plazzed?"

"No."

"They're supposed to be pretty close to uncontrollable. One sexual remembrance and the good old over-memory goes straight for the dick."

Joe said nothing. Brekke grinned again and Joe closed the door. Before the last sliver of hallway vanished, Brekke began to whistle: Chopin, the Nocturne in E Flat. Surprise made Joe hold the door; annoyance made him close it.

The wall screen still held Robin's message. **PURPLE MARTINS FLYING.**

Joe blanked the screen, turned away, turned back. On sudden impulse, he keyed in the ABA net, nonvocal mode.

AMERICAN BAR ASSOCIATION DATANET. ACCESS RESTRICTED. ACCOUNT NUMBER, PLEASE?

Joe gave it, then typed PLAGUE VICTIM INFORMATION REQUEST. LEVEL THREE. CROSS-REFERENCE NAME SEARCH: CATHERINE BOHENTIN. MINOR.

Minor? Had to be. The mother couldn't be more than thirty-five, even allowing for all the cosmetic clinics in the world. Probably she was even younger.

The datanet gave him the unprivileged information almost immediately:

CATHERINE MARIE BOHENTIN LONG
BORN JULY 2, 2012, NEW YORK, NEW YORK
AMERICAN CITIZEN
FATHER, GENETIC/LEGAL: CHARLES GORE LONG
MOTHER: GENETIC/GESTATIVE/LEGAL: CAROLINE
      SUSAN BOHENTIN (KLINE, LONG)
FIRST PLACE DIAGNOSIS: FEBRUARY, 2019, JOHNS
      HOPKINS
CURRENT STATUS: MINOR
                CUSTODY OF BIOLOGICAL
                  MOTHER
                RESIDENT, MEADOWS HOME
                    204 GARDEN ROAD
                    ALBANY, NEW YORK
                    E-POST 16*4288*18j

PUBLIC DOCUMENT HISTORY: ENTER COMMON
      NUMBER
POLICE RECORD: LEVEL TWO ACCESS
MEDICAL HISTORY: LEVEL ONE ACCESS
FINANCIAL HISTORY: LEVEL ONE ACCESS

Joe rubbed his eyes. He was more tired than he thought. Angel's call, Angel's strange voice, hovered at the back of his eardrums. Caroline Bohentin's daughter, who was also the daughter of the man slated to be the next governor of New Jersey, had contracted plague at the age of six. Rubbing didn't help his eyes much; they burned somewhere behind the irises, somewhere he couldn't reach.

He wiped the ABA net. The screen returned to message mode: PURPLE MARTINS FLYING. Joe blanked it, keyed off the incoming chime, thought again and turned it back on. Pirelli might call again. Probably not, but he might.

Joe switched on the box and lay, fully dressed, across the Institute bed. The mattress felt firm under the small of his back. He tried to imagine the newly isolated virus, removed from someone's brain to grow slowly, slowly in a computer-controlled pulpy and artificial culture, while around him the *Brandenburg Concertos* leapt and sped, sure inevitabiities of sound.

3 ROBBIE

Robbie leaned his shoulders against a huge natural sugar maple halfway between the Institute building and Lake Ontario. Leaves as large as his hand rustled in the darkness; behind him, unseen waves broke gently over rock. It was 3 A.M. While waiting for the brainie he had swallowed moments ago to take effect, he stared at the black rectangular bulk of the Institute slicing across the southern stars.

The windows of the first-floor lobby shone with dim ghostly night lights. Above the first floor, only two lights burned, one in the northwest corner of the fifth floor and one slightly west of center on the third. Three windows had been forced open, on the fourth and fifth floors. The screens looked flimsy, but the north face of the building presented few handholds, and anyway there was no need for that much risk. Although it might have been fun.

Robbie reached up and caught a maple leaf, tracing the cool ridged veins with one finger. He could feel the brainie begin to take hold, although not in any obvious way. No rush of light or color, no glorious electrical storm in the limbic or the temporal lobes. Not for this. He shifted his weight to his toes, flexed his knees. He felt light and eager, capable in a quiet way, slightly detached. In control. The feeling said that nothing

55

would be hard to decide or carry out, and that everything needed to be done. It was time.

Moving soundlessly across the wet grass, he rounded the west end of the building and entered the main lobby in careful view of the monitor cameras. A legitimate resident, out for a late-night walk. Nervous about having his brain plazzed three days from now, unable to sleep. Hide in plain sight.

He pressed the elevator button for the third floor, got out, eased open the stairwell door, and climbed to the fifth. The stairwells, he had learned, were monitored for the first and second floors, where visitors and medical staff gathered, but not on the residential floors, where nocturnal wanderers probably wanted sexual anonymity. And the Institute, ever ready to serve client needs, had obliged. Robbie smiled.

The lawyer's door was at the far end of the fifth-floor hall. Poor limping stodge. Tomorrow was his day. Robbie wished him well, even if McLaren did have his balls hard-wired to his cortex. After all, it was the visit to McLaren's room that had given Robbie the excuse to dawdle in traffic coming and going from every room on the fifth floor. He had chatted with two people in the short walk from the elevator to McLaren's door, and three on the way back. Two, both women, had invited him in for drinks. Robbie could have mapped out the entire floor for Hatton—except that Hatton wasn't going to know about this.

In the room across from McLaren's was the journalist, Prokop. Next came the minor British lord—neither any good. Prokop wore a cheap watch, and the aging lord reeked of caution. Robbie could smell it, the stink of a body so desperately clutching the remnants of what was his that he never looked up to see the whole rich array of what wasn't. Poor blighter.

The fourth room, directly across from the stairwell, belonged to Caroline Bohentin. Robbie hesitated. With that pretty blue dress she had worn a gold necklace discreetly set with diamonds, and on her right hand a diamond ring that was a stunner. And one of the three windows forced open to the screen had been hers. She was careless.

But he and Caroline were both here for three more days before surgery, and a month afterward. Robbie knew when women found him attractive, no matter what they said, and no matter what false step he had accidentally taken on the terrace with that stupid plague joke. Caroline would get over her pique. And if she were burgled now, she might feel less interested in sex for a while. Some women were like that. He moved past Caroline's door.

The holovid evangelist, the shabby academic—probably saved for this all his life—the nondescript couple who had held hands at the reception. Rich, but two doubled the risk. He stopped at the last door and pulled out DeFillippo's E-break.

A featureless gray metal square three inches on a side and half an inch deep, it had cost him the calling in of every favor he had ever done for anybody. DeFillippo, who had located the fiberhead who had matched its mysterious inner components to pirated data on Institute security, had sworn the E-break was the best on the street. Robbie didn't know, or care, how it worked. He had tested it on his own room, and it had deactivated the lock without triggering any alarms. DeFillippo was all right.

It worked again now. The square in his hand flashed a brief light as fields tangled, and then the doorknob turned under his membrane-gloved hand. He slipped inside and closed the door.

Utter blackness: curtains drawn, screen blanked of even a message light, not so much as a digital clock. From the bed came a rhythmic swampy cacophony. Robbie grinned; Elle Watt-Davis, the would-be-famous holovid actress, snored.

When he had tried to talk to the bitch earlier, coming on as admiring and ingenuous as he could, she had cut him dead. He had said nothing. Now he felt the brainie coursing through him, experiencing it as a steady stream of certainty: quiet, capable, strong.

The furniture arrangement seemed to be identical for every room on the floor. Robbie eased past the bed, felt for the dresser on the west wall. Carefully he worked the surface from right to left. Makeup jars. Pencils. Comb. Tissues. Wig—he smiled into the darkness—book, micro-vid. Necklace.

It was heavy, made up of separate, large flat plates on an intricate chain. Robbie had seen it on Elle Watt-Davis's slender neck earlier that afternoon, in the lobby: African, worn as a morbid attention-getter, a trendy affront to the good taste that avoided trivialization of Africa's final death by politics, famine, and the AIDS that had been checked in the United States twenty years ago. The necklace was worthless.

The actress snorted wetly and turned over in bed.

Robbie's fingers brushed something wet and sticky. He brought his hand to his nose and sniffed: spilled makeup. He started to wipe his fingers on his pants, stopped himself, carefully held open his pants pocket and wiped his glove inside the pocket.

Cassettes. Pill bottle. Rectangular box.

He felt smooth wood with rounded corners, a simple metal clasp. He frowned. A jewelry box would have an E-lock and metal casings. And the actress couldn't be that stupid—she wouldn't have a whole box of jewelry in her room. Robbie had hoped only for the earrings she had been wearing when she passed him in the hall on her way to her bedroom: long dangling curves of jade set with diamonds. They had swung above her shoulders like glittery scythes.

He pressed the clasp on the wooden box. Immediately the room filled with electronic shrieking, wails that rose and fell and rose again at a pitch to shatter bone. The actress sat up and screamed.

Robbie grabbed the bedspread from the foot of her bed,

yanked hard, and threw it into the blackness where he thought her face should be. The screaming muffled in mid-note; the alarm shrieked on. Robbie sprinted for the door, wrenched it open, and hurled himself through before the woman could pull the blanket from her eyes.

His luck held. The stairwell door slammed behind him just as the first of the doors opened along the fifth-floor corridor. Racing down to the fourth floor, he reached its fire door just as the one above flew open. Footsteps pounded on the metal stairs.

The fourth floor lay quiet. There was a second stairwell in the east wing; Robbie ran toward it through an open social area. A blank datanet screen stared blindly. Pool cues, neatly crossed on green felt, looked like elongated bones. He couldn't remember who roomed on the fifth floor and might be behind him; then he could, seeing the names typed before him in the air, a glowing list traveling along beside him as he ran. It was probably the journalist. Prokop. He reached the second stairwell unseen, sped down the stairs, and emerged on the third floor, where he made himself stroll casually down the corridor to his room.

Even though he was breathing hard, he could feel his mind sliding along smooth, clean grooves of thought—thanks to the brainies. He stripped off the membrane gloves, wadded them small, and put them into the lens disinfector, where they immediately vaporized. Pulling off his clothes, he laid them carelessly across a chair, then climbed into bed and lit a toke.

No one knocked on the door. Robbie began to smile.

A walk outside, the elevator to his room—both camera-verified—then a late toke and sleep. Let even that draggle-footed lawyer prove otherwise.

But—

But what if the actress's room had had infrared security, photographing the outline of his body from the heat it gave off?

For a second the chill penetrated even his brainie. But,

no—the Institute had obviously put its money into external security, keeping out the nuts who bombed plague homes and Gaeist camps: getting *into* this place had been a fucking ordeal. But once in, the well-heeled stodges were expected to behave themselves. There hadn't even been enough security to handle that split-brain Sandy Ochs. Rich people stole from each other in politer ways that he had just tried. And the actress—no one would back her for holovids, her last "movie" had been a wipe, and she had married only nobodies. Next to someone like Caroline Bohentin, she looked like imitation vinyl. She wasn't important enough for infrared.

But maybe she thought she was.

It was all DeFillippo's fault. DeFillippo should have fucking *warned* Robbie that the E-lock field didn't extend to international locks, DeFillippo should have foreseen the problem, DeFillippo should have . . .

No, it wasn't DeFillippo's fault. It was the goddamn infrared tech. Once you got past the people there were always E-locks and once you got past the E-locks there were usually more people and then on top of that to add the infrared and brain-scan tech—not that there would be brain-scan tech in a place like this—was a fucking shame. At least in Liberia you had a sporting chance. You could get shot, but that was part of the program, the zap, the power surge. It was only danger. Infrared was much more—infrared could get you hauled into court, and that could get you into prison.

He jabbed out his toke hard and turned off the light. Prison. Locked in an eight-foot cell, scams run on brutality rather than wit, getting raped for his blue eyes by fags who just might well have the last cases of AIDS. And the same routine day after day. Gray, endless gray. There was nothing more stodge than that, the prison stamped on the gray readouts from infrared and brain-scan tech.

Hatton had had them both.

But the actress *didn't*. He was just paranoid, because of

Hatton. If it hadn't been for Hatton, he wouldn't even be thinking about infrared. It was just Hatton, and the brainie wearing off. He had done everything right tonight, until the damn alarm had gone off, and he had handled that well and gotten out clean, so he certainly wasn't going to panic now. Not over the actress, not over Hatton. After all, if it hadn't been for Hatton, he wouldn't even be at the Institute.

He had been working with DeFillippo in Boston. A deal had gotten wiped, a big one—it was always the big ones that got wiped, somehow—and he and DeFillippo had been desperate to recover some costs. Not a lot desperate, just a little, but enough to try an old-fashioned live run on an estate DeFillippo knew on Cape Cod. DeFillippo spent the last of their Liberia money to buy the estate's security data from his best stodge contact. The estate had an electric fence, electronic surveillance' dogs, and E-locks: nothing too difficult, except maybe the dogs. But dogs liked Robbie, nearly all dogs. He figured it was something in his smell. DeFillippo figured it was crap.

"They'll tear you apart, Brekke. They're fucking *attack* dogs."

"No," Robbie said. He leaned back in his chair in DeFillippo's dirty apartment, enjoying the moment. "They won't. They'll growl and bristle, but they'll hold off attacking until I get close enough to shoot in the tranqs. Dogs like me. Dogs and women."

DeFillippo farted.

"No, it's true. Oh, they'd attack if someone ordered them to, but if I'm alone with them they'll come at me and then slow down and feel uncertain."

"How the hell do you know how a dog feels?"

"I do. They won't chew me. I know it's weird, but they won't. A friend once took me down to a place they train attack dogs, in Georgia, because he didn't believe it either. His brother worked there. I went in with the dogs over and over, and it worked every time. They even offered me a *job* there. I was only seventeen."

"So maybe you lost it since then."

Robbie smiled. "I didn't lose it."

DeFillippo watched him from small eyes the color of dead leaves. A flat purple splotch on the side of his neck seemed to Robbie to have grown larger since they were in Liberia. They hadn't gone anywhere near either the bomb sites or chem zones; maybe it was just Robbie's imagination. A few hairs grew from a wart in the middle of the splotch.

"Sometimes I think you don't know any more than you did at seventeen, Brekke."

"I know I can take out the dogs."

DeFillippo shrugged. "It's your jugular. I can handle the fence, Crispy will get us the E-breaks, the floor plan for the house came through this morning. You enter here. The dining room is off to your left—move closer to the fucking screen, Robbie, you need to memorize details . . ."

Neither the screen nor the surveillance contact had mentioned the infrared tech. It must have caught him as soon as he entered the house, gone on tracking him even after the brain scan took its silent data. Robbie never found out. Hatton had been waiting for him in the shadows at the far end of the dining room, Seymour Hatton himself, with a neat little laser gun in his hand.

"Stop there. Put your hands on your head. Do it now." The voice had been calm and reasonable. Robbie, on brainies, had obeyed immediately.

"Turn around."

Hatton cuffed him, then turned Robbie around again. It was Robbie's first good view. Hatton was in his sixties, a short, powerfully built man with no visible bio-mods. He had white hair and a tan, deep against a white robe of dull, heavy silk. Robbie's first thought had been, *I'd like a robe like that*, a thought he later found incongruous until he realized he was a little bit proud of having had it. Coolness under fire. An eye for quality. DeFillippo never would have noticed the robe.

"Sit down," Hatton said. He pushed a chair toward Robbie, who took it. "Who are you?"

Robbie didn't answer. At the first syllable in Hatton's voice, the brainie melted off every synapse. Robbie could hear it, all in those three words: Hatton was not going to call the police. Something else was running. It was in the set of Hatton's shoulders, the lifting of his brows, the angle of the little gun drooping in his fingers. But most of all it was in the voice, the words, the words behind the words. *Not stodge.* And Hatton was curious about him, curious and interested—more interested than angry.

"How did you get in here?"

Robbie never even thought how to answer. He knew, the answer welling up out of him easily and naturally, with no false fumble, no second-guessing. Pure nerve, pure instinct. As he had always known he could, given the right opportunity, and despite what anyone else said. He had always known it was lying there ahead for him somewhere. Always.

"E-break. Not hard. An outside partner to deal with the fence."

"How?"

"I don't know. He does the electronics."

"And the dogs?"

"They're alive. Tranq gun. In my shoe."

Hatton didn't feel for it. Instead he studied Robbie's face and Robbie felt it all over again. The time, the break, the chance. The big one.

"The dogs wouldn't let you get that close."

"They let me. All dogs do."

"Not these."

"These, too."

Hatton's eyes gleamed. "A useful talent, young man."

"Yes, sir."

"I'm not impressed by deference."

"Certainly not." He let himself almost smile, looking straight at the old man. Hatton shifted slightly.

"What's your name, young man?"

"Robbie Brekke."

"Are you sure?"

"*I* am. You're not."

"I will be. What were you doing in my dining room, Robbie Brekke?"

"Inspecting your George III silver. Suppose you tell me how you knew I was in your dining room."

"Suppose you tell me how you know it's George III."

"I know a lot of things."

"I imagine you do," Hatton said. His eyes gleamed; Robbie felt the excitement spin itself out along his nerves, cool and liquid. This was it, all right. The way he always knew it was supposed to be. As far from DeFillippo's grubby street deals as it was possible to get. Here, now, the real thing.

"Wait here," Hatton said, not even binding Robbie to the chair. But then, why should he? Hatton knew, too, Robbie thought. He had to.

He was gone a long time. When he returned, Robbie first saw the robe, rich white silk materializing out of the shadowed doorway like a slow holovid.

"Robbie Brekke."

"I said I was."

"You run minor scams for Paul DeFillippo, before that for Jose Menezes."

"I never—"

"Then you didn't know it was for Menezes. He operates that way. You've never done time, never logged as much as an arrest. You've been very careful or very lucky, Robbie Brekke. You come from Boston, you live nowhere, you weigh one hundred seventy-five. You spent five months smuggling in

Africa, and your attention curves are interesting in that they're aroused considerably faster than normal."

Robbie said slowly, "Brain scan. You have brain-scan tech—but no, wait, there's no dBase on me anywhere to match it to—"

"Menezes has it."

"I never—"

"You didn't have to. He has it."

When? He couldn't remember. Hatton stood smiling like a trim Buddha. Robbie said, "And you picked me up with brain scan—"

"With infrared. As soon as you reached the side door. Brain scan was later. Just for identification purposes, you understand."

"Usually it's cops who have the tech. And you're no cop."

"Certainly not," Hatton said, mocking Robbie's phrase so exactly, inflections and even the tilt of the head, that they both smiled. Their eyes met. A voice in Robbie's head—not the brainies, better than the brainies—said, cool, and calm, *Partners already*. The moment spun itself out, glowing as crystal.

Then Hatton shattered it.

"Listen to me." His voice had become a little ragged; the breast of the silk robe rose and fell. "There are six people in the house right now. Maybe you already know that. One of them is Donohue, my bodyguard, monitoring me now. The E-break you used to get in here won't get you out; the program changes behind each entry. You're here until I say different. But maybe that's all right with you." He leaned over, laid two fingers against Robbie's cheek, and slowly traced the line of his jaw.

Robbie froze. He had never even met, never even seen, nobody did—they just weren't there, not since the turn of the century and the AIDS hysteria he thought they were all dead or in prison or killed, all the perverts—

Hatton's fingers caressed this throat.

"No," Robbie said, loudly but calmly. He remembered the calm later. His nostrils seemed to fill with Hatton's old-man smell; nausea rose in him like oil. "No!"

Hatton took two steps backward. In a totally different voice he said, "You're a fool."

Robbie didn't answer.

"Did you suppose I was interested in your skills as a *thief?* Caught by a simple infrared and an old man who—contrary to what your over-fevered brin now imagines—is not into anything *you* would recognize as crime?"

"Into." Even his diction was old, was stodge, how could Robbie have thought any different? A rich fag stodge, just hanging on like death to whatever he had put together during a life of the same gray flat paralyzing boredom as everyone else, only Robbie had thought—had *thought:* Just another fat stodge, a fucking plague victim without the plague, done with his living and interested in Robbie only for some filthy sex, it had only been a sexual interest after all—

He sprang off the chair, bringing both cuffed hands up hard under Hatton's chin. The little gun fired, and Robbie went down.

When he came to, he lay on the floor of the same dining room, staring at a ceiling crossed by dark polished beams. His head ached with the peculiar wavery throbbing of nerve stun.

"If you don't move," Hatton said genially from the chair, "the headache won't be quite as bad."

The straight lines of the beams hurt his eyes. Robbie closed them. After a moment something wet and rough touched his eyelids, and he opened them: one of the dogs, licking him. Its eyes, inches from his own, were a flat opaque black. The dog growled softly, deep in its throat, showing a quarter-inch gleam of white teeth.

"You were telling the truth," Hatton said; his voice held

amusement. "If you hadn't been, we'd have had quite a mess on the parquet. Heee, Abigail—heee!"

The dog backed off a foot and lay down, continuing to regard Robbie. He turned his head, which immediately ached worse. Hatton sat smiling.

"Do you know what the term *'un vrai innocent'* means, Robbie Brekke?"

"I can translate it," Robbie said sulkily. At the sight of Hatton, his gorge rose again. Beneath the silk hem of the robe, bare skinny legs crossed at the knee.

"Very good. French picked up in Africa? I thought so. But do you understand the term's religious significance?"

Robbie didn't answer.

"Ah. How about the term 'pratfall lucky'? You take offense, Robbie Brekke. But you must be one or the other to have your remarkably inept crime history combined with your remarkable lack of any formal police record. Quite an achievement. All those scams depending on charm and youthful high spirits, starting so well, finishing so drearily. You were pratfall lucky to get out of Liberia alive, you know. I know Kwambe DeLucas. Down, Abigail!"

Robbie didn't turn his head toward the dog. Hatton recrossed his bare knees in the opposite direction, left over right. Stale smells drifted across the floor.

"Two years at an insignificant college," Hatton went on. "Insignificant but real, not just a data front. You can talk well. You smile well. You dress with the kind of shabbiness women find appealing. And that infallible innocence underneath— women are such sentimentalists, Robbie Brekke, all of them. Yearning to be understood. You give them the illusion that they are."

Robbie jerked his head; pain stabbed behind his eyes like bayonets.

"I told you to lie still. You don't listen when you are told something. But that isn't a large problem—there are many people who know how to make sure other people remember what they are told. Those people generally don't talk well, aren't charming, and could never be accused of innocence."

Through the pain behind his forehead Robbie said, "You're building up to something. Say it."

"I am indeed," Hatton said. He bent down and reached across Robbie to rub the dog's neck. Robbie saw directly above him, a foot from his face, the same expression Hatton had worn earlier, in the doorway to the dining room, the expression that had made him think the old man was more than stodge. Had made him think this was something, was a break, was real. Tied on the floor, Hatton's crepey neck leaning across him, the memory made Robbie writhe. Hatton picked a flea from the dog's fur, leaned back, and crushed the flea between his fingers. He held the minute dead fleck out to Robbie as if it were a delicacy, and smiled.

"How much have you ever thought about reincarnation surgery, Robbie Brekke?"

Robbie punched his pillow viciously and flopped back down across it. The third-floor corridor beyond his door was still quiet. Whatever the two-byte Institute Security was going to do about the attempted robbery of Elle Watt-Davis, they apparently weren't going to do it until tomorrow.

The Institute would be netted to a private police agency, of course. Not that it would matter. Whatever any legit agency had on him—if anything—the Institute would have already researched when he applied for admission. The problem was that when the Institute posted the attempted theft, Hatton would have it. There wasn't a legit police datanet that was adequately defended—why should there be? Information flowed both ways. And even though the Institute had no evidence to formally tie the run to Robbie, Hatton wouldn't need any such legalities. And Hatton had made clear his position on free-lance work while Robbie was getting plazzed.

Christ, Christ, Christ.

Of course, if he had succeeded in getting the jewelry, Hatton's displeasure might have been worth it. Why had he dropped the case? No, that had actually been good sense—courtesy of the brainies. No time to hide it outside his room anyway.

The last of the brainies melted off his neurons. He played it over and over again, thinking he should have done this, thinking he should have done that. Slowly his annoyance at himself faded. You couldn't get it right every time. No one could. These things happened. And he had thrown the blanket over the actress's face so deftly. Not a wasted motion, not a superfluous thought. Smooth. DeFillippo would have approved; that fag Hatton himself would have had to approve. He could still feel the edge of the fabric in his hands, the quick economical turn of both wrists, the sudden deft muffling of her scream. Smooth. Fast. No one hurt.

He fell asleep smiling.

4 CAROLINE

"Ms. Bohentin," said a male voice. Caroline groaned and kept her eyes closed. She tried to put a hand over her face to block out the light but somehow her hand wasn't there anymore or, if it was, she couldn't find it. This cut through the mush in her head faster that the voice had done; she opened her eyes. Her hand lay across her chest, the inside of the wrist thin against the blue hospital gown. The old scars were lacy white ridges. She closed her eyes.

"Ms. Bohentin. Wake up."

"No," she whispered, and could hear the amusement in the voice when it spoke again.

"You're already awake. Come on, now. The anesthetic should be pretty much gone."

"What day is it?"

"Thursday. Come on, we'd like a chance to ask you a few easy questions."

"Who's President of the United States?" Caroline said, and opened her eyes. Brown eyes in a heavy, ruddy face loomed over her: Robert Bulriss, assistant surgeon. Before surgery she had talked with him twice. His directness and warmth had made the whole Institute seem less slick. Behind him stood Dr. Armstrong, sleek dignified blackness; behind her, two strangers, one of them a nurse.

"We could hold the caucus right here," Caroline said, to make Bulriss laugh. He did. Her stomach was starting to tighten, a long slow pull of steel cable from throat to belly. This was it, then. She went on trying to amuse Bulriss.

"So, who am I? Who are I?"

"Who do you want to be?" Bulriss said. The brown eyes—shit brown, dead-leaf brown—were kind. She groped for his hand and he gave it to her. His fingers were plump and warm.

"No one should have to talk philosophy under anesthetic, Doctor."

"Nor have to be funny, either. How do you feel, Caroline?"

"Scared."

"Lucky you, to be able to admit it. You came through surgery fine. Does your head ache?"

"No. Yes. I don't know yet. Am I shot full of brainies?"

"Yes. But you might have a slight headache anyway. You won't be doing much for a few days. Right now Dr. Armstrong is going to make a simple neurological exam, and then we're going to do a brain scan in the awake state. After that, Father Shahid wants to talk to you for a little while. Father Shahid is our resident historian."

"Don't waste any time, do you?" Caroline said. "Give the customer what she wants."

"And you get a free set of drinking glasses when you check out. Bet you didn't know about that."

"Tastefully embossed with cortical diagrams," Caroline said. She felt that she might throw up or—worse—cry. Bulriss squeezed her hand and pulled a curtain around her bed, enclosing her and Armstrong in a cocoon of yellow plastic.

Armstrong's exam was quick and deft; Caroline endured its mild physical indignities in silence. In the black woman's austere presence, all desire to cry left her. Caroline watched the long slim fingers, supple as a musician's, and the wrist bones turning under the polished skin. *What were you in former lives?*

"Everything looks fine, Ms. Bohentin. Excellent reflexes. Please sit up for the brain scan. Do you need help?"

"No," Caroline said. She hadn't taken brainies in years, had sworn off them when she divorced Charles. The calm felt like something anchored just beyond her, a clumsy ship too far from the pier, essentially useless.

The brain-scan equipment came in on wheels. How could they make the wheels so soundless? She didn't ask. She endured having her head held immobile for ten minutes, Dr. Armstrong and her nurse as soundless and efficient as the machinery. Caroline wondered what had happened to Sandy Ochs.

Then her body was returned to her, and she sat back against her pillows. Armstrong and the nurse left; Bulriss and the historian returned.

"Don't you have any more tests, Doctor? Blood sugar? Genetic markers? Lower G.I.? I think I have gas."

"Caroline, this is Father Patrick Martin Shahid. He's done this more times than you've had gas, believe me. I'm going to leave you two now, but I'll be back to check on you this afternoon."

She clung to his fingers a minute—when had she taken them again?—then let him go. Father Patrick Martin Shahid pulled a chair close to her bed and sat down.

He was a small man, Indian or Pakistani; Caroline realized that standing he would barely reach her earlobe. He wore a formal clerical collar and expensive dark suit, with a cross and chain of finely crafted gold. But what caught her were his eyes: In his smooth brown face they were a very soft black, like ash or fur, with a still, edgeless intensity.

"Ms. Bohentin—"

"Caroline," she said. His voice was quiet and courteous, unaccented, but she knew immediately he had not been born in the United States. There was a formality about him, a reserve she had not expected in a Catholic priest; those she had met before had mostly been social cheerleaders of balky and diminishing flocks. "Patrick Martin Shahid"? What sort of hybrid was that?

"Caroline. I know you have been through the presurgery classes here and have been instructed in approximately what to expect. But I want to start by telling you that instruction is not the same as memory. Do not be guided by what you have been told of the experiences of others. Let yourself remember what you will, in the way you will. The existing number of people who have undergone previous life access surgery—" she noticed that he said neither "plazzing" nor "carnies"—"is still very small. It may be your experience will differ significantly from theirs."

"I might for instance remember being male?"

"That has never happened yet. The constancy of gender is one of the most unexpected surprises in my field. But who can say it will always be constant? What I am going to show you now is—"

"Have you had the surgery?" She heard her voice: too loud, too urgent.

Shahid looked at her from his soft eyes. "I am a Jesuit. It is not permitted."

"Yet you counsel others about it!"

"Not counsel. I instruct in facts. And I—we—learn."

"Why? Why does your Church even permit you to be here?"

She thought she saw something move behind his eyes, but she couldn't be sure. The cable pulled tighter in her throat.

"I am on special assignment for the Bishop. The past is a legitimate area of intellectual inquiry, and you are probably aware of the Jesuit tradition of intellectualism. But, Ms. Bohentin, this does not—"

"What kind of name is Patrick Martin Shahid?" Immediately she was ashamed of her rudeness, but Shahid did not seem to take offense. He answered her with patient dignity.

"My father was Pakistani, my mother an Irish Catholic nun with a missionary Order in Pakistan, at the time of the last revolution. She left the Order. But this does not matter, not just now. You don't have to postpone your story by asking mine. You don't have to be afraid."

"How would *you* know?" More rudeness, she just couldn't seem to stop. Shahid looked at her for a long moment before he spoke.

"Do you know Kierkegaard?"

She shook her head, wondering why he would even assume she might. Did she look to him like someone who read Kierkegaard? How could that possibly be? But there was no condescension in his quiet voice, and no assumptions.

"His words on this are truer than he could possibly have known. 'Only the lower natures forget themselves and become something new. The butterfly, for example, completely forgets that it was a caterpillar. The deeper natures never forget themselves, and never become anything other than what they were.'

"In other words. Ms. Bohentin, there is no escape from yourself this way. I hope you did not expect that."

Caroline stared at him. "Let's get on with it!"

Shahid looked at her a moment longer. The soft black eyes gave no reflections. He bent to the floor and brought up a zippered leather case. Caroline had not known it was there.

"What I am going to show you now are very simple artifacts, common to many cultures around the world. For ninety percent of our people, one of these objects will evoke the first memory. A memory, as you know even in this life, can be evoked by anything—the creaking of a door hinge, the sight of a childhood toy, a color, a scent. It happens to us all the time. The only difference is that now we will evoke memories from your other lives."

From the leather case Shahid drew a red clay pot and handed it to Caroline. It felt rough and cool. She held it in her left hand and ran her right index finger over the curving unmarked sides, uneven neck, flared lip. She shook her head.

"Nothing. All I think of are museums."

Shahid showed no surprise. He slipped the clay pot back into his case and handed her a knife with a plain wooden handle and dulled, six-inch blade.

She stood at the table, chopping onions. The chimney was smoking again. Smoke irritated her nose; she sneezed. "Mathilde!" he called sharply, from beyond the window. "The cow!" and she chopped faster, peat smoke and onion fumes burning her eyes . . .

"Oh," Caroline said. "*Oh . . .*"

"Where are you?" Shahid said. He leaned forward. "Where?"

"The kitchen. My . . . My stepfather just led the cow back to the byre and I have to milk it. And the stew is not started because I fell asleep and Mother will be angry again—"

Caroline fell back against the pillows. "Mathilde. I am Mathilde Ferrars. I am nine years old."

She savored it. Mathilde. She could see the kitchen, *feel* it: the smoky walls, blackened with generations of fires; the trestle table pulled close to the hearth; the tallow candles already lit against the frozen gray of a late afternoon in November. The kitchen smelled of onions and tallow and peat and wet dog, and when the door opened and Père Henri came in stomping snow from his boots, the warm reek of the cow byre came with him. She chopped faster, her thumb feeling for the deep nick that had always been there on the left side of the knife handle . . .

There was no nick in the knife in Father Shahid's hand.

Caroline put both hands over her face, then just as quickly lowered them.

"The confusion only lasts a moment," Shahid said in his courteous voice.

"No, it's not that. It's that it's so . . . I can feel it inside me, smell it even, but it's still . . ."

"A memory. Your memory."

"Yes. Only not really me . . . oh, it's me, but even the—
I have blond braids, looped up and caught with ribbons,
Mother ties them every morning. And I am betrothed to
Guillaume de Chatelot." She flung out one arm. "I am nine
years old and I'm betrothed. But I don't say it that way to
myself, I don't say it any way. It's just there. Like the table, the
onions. A memory."

"You didn't think it would be like that."

"My memory," Caroline said painfully. "Mine, and not
mine."

"What did you think it would be like?"

"I thought I would feel more . . . connected to the memories. To the lives."

"You thought they would feel more immediate."

"Yes!"

"I want you to do something now," Shahid said. "It is very
simple. Forget young Mathilde for just a moment and try to
remember something that happened to Caroline Bohentin
when she was nine years old. Something small but very clear,
that for some reason has detached itself and traveled along with
you since you were nine. Do you have such a moment?"

Caroline thought. "Nine . . . yes."

"Tell me about it."

"Colin is opening in a new play in New York, and my
grandmother is taking me shopping for a new dress. I have
never seen my father act before, my grandmother had already
decided he was the devil incarnate and never let—anyway, we
went to the old Bloomingdale's, on East Fifty-ninth, and a
saleswoman came in carrying a dress for me to try on. I remember thinking 'sea foam green,' immensely pleased with my
own poesy, watching the woman fumble with the leather belt
when it caught on the zipper . . . Now why should I remember
that dumb moment so clearly?"

"Why doesn't matter," Shahid said. A film of oil glistened

on his brown skin. "Does the moment feel *intimate?* Do you feel you *are* that child again?"

Caroline said slowly, "No. It's just a memory. I'm a different person now."

Shahid watched her, his small strong hands still holding the dagger.

"Then what's the *point?* Why go through this, why even remember this life, if it's going to be so *detached* . . . do you know how much fucking detachment I already have in my life? God . . ."

Her outburst seemed to turn Shahid even more formal. Even his voice changed. "Memory shapes us, Ms. Bohentin. You are a different person now, but the person you are has been shaped by that moment in Bloomingdale's, and the moment in Bloomingdale's was shaped by young Mathilde in her kitchen. Do you understand? It's good to know what shapes us."

"And that's it? A Freudian history lesson? That's *it?*"

Shahid returned the dagger to the leather case and zipped it. "You're angry."

"That's it? Tell me the truth!"

"How did Mathilde die?"

"Die?" She had to think. At first no memory came; then it did. "Why . . . she died . . . I never did marry Guillaume. I died at eleven years old. Of the Black Death."

She frowned. That memory, like the others, felt curiously detached. Yet it was death, her death. Her throat swelled, she couldn't swallow, and everywhere lay the stink of dying, choking her . . . She realized what that memory might feel like without detachment.

"If death felt as real to us as life, we would all despair," Shahid said, and she caught in his voice some undertone strong enough to pull her gaze to his face. He fingered the gold cross at his breast, but all he said was, "The Black Death came to Europe in the fourteenth century, and again in the seventeenth. Do you know the year Mathilde died?"

Caroline shook her head. "She . . . I . . ." A sudden vertigo swept her, a swooping black faint, passing over her like a wave. She put her hands over her face and laughed shakily. "It's not easy being two people, one of them dead. If I added"—the hysteria began, deep in her throat, effervescent as champagne—"if I added . . . added a third . . . I could be a holy Trinity!"

"Ms. Bohentin—"

"In the name of the m-mother, and the grandmother, and the h-h-holy holographic spirit— A-a-a-men!"

"Pull yourself together, Caroline."

"No, it's hilarious, don't you see? I could start a whole church—I could . . . I could . . ."

She couldn't control it. The laughter came, and between whoops all she could do was put her hand on Father Shahid's arm and hang on.

"I could be the whole fucking *Church*, everybody, clergy and worshippers and choir all by m-myself . . . I used to sing . . . do you s-s-suppose that the Catholic Trinity got started because someone had a spontaneous plazzing and c-c-connected . . . his own over-memory . . ."

"Yes," Shahid said, surprising her. He was not smiling. "Do you know the year young Mathilde died?"

In another minute she had stopped whopping long enough to answer him. "No. She didn't know the year, I couldn't read—"

"Who was King?"

Trying to remember sobered her. The answer surprised her by coming out tinged with a reverence she didn't feel. "His Majesty Philippe of Valois."

"France. Philippe VI. He ruled from 1328 to 1350." Caroline looked at him with new respect. The little priest didn't seem to notice. "Soon someone will show you how to use the global reincarnation datanet. You can find out if anyone else has come from the same decade, or the same village. What was it called?"

"Mur de Ronce." She tasted the strange name on her tongue. "But the chances of another carnie being from there, out of all the billions of people who ever lived—"

"Are better than you might think," Shahid said. Suddenly his smooth brown face pulled into lines of strain. Why strain, Caroline thought. Her own skin felt fragile, like thin paper.

Shahid said, "Let's continue. You will remember this." From his case he pulled a covered porcelain box, Chinese, glazed in an uneven blue. Its corners were rounded, and slightly irregular. On the lid, a few lines in black enamel sketched a flowering branch growing from a rock.

"Oh," Caroline said. "*Oh . . .*"

The box exactly fit over her right palm. She closed her eyes, and her other hand twined roughly into the bed sheet.

"Yes?" Shahid said expectantly.

"The *flute*. I hear Tsemo's flute."

"What is your name?"

"Linyi. I am Linyi." Her eyes flew open. "No—I am Caroline!"

Shahid smiled. "That memory must be much stronger than your Mathilde."

"I am *so happy.*" Shahid's expression sharpened, but Caroline barely noticed. She stood at the edge of the little courtyard, the pretty goldfish flashing in the little pool under the long golden shadows of late afternoon, the comfit box cool in her hand and the air filled with the sweetness of Tsemo's flute. In the adjoining courtyard her children played, their laughter silvery and high. Tsemo turned and took the flute from his mouth and smiled at her . . .

"Don't cry, Ms. Bohentin," Shahid said quietly.

"I'm not." She swiped at her cheeks and laughed. "But the order and the peace, I couldn't begin to describe to you the sense of *peace*—and then do you know what I thought of the next second after Tsemo and the flute? This cartoon I'd seen in the newspaper a few days ago. An air conditioner is saying, 'Oh, my God, I just remembered that during the Ming dynasty I was an ivory fan!' Don't you just love it?"

"Ms. Bohentin . . . Caroline . . ."

But she was off again, the uncontrollable laughter scraping at her throat. "Computers that remember being abacuses . . . and—please excuse m-me, Father . . . m-moon shuttles embarrassed over l-low-class roots as Sopwith Camels—"

He waited until she was done. And throughout it all, throughout the whole disgraceful and ridiculous performance, they were *there*, waiting: the little courtyard with the goldfish flashing in the slanting sun, the comfit box cool in her hand, the children laughing, Tsemo playing the flute like all the sweetness in the world gathered into plaintive high notes on the golden air.

Shahid said, "Do you always react this intensely to things, Caroline?"

She shook her head, nodded, made a futile effort to smooth her hair. "Do you know . . . is there somewhere I could buy a box like that?"

"You may have this one. It's only an inexpensive copy of a Ch'ing Dynasty piece."

She opened the box. The cover fit tightly enough to come off with a soft pop, like a sigh. Inside, the porcelain was less smooth. "How did you know I was once Chinese?"

"Shahid smiled. "*Everybody* was once Chinese."

Caroline went on studying the comfit dish, without really seeing it. The flute, and the courtyard . . . she could feel something shifting deep inside, the hidden movements of dark subterranean rock.

Shahid's fingers closed over the comfit box, drawing it away from her gaze. "Let's look at something else."

Reluctantly she let her hand be drawn to her side. From his

case Shahid pulled a length of cloth, rough woven material in undyed wool. Caroline shook her head.

Without comment, Shahid put away the cloth and showed her a small straw doll, its head and arms formed by strings tied around the yellow straw. Something stirred at the edge of Caroline's mind, flickered, and died. She shook her head.

He brought out a wad of string. Spread wide between his outstretched arms, it became a knotted net. A faint smell of fish drifted toward Caroline.

Her eyes widened. Against the hospital gown her nipples tightened and tingled, and a wave of desire pulsed through her so strong, and so unexpected, that she drew a sharp breath. But the breath was full of water, and she was sputtering and laughing and gasping, and Carlos was laughing too as he covered his mouth with hers so that she tasted both him and the sharp salt of the waves. The net tangled between their bodies, gritty with sand and slick with the oil of fishes, and that struck her as funny enough to pull her mouth from Carlos's and laugh again. He rolled her over onto her back and leaned above her, the flash of his teeth very white, his dark head haloed by the sun. One hand closed on her breast while the other fumbled at her skirt. She spread her legs eagerly and reached to draw him toward her, both of them tangled in the fish net, the sea thrashing around them, his fingers moving in her dark, sweet fish-smelling place between her legs . . .

Orgasm shook Caroline. She gasped and leaned forward. When the last spasm had passed, she realized that she sat against the headboard with her hospital gown yanked to her waist and her hand between her legs. Shahid had left his chair and stood at the foot of the bed with his back to her. Caroline jerked at her gown with her hand—it was very wet—and pulled the bedspread to her chin. Her face burned. "Father Shahid . . . I'm so sorry . . ."

He waited a courteous moment longer before turning.

"Don't be. It's normal. The doctors told you, did they not, that of all memories the sexual ones would be strongest, almost impossible to control without training?"

"They didn't say it would be like that!"

"You would not have believed it. The reasons are physiological. Evoked sexual memory sets up an electric storm near the limbic, not unlike some forms of epileptic seizure. Your training will include various controls: biofeedback, alpha-wave concentration, meditative techniques, Linsay-Barr grips. For the more impatient, sex suppressants, although I am told those also interfere with conventional response. Biofeedback is usually the preference."

She recognized that he was giving her time to overcome her embarrassment; she was grateful. Embarrassment yielded to hilarity. No, no, not again—she couldn't start whooping again. "A fish net . . . !"

"I admit that no one else has responded to the fish net in quite that way."

"What *else* have you got in that zippered time capsule?"

"Nothing for you. That's enough for today, I think. Would you like me to call a nurse to sit with you? Or an Institute hostess?"

"God, no."

"Dr. Bulriss will be back shortly."

"Fine." She wanted suddenly to be alone. A lightness filled her, a new necessity, urgent as the pull of sex.

"Before I go," Shahid said quiet, "I would leave you with a paragraph from a great Indian leader of the last century. India has been no friend to my country, yet I have never read a single word of this man's that is untrue. He wrote, 'It is nature's kindness that we do not remember past lives. Where is the good of having in detail the numberless births we have gone through? Life would be a burden if we carried such a tremendous load of memories. A wise man deliberately forgets many things.'"

Caroline stared at him. "You believe this? Yet you work *here*."

"Yes," Shahid said, and she saw for the second time that flash of inexplicable tension, this time deep enough to be pain. "Do not let the past overwhelm your present, Caroline."

She nodded, but without real attention. The lightness claimed her, heady as champagne. She scarcely noticed when Shahid left the room.

I am Mathilde. She saw again the farm kitchen, walls blackened with smoke, tallow candles flickering on the trestle table. Other memories followed, pulled one after the other, like the inevitable chords of strong music. The notes of Mathilde's life: her life. The stiffness of her first linen coif at the sides of her cheeks. Round yellow cheeses, heavy as stones. The birth of a calf, its front legs breeching its mother at the exact moment that the angelus rolled across the spring sky from the bell tower at the Priory.

I am Pilar. A much different life, all bright, careless memories, nights of wine blood red in wooden goblets and dark-eyed men smelling of goats and sweat and tasting of laughter . . .

Caroline felt herself flush and wrenched her thoughts away before her body could respond.

I am Linyi. The courtyard, and the slanting tranquil light on the goldfish, and Tsemo's flute. The peace. The children's laughter.

Shahid, she thought, had been wrong. The sexual memories were not the strongest. She remembered nothing, in any life, with the force of that lost sweet tranquility in the Chinese courtyard. Linyi, and Tsemo, and the flute. And she had children, two healthy, strong, laughing sons, Shujen and Piao with the fat smooth cheeks . . . more, she had had peace. Like a flawless Sung porcelain, Linyi's narrow life had been finished, complete, graced with the perfection possible only to the miniature. Linyi . . .

Someone came into the room, spoke to her, went away. Caroline lay unmoving, her hand on the imitation comfit box, her eyes opened so wide that after a while her vision blurred, and even her own feet, taut under the far end of the light bedspread, looked like something alien and strange.

5 JOE

Two and a half weeks after Joe's surgery, the medical staff insisted on what it called "guided small-group outings for post-surgical candidates." The idea, Joe gathered, was that outside of the shelter of the Institute's protected and boring routine, new memories might become completely overwhelming and cripple the newly plazzed to the point where they could not function without the immediate intervention of the institute staff. This sounded like rank nonsense, and the "guided outing" sounded like a sixth-grade field trip. He only agreed to go when he discovered that his small group would include Caroline Bohentin. He then cursed himself for his stupidity.

The group voted to go shopping.

"For what?" Joe said. "What is there to buy in Rochester that we can't buy just as easily wherever we don't have to transport it back to?"

Caroline glanced at him with amusement. She wore a blue dress made of what looked to him like paper, although it probably wasn't. The blue was pierced with thousands of tiny holes in subtle, swirling patterns which he suspected to be engineered subliminals. With it she wore a plain white silk headband and sandals. Her legs were bare. It was July, a July less steamy than Washington but still hot and somehow not less uncomfortable.

"There are supposed to be some quite good shops southeast of the city," said the other woman in the group, a British woman with a tight smile and a very long nose. Lady Alison. "American glass-making, I believe."

"That's in Corning," said Bill Prokop. "Southeast of the entire fucking county by one hundred miles." The British woman shrugged. Prokop was nervous, edgy. Joe had not seen the journalist since Prokop's surgery, but it seemed to him that Prokop was subtly altered. He carried a small portable terminal with him everywhere. Once at dinner Caroline had asked him a casual question about his new memories; Prokop had gotten up and left the table.

Caroline was the only one who did ask. A strange unwritten code of conduct had sprung up among the newly plazzed: The new memories were never discussed except among people alone together. Memory had taken on the privacy of sex and the preeminence of breathing. Someone would halt in the middle of a sentence, his or her face suddenly out of focus, mouth open, the surprised half smile Joe had come to think of, derisively, as "the memory-access moment." Everyone else would look away.

At first he had assumed this weird code had evolved because people were afraid the memory would be sexual, leading to overwhelming desire that would supposedly embarrass everyone. But then he saw that the code applied to any memory, sexual or not. Even the most casual touch of the past was tinged with a complex and hesitant embarrassment: Was that me, that I didn't really know about before?

It seemed to Joe that only he and Caroline reacted differently. She spoke eagerly about her other lives, with a total disdain for others' distaste that Joe found both appealing and off-putting. The frankness and eagerness were appealing; the sense of being above the need for approval reminded him of rich people he had known at law school. A separate club, so far above the toilers below that the reactions of the hoi polloi didn't count. Did one ask opinions of one's dog? He wondered if someone like Caroline ever remembered being a washer-woman. The thought, which he had had more than once, gave him a mean pleasure of which he was intermittently ashamed.

Joe had been a little surprised to find that very few memories came to him, and that these were fleeting and remote: a choppy day at sea in a life as a Greek fisherman evoked by high waves on Lake Ontario; the sound of an evening call to prayer from a long-ago minaret echoed in the cry of a wheeling gull. After a few days he admitted his profound relief that the memories were not stronger, or more abundant. Admitting the relief meant admitting the prior fear that he would be somehow changed. He was not. His multiple sclerosis symptoms had eased, but they had done that before in various times of re-mission; it was too soon to see if the surgery had done all it promised there. And as for the rest—an over-sell, another hype, not as vicious as the plague "cures" he fought in court, but running off the same dBase. A bells-and-whistles diversion for the emotionally needy, used to enrich the greedy.

Like the Gaeists.

Robin had called three more times in the last two weeks. Joe had refused to take any of the calls. One memory still savagely clear was the night she had left for a Gaeist commune with her young blond lover. *They're as corrupt as people come*, Joe had shouted at her. *A cover for corporations who need a warm-fuzzy public rationale for polluting the environment with in-dustrial chemicals—don't you see, Robin? Corporations finance Gaeism, it makes it religiously all right to destroy whole ecologies under the guise that the biosphere will compensate—are you so stupid you can't see?*

Purple martins flying . . .

"We don't have to go shopping if it's going to make you look like that," Caroline said to him, smiling. "We can make this 'outing' to somewhere else."

The British woman sniffed. "Such as where? Mr. Hasfried,

what else is there to 'do' in Rochester, New York? Can you tell us?"

Hasfried, the medical attendant whom everyone but Lady Alison called "Sonny," looked unhappy. He was a big, slow-moving man of indeterminate age and the jowly, gloomy expressions of a hound. Caroline glanced mischievously at Joe, to see if he had picked up on the fact that Hasfried was afraid of Lady Alison. Joe found himself unwillingly smiling back. It was Brekke with whom she usually shared such glances; he, Joe, was only a stand-in. He looked away.

Hasfried said slowly. "I don't know what else there is to do, ma'am. I'm not really from Rochester."

"What the hell does it matter what we do?" Prokop snapped. "The point is to just get out; let's get the hell out."

"Then we'll go shopping," Caroline said decisively. "There *is* a 'glass shop' on East Avenue, Alison, but it's not American. It's Chinese porcelain. I really want to see it. So if no one else objects . . ."

Joe had expected that they would take a taxi, or that Hasfried would drive a groundcar. But instead Hasfried unhappily led the way to an aircar with uniformed driver waiting just inside the Institute gates. Caroline greeted the driver cheerfully; Joe realized the car must be hers. He was obscurely angry with himself. He had thought he had fought the battle over the relative importance of money in his view of people long ago. He had even thought he had won. He sat on the circular leather banquette as far away from Caroline as possible, and watched the city roll by underneath.

From the air, Rochester looked depressing. Twenty years ago the city had taken a lot of AIDS rioting—not as much as New York or Denver, nowhere near the violence that had all but destroyed San Francisco. But the early precure treatment centers had had their pathetic little efforts bombed "clean" of viruses; AIDS homes for the dying had burned; counterdemonstrations by the liberal hopeful had raised banners on both sides. DEATH TO THE FAGGOTS THAT BROUGHT IT TO US. BURN THE BUMS. AIDS: AMERICANS INTO DEADLY SEX. And on the other side: COMPASSION FOR THE DYING. JUSTICE FOR ALL. VOTE AGAINST ANTI-GAY LAWS. The compassionate, it seemed, were never as good at slogans as the haters.

"I was fifteen when Rochester burned," Prokop said to Joe. He shifted restlessly on the aircar seat. There was an odd note in his voice that Joe couldn't name. "I was terrified. I had never slept with a girl, and I went right out and persuaded one into it. The whole time I was on top of her I saw the faces of the rioters on TV, screaming their drivel about needing stupid anti-gay laws."

Joe was irritated. "The laws weren't anti-gay as such. The intent was to limit choices harmful to the public health, not condemn inner feelings and desires."

"I forgot. You're a lawyer. You split hairs to make distinctions."

"The distinction is important."

Prokop said, "Only to lawyers."

"All laws are based on limiting freedoms for the good of the greater community."

"Depends on your definition of 'good.' "

"Of course."

"Are you saying you're in favor of the sodomy laws?"

"Yes," Joe said, and braced himself for a fight. But Prokop only threw him a look he had come to recognize: the intolerant contempt of the man who made a god of tolerance. Prokop looked pointedly out the window, at Rochester reeling by underneath. Caroline, however, leaned sideways, making an end run around the badgering of the unhappy Hasfried by Lady Alison.

"Joe—do you really think gays should have to stifle their sexuality their entire lives?"

"I think they must make that choice for the greater good, at least until the virus is completely and totally stamped out.

You know as well as I do that the cure acts as slowly as the original virus, and that the economic and social burden of AIDS is still enormous. Just more hidden than it was. And not as fatal."

"But to deny what really satisfies them sexually? For their whole lives?"

"Is that any different from anyone else whose real sexual satisfaction would be socially destructive denying it their whole lives? Say, for example, pedophiles?"

Caroline didn't answer. Joe felt that she was not really interested in the subject, or that she considered him some sort of fascist for not believing in the Eden of unrestrained choice. Prokop continued to look out the window; the memory-access moment flitted across his face and it went slack and open-mouthed. Lady Alison talked through her nose at Hasfried, who nodded dumbly, his eyes like a hunted basset. Joe folded his arms across his chest and wished he had stayed at the Institute.

The aircar set down on a flight platform surrounded by a sea of Gaeists.

Three streets formed a green triangle, a little park planted with beds of marigolds and zinnias. The flight platform sliced across one side of the triangle. Its existence was an unnecessary amenity; aircars equipped with Konig "hummingbird" generators could stop in mid-flight, hover, and set straight down almost anywhere. This platform was made of genuine burnished hardwoods, golden in the sunlight. Did they put a tarp over it every time it rained? Joe wondered. What about Rochester winters?

A uniformed guard idled between the platform and the demonstrators; more guards patrolled the expensive shops lining all three streets of the triangle. The Merchant Association's private security, Joe guessed. The cops watched the demonstrators sourly, aware that the Gaeists had every right to be there but that if they scared away so much as one rich shopper, the MA would have security's asses. Jeffersonian democracy meets contemporary neo-Libertarianism.

Caroline was watching the Gaeists with frank interest; Lady Alison with patrician disdain; Prokop with a curious slack-jawed intensity that suddenly made Joe queasy.

There were maybe two dozen of them, all but two in their late teens or early twenties. An older man with shoulder-length gray hair held the hand of a little girl. Everyone wore white robes, either in the full-length version or the abbreviated mini Joe had noticed mostly on girls with good legs. Some sat on the benches, smiling beatifically; some seemed to be forming a circle for dancing; some offered shoppers the pink brochures stamped with the emblematic blue-green rose that could still, all this time after Robin had left him, make the skin on the back of Joe's neck crawl.

"Should I wait here, Miss Caroline?" the driver asked.

Joe jerked his gaze away from the Gaeists, but apparently Caroline didn't find the obsequious "Miss Caroline" as ridiculous as he did. She merely said, "No, I don't think so—it's a pretty small park. Come back in an hour, please, Jason." The driver nodded and released the latches on the aircar doors.

As soon as he stepped outside, he saw the winfoam. Two Gaeists, teenagers, were feeding it into the pneumatic tubes of the Merchants Association's garbage ducts. They were very meticulous; carefully disposing of every bit of the white winfoam boxes in which their lunch had been delivered, the pink winfoam cartons in which fresh roses—the dew was still on them—had undoubtedly been just flow in by expensive aircar, the thin gray winfoam capes designed to be worn once when the morning was chilly and then thrown away. Joe felt rage in him like a knot.

"Do you know what that stuff *is?*" he said harshly to the two Gaeists. They turned to look at him: friendly, smiling, a beautiful blond girl and a black boy with the gentle smile of a religious martyr.

"Garbage, Brother. Life of the earth."

He wanted to hit them, but forced himself to speak quietly, forced himself to talk to the boy, who—unlike the girl—didn't seem to be on brainies. "Not *that* garbage, Brother. That's not the life of anything. It's made of fluorocarbons. It decomposes into compounds that destroy ozone in the air."

The boy's smile widened. He already knew all that, just as he would already know that up until President Diane Caswell's administration, winfoam hadn't even been legal. Now, of course, it was; Caswell had big-business political support. Joe was punching at air. But he didn't stop; he never could.

The boy said gently, "Sure, winfoam destroys ozone. And then Mother Gaea compensates for us. You know how she does that, Brother?" He had a soft voice, sweet with reason. "She dramatically reduces the amount of nitrous oxide made by microorganisms in the sea and soil. Nitrous oxide decomposes in the upper air and one of the results of that is to break down ozone. Less nitrous oxide, less ozone break down that way. You see, Brother? Winfoam breaks down more ozone, Gaea breaks down less. She *adjusts* for us."

The girl said, "The biosphere is self-regulating. Gaea takes care of us. We're all part of a single healthy organism."

The boy put a hand on Joe's arm. "There isn't anything humans can do that isn't just part of the biosphere. You *belong*, Brother."

Joe had to struggle for calm. "There are bayous in Louisiana so thick with mercury they shine from a mile away. There are continental shelves being aqua-farmed to the point where all the anaerobic organisms are being destroyed—the same little stodges that produce methane to keep oxygen from increasing in the air. And so *it is increasing*. Do you know what that means—'Brother'? It would take only a four percent increase in the amount of oxygen in the air to send the whole world up in one huge global forest fire!"

"Gaea will compensate," the boy said.

"She always does," the girl said. Her hair shone golden in the sun.

Even through his anger Joe saw that Caroline and Prokop had drawn closer to listen. For the first time he realized that the blue dress he had admired on Caroline was probably not paper but winfoam. "You are preaching pollution of the biosphere, and all because—"

"No," the boy said with surprising force. "We *are* the biosphere, all of us. From bacteria to redwoods."

"You, too," the girl said.

"—all because you don't see that your funding comes from people who gain economically from having no government regulations on pollution! Gaeism was *started* by a corporation CEO and chief stockholder, Samuel DeLorio, for God's sake!"

The girl smiled at him with pity. She had the perfect teeth of someone born to afford bio-miracles: tooth implants, gum culture. Joe thought that, despite her jargon, she probably thought a continental shelf was Parisian decor. He concentrated on the boy, feeling his desperation rise, knowing how senseless the whole thing was. "Gaea is real, yes. A real, proven natural phenomenon. But your movement *uses* that, justifies environmental rape—"

"Acid rain—Brother, how about acid rain?"

It was always their big trump card. Acid rain—the environmental scourge of the last century, product of burning fuels like gasoline and oil, killer of freshwater lakes and streams. And then the killing had slowed, halted—reversed. Now fish swam again in ponds in the Adirondack Mountains, and Gaeism rode on their finny backs as the richest quasi-religious movement in the world.

"Ammonia, Brother," the boy said triumphantly. "The acid rain got too bad—Gaea increased the natural production of ammonia to interact with the sulphur in the atmosphere before it got carried back down as rain. Balance, Brother. Gaea restored the balance."

"The world ran out of fossil fuels and switched to nuclear and solar!"

As soon as he had said it, Joe saw how he had played into their hands. The boy's face positively shone, a radiant black sun. "Of course we did. Of course we ran out of fossil fuels. It was necessary we be directed to find some other way, right then. *Our* actions are part of Gaea, too, Brother. *Our* waste products are just as 'natural' as that methane from anaerobic organisms buried in the continental shelf mud. *We* are part of Gaea, too. You belong, Bro. Don't fight it."

The girl held out to him a blue-green rose.

Joe turned away. It was a moment before he could see straight, and then he found that he was actually clenching his fists at his side. Feeling an absolute fool, he made himself loosen his fingers. The boy's final words—they were the last thing Robin had ever said to him, just before she climbed into the aircar with her Gaeist lover, into the long, expensive white van with the blue-green rose in bas relief on the driver's door. *Don't fight it.*

There was no way to fight Gaeism, because everything *was* Gaeism. All acts were part of the biosphere, were balanced by other acts in the biosphere, were part of the global ecology that had sustained life for three and a half eons—and therefore always would. You couldn't argue with the fuzzy-warm Mother image, because you were product of her loins, beloved son. Even AIDS, that last-century scourge that more than anything else had shaped the politics of this one, was part of Gaea. Population control, balanced in time with the discovery of the cure from among the same "natural" slow viruses that started the disease in the first place. Balance. A place in the cosmos. Belonging.

And yet it was the AIDS disease that gave the Gaeists their one enemy. To the haters who still hunted gays, it sounded as if Gaeists were somehow in favor of AIDS. Deadly viruses, too, were part of the biosphere. Everything deserved to be loved. Don't fight it, Bro.

The teeth-rattling worst of it, Joe thought bitterly, was that you couldn't move Gaeists with any lever, no matter how long. Not when they had appropriated the entire planet. There was nowhere left to stand.

Joe had expected Caroline and Prokop to still be listening; he was half relieved to see that they weren't. Prokop was deep in conversation with the older, gray-haired Gaeists whom Joe guessed to be the chapter leader. As Joe watched, Prokop took out a recording computer and started to ask the man questions. The peculiar overheated intensity twisted all his features.

Caroline had walked a few yards away to talk to the one child demonstrator. The little girl, whom Joe guessed to be seven or eight, stood with her back to him. Chestnut hair cascaded down her back. Her feet, in winfoam sandals, had a daisy-shaped bandage over one heel. Caroline knelt down to the child's level, her face so hungry that for a second Joe looked away. He remembered that Caroline had a daughter just a few years older than this, a daughter with Memory Formation and Retrieval Disorder.

The child handed Caroline a rose. In a sweet, high voice, clearly parroting the words and yet without any annoying singsong, the little girl said, "Did you know that roses really bloomed *better* in smoggy cities? Sulphur dioxide killed the fungi that hurt the roses. This is a blue-green rose, symbol of our planet. It's for you."

Caroline took the flower. Joe looked at her face, grabbed her arm, and steered her toward the street. Lady Alison and Hasfried had already crossed. "Come on," he said, more roughly than he intended. "You came here to shop. Let's shop."

Hasfried's back was just disappearing through the infrared-scanning door of the porcelain shop. As Joe pulled Caroline inside, he had one of his fragmented, infrequent PLAS memories:

The Imperial factory at Ching-te Chen. The smell of lime and bracken ashes; the rows of men cross-legged on the floor, each painting a different motif on the porcelain wares; the heat from the kilns. Each kiln took 180 loads of pine fuel. The kiln door was opened, and the porcelain and cases were found converted to a solid mass: Some fool had overheated the kiln again. He would be punished for his stupidity. Anger crackled through him. It would be *he*, Ts'ang Ying-Hsuan, director of the Imperial factory, who would be held responsible, not the cursed worthless workman . . .

The force of the anger made him stop walking. It was the first memory that had ever felt even remotely real. To his left Caroline said, "You remembered something just then."

Joe turned to look at her. She still looked pale. Before he could speak she said, "You remembered that you were Chinese."

"How did you know?"

She smiled oddly. "Everybody was Chinese. Look at that vase."

The store displayed only a few carefully chosen objects; they looked expensive, but Joe knew they were pieces that could afford to be broken. The priceless porcelain would be brought out for collectors. A salesman scanned their group and immediately hurried over to Caroline. How did they always know, Joe wondered.

"I would like to see any Yung Cheng pieces not larger than this," Caroline said, cupping her hands around an imaginary ball six inches across. It seemed to Joe an odd way to request china, but the man immediately nodded and smiled. Joe's eye fell on a tall, ugly vase of gray-green, and again the Imperial factory flashed through his mind, smelling of lime.

The salesman—curator, whatever he was—brought Caroline two small saucers, pink with drawings of branches and birds on them. He tipped them over to show a period mark, six characters in three rows of two each.

"No," Caroline said.

"That is the Yung Cheng mark," the salesman said smoothly. "If madam wishes—"

"The drawing is too stiff," Caroline said, "and the *famille rose* glaze has that orange-peel effect that they—see? There was so much imitation Yung Cheng fired at the end of the nineteenth century."

The man looked at her with new respect. "Just a moment, madam." He took the sauces away.

"Trying to cheat you?" Joe said.

Caroline smiled. There was an intense gleam in her eyes that reminded him uncomfortably of Prokop. "No, trying to test me. The next pieces will be genuine Yung Cheng. They . . . oh!"

Another man approached them, carrying two tiny bowls. Joe knew immediately that he was the shop manager. The bowls were glazed a delicate pink, each asymmetrically painted with a single flowering branch running from the outside to the inside. Caroline cradled one in her palm, and Joe knew from her whole stance that she was remembering. He looked away. She had just brought up the fingers of the other hand to caress the porcelain taste bowl when the plastic explosive hit the window.

The window didn't shatter. There was a sudden clear ringing, almost like a bell. Green plastic splattered in a web across the outside of the window. A fraction of a second later alarm sirens wailed, people screamed, and more explosions rocked the park outside.

"Down!" Joe shouted. He grabbed Caroline and pulled her to the floor. More explosives; the screaming outside reached the same pitch as the sirens. Someone rattled at the door handle, howling, but the door had sealed itself at the first hit on the window. Joe shifted position to see better. Two Gaeists tugged at the outside of the door, crying and hanging onto each other; their faces were contorted and openmouthed but their shrieks were lost in the terrible onslaught of sound.

Between their legs, shoving aside their long, bloodstained robes, the face of the little girl pressed desperately against the glass door.

Caroline jerked out of Joe's grasp and crawled on all fours toward the door. The manager turned his head, saw her, and shrieked, "No—from the inside it will *open!*" He made a grab for Caroline's leg. But he was clutching both Yung Cheng bowls to his chest, and Caroline kicked free of him. She jabbed at the emergency lock on the door, a nonspecific E-lock designed to be opened fast by anyone on the inside. But not fast enough— just before she reached it, the child's mouth opened in an unheard wail of despair and she darted away from the glass door. Caroline flung open the door and tripped over the body of one of the two Gaeists. His leg ended at the knee in a bleeding stump.

"Caroline!" Joe called. The other Gaeist fell into the shop, crying and cursing, and pulled in her companion. The manager, now without the porcelain taste bowls, tried to jam the door shut again. Joe pushed him. The man stumbled sideways, and Joe scrambled over the two screaming Gaeists to the sidewalk.

The park was a battlefield. A dozen young men in scarlet and black leather fired the plastic explosives from tiny, cheap, spring-powered blowers. The plastic rings flew into people, buildings, grass. When they struck something of sufficient hardness, they exploded. Otherwise they lay there, ready to be stepped on, ready to be picked up and squeezed. Bodies writhed on the grass, sobbing and screaming. The burnished wood of the flight platform was smeared with blood at one end, was nonexistent at the other.

Joe was stunned to see the Gaeists fight back. Under their robes some of them carried guns—more precise than the cheap explosives over a longer range, but heavier to maneuver. A man in a short robe, tears pouring down his face, swung his gun awkwardly and sprayed bullets in a wide, ragged arc. Joe dropped flat to the sidewalk.

He saw Caroline huddled against the closer end of the bombed flight platform, shoving the little girl under a shallow lip of newly splintered wood and shielding the small body with her own. Something sang past Joe's head. He hoped it was a bullet and not a plastic explosive. A splat sounded in the wooden wall somewhere behind him, but no explosion followed: a bullet. He started toward Caroline.

Before he had crawled more than a yard, it was over.

A teenage boy in skin-tight black leather pants and scarlet shirt leapt over Joe's back, ran to the platform, and jabbed a pole at the polished planks. Thin metal girders sprang out from the pole and anchored themselves in a tripod, at the same moment that a rigid banner of thin white plastic shot sideways from the top of the pole. Then the boy was gone. They were all gone, attackers and Gaeists and shoppers, except for the dead and wounded crying and twitching on the bloody grass.

Neither Caroline nor the child had been hit. Joe couldn't see how not; it seemed a kind of miracle. Caroline looked dazed, letting Joe hold her up with one arm without looking at him, without seeing him at all. After a moment he understood; a memory had tripped. She wasn't here at all. The carnage had brought back some other war, some other horror. Her fingers clutched and unclutched the flesh of his arm.

"Caroline . . ." She didn't hear him.

The tall Gaeist with gray hair staggered up and grabbed the little girl. As soon as she saw her father, the child threw herself at him and began screaming hysterically.

"Caroline!" Joe said. She turned blind eyes toward the sound of his voice. He was about to slap her when her driver came running up—followed, it seemed to Joe, by most of the city. Police. Medics. Witnesses. Moaning shoppers. And behind them, faster than even Joe would have believed possible, the journalists.

"This way, sir," Jason called. "Bring her this way." His uniform was clean and whole. Joe wondered where he had been during the attack.

Jason led them around the corner, through a brick-lined passageway too well lit to be called an alley, to a parking lot where the aircar waited. Lady Alison peered through the window. When Caroline was inside, Jason looked around uncertainly. Clearly he felt his duty was to Caroline, not to the missing journalist and medic from some crazy hospital. A police aircar landed at the far end of the lot; two cops ran from it toward the park.

"Wait here," Joe told the driver, putting into his voice all the authority he could muster. "I'm a lawyer. I'll get the other two and deal with the cops if necessary."

Jason nodded, obviously relieved. Joe pushed his way through the nonalley, which was suddenly full of people, toward the park. In front of the porcelain shop he found Hasfried dragging Prokop in a half nelson.

"Did you see?" Prokop shouted at him. "Did you fucking *see?* Just like in the beginning! But I still can't remember!" He lunged against Hasfried and nearly broke free.

"Help me with him," Hasfried gasped. Joe grabbed Prokop's other arm. The journalist turned his face into Joe's, inches away.

"I still can't remember!"

"Easy," Joe said. "Easy." They got Prokop through the crowd and into the car. Hasfried slapped a patch behind Prokop's ear and he slumped against the seat. The medic then turned to Caroline, who shook her head.

Jason lifted the car and flew low, veering off at an angle to the park. Even so, Joe got one clear view of the rioters' banner, still at rigid right angles to its pole on the flight platform. It said

FAGS AND THEIR DEFENDERS—NO PART OF MY EARTH. White Gaeists robes writhed over the green beyond the sign. From even this low height they looked unreal, like worms.

Sickened, Joe looked away. As he did, something flashed him back to the Imperial factory, and he remembered about the workman who had overheated the batch of porcelain in the kiln. He remembered that the ruined ceramic had been intended for dragon bowls for the palace garden of K'ang Hsi. He remembered that he, newly appointed Imperial servant Ts'ang Ying-Hsuan, director at Ching-te Chen, was indeed held responsible for the failure to manufacture the dragon bowls. He remembered the worker cowering before him in a soiled white robe of cheap cloth. And he remembered giving the order to have the man killed.

Dinner was roast beef with wild rice and a salad of some curly green leaf so bright and picturesque that it had to be yet another new genetic miracle. The meal was brought to Joe's room on a tray without his having requested it. Maybe the medical staff had decided a riot disinclined people for social dining. Maybe they were right. Joe poked at the beef, wondered where—and in how many toxins—the rice had been grown, and poured himself a cup of coffee from an antique pewter pot. The cup was eggshell china. He counted how many more days until he could leave the Institute behind.

While he drank the coffee, he sat at the room terminal and cleared up his messages. An interim report from the Plague Commission's medical team; they were making satisfactory progress on culturing the plague virus, but were not yet ready to release an announcement to the newsnets. Nothing directly from Pirelli. Routine documents from his office about cases pending—but not nearly enough of them. Joe scowled at the screen, requested a hard copy of his deadline calendar, reviewed the documents again. Several key ones were missing. One was mislabeled.

Angel never fucked up this bad.

Was he running some sort of addiction? Was he in trouble? It had always seemed to Joe that Angel's flash—the brashness, the partying, the old-fashioned Hispanic machismo—was as much deliberate parody as anything else. Under it, Angel had the most efficient administrative brain Joe had ever seen. It was a talent, keeping track of details, as clear and marked as perfect pitch, and like any other strong talent, it wasn't really affected by surface style. Angel in parti-colored pants and a headband of antique circuit wires was still an administrative pro. So what the hell was going on?

He punched in the code to pay for live visuals and keyed in the override number direct to Angel's work station at the law office. It was six o'clock; most everyone should have left, but Angel frequently worked late. Joe might just catch him.

Angel answered on audio alone. "Hello. McLaren and Geisler."

"Joe here. Key in the visual, Angel."

A brief pause. *"Hola,* Boss. Visuals are down."

Joe coded swiftly. A pocket of cold formed in his stomach. "No, they're not, Angel. What the fuck is going on?"

There was another silence, then Angel's voice shrill and angry. "You got remote diagnostics you never told me about?"

"Key in the visuals."

Angel did. His face filled the screen, less than six inches away, glaring. Despite everything else he had seen that day, Joe was shocked. The weight had melted off Angel's face; his eyes were spiderwebs of red in deep sockets. His skin had gone pasty, mottled now with anger. "What the fuck you doing, Boss?"

"Just what I'd like to know. This file is a mess, Angel. Where is the Henderson versus State of Virginia *amicus curiae* brief from that William and Mary bio professor? And where is—"

"I got to go."

"Go? Angel—"

"I got to go, man!" Angel shrilled, and Joe caught the sound of a door closing. Angel's office door, out of sight behind the secretary's looming, gaunt face.

"Angel, what's wrong? What kind of trouble—"

The screen blanked. Joe called back; no one responded. He made the connection by remote override, but all the screen showed him was the office ceiling. Angel had tilted it horizontal when he broke the connection.

Joe sat rubbing his chin. The smell of the beef on the silver tray was suddenly making him nauseated. He keyed in a call to Bill Geisler, his law partner; they weren't really friends, and Bill had his own secretary, but he might know what was going on with Angel. Bill wasn't home. Joe tried Juana Sullivan, Angel's married sister in Georgetown, the only relative Angel had ever mentioned. She wasn't there either. The wild rice had begun to congeal on the plate. Joe blanked the screen and went to knock on Caroline's door.

She had changed from the blue dress with holes to jeans and a yellow cotton blouse with a gray leather headband. Her face when she opened the door looked unfocused, but sharpened when she saw it was Joe. A small warmth melted the edges of the ice in his stomach.

"I came to see how you are."

"Oh, fine. The doctor was in to see me—Queen Armstrong herself. Then Housekeeping was in to see me about a dinner tray suitable for the survivor of a riot. Then Shahid was in to see me—although of course he was the only one I really wanted to see. Father Patrick Martin Shahid. What an enigma. Do you talk to him much?"

"No," Joe said. Although he had been through memory sessions—mostly nonproductive—with the staff historian, he felt he barely knew him.

"You should," Caroline said. She smiled, still holding the door less than two feet ajar. Joe held his ground. After a moment it seemed to dawn on her that it had been a contest;

a gleam of appreciation came into her eyes and she stood back. "Come in, Joe. Sit down."

Inside her room, he couldn't help blinking. Every surface held a piece of Chinese porcelain. A tall slim vase painted with silver pheasants. A pair of bright yellow bowls with iron-red bats. An ewer with curves as flowing as drapery. And on the dresser, a half-dozen covered porcelain boxes, from one as large as his hand to a tiny, exquisite, powder-blue ring box.

"You're an antique dealer?"

Caroline laughed. There was some embarrassment in the laugh, and also a small spark of anger Joe didn't understand. "Yes, but not of Chinese porcelain. I deal in antique doll houses. I told you that once. The porcelain is . . . for something I remember."

A past life. He didn't want to hear about it. "Do you want to take a walk along the lake?"

"Sure. Let me get a sweater."

Joe gave the porcelain a last look, trying to calculate how much money was sitting there in breakable indulgence. Caroline was silent in the elevator. Outside, the sun had just finished setting, and the sky was a pure slate blue. They strolled across the lawn toward the lake.

Caroline said abruptly, "You don't approve of me, do you, Joe?"

He wasn't sure how to answer. Caroline smiled. "No, you don't. You think that because I didn't come from the maintenance projects of Pittsburgh I'm not in touch with reality."

"How did you learn I come from Pittsburgh?"

She smiled again, giving him a sideways look of angry amusement that somehow seemed directed as much against herself as him. "After this afternoon, do you still believe in the anti-gay laws?"

He was staggered at her wrongness, until he saw that it was deliberate. She was trying to provoke him; she wanted to fight.

With elaborate and artificial patience he said, "I told you—they're not anti-gay. They're pro-community. Curtailing potentially harmful behavior for the greater good. And yes, I still believe in the power of that choice."

She was silent. He had just decided that the walk was a mistake, that she was interested in playing games he didn't like, when she said quietly, "The porcelain is real, yes. You were wondering. It's all from the Yung Cheng period of the Ch'ing Dynasty. I lived then, and I was very happy. I had a perfect life, then."

Joe said automatically, "Nobody has a perfect life."

Caroline stopped walking and turned on him. They were half way between the Institute and the lake, under one of the huge spreading maple trees. A single star gleamed low over the water. "Why not? Why shouldn't someone, somewhere, have a perfect life? If statistics say everything human occurs on a bell-shaped curve, why shouldn't someone be out there at the far end, and be completely happy? Why not?"

Joe had no answer. He was startled by her vehemence. She stood rubbing one forearm with her opposite hand, waiting. After a moment he shrugged and spread both palms upward in surrender, and Caroline laughed unwillingly.

"That's not a gesture I'd expect from someone as rigid as you."

It hurt. She must have seen it; she stopped rubbing her forearm and put one hand on his shoulder.

"I'm sorry."

"It's all right."

"No, it isn't. It was a stupid thing to say. But anyway"—her mood mutated so swiftly that, watching, he felt a little dizzy—"*anyway*, rigidity is actually an admirable quality. Knowing who you are. I understand they're thinking of giving an Oscar for it. 'Most Principles in a Long-running Reality.' And the winner *is* . . . Not like poor Mr. Prokop. I talked to him after that carnage this afternoon."

Joe had forgotten Prokop's strange behavior. "He said, 'But I can't remember. Just like in the beginning, but I can't remember.' "

Caroline regarded him with amusement. "Yes, but not in that voice. You're a lousy actor. I think that's wonderful, you know. I despise actors."

"Why?"

Caroline didn't answer. Instead she said, "Prokop went on saying that, after you left the car at the city hall. 'But I can't remember, but I can't remember.' I think he was . . . not in a memory, but trying to be in one."

"Maybe," Joe said shortly.

"So later I asked him what life it was he thought he should remember. He said, 'Armand Kyle's.' "

Joe stopped walking. *"What?"*

"That's what he said. He believes he was Armand Kyle."

Joe looked north across the water, toward Canada, sixty miles out of sight. He felt stunned, although he wasn't sure why. Armand Kyle had been a respected scientist, a genetic engineering genius working out of the University of Southern California. He had also been the close friend of Sam DeLorio, the financier-turned-renegade-evangelist who had founded the Gaeist movement. Single-handed, DeLorio had turned a tentative scientific hypothesis into a dangerous sideshow religious movement. No, not single-handed. Press speculation had Kyle as the brains behind DeLorio's flash. DeLorio's corporations—he had been on the boards of a number of interlocking directorates—gained from the lessening of government regulations brought about partly by a public clamor for AIDS cures—even mostly untested AIDS cures—and partly by Gaeist lobbying. DeLorio had been an unstable, tainted, even corrupt figure—except of course to Gaeists.

Kyle had gained, too, from the neo-Libertarian's coming to power. Government restraints on research had melted. Kyle had been working on slow viruses when he died, murdered by an anti-gay group never actually identified. The murder had made international headlines, a sickening mixture of butchery and money. Kyle's young lover, Paul Winter, had disappeared that same night and his body was never found. Some lawyers had speculated that Winter had done the killing, although from Joe's study of the case in law school, there wasn't much evidence for that. Nobody had ever come to trial. The whole murder had become a totem for the nineties, mixing AIDS backlash, Gaeism, social fury, neo-Libertarian politics, and press coverage in the new media of holovid that made everything larger than life in living three-dimensional laser.

Joe said, "What year was Kyle murdered?"

"1996."

"Is Prokop my age, in his thirties? I was six years old when Kyle died. Prokop looks older."

"He *is*. That's what makes it so weird. He's fifty, and there's no way he could be Armand Kyle. Kyle wasn't even killed until twenty-four years after Prokop was born. But he's convinced himself that we don't know shit about how plazzing really works, and that sometimes rebirth comes into an already existing mind. Apparently he had some sort of religious experience when he was ten. Had a vision, fell down, talked in tongues."

Her tone was dry. Joe understood; even the term "rebirth" sounded foolish. Previous Life Access Surgery was not supposed to be mystical; it was supposed to be scientific reality. It was sold that way. Mysticism made people uncomfortable. Except, of course, for Gaeist people.

Robin had loved it.

He said, "The Institute really does one hell of a job on their psych screening."

"Well—Prokop seemed normal enough. To me, anyway." She laughed suddenly. "For what that's worth."

Joe said quietly, "You've had a rough time." He wasn't sure what had made him say it, but the moment the words were out, he knew they were a mistake. Caroline kept strolling beside him, but he could feel her disappear, pull herself into courteous composure as into a fortress.

"No, you're quite wrong. A great many people have had a much rougher time than I have."

Joe couldn't stop himself. He wanted to know about her. "You were married twice?"

"Yes," she said, without warmth. "Once, at eighteen, to an actor and would-be playwright named Jeremy Kline. A very bad actor, unfortunately. We were divorced two years later. Three years after that I married Charles Long and had Catherine. We're also divorced. The suicide attempt, which I know you want to ask about because you glanced at my scars, happened when I had to institutionalize Catherine with plague."

"I didn't mean to pry," Joe said awkwardly.

"No, you didn't mean to."

"Does your ex-husband—Catherine's father—know you're having PLAS surgery?"

She glanced at him. "What an odd question. Yes, I told him. I called and said I was having surgery, and he said, 'Are you ill?' the way he always does. I told him no, and he said nothing, the way he always does. It's strange. He always ask after the physical, and if nothing is wrong there, he doesn't ask about anything else. It's as if he still felt a connection to my body, having been married to *it*, but not to the rest of me—mental, spiritual, emotional, whatever. It's an odd kind of divorce."

Joe didn't know what to say. He was disconcerted by how freely, unguardedly, she talked. Finally he repeated, "I still think you've had a rough time."

"And I still say—not as bad as a lot of other people. I have enough money to care for my daughter, enough legal advice to make my own marital choices. I have actually been very lucky."

"I only meant—"

"Yes, but you were quite wrong. Although I appreciate your concern." She turned her head to give him a cool smile, deliberate as a slap. "Oh, look—here comes Robbie."

Joe swore inwardly. Brekke walked toward them from a clump of maples. When he left the trees, a hidden floodlight momentarily gilded his blond hair. He wore a light green jumpsuit and headband and carried a drink cluttered with summer fruit.

"There you are," he said to Caroline. "Lady Alison was telling me about your adventure. The massacre is all over the vids. Are you all right?"

"Adventure." The airhead thought a massacre was an adventure. To avoid looking at Brekke, Joe focused on the drink in his hand. Something pale gold, and on the bottom slices of lemon and orange speared with a yellow stirrer . . . The hotel room swam into view just behind his eyelids, brass bed and straight white curtains blowing in the breeze from the square. Julia held an Old Fashioned to her lips, drank, and came toward him, unbuttoning her blouse with her other hand. She sang along with the radio, an American song she had brought with her on her last crossing: "When deep purple falls/Over sleepy garden walls . . ." Her breasts were deep and white. She pressed against him, the cold glass between her bare chest and his shirt, and he . . .

"Leave him alone!" Caroline said sharply. Joe lay on the grass on his back, his pants still half-zipped, soaked at the crotch. The thick white semen covered his hand. Caroline looked out across the water. Brekke straightened lazily. He was smiling.

"Just trying to help. That must have been quite a memory, McLaren."

"Robbie, for God's sake—"

"Your first sexually triggered episode?" Brekke said. The amusement in his voice brought Joe fully back. He jerked on his zipper, smearing stickiness on the fabric. Humiliation flooded him. He scrambled to his feet and staggered from sudden dizziness. Brekke put a hand on his arm to steady him. Joe shook it off.

"Don't be embarrassed," Caroline said gently. "It happened to all of us. Mine—this is terrible—was in front of Patrick Shahid."

Joe was too humiliated to be reached by her kindness. Without looking at either of them, he started off across the grass toward the Institute. Behind him he heard Caroline's voice, low and angry, rumbling at Robbie. He had nearly reached a side door of the Institute when she caught up with him.

"Joe. Listen. It really is all right. You're not the only one."

He managed a brief nod, wanting only to get away from her, to be alone. But then her mood mutated again—he could hear it in her voice: the sudden lilting mockery, unexpected and therefore irritating as sudden rain.

"Did you ever realize how much you and I look alike? No, it's true—we're nearly the same height, our hair is the same color, or would be if I left mine alone, and there's a distinct similarity in the shapes of our left nostrils. Everyone remarks on it. You could be my long-lost clone."

For a crazy half second he wondered if she could have a long-lost clone.

"No, I don't," Caroline said. "And of course cloning attempts are wildly illegal. But of course you're convinced that among the people I come from, that wouldn't matter."

He was forced to finally look at her. She was grinning strangely.

"Caroline—"

"And you're right. It wouldn't matter. But the technology doesn't work. So the fact that we look alike is just coincidence. Do you believe in coincidence, Joe?"

"No," he said. But he felt his own reluctant smile.

She laughed. "Then you're stuck, aren't you? Either you believe in coincidence, or we're related."

"Good night, Caroline."

"Good night, Joe."

"Don't listen too long to Brekke."

"And don't you immediately wish you hadn't said that?"

He did. He left her at the door, climbed the fire stairs to the third floor, and changed his pants. Then he called Room Service and sent down for an Old Fashioned.

"A what, sir?"

"An Old Fashioned. It's a drink. Whiskey and—" He suddenly couldn't remember. "Just bring me some Scotch and water."

"Yes, sir."

"With a cherry and lemon in it."

"In a Scotch and water?"

"Yes!"

"Yes, sir." The man's voice spoke volumes.

When the drink came, Joe put it on a small table in front of his chair and stared at it. The hotel room, the brass bed and straight white curtains blowing in the wind, Julia coming toward him unbuttoning her blouse . . .

When he came out of it, his fresh pants were also stained, although not very much. Not much fluid left, he thought grimly, washed his hands, and gazed again at the drink. Julia, unbuttoning her blouse over the deep white cleft between her breasts . . .

The third time there was no fluid, only an ache deep in his balls.

The fourth time he came out of it after a few minutes, before reaching orgasm.

The fifth time the same thing happened, but somehow Caroline's face became tangled with Julia's.

The sixth time he ached as he hadn't since he had been fourteen, trying to persuade Robin underneath the overpass of some interstate with a number like a Bingo card stalled in the second column.

The seventh time he stared at the drink and felt a great

weariness spread through his mind. Julia came toward him, unbuttoning her blouse. There was a mole on her left breast, and he had to get up early in the morning.

Joe dumped the drink down the toilet, fruit and all. He wondered if he would ever be able to taste Scotch again. Then he fell across the bed, aching groin cradled against a pillow, and slept as he had never slept before.

When he woke, the clock said 2:14 A.M. He lay there a while, remembering the day. Massacre and sexual humiliation. Then he turned on the lights and the room terminal.

Even lighted, the room had the shadowy, deserted feeling of late-night spaces that are not home. Beyond the window a full moon shone on the water. Joe sat in front of the terminal and keyed in the global reincarnation datanet for the first time.

He wondered why he was doing it. No answer came, except that it had something to do with Caroline's remark that he did not believe in coincidences. All her mockery was like that: too acute to be really lighthearted, too warm to be petty needling. He didn't understand, and knew it, and disliked it, and called up the datanet in English.

It was the only net the Institute carried with audio. "WELCOME TO THE PREVIOUS LIFE ACCESS GLOBAL DATANET," the program said in a warm, reassuring voice that was neither male nor female. A slowly spinning globe appeared on the screen, replaced in a few minutes by brain graphics Joe recognized from the first night's orientation presentation. On this much smaller screen, they were not nearly as impressive.

"PLEASE KEY IN YOUR RESPONSES MANUALLY. WOULD YOU START BY TYPING YOUR PASSWORD AND YOUR LEGAL NAME?"

Joe grimaced. Password access programs were never very secure, although of course there was no reason why the designers would think this one had to be. After all, only Constitutional privacy was involved, not money. He hadn't even been asked for his federal ID number, the one identifier held by all American citizens. He could imagine Pirelli's professional scorn for the whole thing.

"THANK YOU, JOSEPH RICHARD MCLAREN," the program said. "I'D LIKE TO ASK YOU A CONFIDENTIAL QUESTION. CAN YOU READ? BECAUSE IF THE ONLY WORDS YOU CAN SPELL ARE YOUR NAME AND PASSWORD, THAT IS TRULY NOT A PROBLEM. I'LL JUST SAY ALOUD ALL THE POSSIBLE AN-SWERS TO EACH QUESTION AND TELL YOU WHAT COLORS TO TYPE, INSTEAD OF DISPLAYING THE POSSIBLE AN-SWERS ON THE SCREEN. THAT METHOD WILL BE A LITTLE SLOWER, BUT JUST AS EFFECTIVE. SO PLEASE ANSWER FRANKLY BY HITTING 'RED' FOR YES AND 'BLUE' FOR NO— CAN YOU READ?"

Joe hit red.

"THANK YOU, JOSEPH MCLAREN. WOULD YOU PREFER I CALL YOU 'JOE'? OR SOME OTHER FORM OF JOSEPH? JUST TYPE IN YOUR PREFERENCE."

He typed in SCHMUCK. To his surprise, the program chuckled.

"I THINK WE'LL STICK WITH JOSEPH. NOW, WOULD YOU PREFER TO START BY SEARCHING THE DATA BANK FOR INFORMATION, OR BY ENTERING SOME OF YOUR OWN PAST-LIFE EXPERIENCES?"

The brain graphics vanished. The screen displayed two figures, one rumaging through hard files from which sprang Roman centurions, Japanese geishas, Argentinian gauchos. The other figure showed identical icons flowing from its head into a computer. The first figure was blue, the second red. Both figures looked inordinately pleased with themselves. *Give me a break*, Joe thought, and pushed the red coding key.

"THANK YOU, JOSEPH. SINCE YOU DO WISH TO ENTER DATA, YOU MUST HAVE A CLEAR MEMORY FROM A FORMER

LIFE. DO YOU KNOW WHAT YEAR, BY CONTEMPORARY CAL-
ENDAR, THE MEMORY TOOK PLACE? IF NOT, THAT'S NOT A
PROBLEM. JUST TYPE IN " 'NO.' "

He had only two that could even remotely be called "clear": the Chinese porcelain factory, and Julia. For a moment he let himself picture Julia. Nothing physical happened. Smiling, Joe entered NO.

"DO YOU KNOW WHAT YEAR THE MEMORY OCCURRED
BY SOME OTHER CALENDAR, PLUS THE NAME OF THE CAL-
ENDAR?"

He keyed in TWENTY-SECOND YEAR OF THE REIGN OF THE MOST GLORIOUS SUN OF HEAVEN K'ANG HSI OF THE HOUSE OF CH'ING.

For a long moment he stared at the screen, surprised by his own answer. The flowery words had seemed to flow through his fingertips from somewhere else than his conscious brain.

The program immediately displayed the Imperial seal of K'ang Hsi. Despite himself, Joe was impressed.

"VERY GOOD, JOSEPH. THE YEAR WAS 1683 A.D. BY THE CURRENT WESTERN CALENDAR. DO YOU KNOW WHERE THE MEMORY OCCURRED? TYPE IN WHATEVER INFORMA-
TION YOU HAVE: THE CITY, THE PROVINCE, THE NAME OF THE STREET OR MARKET—ANYTHING AT ALL."

He smelled again the odors of the factory: lime, bracken ashes, pine smoke from the kilns, the sweat of the workmen, the sweet incongruous fragrance of the plum blossoms growing over the wall. His fingers curved with the curve of porcelain vases broken now for three and a half centuries. He uncurved his fingers and typed: THE IMPERIAL PORCELAIN FACTORY AT CHING-TE CHEN.

The computer's deliberately androgynous voice sounded pleased. "GOOD! WE'RE DOING FINE! WHAT WAS YOUR NAME?"

As he typed, he could suddenly see other hands: brown, hard, small, decked with rings. The sensation almost made him quit. I WAS TS'ANG YING-HSUAN. DIRECTOR OF THE IMPE-RIAL PORCELAIN FACTORY.

The program said, "THAT WAS CERTAINLY A RESPONSI-BLE POSITION!" and Joe blanked the screen. He got up, walked to the window, stared at the moon, and reactivated the screen. It had noticed his cut-off.

"I THINK YOU MIGHT BE A LITTLE NERVOUS, JOSEPH. PLEASE DON'T BE. ANYTHING YOU DISCOVER IS ONLY A MEMORY. BUT IF YOU WANT TO TALK ABOUT IT, THESE NUMBERS ARE PLAS TELEPHONE AND TERMINAL HOT LINES. OR, SINCE YOU HAVEN'T YET LEFT THE INSTITUTE AT OUR ROCHESTER LOCATION, YOU MIGHT PREFER TO JUST PHONE YOUR RESIDENT HISTORIAN. FATHER SHAHID WON'T MIND, EVEN THOUGH IT'S 2:38. TRULY HE WON'T."

The screen displayed undulating patterns. Joe knew about them from Pirelli: they were research-verified calming patterns. He jabbed at the keyboard: DON'T PATRONIZE ME, YOU BASTARD!

Almost without pausing, the voice changed tone. "I WASN'T. DO YOU WANT TO CONTINUE OR NOT?"

What caused the program to switch to the less cloying tone, Joe wondered: the anger implied in the word "bastard" or the diction level of the word "patronize"? He had underestimated the programming team. He typed YES.

"GOOD," the computer said brusquely. "BEFORE WE CON-TINUE WITH YOUR PERSONAL MEMORY, ARE YOU WILLING TO ANSWER A FEW QUESTIONS TO HELP FILL OUT OUR KNOWLEDGE OF THIS PERIOD? YOUR COOPERATION HERE IS PURELY VOLUNTARY. WILL YOU?"

He typed YES, knowing that the placement of the request must vary with the user, and that he was being asked this now to increase his trust not in the program, but in himself as a contributor of unassailable facts. Rational. Academic. A part-ner.

The screen showed him a set of three Chinese court robes,

elaborate and costly. "DO ANY OF THESE LOOK FAMILIAR, JOSEPH? CAN YOU TELL US WHEN YOU MIGHT HAVE WORN ANY OF THEM? ARE THE DETAILS RIGHT?"

He keyed in answers about the robes. The program asked him about court rituals, then about the houses of the period. About the factory. About the people he had known. The places he had seen. Each question, each graphic, brought to him a fresh memory, drawn by the end of the memory before like a snake with its tail in the mouth of another snake being fed on by another. *I lived in that house, no the sash was always blue, I took another concubine that next year, the rains failed and the land was dry, the workman painting lotus blossoms was called Wang*. The program took it all, emptied him, asked for more, emptied him again. And over it all, like a trance, lay the strange numbing of duality: someone else's memories in his brain, someone with alien perceptions and reactions, someone who kissed the ground at an Emperor's feet, bought concubines like pets, and ordered to be beheaded workmen who ruined ceramics. Someone who was nonetheless still him. Me/not me. "The past is a foreign country; they do things differently there." When he looked up, it was dawn.

The moon was gone. Clouds blocked the sunrise. Dazed, Joe hit the FINISH code. The program had an internal override. It came back up and said to him, "THANK YOU, JOSEPH. YOUR HELP HAS BEEN INVALUABLE. I KNOW YOU MUST BE TIRED, BUT BEFORE YOU SIGN OFF, WOULD YOU LIKE TO KNOW IF ANYONE ELSE WHO HAS REGISTERED ON THE NET HAS LIVED IN THE SAME TIME AND PLACE AS THIS MEMORY OF YOURS?"

He didn't. He wanted nothing to do with any of this, ever again. He had proved to himself that he could handle the net, and that the net had nothing to offer him. It was an escape: more personal than holovids, more intellectual than brainies, more sophisticated than mysticism. But essentially no different. He didn't need it.

Joe stood and stretched. His muscles had cramped from the long sitting. He felt arid and dry. The excess interaction with the computer had left his mind as drained as his earlier excess masturbation had left his groin. The juice was gone.

While he was stretching, arms above his head and back arched, the program spoke. "YOU HAVEN'T SAID NO, JOSEPH. SOMETIMES PEOPLE ARE SHY ABOUT ACTUALLY MAKING THE REQUEST. AS IT HAPPENS, YOU ARE TO BE CONGRATULATED. SOMEONE ELSE REGISTERED ON THE PREVIOUS LIFE ACCESS DATANET HAS LIVED IN THE TIME AND PLACE OF YOUR MEMORY. WHETHER YOU CONTACT HIM IS ENTIRELY YOUR CHOICE. I HOPE TO HAVE THE PLEASURE OF WORKING WITH YOU AGAIN SOON."

Words started to appear on the screen, letter by letter, accompanied by muted, solemn music. Cheap theatrics again. Joe grimaced.

LANG LI, 1664–1690 A.D., BORN, LIVED AND DIED IN CHING-TE CHEN, CHINA. WORKMAN AT THE IMPERIAL POR-CELAIN FACTORY.

Joe lowered his arms slowly. Lang Li was the workman he had remembered just before the Gaeist massacre, in the porcelain shop with Caroline. The workman that Joe, as Ts'ang Ying-Hsuan, had ordered beheaded for overfiring a batch of dragon bowls. That he was responsible for killing.

The music swelled in volume. Below it appeared Lang Li's name in this life, with birth date, last-known address, phone number, and mailnet code: ROBERT ANTHONY BREKKE.

6 CAROLINE

Caroline sat back on her heels, her hands flecked with soft mud to the wrists, and regarded Bill Prokop. The journalist—or ex-journalist, it was difficult to tell what he was, he had changed so much since being plazzed—sat a few feet away on a lawn chair. He had dragged the chair all the way from the Institute building to the flower bed Caroline was planting at the edge of the small woods at the eastern edge of the grounds. Prokop sat on his chair, she thought, as if it were made of particularly hard concrete. His pants, shirt, and headband, all of cheap synthetics in an unflattering shade of brick, looked rumpled. He smelled faintly unwashed. He looked tense and unhappy. But he didn't look crazy.

"I don't remember what lives I had in the last century," Caroline said. "I seem to only remember much earlier ones. I told you that already."

"None of them? When were you born? Into this life?"

"In 1988. I'm thirty-four."

He nodded distractedly. "But you were there, Caroline. I know it. When I was Armand Kyle, you were somehow involved."

She didn't point out that he couldn't "know" that: She had registered nothing for the last two centuries on the datanet, and even Prokop's own registrations had been removed from the

118

statistical uses of the data. Shahid had told her that. Inaccurate data; tainted data. Fantasy memories, of a life that never existed at all.

A kind of plague-in-reverse.

"Look, Bill, I'm rather busy just now . . ."

He leaned toward her from the lawn chair, all rigid intensity. "If I could just show you some pictures, it might help you to remember!"

She gave up. Whatever else Prokop was, he was harmless. She knew. After Jeremy, after the night he had lost a role and gone berserk in their New York apartment, she always knew. "Oh, all right." She dried her hands on a towel, threw a regretful look at the marigolds, and took the stack of pictures he held out to her.

To her surprise, they were two-dimensional enhanced holograms, very expensive, very professional. Prokop couldn't have taken them himself; Caroline remembered his telling her that he was not a good photographer. The first picture was labeled "Armand Kyle." The picture showed a thin, balding man in his fifties or sixties. He radiated sharpness: sharp collar bones exposed by the old-fashioned open shirt, sharp beard trimmed to a point, sharp eyes like needles. Caroline knew just how he would stand, move, talk. He would be the kind of man who engaged strangers in conversation only long enough to feel the glow of his own intellectual superiority. An eminent scientist, a social boor.

She shook her head at Prokop. "Doesn't trigger any memory."

"Try the next one."

It was more interesting. "Paul Winter," Kyle's young lover, looked no more than twenty-two or -three. Dark wavy hair, beautiful eyes. He was extravagantly handsome, but she would have expected that. What was unexpected was his sideways glance at the camera: almost annoyed, as if he didn't like being photographed. Given the ferocious anti-gay climate of the time, perhaps he hadn't. But it seemed to Caroline that the impatience on the strong-jawed young face sprang from something else, some innocent arrogance so unquestioned that it did not need to see itself reflected in plastic and light.

"Yes?" Prokop said eagerly. "You're looking at it a long time—anything?"

"He wasn't an actor."

"No. How did you know that?"

His eagerness depressed her. "I don't recognize him, Bill. No memories."

"Look at the last one."

She shuffled the pictures, made a sudden noise, and dropped them. It was the murder scene. Kyle lay decapitated in pools of blood, a laboratory reduced to wreckage around him. DEATH TO FAGS was scrawled on the whitewashed wall behind the mutilated body. Caroline glared at Prokop.

"I'm sorry," Prokop said, surprisingly humble. He bent to pick up his hologram. "I just thought seeing it without any warning might trigger—"

"It didn't," Caroline said coldly. "I can't help you."

"I just thought—"

"I'm sorry. Please let me finish my planting."

Prokop left, dragging his lawn chair under one arm, carrying his pictures under the other. He *was* crazy—to want to be that mutilated body . . . Caroline turned back to her marigolds, gouging a hole in the dirt with her trowel and jabbing a plant into it. A shadowy, unbidden memory came to her; planting rice somewhere warm, scratching at the earth with a pointed stick . . .

"Good God, what are you doing?"

Robbie. "What does it look like I'm doing? Planting marigolds." She had to laugh; he looked genuinely horrified.

"*You?* What for?"

"I want to."

"Why? And does the Institute know you're mucking up their flower beds?"

"I'm not mucking them up; I happen to be an excellent gardener. I once won a prize for azaleas. And the Institute, in the form of Father Shahid at least, would probably consider this good occupational therapy." She waggled her fingers, and bits of damp earth fell on Robbie's shoes. He jumped backward. She shook her head, smiling. "Robbie, Robbie. Didn't the women where you come from garden? Don't you know that growing flowers is very fashionable, and that it isn't customarily left to servants? You're giving yourself away."

He looked interested, rather than offended. It was, Caroline reflected, a large part of his charm: He neither hid his desire to climb socially nor felt diminished by it. He was the perpetual outsider, yet so sure of someday coming inside that he could afford to be casual, unhurried, even spontaneous. She watched him file away this new information behind the blue eyes and felt a burst of pointless affection.

"I used to maintain a whole kitchen garden, you know. When I was Mathilde. I grew enough vegetables to keep us all winter, even though my hands got chilblains and when they broke, they bled horribly—" She curled her hands together and blinked. The lake was too bright, hurting her eyes. But how could there be a lake, there wasn't any lake in the village of Mur de Ronce . . .

"Caroline," Robbie said.

No lake . . .

"*Caroline.* You have a visitor."

Mur de Ronce vanished. "Can't be. No one knows I'm at the Institute."

"Someone does. The receptionist asked me to find you."

"Oh, God, *Catherine*—"

"Who's Catherine?" Robbie said, but she was already running across the grass. It had to be Catherine, only her daugh-

ter's Home knew, always, where to find her. They must have
sent a messenger. They would only do that if something were
very wrong. They would only do that if Catherine were dead.

She burst into the Institute lobby. The receptionist, a
middle-aged woman with bright red hair pinned up in elaborate curls like empty tunnels, smirked at her. So it wasn't
Catherine.

Angry with relief, Caroline stalked to the reception desk,
where the redhead sat patting her silly hair and glowing like
Christmas. "Ms. Bohentin, you have a *visitor!*" And, oh, God,
that look—she thought she was done with that look.

She said coldly, "Where did you put him?"

The receptionist's smile faded into confusion. "I thought he
. . . such a famous man . . . I gave him a key to your room
because I thought if I put him in the lounge he might be
bothered, autographs or something."

She looked ready to cry. Caroline took a breath and reached
for a gracious smile. It wasn't there. And in another second the
ridiculous woman would start to sulk; Caroline could see it
coming. Beside her, Robbie stood grinning.

Caroline leaned far over the desk and whispered two inches
from the woman's ear, "Don't be too impressed. He has to have
his pheromones dubbed for all his sex scenes. Not musky
enough. Don't tell anybody."

She left the redhead gaping. Robbie followed her into the
elevator, his eyes dancing.

"Might as well," Caroline said. "You'll be a distraction."

"I'll be a buffer. I promise. Although this is the first time I
ever saw you need one."

She jabbed at the CLOSE DOOR key. "My famous father and I
don't do well together."

"So I see. Not that you've ever told me anything about him
except that you're his daughter. What did he ever do to you?"

She didn't answer. Robbie said. "Did you really win a prize
for azalers?"

"*Azaleas*. Yes, I did. In the stodge part of my life, when I was growing up with my grandmother Bohentin."

"What other parts of your life were there?" The elevator reached the fourth floor. "Two marriages, I know. What else?" The door slid open. "And 'Catherine.' Who's Catherine?"

She turned to face him. "What my father did," she said, each word careful, "was sleep with me. And when that didn't work out, marry me off to a fourth-rate imitation of himself. And in between, try to have an illegal clone made of the fun-loving little daughter he had somehow alienated."

Robbie's eyes widened. Immediately Caroline felt better. So that was why she had told him—for that second of genuine shock, that momentary connection to someone on her side. However briefly. How strange.

"It's all dead past now," she said. "Don't worry about it. Let's go see what the son of a bitch wants."

Colin Cadavy stood with his back to them, bent over the Chinese porcelain on Caroline's dresser. As they entered the room he turned and held out both hands. "Callie!"

Caroline felt herself receive his hug, raise her cheek for his kiss, and felt, too, Robbie's surprise. Well, why shouldn't he be surprised, after what she had just told him? And why did she let Colin kiss her? But she always, always did.

"Callie," he said again, more softly. "Too long, too long." He still held her; warmth flowed from him like sunshine. She pulled away and looked at him. There were more lines around the eyes, artfully sculpted to reflect an age ten years below his own. The famous green eyes, implants before eye jobs had become common, still glowed with the same pointless fervor. He had kept his tall body hard and slim. Every time she saw him, it was the same: She immediately wanted to let herself become fat and old. *But I never will*, she thought, and felt the old familiar noose tighten.

"Colin, this is Robbie Brekke."

"Hello." She watched him take in Robbie, dBase him to the

last betraying position of the last facial muscle, and turn on the warm physical presence that meant Robbie had been dismissed. "It's nice to meet you, young man."

"Happy to meet you, sir. I've admired your work for a long time."

Colin laughed: pleased modesty, measured out in just the right dose. "My work has been around much longer than you could have seen it, I'm afraid."

"Not really." They both laughed. Caroline couldn't stand it.

"I'm impressed," she said in a shrill voice she immediately hated. "You didn't immediately pull off that silly headband. In my father's presence young men are always pulling off inappropriate items of clothing. I'm really impressed."

Both men looked at her. Caroline turned away. "Coffee? A splash?"

"No, thank you. I'm afraid this is rather a flying visit, Callie. The car is waiting. I have to be back in New York for rehearsal, but when I heard you were here—"

"How did you find out?"

"From Charles."

"*Charles?*"

"I called the Home to check on Catherine—don't look at me like that, Callie. She's my only grandchild. Why do you find it so strange that I worry about her?"

"Catherine is beyond your worry."

"Callie, Callie," Colin said, his voice beautiful with that infinite sadness that a good actor can summon at will. Or maybe the sadness was genuine. No bouncing young granddaughter to travel with, to laugh with, to play scenes at. To court. No young princess to justify Colin Cadavy's perpetual, frivolous, monstrous youth.

None of that was true.

Or maybe it was, and she just couldn't tell anymore. With Colin, any conclusion she came to was going to be too simplistic, too flat. Whole layers of experience would slip sideways and be left out.

"Robbie," she said in that same hateful voice, "your turn. Why don't you say something else obsequious and obvious. Tell Colin you thought he was wonderful in his last play."

"I did," Robbie said, so quietly that she felt ashamed. He handed her a drink. She sipped it, tears suddenly stinging behind her eyelids. Tears of gratitude for a drink—was there anything more pathetic than that? But had he even seen Colin's play? Even heard of it?

"Thank you," Colin said with his beautiful sadness. "Anyway, I was worried about Catherine. There was another bombing in Poughkeepsie, or somewhere here upstate. Those terrible political people. I called the Home, and Charles just happened to be there. He told me where you were. I don't know why."

"Yes, you do," Caroline said. "Spite."

Colin shrugged, a gesture of fluid grace. "Maybe. At any rate, I became worried about *you*. Caroline, what's it all about? Why did you come here? What do you want with past lives?"

"You wouldn't understand."

"Try me," he said, the famous voice now drier and harsher. Caroline had a sudden memory of him scolding her for some childish infraction. They had been standing on the steps of some recording studio; he had turned his back on her right there. The memory felt no different than the over-memory flashes she had a dozen times each day.

"Please, Callie. Please."

She laughed. "Come on, Colin. Save that for your fans. I'm immune."

He went on looking at her, his expression complex but unreadable. He was the only one she had never been able to dBase. Finally he transferred his gaze to the clutter of Chinese porcelain on the dresser. He picked up a small vase, blue glaze without additional trimmings, the lines so pure it had made her throat close up the first time she saw it.

"Yung Cheng," Colin said, "but a copy of something Sung."

Memory hit her like a blow. She was a very young child, no more than four, on the first visit her grandmother had permitted her to the widowed son-in-law she disliked so much. Her father stood holding a curvy blue bottle he wouldn't let her touch. "You collected," she gasped. "You *collected* . . ."

"Not for decades now."

"I forgot. Somehow I completely forgot. I forgot . . ."

Robbie was watching her keenly, Colin quizzically. He still held the porcelain vase. The sight of it in his long fingers made her suddenly dizzy.

Colin said dryly, "You forget a lot of things, Callie. Is that what this carnie run is for? To remember? Or to forget?"

The dizziness passed. She realized that Robbie's hand was on her elbow, steadying her.

"It's because of Catherine that you're getting plazzed, isn't it?" Colin continued. "Somehow. I sense that, but I don't understand."

Caroline crossed the room to the dresser. She opened the top drawer and began placing each piece of porcelain inside, one by one, on top of the shirts and headbands and folded nightdresses.

"You're my child," Colin went on in his beautiful voice, "and I only want to help. I tell you that, each time, and you never accept it. I only want to help."

She cleared the last piece of porcelain from the dresser and turned toward Colin. Without looking at his face, she took the blue Yung Cheng vase from his hands and laid it in the drawer.

"Damn it, Callie! You're my daughter!"

Caroline closed the drawer. It made a small clunk. "I think you better leave now, Colin."

"Callie . . ."

"I'm fine. Catherine is fine. We're all fine. Nobody needs any help. Please leave."

Colin looked at her, helplessness and pain on his expressive face.

"God dammit, get out of here!"

His face changed; he was finally angry. The anger pleased her. Then it suddenly didn't. Was she that petty, that she could be pleased just because he wasn't? Still? After all this time? What did that say about her?

"Good-bye, Callie. Brekke."

The two men did not shake hands. Colin left. Caroline resisted the sudden crazy impulse to call after him: Beware the love-struck receptionist downstairs! Once, it would have been a cause for muffled giggles, endless scheming, gleeful smuggled notes. Lovesick receptionists, backstage catastrophes, absurd escapes in speeding taxis . . . Memory overwhelmed her.

Robbie stood very close, holding both her hands hard. "Don't look like that. Caroline, don't look like that."

She couldn't think what he was saying. The words made no connection to each other. Robbie let go of one of her hands and slid open the dresser. He pulled out the first porcelain he touched and wrapped her fingers, one by one, around it.

The comfit box was cool and glassy. She stood in the small courtyard, listening to the flute, watching the long slanting sunlight gold on the little pool. Tsemo turned and smiled at her. In the next courtyard her children laughed, their voices high and sweet on the still air. Her children . . .

"Caroline," Robbie said.

She looked up, startled. She was sitting in a chair. The room was much dimmer. Beyond the window the shadow of the building stretched halfway to the lake, and beyond that lay long slanting bars of sunlight between the trees.

"Caroline."

She stood up. Her legs wobbled. "What time is it?"

"After six."

"It can't be!"

"You've been sitting there over an hour."

Caroline shook her head.

"Yes. I watched you. You wouldn't talk to me." In the gloom his voice was very quiet. "Where were you?"

She shook her head again, this time to clear it. *I should be afraid,* she thought. *This wasn't supposed to happen.* But instead she felt calm, refreshed. The flute.

The courtyard.

The children laughing . . .

"I'm going to call Father Shahid," Robbie said.

"No," Caroline said. It came out in a gasp. "No, don't, Robbie. I'm fine." The last of Linyi slipped out of her mind, but Linyi's glow remained. The flute. The courtyard. The children. Suddenly Caroline felt wonderful: happy, reckless. She laughed. "Truly! I'm fine. I'm also starved. Let's go get something to eat!"

"Caroline—what just happened to you?"

"Nothing. Everything. Let's get something huge and non-nutritional and fattening!"

Robbie took a step closer, out of the gloom. She realized that she had never seen his face like this: still, troubled. He put his left hand on her shoulder. "What happened? You looked . . . lost. In a past?"

"Yes," she said gaily. On impulse she stood on tiptoe and kissed the end of his nose. He took a step backward.

"Will that happen to me?"

Caroline laughed again. His self-centeredness was as frank and innocent as a child's.

"If you're lucky, maybe."

"That's not what the past is for. Getting lost."

"What is it for, Robbie? Who knows? You?" She was suddenly enjoying this: thrust and parry, challenge and response.

What she should have done with Colin, instead of getting drawn into his theatrical and insincere can-I-help's.

Robbie said, a little angrily, "Yeah. I know what the past is for."

"You do? What?"

"For profit. Like everything else."

"Well—yes." That threw him off-balance; she could just make out his quizzical expression in the shadows filling the room. He took a step forward, bringing him close enough so that his breath stirred the hair beside her left cheek. "Of course, it depends what kind of profit you're after, doesn't it?"

The quizzical look deepened; then, all at once, it vanished. Caroline saw the exact instant he escaped the conversation. His blue eyes suddenly sparkled, and he moved his hand from her shoulder to tuck her loose hair behind her ear.

"You're beautiful."

"Am I?"

His arms went around her. Caroline let her body relax against his. He kissed her, his hands moving strongly over her back. She opened her mouth. But when his right hand moved to her breast, it suddenly hit her:

Wrong.

It swept into her mind in a great blown wave: *wrongness.* There was no other word to describe it. Caroline tore her mouth from Robbie's and pushed him away. *Wrong, wrong.*

Robbie stepped backward, his eyes narrowing. "What was that for?"

"I don't know. Oh, I'm sorry, Robbie, I don't know what happened . . . it just . . . it's wrong."

"Wrong?"

"Yes. You and me. I don't know how it . . . I meant to—it just—"

"A verb, Caroline. Give me a verb."

"You have a right to be angry. I just . . . I don't know. It would be all wrong. You and me. I don't know why."

They stood two feet apart. Caroline reached out to touch his arm. "I'm sorry. I wasn't teasing. I just had this sudden sense of wrongness, filling my mind. That sex with you would be a terrible mistake for some reason."

Robbie turned and poured himself another drink in the same glass he had used when Colin had been there. Caroline glimpsed the rounded curve of his cheek against the light from the window. Was he even the twenty-six he claimed to be? The firm, rounded skin reminded her suddenly of Catherine. But that was absurd.

"Look, Robbie, it's been a rough day. I was on the carnie net all morning. And then Colin—"

"You told me something the first night we were here. Out on the terrace. You said you'd been vaccinated against my 'type' by your first husband. But that wasn't the truth. It was by *him*. Your father."

Caroline shrugged. "Oh, I suppose so. They're very much alike, both actors—except that Colin has talent and Jeremy didn't." She heard her voice make the distinction as if it were a minor one. "Will you pour me a drink, too?"

"You're not ever going to go to bed with me, are you, Caroline?"

She had a sudden flashing picture of the two of them naked, Robbie's beautiful body lowering onto hers, and again the brown wave washed through her mind. *Wrong*. Mutely she shook her head.

Robbie, smiling, handed her the wine. He crossed the room and hit the light switch. Blinking against the sudden increase in brightness, Caroline nonetheless saw that again he had erased a troubling conversation, just dumped it out of mind. He smiled, and his eyes danced. He held out her wine glass, and for the first time she realized that she was still holding the porcelain comfit box and had been ever since Colin's visit. She looked down at it in her right hand, and Robbie made a little mocking play of pretending to pour the wine over the green-glazed cover.

"Robbie! It's priceless!"

"Obviously not, or you couldn't have bought it. From where, Caroline? Was that the armored truck that pulled up here yesterday?"

"You don't miss much, do you? But you're going to miss this box." She met his eyes deliberately. "Because I would."

He grinned. "You do me an injustice."

"I don't think so."

"Oh, but you do. I would never rob you. And I can prove it."

"How?"

He drank her glass of wine with one gulp, his head thrown back in a mocking flourish that reminded her of Jeremy. She saw that his mood had changed yet again. He was about to take some outrageous chance, something that would balance her refusal to sleep with him. The blue eyes sparkled.

"Your jewelry is in a small black safe anchored by an E-field to the back of your bottom dresser drawer. The safe has an E-lock set at a different frequency from the anchor field. Inside is a heavy gold bracelet worked in curlicues, a pair of diamond pendant earrings—"

Caroline drew in a sharp breath. She had not even worn the earrings since coming to the Institute.

"—a dinner ring set with a square-cut emerald, an antique bracelet, two other pairs of earrings, and the hard copy of a document file."

Caroline dropped to her knees and yanked open the bottom drawer of her dresser. She used a keyed code to turn off the Institute's wall field and her thumbprint to turn off the safe's, and opened the safe so hastily the contents spilled out onto the rug: necklace, ring, bracelet, three pairs of earrings, a single folded piece of paper.

"All there, you see," Robbie said blithely.

"Did you read the letter? *Did you?*"

"No."

"The lock is keyed to my thumbprint—only mine. How'd you get in?"

"You're angry."

"How?"

He shrugged, his eyes dancing. "Professional secret."

"And why on God's polluted fucking earth did you tell me?"

"To show you how wrong you are about me."

"Wrong? Do you think I'll change my mind about going to bed with you just because I know you flirted with the idea of stealing my jewelry?"

"Flirting ain't marriage. And I don't expect you to go to bed with me. Merely to acknowledge my skill. That's a Yale-Ulrich E-lock."

"God, you take risks to be pleased with yourself!"

"That's because I'm already so pleased with you."

She had to laugh, less at the fatuous words than at the expression on his face. Cat in the cream. But the laugh felt tired to her, felt old. Slowly she gathered up her jewelry and put it back into the safe. It occurred to her than Colin would have loved this. Robbie was half right; she was immune, but not in any way he—or Colin—would have understood. She didn't actually disapprove of Robbie's risky outrageousness. It was just that too much of it bored her.

He sat beside her on the rug, lounging back against the side of the bed, his long body loose with expansive pleasure. "Who's the letter from, Callie?"

"Don't ever call me that."

"Caroline, then. Who's the letter from? Ex-husband number one? Number two? Daddy?

"From my daughter." She lay the letter in the safe last and closed the door.

He touched her knee. "The one with plague."

"How'd you know that?"

"McLaren."

Caroline thought he was probably lying; Joe was a man who kept his own counsel. But Robbie's tone was gentle and she felt herself responding to it, even though she knew the gentleness only floated at the surface of his mood of jaunty recklessness. Bread on the waters.

Robbie said, "Her name is Catherine, isn't it?"

"Yes. Catherine."

"Must be rough." He put his arms around her from behind, and because she felt in them this time no sexual urgency, she leaned back against him, her head on his shoulder. His chest was broad and warm against her back. But she could feel his grin in the movement of his jaw against her ear, and after a moment his foot began to tap, a bright little restless rhythm.

Caroline said despite herself, "It was the last letter she was ever able to write. Before the plague got too bad."

"I'm sorry," Robbie said, almost carelessly, and she saw that he had no idea of what to say about this, or how to say it. This bright brashness was the best he could do. And yet he had been perceptive and supportive about Colin, steadying her as if he actually understood the quicksand of parent-child treacheries, the intermittent and hysterical bogs, the unseen and shifting footings below the surface. But he hadn't understood; how could he? He was a child himself.

On impulse, she said, "Colin didn't seduce me; it was the other way around. It was me that crept into his bed one night when he'd been doping, and I wouldn't take 'no' for an answer. I was fifteen, and wanted desperately to think I was wild. At least, I think that's the way it was. The memory . . . slips."

This time she had not shocked him. His foot, stretched out on the rug before her, went on tapping its jaunty rhythm.

"I loved him," Caroline said. "Or something. I was fifteen."

Behind her, Robbie nodded. She felt his chin brush the top of her head. He didn't, she knew, have the faintest idea what she was telling him. Caroline smiled: an immense effort, a smile dragged by force from some deep place she didn't want to visit. She picked up the safe, pressed her thumb into the E-lock, and drew out a pair of earrings. Not the diamonds. These were gold, curving heavy crescents meant to hang from the earlobe halfway to the shoulder. She held the earrings out to Robbie, an awkward backhanded offering.

"For you."

He was still behind her. She drew away from his chest and turned to face him. "I mean it. I want you to have them."

He made no move to take the earrings. Caroline held one up to his right ear, mock-hooking through the nonexistent hole. Men's fashions had changed; Robbie was too young to have the pierced ears of Jeremy, of Charles. The gold crescent swung gently against his neck.

"Why?" Robbie said.

"Just because."

"Just because I didn't steal them?"

She thought about it, the earring still held to the side of his head. His neck felt warm. "No."

"Then why?"

"What do you care? They're valuable."

He reached up, took the earring from her, and studied it as it lay on the palm of her hand.

Caroline said, "You're thinking that women don't just give away expensive jewelry. You're thinking there's a catch. You're thinking I'm crazy. Well, they don't and maybe there is and could be I am. Take them anyway, Robbie."

Robbie still looked down at the gold on his palm. "What *is* the catch? What are you trying to buy, Caroline?"

"Nothing."

"I don't believe you."

She shifted on the floor, sitting with her back against the dresser, facing him and stretching out her legs. Their toes, his in leather boots and hers in the canvas espadrilles she wore for gardening, almost touched. She realized she had begun to enjoy this. He looked so amazed. The startler startled.

"Well," she said, "what *am* I after, then? Not sex, obviously; I just turned you down. Not 'profit'; I already own the earrings. Not partnership; I've consistently refused to even listen to your wonderful smuggling activities in Liberia or your street career in Boston. So what *could* I be after then, hmmm?"

He said quietly, "Absolution?"

Caroline went rock still, then jerked her head angrily to meet his eyes. "Yeah? For what, supposedly?"

"How should I know? For incest with your father? For two smashed marriages? For your daughter's plague?"

She had been sitting on the floor too long, her legs had numbed, they buckled under her. She staggered to her feet. The door handle slipped and slid from under her hand as she jerked open the door. "Get out."

"Caroline—"

"Get out."

Robbie picked up the second earring from the rug and stood with both on his outstretched palm. "How did your daughter get the plague?"

"Nobody knows how anybody gets plague! That's one of the great puzzles about the whole damn thing—you know that!"

"And so do you. It can't possibly be your fault. You didn't do it, Callie."

She saw from his face that the name had just slipped out, but she didn't care. Fury tore through her like a gale. "What do you know about fault? You've never admitted to a fault in your life, never felt guilt, never had the least idea what connection to another person involves or implies or does to someone. You romp through the plague, telling jokes and baiting people and strutting as if you were immortal yourself— and not only immortal but above reproach, blithe and bright as a village idiot who doesn't know the whole town's laughing at him—"

"And," Robbie said, his eyes glittering, he was finally angry—good, she was glad he was angry—"I don't slit my wrists, either. Now *there's* a fine measure of social concern for the welfare of America's victims."

Caroline stood very still. Robbie picked up both her limp arms and turned them palms up. The long white ridges shone faintly where the thickened scar tissue reflected the light. Across the hall the elevator opened and two voices sounded: Joe McLaren and Lady Alison Ogilvie. Caroline didn't move. The voices drew closer. "—had to have been someone who saw—" Finally Robbie reached behind her and closed the door.

The silence in the room sounded overwhelming to her, like the sudden cessation of a great din, even though the voices in the hall had been low, and only heard for perhaps fifteen seconds.

Eventually Robbie spoke. "I'm sorry, Caroline."

All anger had left her, disappearing into the strange huge silence, and replaced with a kind of distant tiredness. She wanted him to leave. She wanted to lie down. "I started it. I should apologize, too, I guess."

"Here. Take your earrings." He dropped her arms and held them out to her. At that angle the curved gold crescents looked like miniature scimitars. Lunar blades.

"Keep them, Robbie."

He said nothing.

Caroline smiled tiredly. "A memento of moments gone wrong, if nothing else."

He smiled, too. A slow, reluctant smile, without volition, and in his blue eyes, narrowed still against the light, she glimpsed the sudden memory of other moments gone wrong, other bungles and failures and fucked-over chances. So not all his memories could be ignored, at least not all the time, no matter what he said.

"Keep 'em."

"Thanks. I will."

He closed his palm tight around the earrings: another involuntary gesture, she guessed, the conditioned clutch of a man who never had much money. But the close of his fingers continued until his knuckles turned white and she saw, startled, a drop of blood drip between his fingers where a gold point pierced his palm. She jerked her gaze to his face. Wide-eyed, slack-jawed, turned inward in sudden surprise—she had seen that face in her own mirror. He was having a powerful flash of a previous life, perhaps his first, or at least the first to matter to him. His fingers tightened even more convulsively on the earrings, and another drop of blood squeezed from between them.

"Robbie . . . where is it? When?"

He didn't answer. She tried, without success, to loosen his grip on the earrings. "Robbie—they're *sharp.*"

Still he didn't answer. Caroline took a step backward and waited, watching him curiously. What kind of memory would mean that much to a man like Robbie? What kind—the thought came unbidden, unwelcome—would it take to mean anything to Colin?

Suddenly Robbie shouted out loud. She reached out a hand to steady him. "Rob—"

He shouted again, and this time she realized the shout was a laugh. He caught Caroline in a hug, picked her up, and whirled around the room with her.

"Robbie, for Christ's sake—"

That seemed to amuse him. He whirled harder, then laughed again, and kissed her full on the lips. For a second she was afraid his triggered memory was sexual and he would not be able to control his reaction, but then she realized that the kiss was just exuberant high spirits, sudden hysterical release which had nothing to do with her. Which gave her, in fact, the odd sensation that she wasn't even there.

"Put me down!"

He did, then leaned forward and kissed her again. Caroline shrugged away.

"What the hell are you doing? Where are you?"

"Wyoming," he said, and laughed again.

"Doing what?" she said tartly.

"Getting rich!" His eyes shone; he was a sudden flood of energy, picking up his jacket from the chair, thrusting her earrings into his pocket, reaching for the doorknob. She slid herself between him and it.

"Robbie, what is it? What did you remember about Wyoming?"

"I'll come back and tell you someday."

"Come back? You can't leave the Institute yet, you haven't even paid attention to the little training you've—"

"Sure, I can. I can do anything. Haven't I been telling you that right along?" He grinned down at her. Triumph flew off him like sparks. "I'll see you next week."

"Next week? But you can't—" She saw that he could, and would. "Be careful!"

"And wear my sweater when it's cold, and brush my teeth. Bye, Caroline" He picked her up, set her to one side, and closed the door jauntily behind him. Caroline thought, with irritation, that she had never seen him look so fatuously adolescent. This was a man she had nearly gone to bed with? What had he remembered?

She bent to pick up the safe, again opened. But instead of straightening up, she sank down to the rug and pulled out Catherine's letter.

It was written on lined paper, with an eraser smudge in the upper right-hand corner and a tiny tear one third of the way up the left edge. The writing, careful block letters, was that of a seven-year-old. But Catherine had been nine, and the letters were too careful: squared corners, precise uprights. How long had it taken her to draw each part of each letter, scrutinize it, draw the next part, scrutinize, draw? On and on, from a memory that remembered parts but no longer wholes, a memory nearly incapable of recognizing anything new.

> DEAR MOMY,
> HOW ARE YOU? I AM GOOD. I HAD CAKE WITH LUNCH. MS. HARLOW KNITTED ME A RED SCARF.
>
> LOVE,
> CATHY

Catherine had written that letter a few months after she had gone to live in the Home in Albany. Caroline had waited, hoping without cause. She had known it was without cause, even then. It hadn't, somehow, stopped the hope. The genesplicers had found a cure for AIDS, maybe there would be a cure for MFRD. The number of children who contracted plague was very small; maybe the disease would burn itself out in the very young. The brain was still a largely unknowable organ; maybe something in Catherine's brain would snap, would right itself, would begin to recover its ability to respond to the new. Then the letters had started coming, one every week or so at first:

> DEAR MOMY,
> HOW ARE YOU? I AM GOOD. I HAD CAKE WITH LUNCH. MS. HARLOW KNITTED ME A RED SCARF.
>
> LOVE,
> CATHY

After a month or so, the letters started coming every other day, and then every day, as Catherine's brain closed down to new stimuli and settled into the fixed cycle it would run the rest of her life. Caroline had opened each letter in an apartment full of the packing boxes and bitter spaces of her and Charles's divorce, tearing at each envelope as the days lengthened into weeks, searching for one in which Catherine had gone to the park or played with her doll or had something else for lunch—

> DEAR MOMY,
>   HOW ARE YOU? I AM GOOD. I HAD CAKE WITH LUNCH. MS. HARLOW KNITTED ME A RED SCARF.
>
>   LOVE,
>   CATHY

—one in which she had a cold or a tummy ache—

> DEAR MOMY,
>   HOW ARE YOU? I AM GOOD. I HAD CAKE WITH LUNCH. MS. HARLOW KNITTED ME A RED SCARF . . .

—one which had Ms. Harlow crocheting or tatting or fucking or anything else but knitting endless red scarves for a child eating endless cake—

> DEAR MOMY,
>   HOW ARE YOU? I AM GOOD. I HAD CAKE WITH LUNCH . . .

—one where someone took the goddamn trouble to correct her spelling of "Mommy," surely that wasn't too much to ask for what she and Charles were fucking *paying* for the place—

> DEAR MOMY,
>   HOW ARE YOU? I AM GOOD . . .

—one without the same eraser smudge in the same corner and the same tiny tear, faithfully duplicated, one third up the left edge—

DEAR MOMY,
     HOW ARE YOU?...

—one—

DEAR MOMY,

The letters had finally stopped. Charles had seen the pile of them in her bedroom, and exploded at her "secrecy" and "theatricality" in keeping them all to herself: *Really, Caroline, you get more and more like your father every day.* And Colin, with macabre timing, had tried to visit her for a dramatic reconciliation: *Callie, in this your time of sorrow I only want to help*— And Caroline had gone in an ambulance, screeching and flashing through the New York night, to Mount Sinai with a paramedic leaning on each wrist. And when she had finally come home, only this one letter had remained, this first one, in the safe with her grandmother's jewelry and the curving gold-crescent earrings Colin had given her on her fourteenth birthday.

Caroline refolded the letter and put it back in the safe. It was past dinnertime. She thought of having a tray sent up, but she wasn't hungry. Then she thought of asking Joe McLaren if he wanted to have a quiet drink with her in the small bar at the top of the building where a pianist played from nine to eleven every night, tinkling out requests that often made funny looks come over people's faces as they either remembered past lives, or didn't. But McLaren had been distant and brusque the past few days. He obviously had something on his mind. She thought of dropping in on Patrick Shahid; when the little priest wasn't brooding over his data, he had a sharp, dry sense of humor she enjoyed. But Patrick, she remembered, had left for the weekend, gone visiting somewhere he had declined to specify.

Caroline replaced the safe inside the bottom drawer of the dresser and reactivated the E-fields. Then she reached for the blue vase with silver pheasants and leaned back against the bed, where Robbie had sat a half hour ago. Her thumb moved over the pure curves of the vase. One like it had stood on a small carved table just inside the door from the courtyard, holding a spray of peach blossoms, of quince or pear . . .

The courtyard.

The flute.

Tsemo, and the sound of her children's laughter . . . always, always, the children . . .

Her fingers moved hypnotically over the blue porcelain, and she smiled.

7 ROBBIE

It had been pure luck that had led him to Johnny Lee Benson in the first place.

That was the thing Robbie marveled at most—how much aces-high, random-access luck had been involved. For that matter, it had been just luck that he remembered it, any of it, now. If Caroline hadn't given him the earrings . . .

He packed them last, letting them lie on the blue Institute bedspread while he stuffed shirts and pants and headbands into a soft rectangular case of imitation leather. At one side of the traveling case was the usual detachable, protected pocket for software; he would keep the earrings in there, along with DeFillippo's handy device. Robbie never carried software.

Or maybe he would wear the earrings. One, anyway. He could jab a hole in his ear with the sharp part of the earring backing. The fashion was twenty years out-of-date—but who cared? It might look jaunty, at least on someone his age. Women might just like it.

Women had certainly liked Johnny Lee Benson.

Folding a dark red shirt threaded with silver wire at the wrists, Robbie grinned to himself. He could visualize Johnny Lee completely, after weeks of visualizing nothing at all. Everyone else at the Institute seemed to remember past lives so easily. Anything could set them off. He himself, it seemed, was always setting someone off. Caroline would catch sight of a shirt he had just changed into, or that ice man McLaren would hear him whistle a fragment of Bach, or the crazy journalist Prokop, who thought he was some dead millionaire, would be walking along the lake shore while Robbie swam and suddenly get that look on his face that meant a memory from another life was surfacing in this one: eyes slightly unfocused, smile briefly frozen, head held as if listening for echoes. They all got that look several times a day. Except for him.

He had had only four memories since his surgery three weeks ago, all of them worthless. Once he had been a sick child. Once a boy riding on an elephant. Once a laborer in China. And once a man, a very hungry man, digging potatoes with a pointed stick. None of them had been connected to any situation at all that could turn a profit, even though he had entered all three in the global datanet with full dates and names and bells and whistles, hoping for some fuller information that might be useful. *Nada*.

"You have a high trigger threshold for memory," that damn Shahid had said in his quiet voice. Robbie never trusted men that spoke that quietly. "It is the same as some people having a high threshold for pain. It is normal."

Robbie had been irritated. What kind of name was Patrick Martin Shahid anyway, especially for a priest? "How can you tell what's 'normal' for a tech that's only existed barely twenty years?"

A strange look crossed Shahid's face: strain, too great for the situation. Way too great. Robbie had been interested, but all Shahid would say was, "We already have a surprising amount of data on what is normal. Your memories will come."

"I'm not worried."

Shahid had regarded him thoughtfully, for an unnecessarily long time. "Good."

And he *hadn't* been worried. But just the same, when his fingers had closed around Caroline's earrings so hard that one of the pointed backings had drawn blood, that had been it. The trigger. The memory. The pay-off.

And Seymour Hatton wasn't going to know anything about it.

No reason. Hatton might get inside the Institute; Robbie had no doubt that of the array of service people passing in and out daily, at least one transmitted reports of Robbie's continued presence over some datanet or other. Hatton might even have gotten inside his room; maids and waiters came cheap, cheap enough even to justify spending on a speculative sideline like Robbie. But Hatton couldn't get inside his head.

That was the real beauty of this past-life deal. No one could know what he had remembered of another life, or where, or when, unless he blabbed it on the net. Any standard psych program Hatton might be having some underling use to predict what Robbie would do next was utterly invalid. It could extrapolate the movements and actions of Robbie Brekke—but not of Sean Malcolm Callahan.

Mallie Callahan. That's who he had been when he met Johnny Lee Benson. Fifteen years old and still raw from his father's last beating. God, it was all so clear!

Robbie shoved the last of his underwear into his travel case, pressed his thumbprint into the lock pocket, and hoisted the bag. A sudden uneasiness shot into his mind. It came from nowhere: from no thought or anxiety he could identify. And then, just as suddenly, it was gone.

Everything was all right. Everything had to be all right.

Robbie frowned. Now what the hell did that mean—and where had it come from? Of course everything was all right. Everything, in fact, was perfect.

He locked his door on the rest of his things; he'd be back in just a few days. The corridor and elevator were both empty. In the lobby the receptionist barely looked up from her terminal as he walked past. Two other carnies he knew only by sight glanced curiously at his traveling bag but said nothing. Out-

side, the September air smelled cool and sweet. No one
stopped him until he reached the gate.

"Can I help you, sir?" The security guard emerged from her
kiosk. In the plastic windows and door Robbie saw the watery
reflections of flickering screens.

"No, thank you. I have a taxi coming."

"May I have your visitor's pass, sir?"

"I'm not a visitor. Excuse me, my taxi is here."

"May I see your staff or client ID, sir?"

"No, you may not. Nor my thumbprint, nor my infrared
scan, nor the size of my light pen. My taxi's here."

"Please wait just a moment, sir." The woman stepped back
into her kiosk and closed the door. She stood facing both
Robbie and a screen he couldn't see; he watched her lips move
soundlessly. The gate, of course, was charged. The light poles
undoubtedly held the cameras. Robbie tilted back his head and
waved.

The guard opened her door. "Dr. Shahid will be here in just
a moment, Mr. Brekke."

"Will he pay for the meter running on the cab?"

"Dr. Shahid will only be a moment."

Shahid arrived by maintenance car, a ridiculously tiny open
vehicle powered by solar energy. He was the first person
Robbie had ever seen who did not dwarf the seat. His smooth
brown face looked unruffled but Robbie, amused, clearly felt
the tension as the historian stepped out. Historian, priest,
whatever, Shahid was definitely stodge. Sometimes it was fun
to match a stodge courtesy for courtesy, playing it their way.
Robbie smiled: What would this stiff, pious historian have
made of Johnny Lee Benson?

"You seem happy, Mr. Brekke."

"I am, Dr. Shahid. How charming of you to come down to
the gate to wish me good-bye."

"You are leaving us?"

"For a few days."

"May I ask why?"

Robbie grinned. "No."

Shahid smiled back. "I'm afraid it's not wise for you to leave just now, Mr. Brekke. You haven't completed your training in handling your new memories."

"How charming of you to be concerned."

"I am concerned, Mr. Brekke. Clients who have left us too early, thinking that they have mastered their new dimensions of mind when they have not, have sometimes regretted it. They have found themselves overwhelmed by disturbing memories without sufficient guidance in integrating them with their present beliefs. Emotionally overwhelmed, morally overwhelmed."

"But only sometimes."

"In your case, I think likely."

"Do you? I'm sorry to hear that. Now if you'll order the gate discharged . . ."

Shahid's smile vanished. "You can't leave."

Very slowly, Robbie moved toward Shahid, not stopping until he stood so close their shoulders touched. The top of Shahid's head didn't quite reach Robbie's chin. Courteously, softly, Robbie said, "Don't bluff, Doctor. You can't keep me here and you know it. Not legally, not emotionally, not morally." He put a faint and gleeful emphasis on the final word, knowing that Shahid would catch the mockery.

The historian took a step backward and looked up to meet Robbie's eyes. Shahid's black ones looked flat and opaque. "No. That is true. I can't keep you here. But I can warn you in the strongest possible terms what might happen if you go. In the past weeks you have not attended even half of the training classes you were scheduled for. Now you have remembered something, something exciting and pleasurable. You think it will always be as easy as this memory, whatever it is. But you have demonstrated a high memory threshold, which usually means internal conflict of some sort. Your psych profiles indicate a pronounced ability to disregard any reality you do not choose to see, plus a strong talent for self-deception. Given those characteristics, any difficult recollections of—"

"That's enough," Robbie said. The bastard was spoiling the whole mood. And it was partly Robbie's fault. Any day he let a little two-bit Freud-fly get to *him* . . . "Open the gate."

Shahid looked at him, steadily and for a long time. Then he motioned to the kiosk. The gate flickered blue, signaling the collapse of its E-field. The guard swung open the ornate wrought iron.

"I ask you once more to reconsider, Mr. Brekke. You are not as protected as you suppose. Because memory resides inside your skull does not mean it can't be at least partially detected from outside."

The little man was trying to spook him. Robbie shot Shahid a contemptuous glance and moved toward the gate. Behind him the historian said quietly, "What you have remembered occurred in the nineteenth century, in an English-speaking country, during which time you were either a military man or engaged in some other armed activity."

Robbie spun around. Shahid smiled wearily. "You used the word 'charming' twice, in two separate comments. 'Charming' has not been casual usage since the last century. Such linguistic carryovers only happen when a past life spoke the same language as the present one. And when you clenched your fists a moment ago, your right hand moved toward your hip to where a gun or sword would be worn, but only by those with no need to conceal their weapons. Soldiers. Guards. American cowboys."

Robbie stood completely still. Then he shook his head and smiled. "Parlor tricks, Shahid. I'm going."

" 'Parlor,' Mr. Brekke?"

The taxi let out an impatient blat. Robbie walked through the gate, forcing himself to smile dazzlingly at the woman in the kiosk. She smiled back, but then glanced apprehensively at Shahid.

This tiny incident suddenly cheered Robbie. Poor little girl—afraid of a dried-out academic God-spouter, of all things. He, Robbie, could show her different. Too bad she wasn't prettier.

"Beautiful morning," the driver said.

"Always," Robbie said with such force that the man twisted briefly in his seat to glance at him. Robbie laughed. The cab lurched into a U-turn and swung into traffic, leaving Shahid a small brown blur inside the reactivated gate.

Rochester International teemed with Gaeists in the midst of a major demonstration. Someone important, Robbie thought, must be due either to arrive or to leave. For a minute the only name his mind would bring up was Sam DeLorio. Robbie shook his head to clear it. That was Prokop's doing—all his questions about DeLorio and Kyle and all Robbie could think of was the dead corrupt industrialist who was father to this band of white-robed chanters with expensive electronic signs.

The demonstrators were grouped in three locations. In the center of the huge open terminal lobby—built twenty years ago when the AIDS panic had led hordes of people to see Rochester as a comparatively "safe" city to live in and so swelled the population—Gaeists danced. They wove in and out of ever-shifting circles that were, Robbie knew, supposed to represent shifting biological harmony on the earth. In front of the ticket terminals, Gaeists demonstrated, their signs flashing in blue-green: LET THE EARTH BREATHE. YOU ARE PART OF ALL. THE DESIGN ABIDES.

Next to the security fields, watched by scowling guards, Gaeists handed out literature. Robbie recognized the green pamphlet he had found in his pocket the day he arrived at the Institute. For a lark, he had brought it one night to dinner and read it aloud in an interested, mock-respectful voice that had

Joe McLaren steaming into his creamed corn soup. Robbie grinned.

Both television and holovid equipment, all trained on the demonstrators, obstructed what was left of the floor space. Robbie made his way through the tumult to a TWA terminal booth, which turned out to be equipped with voice response but only manual input. In Boston, of course, everything would have been handled by voice. Robbie keyed in information-only mode and requested the name of the airport most convenient to Salt Wells, Wyoming. The terminal informed him, in a soft courteous voice, that there was no Salt Wells, Wyoming.

His fingers hung motionless over the keyboard. No Salt Wells, Wyoming. A whole town gone, disappeared, since he and Johnny Lee—not that it had been much of a town. But what the hell was the one before it on the Union Pacific Railroad, the one he and Johnny Lee must have ridden through before they stumbled off the train at Salt Wells? He couldn't remember.

Robbie closed his eyes and tried to concentrate. The chanting of the Gaeists distracted him. "Earth our mother, cradling our life . . ." He had to remember. He could see Salt Wells so clearly, the wooden railroad platform and the homesteader family and the ragged squaw with her papoose and that Chinee, that ridiculous Chinee, and Johnny Lee had said—

Trying to remember made his head hurt, an actual physical ache just behind his eyes that suddenly blossomed into vertigo. Queasy dizziness washed over him and he sagged against the sides of the terminal booth. The unease that had invaded his mind in his Institute room returned. Robbie grabbed hold of the edge of the booth to keep from falling.

Everything was all right. Everything had to be all right.

Thayer. The town just before Salt Wells. Thayer.

Robbie straightened, the vertigo gone as swiftly as it had come. He shook his head. Maybe he was coming down with something. But he was never sick. Maybe he should eat something. That was probably it—he had skipped breakfast, and then had come that whole bizarre afternoon with Caroline going into her weird trance, and he hadn't eaten since last night.

He requested the airport most convenient to Thayer, Wyoming, and got Rock Springs. Then he asked for information on aircar rental in Rock Springs and was told there was no aircar rental available in Rock Springs, only ground vehicle or light plane rental. In the twenty-twenties? What the hell kind of place was Wyoming?

He only knew what kind of place it had been.

The closest airport with aircar rental was Rawlins. The terrain, the terminal told him sweetly, was very rough for aircar travel, but many tourists and historians found it enjoyable to drive above the old Union Pacific tracks toward the western part of the state. Accommodations in Rawlins, the terminal added, were comparable to any other major city.

Robbie, who remembered glimpsing Rawlins from the steam cars in a haze of whiskey and cigar smoke, blinked. Major city?

He booked a flight to Rawlins and reserved an aircar there, paying for the plane ticket with cash from the sale of Caroline's earrings at a Gold Exchange on the way to the airport and giving a false name. Paying cash, he did not have to give an ID or credit number. The plane would leave in two hours. As he left the booth, a Gaeist stood waiting, smiling and holding out a rose.

This Gaeist was nothing like the girl with the holo rose on her ass. Robbie felt immediate dislike: for the boy's gold-irised eyes, implants shining with legit and stodge family money. For the faint arrogance in the set of his lips. Most of all, for something effeminate that reminded Robbie suddenly of Hatton. He had heard that Gaeists had always been soft on gays, that they even considered AIDS a part of the self-regulation of the planet. And if you believed Prokop, DeLorio and that crazy murdered millionaire Prokop kept

trying to be, had once even maybe been, who knew . . .
Robbie grimaced in distaste.

"Grown in shit, brother," the boy said, flapping the rose
languidly. "Just as man's so-called pollution gets turned into
gain by the self-regulation of Gaea. Keeping conditions on the
planet favorable for life."

*The most dangerous movement to the fate of the earth that
has ever existed,* McLaren had said at dinner, his face filled
with bogus pain. Trying to impress Caroline. Robbie had gone
on reading from the green pamphlet.

"You are part of the biological design," Golden Eyes said.
His expensive irises were framed by thick bristling expensive
lashes.

"I spritz myself with aerosol cologne," Robbie said, remembering McLaren's argument, "destroying ozone—and that
makes me part of a biological design?"

"And Gaea compensates by decreasing the amount of nitrous oxide produced by microorganisms on the continental
shelf. Nitrous oxide also destroys ozone, in the upper atmosphere. You do more, Gaea will do less—to keep the world
steady for life."

The boy's startling eyes glowed. He put a hand on Robbie's
arm. "Everything man does is *part* of nature. We can't be—"

"Fuck off," Robbie said, shaking his arm loose. He strode
away from the boy, toward the airport restaurant. Fag. Rich
fag. Maybe McLaren had been right just this once, and this
whole movement was rotten with unseen money, making it
easier for corporations and governments to vote down expensive environmental controls—but why the hell should he care
one way or the other?

After eating a soyburger and some greens—the aircar
would be fabulously expensive, and the Gold Exchange had
cheated him on Caroline's earrings but he hadn't had time to
shop for a better deal on the street—his mood lifted. By the
time he boarded his flight, he was smiling again. After all, there

was more than one way to afford gold eye implants. He was on his way to a fortune. Even more, he was on his way to some unstodge action. God, how had he stood all the weeks in that Institute, the polite meals and careful routines and all the bullshit from wispy careful people like Shahid? But Shahid hadn't deterred him, and the crazy feeling in his room and in the TWA booth hadn't deterred him, and not even Caroline had deterred him. She had given him the earrings, but he was the one on his way to the action, on his way to the big one. This belonged to *him*—to him and to Johnny Lee Benson, who had been dead nearly a century and a half but who had been the most alive person Robbie could remember ever knowing. In any life. Johnny Lee, scheming and laughing and whoring and fighting his way from San Francisco to St. Louis and back to Wyoming, where . . . where . . .

Everything was all right.

His head hurt again. He couldn't remember it all. Memory went so far and then stopped, abruptly, as if his brain had slammed into a stone wall. But he remembered everything that counted, everything he would need in Wyoming, and enough of Johnny Lee to almost see him here, shimmering in the seat beside him as the plane lifted straight into the air. Johnny Lee stood six feet high for all that he was only seventeen years old, with black curling hair and bright blue eyes. His own eyes—his, Mallie Callahan's—were blue too, but he had plain brown hair and a body like a barrel and it just wasn't the same. Women didn't think so, and Mallie didn't either. There wasn't anybody like Johnny Lee.

Johnny Lee was clear to Robbie. And so was he himself, Mallie Callahan, fifteen years old and a runaway from home, standing on a trolley car in St. Louis with his fingers stuck through the bottom of his sack coat and into the purse of a seated blond lady with a nose like a hatchet and small, mean, rich eyes.

*   *   *

The loose sack coat, made of checked wool, came to just below Mallie's hipbone. He had bought it a half hour ago with money Johnny Lee had mysteriously produced, enduring the giggles of the shopgirl—what call did she have to giggle at him?—along with the rumblings in his own stomach. He had wanted to spend some of the mysterious money on food, but Johnny Lee had only laughed and said there would be plenty to eat once they were on the cars, the important thing was to do the job first. So Mallie had put on the checked coat, boarded the crowded trolley, and made his way to stand next to the small-eyed blonde in the rich-looking green taffeta dress and short black cape.

As the trolley became more crowded, Mallie edged closer to the woman. With his left hand he reached up to grasp the leather strap hanging from the ceiling. His right hand reached into the pocket of his coat.

The blonde glanced up at him suspiciously. Mallie pulled his handkerchief, white linen as new as the coat, from his pocket and blew his nose with much loud honking. She jerked her gaze away, mouth pursed. Mallie snorted a few more times, thinking of the explosion her own sharp nose must make when she blew it, and trying not to laugh.

More people boarded as the trolley neared the river. Mallie was pushed from all sides, until he stood with his chin directly above the woman's tightly knotted hair and tiny black chip hat. The edge of his sack coat lapped over the blonde's short cape.

Mallie put his handkerchief back in his right pocket. His hand found the slit Johnny Lee had cut in the coat lining across the back of the pocket. His fingers slipped between the lining and the checked wool. In a coat this cheap, the two had not been sewn together at the bottom. Carefully, Mallie thrust the tips of two fingers below the edge of his coat and began to pull up the bottom edge of the blonde's short black cape.

Little by little, the black fabric inched upward. The woman had turned her face away from the press of bodies in the center of the car, her nose wrinkling fastidiously. Town women always did that, Mallie thought contemptuously. It almost made the whole thing too easy. Not that Johnny Lee saw it that way. "Be glad you're a moll buzzer, it's easy," he said when they met, and laughed, and passed Mallie the bottle he'd never been allowed to have at home, not ever, not even when that old stinking skinflint his father had passed it to his brothers. *You ain't hefty enough to farm or steady enough to hunt, and I can't see that you done anything today to earn it. You'll be whining poor all your dead-lazy life, but not on my liquor.* Well, the last laugh was on the old dung. Mallie wasn't whining; since he met Johnny Lee he wasn't lazy; and in another fifteen minutes he wouldn't be poor. Again.

The cape was pulled up far enough for Mallie to feel the woman's leather pocketbook through her taffeta pocket. He was surprised to feel that it was a man's wallet, what Johnny Lee called a pittman. It fit snugly inside the pocket. Using two fingers, bending first one and then the other, Mallie began to work it free. He just had the leather reefed enough to draw it up through the lining of his coat and into his own pocket when it all happened at once:

The trolley started to slow down.

He felt something hard and bulky inside the wallet.

His stomach rumbled—hugely, loudly, a rumble of hunger so wet and explosive that heads turned all over the car.

One of them was the blonde's. She turned to glare directly into the offending stomach, her free-floating sourness momentarily fixed on a definite object. Her eye fell on the edges of her own cape, pulled up into a pleated arch that only partially collapsed back into smoothness after Mallie had withdrawn his fingers.

She clapped a hand over her pocket. "Thief!" she shrieked. "Thief! Stop him!" She lunged at Mallie with both hands but he was already moving, shoving with his shoulder through the bodies crowding the trolley. A few men at the back had already stepped onto the platform, easing the press slightly. Frantically Mallie jammed himself toward them.

"Thief! Stop him! Stop him!"

Hands reached toward Mallie, none of them more than tentative. Heads jerked in confusion. Someone called something decisive, but not even decision could be heard above the storm-wind shrieking of the blonde and the cacophony of questions. Only the motorman seemed to know what to do: The trolley suddenly sped up, trying to keep the thief from leaping off before he could get caught. Bursting out onto the rear platform, Mallie saw the trolley stop flash past, the upturned surprised faces of the waiting passengers-to-be like so many frozen white lumps.

A man on the platform lunged toward Mallie, who kicked him sharply in the groin. The man cried out and collapsed against two others standing below him on the steps; all three tumbled off the car. Mallie bent his legs, gathered himself together, and leapt.

He hit the ground rolling, landing on bare earth softened by recent rain. Mud splattered against his closed eyelids. Then he was up and running away from the tracks and the levee, toward the warehouses that lined the Mississippi, while behind him the trolley brakes screamed and the air filled with shouting.

Skirting the corner of a warehouse, he came to a great busy square. Desperately he looked for someplace to hide, someplace where his mud-soaked clothes wouldn't attract attention. Negroes carrying crates on their shoulders looked at him somber-faced. Buggies carrying warehouse buyers drove past. Mallie dodged them as best he could, until a semi-open carriage with huge red wheels drove through a deep puddle in the middle of the square, narrowly missing him and sending a spray of water furling high enough into the air to soak his head and shoulders with filth.

Somewhere a voice inside Mallie's head said: *Hold still. Now. Play it.*

The driver of the carriage pulled up his horses and leaned around the deep mudguard. He was a big man with a very red face. Mallie had a flashing impression of white ruffled shirt with a diamond stickpin. "Oh, I am sorry!"

English. The accent was English. Mallie made himself take only one step toward the carriage, scrubbing with his hand at the mud on his coat, widening his eyes. Somewhere behind the lines of Negroes with crates, people shouted.

"I didn't at all see you!" the Englishman said, irritation beginning to creep into his voice. "Where the devil did you come from?"

"My father's," Mallie said humbly. "Preacher Dodson, sir. From buying me my new coat for Sunday meeting . . ." He scrubbed again at the muddy coat shoulder, trying to look as if he were holding back tears.

The Englishman frowned. Mallie saw the doubt at the edges of the frown, and he didn't push. He stood with his head down, dirty shoulders sloped, letting his hands dangle loose at his sides. Finally the Englishman said tightly, "Then let me replace the cost of your new coat, lad. How much?"

"Oh, I couldn't," Mallie said, lifting his head.

"I insist. Here." He thrust a bill at Mallie, who let it stay at the end of the Englishman's outstretched arm.

"I couldn't take money for no accident you didn't mean, sir. It wouldn't be right. But if you could . . . could just see your way clear to drive me to where I was supposed to meet my father . . . It'd be right embarrassing to walk through town in my shirtsleeves and the coat's so dirty . . ."

"Get in," the Englishman snapped. Mallie went around to the other side of the carriage and climbed in. A knot of shouting men appeared from behind a stack of cotton bales. Mallie stripped off the dirty coat, put it under the seat, and leaned far back into the semiclosed carriage. The Englishman flapped his reins and the carriage started forward.

Mallie's belly gave another huge rumble. The Englishman's

mouth twitched, but all he said was, "And where are you supposed to meet your father?"

"At the railroad depot, sir." The carriage passed the men from the streetcar.

The Englishman said nothing until they reached the station. When Mallie climbed out, he heard the amusement in the man's voice. "If walking on the street in your shirtsleeves is the worse embarrassment you ever face, young man, yours will be a very easy life."

"Yes, sir. Thank you, sir." He was careful to keep his head down until the carriage had driven off, and when he finally looked up, the grin bursting out of his head, there was Johnny Lee Benson grinning back, his blue eyes sparkling and his hat pushed so far back on his black hair that it seemed it must fall off, although it never did. Under Johnny Lee's grin Mallie felt himself expand and glow, felt the laugh break out of him, and that was right, was as it should be. For it had been Johnny Lee's voice in his head saying *Now. Play it,* and Johnny Lee who had taught him how to reef a pittman in the first place, just as Johnny Lee had taught him everything else that made this new life such a fast, hot ride that every day Mallie woke up tingling and every night he went to sleep laughing and drinking and staggering alongside Johnny Lee.

"What'd you get?" Johnny Lee demanded.

"Let's look," Mallie said. "Wait till you hear!"

They went down a little alley formed by the side of the railroad station and a livery stable beside it. The alley was filled with broken bottles and the smell of manure, but Mallie didn't care. He pulled out the wallet he had taken from the blond woman. For a moment he held it unopened: For that moment the wallet might hold anything at all, *did* hold anything, and the anything was something he had won that Johnny Lee couldn't wait to see. He, Mallie, could see it in the strain of Johnny Lee's body forward onto the toes of his boots, in the expression on his sunburned face under the pushed-back hat brim. And he, Mallie, held the unopened wallet . . .

Johnny Lee grabbed it. "*Open* it, for Christ's sake!" He fumbled at the leather, tipped it up. Something fell to their feet.

Inside the wallet was $2,000 in large bills.

Johnny Lee whooped, looked around, and clutched the wallet. No one was in sight. He looked at Mallie, a sudden look so hard—so unexpected in his speculative hardness—that Mallie first stood still in surprise and then bent to retrieve whatever had fallen to get away from Johnny Lee's eyes. When he stood up, the look was so completely gone that he thought he must have imagined it, and a pair of earrings lay on his outstretched palm.

Gold. Five gold balls to each earring, with little gold chains between them and sharp gold crescents at each end, the pair tied together with pink silk. At the sight of them the hard look appeared once again on Johnny Lee's face. This time Mallie had plenty of time to see it. It settled over the top point of his mind like ground fog, muffling everything in murky white.

"Jesus Christ," Johnny Lee said softly, almost reverently. Mallie thought of his father. Orin Callahan didn't hold with cursing. "Who *was* he?"

"She," Mallie said. Johnny Lee's head jerked up and the unholy glee came back into his blue eyes. "She? You was moll buzzing again?"

Mallie nodded. Johnny Lee's eyes danced and he threw back his head and laughed. Still his hat didn't fall off. And then Mallie was laughing too, and the white fog swirled away.

"A female stall!" Johnny whooped. "Had to be! You reefed a thief!"

He clapped a hand on Mallie's shoulder, hard enough to knock him against the side of the stable. On the other side of the wooden wall, a horse stamped and snorted. The two young men whooped and gasped. Somewhere Mallie felt a stab of alarm: Wouldn't people who had lost that much money be pretty thorough about looking for it? But Johnny Lee was still laughing, and probably they would leave St. Louis right away on the steam cars and outrun any danger, and anyway nobody could see the wallet because it had already disappeared into Johnny Lee's clothes and not even Mallie had noticed where. So he went on laughing. His hand closed around the gold earrings, hard, and the sharp-pointed crescents cut into the palm of his right hand.

Robbie stirred in the narrow seat. Directly in front of him, soothing patterns in various shades of green played across the plastic back of another seat. The flight attendant holos appeared in the aisle: one per six passengers, all identical. She rotated slowly to smile at each passenger in turn while making her spiel: drinks, dinner, brainies, sleepcaps. She had dark curls, a trim gray uniform, a red headband with the TWA logo. Robbie noticed that she smiled at the empty seats as well as the occupied ones.

He wondered if she were actually aboard. Sometimes on domestic flights the holo models were actually aboard, since it was the younger attendants who received both the holo bids and the duller flight assignments.

She smiled at him again. Robbie realized that he didn't really care whether she was aboard or not.

He ordered a brainie and a sleepcap, which were brought to him by a male attendant who looked harassed. Robbie set the sleepcap for three hours, no REM monitoring, no audio. He shifted in the narrow seat, trying to get comfortable.

Just before he drifted off to sleep, he heard the voice again, soft-edged from the brainie, distant as a far country.

Everything was all right. Everything had to be all right.

"Fucking *true*," Robbie said out loud, and slept.

8 JOE

"We did not admit Mr. Whittaker inside the Institute gate," the receptionist said primly. "You know the rules, Mr. McLaren."

Christ on a ramchip, Joe thought, and glared at her. The woman pursed her mouth into a tight wrinkled O—that same mouth that only an hour ago Joe had observed soft and smiling at Colin Cadavy's unexplained presence—and glared back. Joe made a conscious effort to soften his expression.

"Then where is he now?"

"At the front gate. The Institute does not admit just anyone on their own word, Mr. McLaren."

"I left *my* word. Angel Whittaker is my secretary, and I'm sure he was carrying the proper ID to verify that. And you seemed to admit Colin Cadavy fast enough."

"Mr. Cadavy is a relative of Ms. Bohentin's."

Joe tried not to show his surprise. Which, he realized a moment later, was not as great as it should have been. Caroline herself was half actor, every moment of her life.

"Her father?" he asked the receptionist, but the woman merely leaned toward her terminal screen and ostentatiously studied it.

Brekke would have known how to get her to answer. Charm. Bribery. Pheromones. He had seen Brekke and Caroline go together toward her room just after Colin Cadavy's arrival. Cadavy had left; Brekke had not.

Joe walked out of the lobby and along the driveway toward the gate. Beyond the bulk of the Institute, just before the driveway curved into the trees, he caught a glimpse of Bill Prokop walking along the edge of the lake, carrying some sort of portfolio. Joe quickened his steps. Prokop had become increasingly strange in the last few weeks, badgering people for memories of Armand Kyle, of Paul Winter, of Sam DeLorio, all dead. What were Armstrong and Shahid and the rest of the high-powered Institute staff doing about it? Nothing, as far as Joe could see. Hazard of the operation. Unforeseen and unfortunate result of free choice. Prokop had the right, they would probably say, to quietly go crazy in whatever life he chose. Even one he hadn't actually had.

Angel waited beyond the security gate. Joe thought about hassling the guard to admit him, but decided against it and went outside. His very first glance at Angel disturbed him. Instead of sitting cross-legged on the taxi hood or haranguing the guard, Angel stood stiffly at the curb. His headband was crooked and there was a food stain on the front of his shirt—Angel, who usually paid inordinate attention to, and money for, his beautifully cut clothes. Joe had known him to spend one month's pay on a jacket and then eat soyburgers for the next two. He waited for Joe to walk over to him.

"*Hola*, Counselor."

"What is it?" Joe said quietly. Up close, Angel looked even worse: café-au-lait skin mottled, eyes puffy.

But Angel chose to misinterpret his question. "It's from Jeff Pirelli," he said, holding out a thick package stamped CLASSIFIED and electronically sealed. Angel never said "Mr. Pirelli"; he scorned all titles except the most exalted. When President Caswell had unexpectedly called Joe because she was unable to reach Pirelli with a question about the Plague Commission, Joe had held his breath in half expectation of Angel's calling her

"Diane." Now, however, Angel's jocular informality sounded hollow.

Joe took the package. "What is it, Angel? What's wrong?"

"Nothing."

"You look like that and nothing's wrong?"

"Just because I work for you," Angel said through tight lips, "doesn't mean you have a right to pry into my life."

There was a long pause. Joe said quietly, "I'm sorry."

Angel made a gesture that might have meant anything, a sudden upflung arm just as suddenly dropped. "Brad Howell wants you to call him on the Spicer case. The court granted an appeal on *Juddson versus Maryland*—you're on the docket for next February. And besides all that stuff there, Jeff Pirelli wants you pronto. He's been calling all day, and calling you up here as well. He says to call him right away, if you can."

"If I can? What does he think they've done to me up here?"

"You're asking me what Jeff Pirelli thinks?"

That sounded more like Angel. "Nah," Joe said. "Nobody can figure out what Pirelli thinks. That's why he's so good at what he does. Tell him I can still make phone calls, pace the floor, and do his homework at the same time."

Angel studied him; it was the first time the dark eyes had met his directly. "Have to say you don't look any different, Counselor."

"What did you expect? A different face? Twenty different faces?"

"Not sure."

Joe was irritated; mention of the plazzing always seemed to do that to him. Out of the corner of his eye he saw Bill Prokop round the corner of the drive. "The MS symptoms are receding. It feels like another remission, is all. Otherwise, I'm not anybody I wasn't before. The operation to pull that off doesn't exist."

Angel surprised him by saying harshly, "Maybe that's too

bad. For some of us." Joe looked up, but he saw that Angel had not meant the bitterness for him. Angel stared, uncharacteristically, at the ground. Abruptly he again busied himself with passing Joe bunches of papers.

"These are for the Franzen case; the uncle is countersuing. And these here need your signature, now, on this great desk they gave you in the driveway."

Prokop approached them. "Hello, Joe."

"Hello," Joe said distantly.

"Nice day."

"Yes. Bill, this is my secretary, Angel Whittaker. Angel, Bill Prokop. Bill, we're busy just now so if you don't mind—"

"Kyle," Prokop said pleasantly.

"What?"

"I go by the name of Kyle now. Armand Kyle. Joe, I appreciate that you're busy, but would you mind taking just a second to look at these pictures?"

"Not now," Joe said as courteously as he could. Christ— *Armand Kyle*. But the man didn't look crazy, standing there in his conventional clothes and smiling politely. "Perhaps later."

"It will only take a moment," Prokop said, pulling out a pile of holos, and Joe remembered that he had been a journalist. Used to pushing for information.

Angel said tightly, "Armand Kyle?"

"Yes," Prokop said pleasantly.

"The gay who was murdered by that mob? Back in the AIDS time?"

Prokop's eyes sharpened. "You know about that?"

Angel folded his arms across his chest. His face wore a look Joe had never seen on anyone outside of a witness chair: deliberate unreadability laid over anger so fierce that Joe took a step backward. But Prokop said eagerly, "Have you been plazzed? Did you know anything about Kyle or Winter in their lifetimes? Or even about Sam DeLorio, the founder of the Gaeists?"

"I don't know nothing," Angel said. "And I never been plazzed. Fuck off."

Prokop eyed Angel keenly. Joe said nothing; he had never heard Angel speak like that before, not in that tone or with that grammar. He knew Angel had never had reincarnation surgery—had never, so far as Joe knew, expressed any interest in it, or in murders over twenty years old, or even in history in general. And he knew damn well that Angel was no Gaeist; he wouldn't have hired him if he had been.

Prokop, when it became obvious that Joe was not going to speak, walked away. Joe had no idea what to say. The exchange bewildered him. Angel jerked a pen from his pocket and said, "Sign this one, and this one, and you better read that one first."

Joe signed, balancing the papers awkwardly on one upraised knee, thinking how much Pirelli would have relished the scene. *Who works for who here, boy?* But there were deep circles around Angel's eyes, and when he turned to walk back to the waiting cab, Joe saw a tiny rip in the back of the jacket he had paid two months' salary for.

"Angel—wait." Joe took a slow breath; he knew he wasn't good at this. "Listen. If you don't want to tell me what's wrong, I won't push. But if I can help at all . . . if I can, please tell me."

Angel stared at him from dark eyes. "You can't." He waited a moment, then added, "With what you believe, you can't."

With what I believe about *what*? Joe wanted to say, but Angel was already walking toward the cab. Halfway there, he stopped and turned a final time. "You got another message from Robin Nguyen. This one in person. She said she flew in from California to see you, and when I said you were on vacation and unavailable for another month, she said to please tell you, 'Purple martins flying.' 'Please, please, please,' she said. Three times. Like a kid."

Robin in Washington. Looking for him. Joe watched as Angel climbed back into the taxi. The packet from Pirelli felt smooth and heavy in his hand.

*　　*　　*

He opened it in his room, wanting to avoid any more talk with Prokop. Lady Alison Ogilvie and Elle Watt-Davis got off the elevator at his floor; Joe forced himself to chat with them until he reached his own room. Caroline's door, he noticed, closed abruptly as he and the women approached. Joe looked away. It had been a male hand that pulled it closed. Brekke?

INTERIM REPORT: ISOLATION OF MEMORY FORMATION AND RETRIEVAL DISORDER PRIMARY VIRUS. "Primary"? Did that mean the medical team now thought there might be more than one cause for the plague?

Joe settled himself at his desk and began to read. It was slow going. He understood why Pirelli had not wanted to risk sending the data electronically to the Institute system; he would consider its attempts at security a feeble joke. He understood, too, why Pirelli would trust Angel as courier with the hard copy. What he didn't understand was why Pirelli wanted him to read the masses of undigested detail in these reports, much of it in medicalese, some of the rest in mathematical equations. Even the "executive summaries" were written in the dense prose that seemed to be a requirement for probability scanners.

He turned to the legal sections. With the plague virus identified, Carl Esparza's team of lawyers had been able to zero in on the patent issues involved in creating both testing serums and potential vaccines. From the beginning, the legal team on the Commission had worked on the other ramifications of a testing program. How widespread could it be without violating civil rights? For whom could testing be mandatory (the armed forces presented no problem) and for whom would it need to be voluntary? Until now, of course, all the lawyers' recommendations had been provisional; there was no test to administer. Now the theoretical had become real.

Joe had lobbied hard for mandatory testing of everything that moved. Completely unrestricted choice, he argued, was not compatible with a society that valued its members enough to structure government-supported programs to care for the ill. If you wanted the benefits of care from others, you must be willing to accept control from others. The Constitution, he had argued, was based on just such a system of balances in both spirit and design. He had not been listened to. Testing, when it was implemented, would be voluntary.

He turned back to the medical sections and read them again, this time more closely, wanting to understand. The slow virus, he finally decoded, attacked the part of the brain called the hippocampus. The hippocampus was crucial in the search for novelty. When a person was immobile, it barely showed any activity, as measured by neural firing, at all. When the person was engaged in familiar and routine activities, the hippocampal scans showed a low level of activity. But when the person was doing something new, there was a high level of hippocampal firing. That much, Joe gathered, was not new research, although some of the pages of equations seemed to represent new findings about old concepts.

What *was* new was the careful chemical mapping of how the hippocampal function interacted with both cortical and limbic memory. Apparently the hippocampus, concerned with novelty, was what "turned on" the brain to form memories. As the slow virus altered the hippocampus, the plague victim lost all interest in doing new things. Slowly the memory became affected, so that even when new activities were engaged in, they were not remembered. Finally, in the last stages, hippocampus and memory had "frozen" in a single sequence of memory repeated over and over and over. No new stimulus could get in, unless it was forced in, and forcing a victim to do something new—such as, for instance, physically dragging him away from writing a letter to take a shower—produced panic and hysteria. If it could be done at all—many plague victims would simply go on writing the letter in the shower, sans paper or pen or any awareness that there was a new stimulus to be noticed.

Left alone, of course, unable to remember to eat or drink, they died.

The test serum, Joe finally deduced, was not going to be difficult or expensive to synthesize. That was a break, perhaps the first one the Commission had ever gotten. The first subjects would all be volunteers with good security clearances. Nothing would be revealed to the public until there was a firm program in place. Irresponsible groups had already dispensed too much false hope—among them the most irresponsible of all, the Gaeists. "Viruses, too, are part of the biological design. Gaea eventually compensates for all imbalances in the design." Bullshit. He couldn't even think about it without getting angry all over again.

Joe pulled out his lap computer and began composing short, clear summaries of what he understood from the pile of documents. The summaries would save other members of the Commission—and of the administration—from having to wade through as much jargon as he had. The wall terminal would of course have been faster, but he didn't trust its security any more than Pirelli did.

After two hours of work, his eyes began to ache. He stood up, stretched, and decided on a walk by the lake. What he wanted, he told himself, was the evening lap of waves on the shore, the smell of damp rocks. It would clear his head. But when he saw that Caroline's door was open a crack, he paused.

By walking past the door, then turning around and heading back toward his room as if he had forgotten something, he caught a glimpse inside. Caroline was alone, sitting on the floor with her back against the bed, holding a piece of her Chinese porcelain. Only her thumb moved, caressing the porcelain, over and over. Her eyes were vague and unfocused. She looked tranced.

"Caroline?"

She didn't answer. Joe pushed the door open a little wider and raised his voice. "Caroline?"

She looked up. "Joe." The name seemed experimental, as if she wasn't completely sure who he was. He came a little farther into the room.

"Are you all right?"

"All right?" Then all at once her face came into sharp focus. "Yes. I'm all right. I'm fine." She started to stand, staggered a little, and sat down on the edge of the bed, looking up at him. "Did I look not all right or something?"

"You looked . . . in a trance of some sort."

She smiled ruefully. The Chinese porcelain rested easily in her fingers. "Sometimes I get a little . . . lost in a past life. For a little while. It's no big deal."

"It's *not?*"

"No. I like it."

He went on watching her and she laughed, her eyes suddenly dancing. "Joe, Joe. Does even such a small breach of control bother you?"

"You should talk to Shahid."

"I have. He says I can learn to control it, with practice. I'm staying an extra few weeks for training."

He sensed that there was more to the situation than she was saying, and more to Shahid's reaction to it. Her jibe about control stung; it was too close to things Robin had said to him during their marriage. *The real reason you hate the Gaeists is because they give up control to a larger power, isn't it? Then you wouldn't be able to think you were making your little so-called rational choices.*

He watched Caroline carry her priceless porcelain to the dresser. Light played over her bent head, highlighting subtle shades in her brown hair. Cinnamon, he thought. Seal. What else? How the hell should he know. He was no artist. And the hair color wasn't even natural. Bought, like the porcelain, like the right to jibe at him.

Caroline said, "Do you want to get some food? I didn't get any dinner." When he didn't answer, she looked at him more closely, and her face changed. "No, you don't want to eat, do you. You want to fight." She shifted forward a little, almost balancing on her toes. Like a dancer, Joe thought. Or a boxer. Ready. The theatricality of it irritated him.

She said, "You didn't like what I said about your being so controlled."

"Not especially."

"Because it's not true?"

"Because it's a cheap shot at a real truth. There's nothing wrong with control. Or with making choices."

"And there *is* something wrong with enjoying memory?" Oh, she was ready to fight, all right. Her eyes gleamed with anger. What surprised Joe was finding how ready he too was to fight.

He said, "There's something wrong with wallowing in memory."

"Really? And what might that be? Do analyze it for me."

"Irrelevance. Escape."

"From what?" She smiled with amusement; apparently her fighting style was to stay cool and superior. He hated that, and it made him say things he might not have otherwise.

"From reality. From any problem too tough to dissolve in money. From the adult responsibility of creating an identity through making choices instead of escaping from them."

Caroline's smile broadened. Above it, her eyes glittered dangerously. "Really. What a fascinating philosophy. Did it take you long to come up with the wording? And what choices am I supposedly escaping from? Tell me, Counselor, from your vast experience in working with plague victims, what choices does the mother of a ten-year-old child with plague have left?"

"I didn't mean that," Joe said. Her calling him "counselor" made him suddenly think of Angel. God, what a shitty day.

"No, of course not. You just hint at it, out of all your great store of the right answers. As codified into law, of course. And so in addition to evading choices—the '*adult responsibility*' to make choices, no less—I'm also evading 'creating an identity.' Well, then, draw on your basic Philosophy 101 program and answer me this one: What the hell do you think identity is but memory? What are *you* except everything you remember, everything you've done in the past shaping the choices you make in the present? Nothing. Nothing at all."

"Not true. I am what I invent myself to be now. Moment by moment. By choices guided by a moral vision."

"Choices you make out of memory!"

"Only as raw data," Joe said.

"Processed by what? Your 'immortal soul'? Come on, Joe!"

"Processed by my rational mind," Joe said. He was a little surprised at the passion in her arguments; he hadn't expected her to have thought much about any of these things. But her white face shone at him like ice. "I invent myself, Caroline. Day by day. Through the consistency of my choices."

" 'Consistency'? *'Consistency'!*" Her voice scaled upward. "You think it's possible for any human being above the age of seven to act consistently? Or desirable? In a world like *this*?"

"I think it's possible to try," Joe said as calmly as he could. Her smiling mockery had vanished; she looked ready to tear him apart.

"I'll tell you what consistency is. Consistency, Counselor, is doing the same thing over and over because you did it before. Consistency is writing letters all exactly the same. Consistency is the plague."

"Not that kind of consistency!"

"What kind then? How many kinds do you fucking think there *are*?"

"At least one other. The consistency of choosing what you believe to be right. Instead of taking the easiest path out."

"Even at a sacrifice to yourself, I suppose."

"Even at a sacrifice to yourself."

Her face twisted in contempt. "You're a prig, Joe."

"And you're a rich spoiled child."

They glared at each other, Joe appalled at himself—how had he lost his temper like that? He felt bruised inside, the way he used to feel after fights with Robin. He wanted to slap Caroline—no, he wanted to reach out and touch her hair, say he was sorry. Only he wasn't sorry. He was—

"All right, Joe. All right," Caroline said wearily. The fight seemed to have abruptly gone out of her. Her face looked pale and tired. "We obviously don't have anything to say to each other about this. Why don't we just drop it. I don't have an education steeped in Constitutional nobility, and you don't have a daughter with the plague."

He said, "I had a wife who left me for the Gaeists," and immediately hated himself: of all the whining, self-pitying, fucking *stupid* things to blurt out . . .

But Caroline looked interested. He saw her mouth, bare of makeup in her strained face, open to frame a question when the phone rang. She picked it up.

"Yes . . . *yes* . . . is she alive?" Joe looked up sharply. "Is she hurt in any way? . . . When did you say? Just what happened?" There was a long pause. Joe watched Caroline's face, until he had to look away. "I'll be there in two hours, maybe less . . . If you have to. But don't under any circumstances let him remove her from the premises, do you understand? I hold physical custody."

"What is it?" Joe asked.

She hung up the phone, activated the wall terminal, and punched in a rapid string of code before looking at him remotely. Her face was calm and set. She snatched up her purse and reached for the door. Joe caught her arm. "Caroline?"

"Catherine's Home has been bombed."

"Is she—"

"All right. Yes. Thank you," Caroline said, as remote and formal as if she were pouring tea for Japanese lawyers. The last time Joe had seen that look it had belonged to a defendant who had bowed courteously throughout a bankruptcy hearing and then shot himself. There were, he thought, all kinds of bankruptcy.

"I'll go with you."

"Why?"

"I'm a lawyer. And as it happens, I've dealt with that Home before."

"Thank you, but I don't need another lawyer," Caroline said with that same cool and remote courtesy. She strode rapidly toward the elevator.

Joe followed. "Who did the bombing?"

"I don't know. Americans for a Clean Country, I imagine." She strained toward the elevator doors, as if that might make them open sooner.

"I'll go with you," Joe said as firmly as he could. "We have nine lawsuits filed against them already for alleged bombings. One right here in Rochester just a month ago." He remembered Sister Margaret, her scorn for him, the bits of bone embedded in the synthfoam wall.

Caroline didn't answer. Joe watched a vein at the side of her neck, just above her collarless yellow shirt, beat frantically. He followed her out of the Institute and into the aircar that had already appeared. Had she summoned it on the terminal, that fast? Apparently. And wasn't anybody going to check her driver Jason's credentials before allowing him to land inside Institute gates? Apparently not. Joe thought again of Angel.

Caroline didn't comment further on his presence. She neither spoke nor moved during the trip to Albany. Joe glanced from her to the scenery below. They were flying pretty high for an aircar, higher than they had on the shopping trip for porcelain. This car must have special modifications. The three other times he had ever been in aircars—all official occasions connected with the Plague Commission—they had flown low enough over Washington to see the expressions on people below. All three cars had resembled public planes: washable seats in muted tasteful colors trying to look roomier than they were, passengers seated for maximum efficiency. Caroline's car had an upholstered fuchsia banquette, a fold-down table of what Joe thought might be teak, and a sound system she did not turn on. Was the car hers? Cadavy's? Her ex-husband's?

Below him, the Mohawk Valley flashed by in a patchwork of fields and towns folded along the bright silver ribbon of the river.

Two thirds of the way to Albany, Caroline said quietly, completely naturally, "Shujen, Tsemo's and my oldest son, could already brush the wood character by the time he was two years old."

Joe took her hand, but said nothing. She turned to him and nodded, unsmiling, then turned back to the window. Her face was calm and composed. Joe thought about the nine lawsuits against Americans For a Clean Country, about the plague-testing program the Commission was developing, about the briefs for various cases that Angel had brought him. He realized that he was concentrating on these things, the furniture of his own life, as a barrier to the sheer quiet intensity of Caroline's pain. But what could he possibly do for her now? Nothing. *Inventing yourself day by day*, he had said to her. *Making choices.*

It was too bad the truth could make one sound like such a pompous ass.

The Meadows Home lay in a wooded area north of Albany. From the air it should have looked tranquil and reassuring: long, low white buildings, too big for cottages but too architecturally interesting for dorms, connected by curving stone paths bright with flower beds. A Japanese meditation garden rested in a small dell. Ducks swam in a blue pond. Half of one building had been reduced to rubble flung over the garden and pond like stone confetti.

The blackened beams of the hall still smoked, but both fire trucks and ambulances had already departed, leaving long ruts across the lawn. A police aircar, small and stark, was parked nearby. A few people stood around the edges of the site—reporters, Joe guessed, and wondered why they had been let in. You never knew what the local politics were. As the aircar dropped softly to the ground, he saw that the knot of people surrounded a man whose face bore the weariness of too many repetitions of information to people who wanted to hear something else.

Caroline jerked open the door even before Jason had completed the landing and jumped out, running toward the intact end of the bombed building. A state trooper yelled after her, "Hey, miss, come here—security check!" Caroline ignored him. The cop yelled again, his face turning red, and started after her. Joe intercepted him.

"She's a parent. Her little girl was in that cottage. Catherine Long. The Home notified her of the bombing and she's here to check on her daughter."

"Who are you?"

"Her lawyer. Need ID?"

The cop ignored him, repeating everything Joe had said into his wrist mike. Soot smudged the trooper's uniform and lay in long welts across his cheek. A woman came running across the lawn to Caroline and led her toward another building at the far edge of the campus.

When the cop had finished talking to the security terminal, Joe said, "Ground bombing?"

"Air."

"Any notes or calls claiming credit?"

The cop said, "Does there have to be? Third one in this state alone in the last three months."

"Ummm," Joe said, waiting. With cops, the politics could go either way. A lot of them resented the increase in taxes that the plague had carried as surely as it carried the newly isolated DNA.

"Bastard sons of bitches. I'd like to bomb the whole Americans For a Clean Country headquarters back into the toilet it grew out of." He looked directly at Joe. "I got a brother with plague."

In that case, there was only one way the politics could go. When it happened to you, then it really happened.

Joe said, "Any idea why this particular Home? It's private, no tax funding." But the cop turned away with the cold scowl of a man who thinks he's already said too much. Joe followed Caroline into the other residence hall.

The lobby was bedlam. Sleek green chairs overflowed with patients, relatives, and harassed nurses. Joe passed an elderly woman in a torn, smoke-blackened bathrobe vigorously mixing a nonexistent cake in a nonexistent bowl. She hummed happily, oblivious to the blood caked on her arm. A younger woman hung over her crying. The older woman never glanced up from her cake.

"Catherine Long, please."

"Room 247," the receptionist said, and turned to a man who rushed up demanding his son.

The staircase dated from the last century, modeled on the one before that: wide curving treads, polished balustrade. Joe thought again of Sister Margaret. He hoped she had found funding to move her charity patients.

In Room 247, Caroline was not crying. She sat on a wide windowsill at the far edge of the large room, stony-faced and smoking, listening to a woman in an expensive tailored suit. Joe had never seen Caroline smoke before. With them, his back to Joe, stood a big man with an overcoat folded over his arm. There were two other people in the room that might have been two separate rooms, so sharply was the space divided by a light blue rug.

The half of the room covered by the rug was filled with toys and children's furniture: white wicker bed, dresser, rocking chair, shelves, small desk with popular-model terminal frozen midway through a computer game. The terminal sang softly. In the middle of the rug a little girl with a thin, intense face sat putting together U-Builds with a concentration too pronounced for her age. Which was ten, Joe remembered. She didn't look it. Blonder than Caroline, she had a different set to her chin: less rounded, jutting more forward. Joe tried to see what she was making with the construction toy, but her hand blocked part of it and he couldn't tell.

Beyond the carpet, the room abruptly changed character. On the synthetic, easy-care floor stood a utilitarian table and three plain chairs, one of them filled by a plump, pleasant-faced nurse reading a newspaper. The table was littered with medical logs, knitting, medicine bottles, a hypodermic, and a newspaper. Hypodermic, knitting needles, and medicine all stood within easy reach of the child. Joe understood; Catherine would never go near them. She would not even see them.

"—after an hour or two," the administrator was saying, her voice low with professional calm. "As soon as she stopped screaming, we just slipped her back into her environment, and you can see now that she's just fine."

"What the hell was she doing outside when the bomb fell anyway?" the big man said angrily. "I thought you preserved her routine perfectly for us!"

"A walk outside is part of that routine. You were told that, Mr. Long," the woman said, not unpleasantly.

"And how the hell did the bomber get away with it in the first place? What kind of security are you people running here?"

"The best we can," the woman said. Caroline pulled deeply on her cigarette, her face impassive.

"And another thing," Charles Long said, "what the hell was that man I saw wandering loose in the lobby downstairs? He was no plague victim. I was told this Home took only plague victims—that was part of your much-vaunted expertise that I'm paying you for. And now I'm accosted by some loony babbling and drooling at me!"

"You were informed by letter of the new patients and staff in Cox Cottage, Mr. Long. We were fortunate enough to obtain a research grant—"

"I was not informed!"

"Yes, you were, Charles," Caroline said in a hard voice Joe had never heard her use before. "Your secretaries probably couldn't get you to read it."

"—a research grant to *help* our plague victims," the woman went on determinedly. "There are definite indications of similarities between the brain wave patterns of patients not yet in the tertiary stage and these new people with Korsakov's syndrome. They—"

"Could wander into my daughter's room and further wreck her stability," Long shouted. Caroline appeared to no longer be listening. She glanced at the time, then watched Catherine. At the same moment, the nurse checked her watch and laid down the newspaper.

Catherine put down her toy, reached for a doll in the bookcase, pulled back her arm, and called, "Mommy!"

"What?" the nurse answered.

"Come here, please!"

Caroline said, "I'll do it." She slipped off the windowsill, ground out her cigarette, and crossed to the table, making a sharp turn to enter the carpet at the exact place the nurse would have. The nurse watched them both.

Catherine said, "Can I have a cookie?"

"Too close to dinner."

"Puh-lease?"

"Don't whine, darling."

Caroline stepped back off the carpet. Catherine wandered over to the computer terminal and idly punched keys. The game flashed and sang. After a few moments she wandered back to the bookshelf, took down her doll, and began to change its clothes. Unobtrusively the nurse went to the computer and returned the game to its previous position.

Joe looked away. The childhood cases were always the worst. In the tertiary stage a child's routines often contained bits and pieces from different ages they had been, different places, different stages of the illness. And children often retained enough emotional responses to panic if everything in their day—every line of dialogue, every small action, every adult response—did not exactly duplicate the pattern now locked into their brains as the only reality. The panic could be overwhelming—as if an adult suddenly discovered mad strangers thronging his living room and babbling in a scary tongue. Reality itself failed. The only other choice was chaos: the monsters and the screaming, alone in the unreal dark.

Caroline, expressionless, returned to her windowsill. Long was still blustering. He half turned, and in his profile Joe caught a glimpse of Catherine's long, jutting chin. Joe slipped from the room.

The harassed receptionist told him that the Korsakov's syndrome patients caught in the bombing were being temporarily housed in Clarement Cottage. Halfway there, he was surprised to have Caroline catch up with him.

"She was starting to write me the letter," she said in a tight, dry voice. "And Charles was making the usual ass of himself. There's no reason to stay any longer. She's all right now." Abruptly she laughed. Joe reached for her hand.

He said, "Do you mind holding the car for me for just a minute? I just want to check on this research with Korsakov patients that the administrator mentioned."

"Why?"

"Connections with one of my cases," Joe said evasively. He didn't want to tell her about the stack of nearly unreadable research Pirelli had sent him; the Korsakov research had played a key role in isolating the plague virus. The probability scanners had worked out a complicated reverse congruence in the mathematical models of brain waves for plague victims and Korsakov's cases. But he thought that Caroline looked too fragile to discuss that, even in general, unclassified terms.

"I'll go with you."

Joe wished she wouldn't, but could think of no way to refuse. He saw that she wanted distraction, and that almost any distraction would do. Her heels tapped tensely beside him on the stone walk. When he realized that he was still holding her hand, he kept it, rubbing his thumb over slim fingers that felt as smooth and stiff as the polished balustrade on the stairway.

Caroline said, "Tell me what Korsakov's syndrome is. I don't even know."

"It's a brain disorder. Patients forget huge chunks of their past. But they keep all their wit and ingenuity and imagination, and frequently they invent like crazy."

"Invent what?"

"New identities," Joe said, and in the quick downturn of her mouth he saw the echo of their earlier quarrel. Nettled, he said, "No, not like *that*. Not consciously, with coherent choices and values. At random, to replace the lost identities they once had. They—"

She cut him off. "In here?"

"Yes."

Caroline dropped his hand and led the way crisply to the reception desk, then had to stand aside while Joe presented his credentials and explained his presence. "Well," the receptionist said, "if you really want to talk to a patient instead of a *doctor*—"

Joe smiled. "Is that so strange?"

The woman stared at him flatly. "Mr. Holiworth is in the garden. Through that door."

The garden was a pretty courtyard surrounded by walls on all sides and furnished with stone benches. A small, beefy man with a wide smile jumped up from a bench and ran toward Caroline, hands outstretched.

"Laura! Haven't seen you in a dog's age!" He seized both Caroline's hands. "You get prettier each time I see you!"

"I'm afraid I'm not Laura . . ."

Holiworth immediately dropped her hands. "Of course you're not—my apologies! But you know, in this light, Mrs. Klein, you look a lot like my sister-in-law Laura—although prettier, of course. How's Tom? Did he get that garage painted yet?"

Joe said, "I'm afraid that's not Mrs. Klein, Mr. Holiworth. Her name is Caroline."

"Of course it is, Doctor. I'm sorry, my dear. You'll just have to forgive a stressed-out man. I've been telling the doctor here for days now that overwork is what's wrong with me, nothing fancier. Think he'll listen? Doctors got no room left for common sense, too much learning in their brains." He smiled hugely, beaming at Caroline, who looked dizzy.

Joe smiled back. He had talked to Korsakov's patients before. "Actually, Mr. Holiworth, your doctor isn't here yet. My name is Joe McLaren. I'm a lawyer."

Holiworth's manner changed completely. He became calm and professional, eyeing Joe shrewdly. "A law office. Well, sir, let me tell you that you couldn't do better than Xerox 1340 to meet your document copying needs. Of course you'd expect me to say that, but I'm not speaking as a Xerox salesman, I'm speaking as someone with twenty-three years experience in this business who hasn't ever steered a customer wrong yet. And I've worked for all of them, Mr. McLaren—Big Blue, Ricoh, Ki-Taik—and in all that time I haven't seen a machine to equal the 1340. Just launched three months ago and to tremendous customer response, especially—if I may say so— among the law offices we're proud to do business with. But you don't have to take my word for it, and I don't *want* you to take my word for it. I want you to judge for yourself just what this revolutionary technology can do for you. This is the paper bin, and over here you set the machine for either an original doc-

ument or an electronic input, formatted or unformatted—"
Holiworth began to manipulate air, opening and closing draw-
ers, pressing buttons, peering at screens and displays with
complete conviction. Occasionally Holiworth glanced at Joe
confidently, smiling with pleasure, a man absorbed and happy
in his work. Joe glanced at Caroline, who stood preternaturally
still.

Finally Holiworth wore down, closing with an enthusiastic
discussion of differential pricing and bid specifications. He
beamed at Joe.

"Thank you, Mr. Holiworth. We'll consider this and get
back to you."

Holiworth blinked. "Consider what?"

"The purchase."

A grin broke out on the man's face; it was like a rising sun.
"You're here to purchase jelly beans! The kids will be pleased—
believe me, they worked hard on this fund raiser, don't let
anybody underestimate the Cub Scouts. How many bags?" He
turned to Caroline. "Mary, go tell Billy and Danny to bring out
their order sheets. *With* pencils."

"Another time," Joe said. "We really have to go now.
Good-bye, Mr. Holiworth."

"And may God go with you," Holiworth said, making the
sign of the cross. "You and your beautiful wife."

Joe took Caroline's arm and tugged it slightly. Holiworth
waved at them with both hands until they had left the courtyard. The one-way security door locked behind them.

Joe said quietly, "That hit you hard. I'm sorry."

"He's not . . . not human anymore."

"Pretty harsh."

"Maybe. No. He has no . . . no center. Nothing connects
him with a real past, that's really his. Except a little bit when
he talked about selling that copier. Then he seemed to settle
down."

"He may once have been a copier salesman. Although I don't think Xerox-Ricoh has manufactured the 1340 for twenty years."

"What causes Korsakov's syndrome?"

"A bunch of things. Advanced alcoholism. Tumors pressing just right on the brain. We even know just where, so accurately that we could probably induce Korsakov's artificially."

"We know just where Korsakov's is," Caroline said bitterly, "and nothing at all about where the plague virus is. How many people have each?"

Joe didn't answer. Jason waited by the aircar. As they climbed in, Joe said, "Not all Korsakov's patients are like that. Some can remember things for weeks before the memories fade. And some are brilliant, especially at things like theater, where it's crucial to both pretend and to believe in your own pretending. I once saw a production of *Henry IV* inside a federal prison, with a Falstaff who had Korsakov's. He gave me the chills. He *was* Falstaff, in a profound way no ordinary actor could ever duplicate."

Caroline said dryly, "Don't underestimate the power of self-delusion of the ordinary actor."

The aircar lifted. As they left the roof of Catherine's cottage behind, Joe realized suddenly what it was that the child had been making with her U-Builds, would be making with them over and over, the rest of her life: flat platform, brief steps, proscenium arch, trap door. A puppet stage.

It was nearly midnight when the aircar set down in the Institute driveway. Father Shahid waited in the lobby. Joe caught the quick, anxious way the priest scanned Caroline's face before his own relapsed into calm.

"Tomorrow, Patrick," Caroline said briskly. "It can wait."

Shahid said quietly, "If you think it can wait, then it can. But, Caroline—don't use the nets tonight. Just not tonight."

Caroline didn't answer. Her heels tapped across the floor. In the elevator Joe said softly, "I didn't know you were Catholic."

She gave him an amused look. "I'm not. We're friends."

Joe digested this. He had never felt comfortable with the priest/historian and had never been willing to examine why. "Why did he say that about the nets?"

Caroline made a dismissive gesture, a quick twist of her wrist that flashed light across the slim bones. "I search the carnie datanet a lot. Too much, Shahid thinks." Joe took his eyes from her wrist.

But at her door, she suddenly put a hand on his arm. "Stay with me tonight, Joe."

It was completely unexpected. Wariness flooded him. She stood with her other hand on her doorknob, the subdued hallway lighting soft on her brown hair, her tired face raised to his. He had no idea what he saw there. Did she want to sleep with him? Where was Brekke? Her touch on his arm felt soft, tentative, but there was nothing tentative about her smile. "You should see your face, Joe. No, we don't have to make love. Or even have sex, if you don't want to. I know you don't approve of me. And no hysterical scenes—I promise. I just don't want to . . . be alone."

He was responding to the break in her voice, reaching for her, when she suddenly pulled back and grinned at him, tense quirky mischief in her eyes. "And I can hardly ask Patrick to come in and hold me through the night." The mischief faded. She stood quietly, waiting. He thought that he had never known anyone who baffled him as much, or made him as wary. The skin underneath her eyes sagged with weariness, making her finally look as old as he knew she must be to have a daughter Catherine's age. There was a tiny rip along the shoulder seam of her expensive leather jacket, which had probably cost more than most of his wardrobe put together. The force of his erection embarrassed him.

He said, "What about Brekke?"

She didn't seem flustered. "Gone. And it was no good, anyway."

Did she mean Brekke had been no good in bed? Somehow, Joe doubted that. His wariness deepened. He foresaw something triggering a sexual memory, alone with her in the dark, and his losing control.

"Sometimes," Caroline said quietly, "there just isn't enough past, some nights. Enough past to hold onto. I know you don't agree. But you were very kind to me about Catherine."

He not only didn't agree, he couldn't focus on what she was saying. His groin ached with sweet, treacherous heaviness. Caroline brushed at her hair and one strand stuck to her cheek, held by makeup or dried tears, a meandering lustrous road. He knew he shouldn't say anything, should just either stay or go, but he couldn't stop himself. "What did you mean when you said it was no good with Brekke? You slept together?"

"No. We might have. But it was . . . no good. Wrong." Her face changed. "I can't explain any more than that. But, then, I don't have to, do I? If you don't want to, you don't want to. Good night, Joe."

He reached behind her and opened the door.

Caroline didn't turn on the light. They lay across the bed, fully clothed, in the darkness. Joe put both arms around her. Her neck smelled of perfume, subtle and costly.

"Talk to me," she said, so gently that he heard it not as a request but a plea. "Tell me about when you were young. In this life, I mean."

To his surprise, he did. He told her about Pittsburgh in the nineties: skating off the edges of the abandoned highway passes, scavenging discarded vinyl records as people replaced them with CDs, playing mock war games on Pirelli's precious, antiquated computer. He told her about his mother, dead in a bus crash while he was struggling through law school. He told her about the night jobs so he could attend classes during the day, the scholarship he might have had except for being a year too late, twelve months behind the date Congress, newly dominated by neo-Libertarians elected by an overburdened middle class, slashed both taxes and most aid to universities.

"So now you argue in favor of moral restrictions and fiscal escalation," Caroline said. "Even though the neo-Libs pulled us out of the worst of the federal deficit."

He didn't want to argue politics with her. Her arguments were too simplistic, and the smell of her neck too disturbing. Instead, he talked more about his childhood, on and on, astonishing himself with his own lack of self-consciousness. He talked about the dances in junior high school, about the few memories he had of the father who had deserted them when Joe was four, the rock concerts he and Pirelli tried to crash, the phone piracy he had caught Pirelli masterminding, the fight they had had until Pirelli agreed to stop it. He told her about the first MS symptoms, while he was still in law school, about the bar exam he had failed because his hand would not hold the keyboard, about the long remission afterward. He told her about everything, except Robin.

He could feel Caroline listening in the darkness, her breath against his forearm. The listening seemed almost a third entity in bed with them, so palpable was it, a breathing separate life, like a precious child. Eventually, however, the breathing changed, and Joe realized that she had fallen asleep.

His watch, glowing in the darkness, said 2:17 A.M. His throat felt hoarse. He stood up, removed his shoes and then Caroline's. She didn't even stir. Joe covered her with a blanket from the closet and, after a moment's hesitation, lay back down beside her. During his long purging recitation (purging of what? a mocking voice asked, but he was too tired to answer), all sexual desire had left him. He twisted and pulled at the blanket until it covered them both.

Sleep came slowly. Bright pictures danced behind his

eyelids, vivid images with no connection to each other: Catherine's hands on her construction toy; the Mohawk River seen from the unusual height of the aircar; Angel's angry, secretive eyes; Mr. Holiworth's Xerox-Ricoh 1340 copier, made of empty air.

He woke to a low cry. The room seemed confused; he couldn't remember where he was, or why. Nothing was in the right place. When his vision cleared, he saw Caroline sitting at the fold-out wall screen, facing him across the room. Her hair hung around her face in uncombed hanks. The curtains had been open and the pearly, thin light of predawn leeched all color from her face. She stared at him wildly from huge eyes that seemed to see something else.

"Caroline . . . what the hell—"

"The carnie dBase," she said in a voice so calm it chilled him. There seemed no way that voice could go with those eyes. "Robbie."

"What about him?" Joe snapped. Obscure anger filled him: *now* what? He sat up, the blanket still around his shoulders. The room was cold but Caroline, in her thin shirt, didn't seem to notice.

She said calmly, "He's my son."

"Was," Joe said, before he knew he was going to say anything. "Whatever the hell you're talking about, it's 'was'!"

She didn't seem to hear him. "My child. My son."

Joe stumbled out of bed. The blanket, tangled around his legs, dragged after him; he knew he looked ludicrous. Caroline's face scared him. He stood where he could see the front of her terminal. She must have had the sound very low; in his sleep he hadn't heard the cloying voice of the dBase. The terminal displayed:

CONGRATULATIONS! YOU HAVE A MATCH!
TIMOTHY HENDRICKSON; 1958–1976 A.D.;

BORN, LIVED, AND DIED IN WICHITA, KANSAS,
USA.
ROBERT ANTHONY BREKKE; BORN 1997; CURRENT
MAIL ADDRESS—

"Caroline," Joe said, "*Caroline* . . ."

"My son."

"It's a malfunction in the program, Caroline. It has to be."
She looked at him. "I'm sorry, but it has to be. It's not possible.
Out of all the billions of people who live or ever lived on earth,
that *both* of us would have known him in a previous life—" He
realized he hadn't told her about his own dBase "Congratulations." Her face looked like rock in the pearly light. He tried
again. "I know the dBase exists in the first place to find matches,
but the astronomical odds . . . and even if it were true—even
if—it's past, don't you see? It's gone, dead, over. It doesn't
count anymore!"

"Why are you yelling?"

"I'm not yelling!"

Caroline stood up. Her forearms had come out in goose-
flesh. She faced him calmly. "A better question might be why
you're trying to spoil this for me. Why, Joe? Are you that rotten
with jealousy of Robbie? Or of *me*? Because you think I've had
a nice privileged, moneyed existence while you've been clawing your way to your present priggish Almighty pinnacle of . . .
of constant *rightness*? Is that it?"

Joe picked up his shoes. Caroline's voice rose higher. "Or
is it that you just can't stand anyone to be happy in ways *you*
don't approve?"

He opened the door and left. The corridor lights were still
on nighttime dim. His own room was cold but not quiet: the
terminal said clearly, over and over, "MR. MCLAREN, YOU
HAVE A PRIORITY ONE RECORDED MESSAGE. PLEASE
READ IT NOW. MR. MCLAREN, YOU HAVE A PRIORITY ONE

RECORDED MESSAGE. PLEASE READ IT NOW. MR.
MCLAREN—"

He turned it off, rubbed his temples with both hands, and
asked for the message. It was from Jeff Pirelli:

URGENT YOU CALL ME IMMEDIATELY. SOMETHING
VERY UNEXPECTED TURNED UP. BUT FIRST DO
SOMETHING FOR ME:
BUY SIX YAMS, THIRTEEN LOAVES OF BREAD,
THREE SALAMI, SIX CARROTS, ONE HAM, TWENTY-
TWO BAGELS . . .

The list went on and on. Joe stared at the screen, mesmer-
ized, until he finally remembered. It was one of their teenage
codes, one so insanely idiosyncratic it had been virtually un-
crackable by even the most sophisticated software. Pirelli had
based it on a completely random association of food items with
words and phrases, each modified by the numerics in ways that
changed according to another random table. How could Pirelli
possibly expect him, Joe, to remember it? And what the hell
was both so important and so secretive that Pirelli should
expect him to try? Anything connected with the Plague Commission would come by government code, or by courier, or by
Angel.

Unless it was something so weird that Pirelli wasn't yet
ready to make it part of the Commission record, and Angel
wasn't available to act as courier. Politics? Or just megaloma-
niacal games playing?

Joe's head hurt. His throat was still hoarse, and the inside
of his mouth felt like something had died in there. Worst of all
was the ache in his chest. What would Caroline say to Brekke?
What the hell *could* she say?

Joe brushed his teeth, drank a glass of water, took a brainie.
Then he sat down in front of the screen with pen and paper.

Memory came slowly. Six yams, thirteen loaves of bread
. . . *Christ*. It was past six o'clock when he was finally sure he
had it; sunlight slanted in long diagonal bars across the floor of
his room. The message was couched in the melodramatic trans-
lations Pirelli had devised for teenage war games complete with
mock prisoners, electronic destruction, swashbuckling stupid
smuggling and espionage and what they had imagined then in
their overheated innocence to be high excitement:

KEEP WITH YOU AT ALL TIMES UNTIL I ARRIVE, DO
NOT LET LEAVE THE AREA, HOLDER OF INFO KEY TO
THIS WAR: ROBERT ANTHONY BREKKE

9 ROBBIE

The sleepcap left Robbie irritable and restless, shifting in his plane seat as if it were a cell. Below him patches of light shone intermittently, insignificant among the great dark masses of the Rockies that in turn were lost in the greater vast silence of night. The holo of the brunette stewardess flickered in the aisle long enough to tell everyone that the local time was 10:03 P.M. Robbie crossed his legs, bumping his knee against the seat ahead, and rekeyed his watch. It gave a sharp little hum and went blank. The central unit was dead. He grimaced and tossed it into the trash chute.

There was something he couldn't remember, something that spread at the edge of his mind like dank air beyond a circle of firelight. Had it been a dream? Of what? He couldn't remember.

At the Rawlins airport the aircar rental counter—not a terminal booth but a real counter, with a real person behind it, a small wiry man with hair like sandpaper—would not accept cash. Perhaps, the small man suggested delicately, the gentleman did not realize how expensive the aircar technology still was? Perhaps he did not understand how the rental company needed to protect itself against the possibly unscrupulous?

Robbie said he understood. They wanted a credit number, they wanted a federal ID number, they wanted a license. All stodge. All traceable through every net in the world. Robbie smiled at the man, who did not smile back.

The credit number Hatton had given him for his Institute bills was out of the question. So was his own. So were the ones he sometimes shared with DeFillippo. The only thing he could do was wait until the morning to rent the aircar, file a false itinerary with the rental company, and take off instantly. Hatton's goons would not have time to follow him, even if they discovered he had gone to Rawlins. Which he supposed they would, eventually, if he used his own numbers.

He paid cash for an airport sleep cubicle, an anonymous light green box with less than a meter between the sliding door and the platform bed. There was a clothes bar with two hangers, a metal wall shelf, and a synthfoam blanket. Robbie would have said he was impervious to surroundings, to color, to even the lack of a terminal. But sleeping in the cubicle depressed him as had no night spent crouching in the wet bottom of a powerboat in Liberia, no gritty and freezing night on the alkali flats with Johnny Lee Benson.

There was something he couldn't remember. Trying to pull the memory toward him in the darkness of the cubicle, turning from stomach to back to stomach again, didn't help. The memory only receded, a small, darting fish in cool, dark water. He had the confused sense that the memory had somehow been closer during the three hours under the sleepcap on the plane than it was now, that it was important, and that he was not going to remember it.

Robbie punched up the pillow he couldn't see in the total blackness of the cubicle. He disliked this: his head full of shifting shadows, cold, dark shapes. This wasn't what they said getting plazzed was supposed to do. He was supposed to remember clearly, cleanly, in bright primary colors—the way he remembered Mallie Callahan.

A little of the confusion and neck ache receded. Robbie shifted more comfortably onto the pillow. Mallie. What would that poor, ignorant kid self of his have thought of the plane trip Robbie had just taken two thirds of the way across the continent? Of tomorrow's effortless journey by aircar across the flats and mountains that had cost Mallie and Johnny Lee their money, their friendship, and finally their lives?

Robbie frowned. Now why had he thought that: That the journey had cost him Johnny Lee's friendship? They had died friends, in the secret cave in the Wind River Range that he remembered with perfect, 140-year clarity. They had died together, which had of course been Mallie's bad luck then but was Robbie's great good fortune now, since it was Johnny Lee who had had the saddlebags. They had died of wounds received in the attack by the pathetic band of Sioux renegades by the Sweetwater River, which again had been bad luck then but was good fortune now. Wonderful fortune. For they had died holding gold worth $5,000 and an eleven-carat diamond worth God knew what, both taken from the overland mail at Black Butler with explosives bought from the sale of earrings moll-buzzed in St. Louis by Mallie Callahan and deployed by the laughing genius of Johnny Lee Benson.

He and Johnny Lee had waited clear until Denver City to sell the earrings. Johnny Lee had gotten himself and Mallie out of St. Louis in two hours, using what money? Mallie never found out. All he knew was that one moment his belly rumbled with hunger behind the livery stable with the gold earrings cutting into his hand, and the next they were eating on the cars, thick beef sandwiches hawked by a man who looked too old to stand up but who Johnny Lee said was probably twenty-five. He said this while they were washing down the sandwiches with whiskey, and Mallie got the giggles. Then Johnny did, and they both ended up going to see the elephant again that night. They were always going to see the elephant, every night, and so all Mallie remembered of Denver City was flashes, like daguerreotypes frozen in hectic color no daguerreotype could ever have had:

—a hotel lobby, all green portieres and real gold, and a stone-faced clerk so stiff and cold saying to Johnny Lee, "I'm sorry, sir, we don't have a room available for . . . you," and Johnny Lee trying to hit him, and then they were both on the street, only it couldn't have been the street because they were going to see the elephant again next to a wall with red paper on it soft under his hand like a girl's dress, and it stood to reason there couldn't have been a red paper wall on the street. So maybe they had a room after all, a room in which to go see the elephant, somewhere.

—a huge building, so wide and tall and handsome it made him think of the Preacher Ronson's talks about the buildings of Heaven, and Mallie had to look away from it. The Windsor Hotel, Johnny Lee said with something sharp stuck in his voice, and it seemed the something sharp exploded because the next second there was gunfire and he and Mallie had dived for it, looking around a wall that had come from someplace to see the most beautiful woman Mallie could imagine leaning out of a third-story window with her breasts falling out of her red satin dress and a gun in her hand, shooting at insulators on the telegraph poles in the street.

—another room somewhere, only this one was small and plain and smelled bad, and it seemed Mallie and the elephant had been in it for days while Johnny Lee "arranged everything." Mallie never found out what everything was, because they had left Denver City in the middle of the night just after that—he thought it was just after that—on another train, Johnny Lee in a sullen rage that Mallie didn't ask about. It had gotten so it wasn't safe to ask Johnny Lee about too much. Sometimes Mallie thought vaguely that there was something he should remember, something about the money from the earrings, but then they would go to see the elephant again and anyway Johnny Lee was arranging everything so it didn't matter.

They had gone to Cheyenne City, and then on the Union Pacific cars to Salt Wells. On the cars they ran out of whiskey; Mallie's first sight of Salt Wells was with him clear and sharp and strong as hard light.

A bare wooden train platform held six people, as neatly arranged as colored stones in a girl's brooch. At one end sat an Indian squaw wrapped in a dirty blanket, showing her papoose to a white woman for two bits. The squaw's face had a settled, barren look like leeched gullies; the woman leaning above her wore a green plaid dress with a huge bustle. Mallie, who had never seen either a squaw or such a large bustle, stared until Johnny Lee nudged him to look at the other end of the platform. Two Chinee squatted on their heels like patient dogs, their hair long like a woman's in glossy black braids that suddenly made Mallie itch for scissors. "Lookee there," Johnny Lee said, but he didn't say more because the two figures in the middle of the platform were Yankee soldiers, carrying dusty blue grips and rifles more battered than Mallie thought wood and metal could get. As he and Johnny Lee crossed the train platform, wind blew the dust up on either side of the platform, framing the six and trapping them like the trapped words in the samplers Missouri ladies hung on their parlor walls.

At Salt Wells Johnny Lee finally got everything arranged. He told Mallie so in a curt voice that warned not to ask any questions. Mallie, sitting in another bare room with his hand cupped around his bottle, didn't ask any. There was vomit down the front of Johnny Lee's vest, and one side of his face was bruised and swollen. Had there been a fight? Had Mallie been in it? He couldn't remember. But he felt the sides of his own face and found no swellings or hurts, only unshaven whiskers and a thin sour film like dirty water.

They picked up two horses and a pack animal at the livery stable and rode north across the empty flats. Toward Black Butler, Johnny Lee said. Where the overland mail crossed nothing special, Johnny Lee said, on its way to what was left of the mining camps. The stage would be out there all alone, carrying, Johnny Lee said, a Wells Fargo shipment, just meandering along like a pretty, Church-going girl in satin petticoats ready to have her dress lifted before she even knew there was anyone around who knew what to do with what was under it.

Mallie blinked. "Wells *Fargo*?"

"The very same," Johnny Lee said. "Get dressed."

Mallie looked at himself, surprised to see that he wasn't. "But, Johnny Lee—they'll have guns. And they'll be better shots than us." After a moment he added, afraid he'd make Johnny Lee mad, Johnny Lee got mad now at any little thing, "Because they're older."

"We're not going to shoot them," Johnny Lee said. "We're going to blow them up."

"Blow up a stage? No, you mean a train. Trains are what people blow up."

"God, you're a dungheap," Johnny Lee said in disgust. "Look at you. I should leave you here."

Mallie started to cry. He hated himself for blubbering, but he couldn't stop. His words came out in little thick pops like farts. "Johnny Lee . . . where's the money from my earrings?"

"Get dressed!" Johnny Lee shouted.

"We don't need to blow nothing up, Johnny Lee. We got money. We got the money from my earrings."

Johnny Lee looked at him from flat blue eyes, and then he came and put his arm around Mallie and Mallie, so grateful was he for the touch and the gentleness in Johnny Lee's voice, didn't even mind that he was naked except for his skivvies, he just leaned back in Johnny Lee's arm and listened.

"Equipment for a big job like this one is going to be is

expensive, kid. It will be all right. Wait and see. Get dressed."
And Mallie had.

They left Salt Wells at dawn, mounted on the best horses
Mallie had ever ridden. He kept putting his hand along the
neck of his big bay just to feel the sleek muscles work underneath the hide. To their right the sun came up red and gold over
the eastern hills.

Mallie had imagined that the overland mail robbery would
stand as the center pole of his life, lifting up all the rest and
giving it some space, some wideness. But all he remembered
after the long boring setting of the explosives and the long
nervous wait was shouting and heat and light and the screaming
of a horse as it died, a shrill agonized rip in the air filled with
flying grit and wood and gobbets of flesh. Later he understood
that he had been hit, but at the time the sharp crack in his neck
seemed only one of all the sharp cracks around him, so that it
seemed the whole world had broken into shards and him with
it and that was only right.

Then he was on his horse and it seemed that he and Johnny
Lee must have gone to see the elephant again because he was
swaying in the saddle and things went in and out of focus, the
baked hard earth becoming the pale hot sky and then back
again. The Preacher Ronson had got it all wrong, Mallie
thought, but he didn't know what he meant by that and all
that would come to him was the sudden, unexpected smell
of his mother's yeast bread, rising in the window ledge under
her sullen eye. The world blackened and paled and blackened
and whirled, and the back of his neck burned with the Preacher's and his father's red brimstone and fire after all, after all,
after all.

Robbie lifted the aircar over Rawlins and headed west. The
aircar was by far the most luxurious vehicle he had ever driven.
He had requested a high-elevation clearance and had gotten
one, but even so Rawlins spread beneath him farther toward

either horizon than he expected in waves of unexpected high towers and shining autobahns. In *Wyoming?* Who would have thought it?

He took the aircar higher and turned southwest. The dashboard began to scold him. "Please note that you are departing from your logged route. This could result in danger to yourself and others in areas with other airborne vehicles. Please note that you are departing from your logged route. This could—"

"Spit it up your superconductors," Robbie said jauntily. But since he couldn't figure out how to turn the voice off, he was forced to listen to it complain.

The old Union Pacific railway tracks were still there, and not shiny in any way that suggested tourists. That was good; the population of Rawlins had made him suddenly afraid of too many people, too little undisturbed wilderness. But the tracks limped away from Rawlins and across the swelling country like weedy varicose veins. Robbie followed them through the swellings in population—*small* swellings, he was glad to note—that were Wamsutter and then Tipton. Somewhere between the two had once been Salt Wells.

Wind blowing across a wooden train platform. Two squatting Chinamen, two U.S. soldiers, a white woman bending over a papoose for two bits a look.

At Thayer Robbie turned the aircar north. "Please note that you are departing from your logged route. This could result in danger to—"

To the north the land changed again. Robbie smelled it before he saw it. The breeze blew toward him, and he gagged. He lifted the aircar as high as it would go and leaned out the window. Below, the ground *crawled*. Mounds of green-gray sludge slowly undulated and shifted, worked from underneath by microbes. Gases spurted from the sludge like misty geysers, gleaming silver in the sun a moment before they dissipated into rotten fog. The dump covered more than a square mile. At its edge, the drowning top of a tree quivered above the sludge. Liquid trickled out, bubbling putridly, and sank into the ground.

It was a long time before the smell left the aircar.

Farther north, the landscape was different yet. Robbie looked down in confusion, searching for the land he and Johnny Lee had crossed with such torture, such despair. He remembered—Mallie remembered—endless alkali flats, rock and sage and blowing grit from the railroad to the mountains, broken only by the slim cold writhe of the Sweetwater River. But below him were *farms*. He couldn't recall ever seeing farms before, not up close. Not in this life, anyway.

Fields of crops glinted with small flashes of silver. Each flash turned out to be a one-chip robot the size of Robbie's thumb. They crawled steadily among the plants, their knifelike tips cutting down weeds and leaving crops. Other tiny robots flew over the crops; as Robbie watched, one turned and flew below him as far as a metal cube labeled IRRIGATION. The robot disappeared inside. Machinery hummed.

"Please note that you are departing from both your logged route and your logged elevation. This could be a danger to yourself and—"

Nothing was the same, nothing Mallie remembered—what if the cave had changed? What if it was now some sort of tourist attraction—See the Robot Pirates!—or a Gaeist condo? But on the horizon the mountains sat stolid, unmoving. Mountains, Robbie thought, were the ultimate in stodge.

It took him less than an hour to reach the Sweetwater River; it had taken Mallie and Johnny Lee two days. To Robbie's relief, the Sweetwater was neither the built-up sprawl nor the manicured resort area he had feared it might have become. The eerie fields, still empty of moving life that was not electronic, spread nearly to the river, separated only by an empty highway. Occasionally the fields parted for a solitary butte which looked as if it didn't belong there at all. Only the mountains, purple under a blue sky, looked the same as Mallie—as he—as *Mallie* remembered.

On impulse, Robbie set the car down between the highway and the river. He got out, bent, and trailed his hand in the water. It felt as icy as before, a wide shallow flow babbling over rocks on its way through the high mountain pass and down the Continental Divide to the North Platte. There was no way to tell where along the Sweetwater the Sioux raid had caught Mallie and Johnny Lee; the riverbanks looked all the same as far as he could see, and nothing else looked the same at all.

There was something he couldn't remember.

The unquiet he had felt on the plane was back, making his head throb. For some reason, he thought of Caroline: Caroline in her blue dress with the thousands of minute holes in swirling patterns, a blue headband tied across her brown hair like an Indian's. The headache grew abruptly worse, a sudden sharp stabbing behind his eyeballs that made him stagger and lower himself to the banks of the Sweetwater. Out of the painful confusion came a name: Paul.

Who was Paul? No Indian would be named Paul. Neither of Caroline's husbands nor her father were Paul. And certainly there had been no Paul in the cave in the nearing mountains.

But somehow thinking the name had eased his head. Robbie flicked his hand; it was dry. The heat had already baked the Sweetwater off his fingers. He had just been blinded, he told himself, by the sun dazzling the river. The bright expanse of water shone and murmured in the sunlight. And the altitude—that did funny things if you weren't used to it. That's what it had been, altitude and sun-headache.

He climbed back in the aircar and lifted it toward the Wind River Range.

10 *CAROLINE*

As long as Caroline could remember, an electronic plaque had hung in Colin Cadavy's dressing room, wherever that happened to be. The plaque was framed in severe gold around lettering that shaded from green to gold and back again but changed style as it went: script to calligraphy to block lettering to a delicate parody of early digital display. "Witty," Colin had called it, while the seven-year-old Caroline, spirited out of her grandmother's house for a custody visit, had moved her lips reading the words:

"MAN'S UNHAPPINESS COMES, IN PART, FROM HIS GREATNESS. THERE IS AN INFINITE IN HIM WHICH, WITH ALL HIS CUNNING, HE CAN-NOT QUITE BURY UNDER THE FINITE."—THOMAS CARLYLE.

At seven, the words had meant only that someone was unhappy, she wasn't sure who, and this uncertainty had made her vaguely uneasy. By twelve, when she defiantly left her grandmother to tour with Colin, they had come to seem to her burningly true, proof that her father, playing Hamlet out front in a London theater while an audience that included the Soviet Premier and Queen Diana sat hushed and respectful, was indeed a great man, deeper than other men, able to discern and appreciate the misery that lay in mankind. In *her*. At fifteen Caroline knew that Colin had never read Carlyle, or anyone else who did not write a part for Colin Cadavy. *"Hypocritical,"* she teased, and if there was an edge to the teasing neither she nor Colin acknowledged it, as they acknowledged nothing in the whirl that had become their life together, the nonstop party of brainies and laughter and private language dBasing the rest of the mundane world.

When the party stopped, the night Caroline crept into Colin's bed, the plaque changed as well. *"Pathetic,"* she screamed at him. *"Melodramatic."* His unhappiness came not from any greatness but from self-indulgence; nothing was ever enough for him, not even her. It was self-aggrandizement, she had shouted at him at sixteen, not any "infinite" that made him so greedy, so theatrical, so *fake*. She and Jeremy Kline, whom she had just met, would never be like that. *They* would be happy. They would live simple and good lives in the real theater, apart from dusty irrelevant plays left over from dead history, because Jeremy was a genius and soon the world would be forced to admit it. Colin had laughed, a laugh filled with such pain—melodramatic pain, Caroline had shouted—that she had torn the plaque off the wall and smashed it on the solid Italian marble floor of a dressing room in a French city whose name she couldn't remember.

Incongruously, Caroline thought of the plaque now. What was the finite here, what was the infinite? Robbie Brekke had been her son. Was that a finite fact, dead in the past? Or was it part of an infinite web, a cord flung across time and space toward her now, coming from the past but as real as her present motherhood of a child whose mind had stopped, stalled, somewhere in her own tiny past? What was cunning here, and what was simply unhappiness?

Or happiness?

After Joe left her room, she sat staring at the terminal screen. TIMOTHY HENDRICKSON. ROBERT ANTHONY

BREKKE. Slowly, so unobtrusively that she was unaware until it had happened, her chest filled with light. Light that glowed; light that lifted heaviness.

Robbie was a grown man. Twenty-six years old. Petty smuggler, inept con man, charming drifter. His life was in no way hers, and he was in no way hers. Not here. Not now.

But he had been her son.

An infinite. That could not quite be buried under the crap.

She showered, washed her hair, dressed in jeans and a soft blue sweater with an angora headband. She wanted to talk to Patrick Shahid, but even after taking as much time with her hair as she could, it was too early: 5:30 A.M. She really couldn't wake him before, say, 6:30. He said a mass in the Interfaith Chapel every morning at 8:00 for whoever showed up—usually it was nobody.

Six-thirty was when Catherine woke up. Day after day.

Caroline opened the curtains. At the east end of Lake Ontario the sky had just begun to streak silver and rose. The air smelled of freshly cut grass and living water. She pulled a chair close to the window to wait.

TIMOTHY HENDRICKSON. ROBERT ANTHONY BREKKE. How long had she sat staring at the screen after Joe left? She couldn't remember. Nor could she remember what she had said to Joe, or how he had reacted. She must have said something, he must have said something . . . Two months ago she would have been amused that she could completely forget something that had happened a few hours ago and so entirely remember something that had happened two lifetimes ago, but now it wasn't funny.

Yes, it was. Amusement was as appropriate a response as any, wasn't it? Better than, say, awe at a suddenly discovered maternity fifty years mislaid?

Now *that* was funny.

"Come on, Patrick," she said aloud, out the window, "wake up. Laugh with me."

She pictured Robbie as he had stood at her door yesterday afternoon, the crescent earrings in his hand. Where had he gone? She would find out, she supposed, when he returned. They would discuss this whole absurd thing, talk about it, maybe send out birth announcements? "Caroline Bohentin wishes to announce the belated arrival of a son, twenty-six, who sprang full grown from her computer—"

But the lightness filling her was not hysteria.

The phone rang. It took her a moment to realize what the sound was, so unexpected were its musical notes. She seized it eagerly. "Hello? Hello?"

"Caroline? Patrick Shahid."

She stared stupidly at the receiver. She had, without reason, expected Robbie.

"Caroline? Are you there?"

"Yes. Yes, I . . . you startled me."

"You weren't asleep."

It wasn't a question. Caroline said, "How did you know?"

"I need to see you, please," he said in his formal, quiet English, as if that were an answer. "Are you all right?"

"Yes. How did you know I wasn't—"

"In the chapel in five minutes?" Shahid said, and she realized that it was the first time she had ever heard him interrupt anyone. "Are you already dressed?"

"Yes. Five minutes is fine. Yes."

The chapel was built into the eastern end of the Institute, with stained-glass windows in abstract patterns facing north and east and a stark black stone altar, completely bare, against the south wall. The walls were whitewashed. In the predawn light they glowed pearly gray, like the inside of some seashells. Caroline sat on an oak pew and watched color creep into the stained glass until Shahid, in jeans and garishly colored Pakistani shirt, slid in beside her. She smiled at his shirt; he never ceased to surprise her. Not until he took one of her hands in both of his did she realize that his skin was like ice. *How weird,* she thought. *Mine must be warm.*

"Are you all right, Caroline?"

"Yes. No. What do you mean, Patrick?"

He watched her closely. "I mean after the bombing yesterday."

She had forgotten. She had *forgotten*.

"Caroline—"

"I forgot. I really did," she said slowly. "I forgot about the bombing at Catherine's home . . ."

"Not even pain can be remembered every minute."

"Apparently not." She heard herself laugh, a horrible sound. Then something else struck her and she twisted in the pew to look at him more closely. The skin under his eyes sagged, dark and thick. She said, "But that's not why you asked if I'm all right, is it? Not really, although you'd like me to think so. How did you know I wasn't asleep, Patrick?"

When he didn't answer, she added, "The carnie dBase is monitored, isn't it?"

"Not ordinarily. But it has instructions to wake me under certain circumstances."

"What kind of certain circumstances?"

"When something significant happens."

"And what happened significant this morning?"

His voice was quiet as always, courtesy interwoven into the words like warp. But Caroline saw the moment, clear as a chime, when he decided on honesty. "You learned that Robbie Brekke was your son in another life."

"And why is that so significant?" Suddenly she remembered what Joe had said to her: *Out of all the billions of people who are or were on earth—*

"Before I answer that, will you answer please a question for me?"

"What is it?" Caroline said, not promising.

"How did you recall that life with that son? What triggered the memory?"

"Why—it was Joe McLaren. He went with me yesterday to Catherine's Home, and I asked him to stay with me when we got back. I didn't want to be alone. A little after three this morning I woke up—Joe was snoring. He was lying with his knees drawn up, hugging his own pillow, like a little boy. And he was snoring. And then all of a sudden I remembered lying in a bed with Timmy when he was little, because he'd had a bad earache. He screamed and screamed, and I couldn't take him to a doctor until morning—" *—lying with his knees drawn up while she rubbed his back in circles and sang to him softly, meaningless little songs like 'Here's a spider, here's another, now there's two, here's another,' until he fell asleep hugging his pillow and began to snore through his poor clogged nose, a soft gentle sound that went on and on in the tiny room like a soft song—*

"And Timmy was how old?"

"Six." Caroline smiled. "What a weird trigger. After all, Joe must be, what—"

"Thirty-two," Shahid said, unexpectedly precise.

"And Timmy Hendrickson was a child. My child. I was Janet Hendrickson, a housewife in Wichita, it was 1965, and my Timmy had an earache." It struck her that Robbie, too, must have had a memory of Timmy, in order to enter him on the datanet. Immediately she wanted, passionately, to know what the memory had been.

Shahid said, "Why did you go right away to the dBase?"

"I couldn't sleep. No other reason."

"What else can you remember about being Janet Hendrickson?"

Caroline frowned. "Not too much. That's strange, considering that with Linyi . . . all I remember is a few flashes from the part of Janet's life connected with Timmy. A birthday party. A Little League game when he was nine. This truck he had, a steam shovel he called Mike Mulligan after a children's book. And his death."

Shahid said sharply, "You remember Timothy Henrickson's death?"

"Yes. But not viscerally. Not like the other memories, the memory is muted the way you told me deaths for other lives usually—"

"Yes, yes," Shahid said impatiently, and she stared at him. "When did Timmy die?"

Outside, the sun was starting to rise. Long fingers of color shot across the floor from the stained-glass windows: ruby, cobalt, ochre. Caroline watched them steadily and let go of Shahid's cold hands.

"He was . . . 'joyriding.' With some friends, in one of his friend's cars. They were drinking. He ran with a wild bunch sometimes, wilder than he was really—"

"When?"

"He was only eighteen. It was the night of his high-school graduation and he—"

"*When?*"

"June, 1976."

Shahid sat back in the pew, his face abruptly smooth and blank. The long bars of colored light began to climb the opposite wall.

"Why is that so important, Patrick?" Caroline said. "Look at you. Why does the date of Timmy's death matter?"

Shahid didn't answer. Before she could ask him again, the door to the chapel opened and Joe McLaren walked in.

He stopped abruptly when he saw Caroline; obviously he had expected to find Shahid alone. He wore the same clothes as last night, now even more rumpled. At the sight of his brown shirt Caroline again felt the smooth fabric against her cheek, heard Timmy's soft snore, felt again the rush of helpless love for her small son with the bad earache.

Who was Robbie Brekke.

Joe said, "Hello. I'm sorry to interrupt. Dr. Shahid, could I see you alone for a few minutes? It's important."

"Certainly," Shahid said, so mechanically that Caroline looked at him, really looked at him. His face was not just blank, it was gray, a peculiar ashy pallor. What had she said to make him look like this? She took hold of the edge of one loose, bright-colored sleeve of his shirt. He didn't seem to notice.

"It's important," Joe repeated.

"Yes," Shahid said. "Of course." He made no move. In his gray face the dark eyes looked enormous.

Caroline said, "Is someone dying?"

"No," Joe said.

"Then in that case, can it wait five minutes? We're in the middle of something important here, too."

"Certainly," Joe said stiffly, unconsciously echoing Shahid. He closed the door.

Caroline said, "We've got five minutes. Tell me why your terminal woke you because I found a carnie connection with Robbie. Tell me why the date of Timmy's death is so important. Tell me *what's going on.*"

Shahid was silent so long she felt anger begin to stir in her. He had no right . . . but when he did answer, it was in a voice so quiet with fear, so obviously intended not for her but for some private and profound part of himself, that her anger died.

"I think what's going on may perhaps be God."

"*God?*"

"Or something I could call God. Perhaps."

Abruptly, he bent his head. Caroline suddenly felt that she was seeing a kind of anguish she hadn't known existed in him, maybe hadn't known existed in the world anymore at all. Beneath the smooth brown face it was a flame, scorching, and in some hidden place he writhed with it. She still held the edge of his sleeve. Her fingers tightened on the rough cloth.

Without raising his head, he moved away from her, farther down the pew.

When he finally looked up at her, the anguish was gone. Caroline saw that she would never be permitted to see it again. Only some unexpected shock had laid bare, for an instant, that bright, tortured core.

Shahid's hands lay quietly on the back of a pew. "Certainly, Caroline, your questions deserve answers. The terminal alerts me whenever anyone—not just you—registers a cross-connection with Robbie Brekke."

"Why?"

"Because it has happened too often."

"How often?"

"One hundred forty-three times."

Caroline caught her breath. "But Robbie hasn't even registered that many memories!"

"Nowhere near that many. He has, in fact, registered four. Each time he registers a new one, the terminal records a rash of connections to it. And of those one hundred forty-three connections, one hundred sixteen were close blood ties."

Caroline felt dizzy. "How many other close blood ties have been found in the dBase? That didn't involve Robbie?"

"One."

"*One?*"

"A woman in Hong Kong and a sixteen-year-old boy in Brasilia discovered that they were once, a thousand years ago, first cousins in what is now the Ukraine. Once."

"But why . . . why Timmy?"

"Robbie," Shahid corrected gently. "Picture, Caroline, a darkness. Living, warm, but closed off from the outer world. In the darkness an entity grows. You can, if you wish, think of the darkness as a womb and the entity as a child, although that is not correct. But think of it that way. What is needed for that child growing in the darkness to burst into the light?"

"It needs to get large enough. Too big for the womb," Caroline said. She looked at Shahid with concern; his face had regained no color. On the chapel walls, beams of ruby and cobalt climbed higher.

"Yes, it needs to get large enough. But something else is needed as well. What if the womb has no path out—if, for instance, the cervix is so small the child cannot be born?"

"It will die."

"Yes. And it will not emerge into its own separate life. So both are needed for the birth—sufficient size, and a path out. Both."

She said, as gently as she could force herself to be, "You're not being clear, Patrick."

"I am being as clear as possible. I said there were one hundred sixteen blood links between Robbie Brekke and other reincarnation surgery clients, and only one other known blood link. But there are hundreds of connections registered on the datanet that are not links of blood but only of circumstance. People who happened to live in the same isolated jungle village. People who served in the same Roman legion a generation apart. People who traded with each other at mountain markets reached by mules once each moon. Hundreds of shared circumstances. Four hundred twelve to be exact, as of an hour ago."

"So?" Caroline said. Her lips felt stiff.

"So how many people do you think have undergone this surgery, worldwide, in the scant twenty years of its existence?"

Caroline shook her head. It seemed to her she had been told how many during her first night here, as part of the introductory holovid presentation, but she couldn't remember the number.

"Fewer than ten thousand. Out of the four billion people now on earth—or the five billion that lived forty years ago, before the first plague. And yet out of those five billion previous lives, the net shows four hundred twelve coincidental overlaps, and one hundred forty-three blood links to one man. That is statistically impossible, if random chance is the operating factor. So it cannot *be* random chance."

"What are you saying? Then what is it?"

"I don't know," Shahid said softly. "But five billion lives is a large growth. A century ago, it was half that. Five centuries ago, only a fraction. Five billion comparatively new memories is a huge living mass to be swelling in the over-memory."

"But it isn't—"

Again Shahid interrupted her. His voice, always quiet, grew so soft that Caroline had to lean forward to hear him. "And reincarnation surgery has provided it with a path out."

Caroline stood up. She took three steps toward the door, turned, turned again, reached the door, and then marched back to Shahid. In her own ears her voice sounded tight and scornful. "And that's supposed to be God? Isn't that a little backward, Patrick? Shouldn't God—if there is such a thing— have come *before* human beings—not be something *we're* just giving birth to *now*?"

Shahid didn't answer. Caroline rushed on, "And it's all too easy to change your analogy. You're a Jesuit, Patrick—you know that analogy is not proof. Pick physics instead of theology. Call it the Big Bang, not a birth. A critical mass of memory, and it explodes. Isn't that just as valid as some theory about God?"

Shahid said, "An explosion is a birth, a birth an explosion. Both create a new center for the world. And nothing remains the same."

"Not all explosions lead to self-consciousness! Why call it 'God' for pity's sake? That says it's a self-aware entity, causing things to happen not by physical laws of chance but by will and motive that affect events—" She stopped, appalled.

Shahid said, "One hundred forty-three connections do not happen by random chance."

Caroline cried, *"But why Timmy?"*

Shahid stood. Behind him, coming in the stained-glass

windows, the sun had risen. Shahid was a dark silhouette
ringed by brilliant color. "I don't know, Caroline. I don't know
why Robbie Brekke. All I can figure is that a critical mass needs
a first atom to fire, a birth needs a first tiny shift down the
canal—everything must begin somewhere. And under your
analogy of random chance, why *not* Robbie Brekke?"

"As a conduit of *God*? Patrick—you know Robbie! He's a
bungler, a charming romantic with no ethics, an adventurer
who always gets the adventure wrong and never realizes it until
it's too late—if then. A conduit to God, Patrick? Robbie
Brekke?"

Shahid said nothing. Caroline made a noise that might have
been disgust, might have been fear; she herself didn't know.
The chapel door opened and she whirled angrily, expecting to
see Joe intruding again, half glad for another target for her
anger. But it was Dr. Maxine Armstrong. Behind the slim Chief
of Staff, Caroline could see Joe standing a little way down the
corridor, leaning against the wall.

"Ms. Bohentin. And Dr. Shahid. I've been looking for you
both," Dr. Armstrong said. Even at this early hour she was
flawlessly dressed, immaculately groomed. But Caroline recognized the note in her voice as professional compassion—
practiced, calm—and she tensed. "Ms. Bohentin, I'm afraid I
have some very bad news. The Meadows Home in Albany
called a few minutes ago. I'm sorry to have to tell you that your
daughter died during the night."

Shahid's hand was on her arm. But it wasn't Shahid's hand,
it was Timmy's, nestled in hers, his breathing finally regular in
the dark. No, it was her father's hand, strong as this one, slick
as ice.

"Steady, Caroline."

"I'm truly sorry," Dr. Armstrong said. "You have the deepest sympathy of everyone at the Institute."

"Thank you," Caroline said. And then, a cry, "It was only
an earache!"

Armstrong frowned, glanced at Shahid, took a step forward. "The little girl died of a cerebral hemorrhage arising as a secondary plague complication, the Home said. It was very quick, Ms. Bohentin. She had no time to suffer."

"Thank you," Caroline said again. She had it straight now: Timmy, Catherine. She felt only a dull ache, just below her breast bone, but she knew that wouldn't last. This was just the beginning, the shuddery mercy of shock. The rest would come later. She wondered how much—even knowing Catherine's death had been inevitable, even knowing it was a release, even knowing—how much it would hurt.

"I sent for your aircar," Dr. Armstrong said. "If there's anything the Institute can do . . ." Propelled on the meaningless phrase, she led the way from the chapel.

Shahid's hand guided Caroline, firm on her elbow. She saw him shake his head at Joe and say something to him, she didn't hear what. About her, probably. "*You have the deepest sympathy of everyone at* . . ." Leaving the lobby by the north door, Caroline saw that the sun had lifted fully above the horizon and sparkled on blue water. Jason wheeled the aircar overhead.

Caroline said to Shahid, "Why . . . why does it matter that Timmy died in June of 1976?"

He said softly, "Let it go until later, Caroline."

"Why does it matter?"

Shahid looked at her steadily. Small waves lapped against the rocks across the lawn. Finally he said, "Someone else was born on that date."

"Who?"

Shahid hesitated. "That's really confidential information. It belongs to someone else's past, someone else's other lives."

"Unless it turns up in the dBase," she said, and after a moment Shahid nodded. Caroline looked away; it didn't really matter. She perceived that the merciful numbing, the gift of shock, was not going to last long after all. Her aircar set down on the grass. Jason hurried out to open the door for her. Beyond the car, in the blinding brilliance of light on water at the lake's edge, someone walked. By squinting Caroline could just make out that it was Bill Prokop, his feet bare on the dewy grass, carrying his portfolio of murder pictures in one hand and with the other skipping flat stones across the surface of the shining lake.

11 JOE

Joe watched Caroline's Aircar lift and turn into the same corridor they had taken yesterday. He stood hidden in the long morning shadow of the Institute building, unwilling to intrude on her grief, uncertain what he would have said if he had spoken. She had apparently refused even Shahid's company. The little priest handed her into the car, leaned forward to say one last thing to her, and closed the door. As the car lifted, Shahid stood watching it, his small body silhouetted against the bright lake, his head tilted backward. By the water a barefooted Prokop, equally motionless, stood in the same position.

The tableau suddenly annoyed Joe. What could Caroline be offered by a reactionary priest and a memory-snapped journalist? His eyes burned with exhaustion and sunlight. Leaving the shadows, he walked toward Shahid, whose face looked as tired as Joe's felt.

"Dr. Shahid."

"How can I help you, Mr. McLaren? You have heard of Caroline's loss?"

"Dr. Armstrong told me."

"Death by cerebral hemorrhage is much more common in child plague victims than in adults."

"I know."

"Of course you do," Shahid said. "Please excuse my lecturing you on your own field. I am very tired."

A rabbit suddenly bounded across the grass, breaking from the woods and dashing at top speed toward a low hedge. Both men turned to watch it. All at once Joe stood on other grass, facing another man with tired eyes, both of them distracted by the dash of a gray rabbit barely visible through the predawn mist. Oak trees loomed over Joe, and the cold metal of a pistol grip added heft to his right hand, which did not feel like his at all. "*Un*," a voice said from somewhere off to the left, "*deux, trois . . .*"

"You had a memory just then," Shahid said.

"Yes. It was—" Joe stopped and scowled.

"You don't have to tell me. You seldom use the reincarnation datanet, do you, Mr. McLaren?"

"Twice. But you already know that, don't you, Doctor? The supposedly confidential information is monitored."

Shahid showed neither surprise nor dismay. "Of course. But only for research purposes. You were never actually told otherwise."

"I suppose not. What's going on here at the Institute, Dr. Shahid?"

Shahid bent to adjust a sandal. "Why should you suppose anything is 'going on'?"

"I can smell it. That's what lawyers do, you know."

"Your field is not reincarnation law."

"Doesn't matter. Smell still works. Go on, you can tell me—it will all be kept 'confidential.'" Shahid showed no reaction to the mockery. Joe waved toward the lake. "Is it concerned with Prokop? Has somebody else actually remembered being the infamous Armand Kyle?"

"I think you are very tired, Mr. McLaren."

"Bet your dBase I am. It's been a rough two days. *Is* it Prokop? Why is he still here when it's so obvious he needs a psychiatrist, not an historian? Does he get sent spinning into ga-ga land by the discovery that somebody else is Kyle?"

"Not to my knowledge."

"Uh-huh. Then if you won't tell me what's going on with Prokop, tell me this: Where's Robbie Brekke?"

Something happened behind Shahid's eyes. He said carefully, "Why should you want to know? I did not think the two of you were friends."

"We're not. He left yesterday. Security told me that, which is a matter of public knowledge, in a voice like crawling ants. Today I need to talk with him, now, this morning. When is he coming back? He hasn't checked out for good; he took only a small bag."

"Is your business with him a personal matter?"

A retort bit Joe's tongue: Everything here was personal, there was never any detached intellectual rigor to anything. He didn't say it.

Shahid said, "You don't approve of reincarnation surgery, do you, Mr. McLaren? You accept it medically but not morally. It seems to you morally indulgent, escapist, a cheap way to avoid planning and choosing one's life."

"It doesn't matter what I approve of or disapprove of, Doctor. I came here for remission of my"— he realized that he had almost said *of my sins*, the old Catholic phrase arising from who-knew-where in his tiredness—"of my multiple sclerosis, and I got that. I have no complaints. Now will you tell me where Brekke has gone and when he'll be back?"

"I don't know."

"Is that the truth?"

Shahid turned his head, locking his dark eyes with Joe's own. Joe realized how his words had sounded.

"I'm sorry. Thank you, Doctor."

"Wait just a moment, Mr. McLaren, before you go." Joe turned back. Prokop walked toward them from the lake. The strain of choosing his words pulled at Shahid's face.

"Escapism is much more complex than you think, Mr. McLaren. So is making choices. It may sometimes happen that our choices are made for us by forces we cannot understand, and that to bow to that is not to evade moral responsibility, but to accept it."

"Tell it to the Gaeists," Joe said.

He walked rapidly toward the building, outdistancing Prokop, beating him to the elevator. His room felt close and stuffy, despite the air-conditioning. Caroline had pried her window open to let in fresh air; this was the first time he was tempted to do the same. Instead he lay down on the bed, ignoring the stuffy air, ignoring Prokop's persistent knock on his door, ignoring the mental image of Caroline's face as she climbed into her car to go to Catherine. Pirelli, Joe thought, had a lot of explaining to do: about the virus, about the testing program, about his melodramatic message concerning Brekke. A lot of explaining. Joe planned to do nothing else, go nowhere else, talk to no one else until Pirelli arrived later this morning to do it.

Jeff Pirelli stood in the lobby, chatting up the receptionist. Joe saw that in the two months since he had seen the data scanner, Pirelli had gained weight. His face was fuller, the skin sleek over cheeks not yet fallen into jowls, the bright brown eyes slightly more hooded by swells of pink flesh. He was taking on the look of a richly oiled Buddha, Joe thought, until he remembered that it was tension that made Pirelli eat too much. A memory flashed by: he and Pirelli, fifteen years old, bent over an ancient keyboard and monitor from the nineties, pizza in one hand and Coke in the other and consuming both with the steady unthinking absorption of boa constrictors. It irritated Joe that this memory felt no different than the earlier flash of dueling in the Bois de Boulogne.

"Top o' the mornin' to you, Counselor," Pirelli said. In one hand he carried an Italian leather briefcase; in the other a computer case gleaming with brass fittings. Joe felt himself smile.

"*Buon giorno, paisano.*"

"No Italian—can't trust a single one of their goddamn bytes," Pirelli said. "You look terrible, old buddy."

"And you look like a suitcase salesman."

Pirelli laughed. "So who am I addressing now, since the Bridey Murphy Time Machine sale? Machiavelli? Do lawyers get more weasely if they discover they've been other lawyers before?"

"Oh, boy," Joe said. "Manic time."

"Yeah, I can see it now. A new law firm: Machiavelli, Cranmer, Nixon, and McLaren. 'Let me consult on that with my senior partner; he's away from his desk just now, bilking out Purgatory.'"

"Vatican III dismantled Purgatory."

"Damn! And I had my reservation in!"

The receptionist, the same one who had been so sour about Angel yesterday, stared at them both. Pirelli said to her, "Did you hear the one about the lawyer and the L-5 colony?" Joe took Pirelli's arm and steered him firmly toward the elevator. Over his shoulder Pirelli called to the receptionist, "We're having a business meeting. Could you tell?"

Joe hit the elevator button. But Pirelli said, "Uh-uh. Let's go outside to talk. I want to see the grounds. Didn't I hear there's a smallish sort of pond around here?"

Joe led him out the north door toward Lake Ontario. Clouds had rolled in since dawn; the lake looked gray and sullen. A cool fresh wind blew.

"Impressive," Pirelli said. "In Washington, that much water would be jammed with sailboats and airdivers. All belonging to the athletic preppy set of our oh-so-elegant laissez-faire prexy, and all ensuring her political survival."

"How do *you* survive in Washington, with that mouth on you?"

"Stodge bastards," Pirelli said genially. "I survive because I'm so damn good."

This was the truth. Pirelli was the best data scanner in Diane Caswell's administration—probably. How did you reliably evaluate a field where wrong predictions could end up more useful than right ones, if they were wrong in the right way? If they affected mathematical models no one really completely understood to make things not happen which no one was sure would have happened anyway? But, on the other hand, Pirelli *had* to be good for his abrasive and high-handed working style to be even tolerated, let alone sought after.

"How's the MS, Joe?"

"Gone, or as close as not to matter."

"That's good," Pirelli said in a completely different tone, "because now I got something else to matter to us. Where's Robert Brekke?"

"Gone."

"Damn," Pirelli said, and from the way he said it Joe knew that Pirelli had already known. Somehow.

He said, "The cross-monitoring here is getting a little dizzying, Jeff old buddy. Not to mention illegal."

"Well," Pirelli said, as if it were an answer. "Where'd he go?"

"No one knows. He's a split-brained adventurer. Gone today, back tomorrow, never really here in the first place."

"Stupid?"

"Well . . . no."

"You don't like him."

"Does it matter?"

"Not in the least." They had walked as far as the stone bench where Joe had gone into sexual memory flash in front of Caroline and Brekke. Pirelli paused. "Let's squat here. I have a lot of data to show you."

"Here?"

"No place better."

"My room is better."

"Your room is bugged. Or at least your terminal is. I don't know about the rest of the room."

Joe stood still. "How do you know about the terminal?"

"Because I bugged it. Oh, Christ on a ramchip, don't look like that, you stodge lawyer you. The Commission has the whole reincarnation datanet monitored, all the Institute outlets where there's a research program, and some other possibly key locations. It's all legal—the Justice Department gave us a dispensation broad enough to monitor the Pope, if we need to."

"Why? And why wasn't I told?"

"You *are* being told," Pirelli said. "I'm telling you. You're on leave, remember? Esparza did the trotting around to Justice. And anyway, this all came up fast, like last week."

"Why a warrant from Justice? Why not just request information from the reincarnation dBase? You could have used my password."

"We tried. This information they're keeping for themselves. They're allowed—private enterprise under the beauteous Diane. Except when it's a question of plague, of course. National defense."

"Why bug my room?"

"Hoping you'd talk with that Irish-Pakistani priest. Shahid."

"What's your interest in *him*?"

"It doesn't matter just now. It's his research, not him personally."

"I don't like it."

"That's evident from your face. But maybe you'll like it better when you see what we've got. This is big, Joe."

"How big?"

Pirelli didn't answer. He laid his expensive computer case flat on the bench, keyed in his thumblock, and raised the lid. Sheets of thin metal supple as cloth opened into precise, complicated folds.

"That's a new one," Joe said, despite himself.

"Full holo capability, laser data transmission up to twenty miles, field data shielding, optic E-scans, and interface modes with everything except the family dog."

"The Commission isn't opting for take-along hardware like that."

" 'Deedy not. This is mine. There's a reason I can't afford a wife." Pirelli glanced at Joe's face and added, "Sorry. Insensitive."

"I'm not going to talk again about Robin."

"I am. But not just yet. Look at this." Pirelli touched various points on the metallic folds, spoke various passwords, finally hit a key on the curiously abbreviated keyboard; Joe guessed that touch points and voice prints activated much of what the equipment could do. The screen glowed, and then projected outward onto the stone bench, creating a three-dimensional hologram two feet square. Joe shifted on the bench to avoid blanking a corner of the holo space, which had filled with a lumpy, irregular rope of violet light tied into a sloppy and intricate knot. The entire length of rope was dotted with pinpoints of deeper purple light. At one point, where several holographic strands met, a larger purple light glowed.

Pirelli regarded the holo with theatrical satisfaction. "Looks like a leprous hyperactive pretzel, doesn't it?"

"My thoughts exactly. What is it?"

"It's the most recent Hofstader model of a polynomial invariant derived from a Komczyc simulation."

"Ah."

"It derives from the data we have about plague occurrences. A field of selected variables about plague breakouts is translated into various three-dimensional analogues, of which this is the most sophisticated. It sums up a lot of different probabilities, most notably the links of blood relationships among people who contract plague. This is the best model we have at the moment of plague occurrences by genetic relationship. You've actually seen earlier versions of this model, when we had fewer plague cases to work with. Now watch this—this is new."

Pirelli touched the metallic folds. The purple ropes vanished. In their place appeared another three-dimensional shape, this one made of what appeared to be orange folds of light, smaller than the Hofstader model had been and far less defined. It was hard to see clearly; the orange light shifted subtly except for one point where it glowed very brightly and steadily.

Pirelli said, "It shifts like that because there's such a high error field in the sample. Squint at it a little; that helps."

Joe squinted. It didn't seem to him to help anything. "What is it I'm looking at?"

"Hofstader model of carnie cross-links registered on the reincarnation global dBase."

Joe stopped squinting. "Cross-links? There are enough to make a model of?"

"Oh, yes," Pirelli said. He sounded grim. "And right now you're asking yourself, what does the PLAS datanet have to do with the plague? Watch."

Again Pirelli gave the computer swift and complex commands. The orange folds of light quadrupled in size, losing even more definition, and rotated in two dimensions. The purple Hofstader ropes reappeared. Each rope fit inside a fold of orange light, following its contours. The fit was very close, although not exact except for the two glowing nodes, purple and orange, which fit into each other exactly.

Joe felt a tightness pull across his chest. "What does that *mean*, Pirelli?"

"Damned if we know," Pirelli said. All levity had left him; his dark eyes were somber under their heavy lids. "But even if we don't know what it means, we do know what it *is*. The models are congruent, at least roughly so. They might be even more congruent if the sample of carnies were larger, or more reliable. But they only fit if the orange model is on the outside of the purple Hofstader. Reverse them and the mathematics just collapse—which they bloody well shouldn't do."

"I still don't understand," Joe said. The tightening in his chest grew worse; it was difficult to breathe.

"There are two implications. One is that the two groups of people—carnies and plaguers—are completely separated from each other. People who undergo reincarnation surgery never get the plague. Never."

"You mean reincarnation surgery prevents getting plague?"

"No, that's not what I mean. I mean that anyone who decides to have reincarnation surgery—even if they choose it at age seventy-three, and a lot of people do—will be a person who never had plague."

"That's crazy! You're saying the decision to have surgery at the end of your life is some sort of backward-acting guarantee that you never get plague earlier!"

"Here's something crazier, the second implication of the data—are you ready for this, old buddy? The occurrence model for plague—who gets it, statistically, which means essentially how it's transmitted—matches exactly the decision pattern for reincarnation surgery."

Joe sat still a second before Pirelli's meaning hit him. "A virus transmission pattern matches a decision pattern? You're saying the decision to have reincarnation surgery is *transmitted*?"

"So says the data."

"Jesus, Jeff, *decisions* aren't transmitted!"

"The equations say this one is."

"Then the equations are wrong."

"So I wish. But I don't think so."

"You think instead that the choice to have reincarnation surgery—a *conscious* choice, even when it's a dumb one—is spread around like a virus? Like the common cold? I breathe in something and suddenly I want to get plazzed?"

"Joe—the plague itself isn't transmitted like the common

cold! You know that. We can't figure out how the hell it *is* transmitted—not a clue. One day three people in Des Moines, the next day a recluse in Butte Top, Montana, who hasn't left her sealed room in sixteen years, the next a prisoner in solitary in Hudson's Bay. When Sholomeis and his med team have test results to see who's carrying the slow virus in their brains, maybe we'll be able to predict outbreaks better."

"Is the test—"

"—in serum form and being injected. Today in fact. I never would have believed a bunch of research docs could move so fast. But what we have now—what we *know* is only what you see here. Plague victims, who made no choice, and people who chose to access their past lives, who made a choice, are never the same people. But the patterns by which the two are linked together by blood *are* the same, and so is the transmission dispersal patterns. *Only*, however, if you include blood links from past lives, which exist nowhere else but the so-called over-memory."

"Are you saying racial memory is somehow responsible for plague?"

" 'Responsible'? Of course not. Christ on a ramchip, Joe, forget you're a lawyer—it's not a question of responsibility. It's a question of connections. Sometimes things are connected in ways we don't see at first. But rattle one end of the chain and the other end clinks."

"You sound like a goddamn Gaeist!"

Pirelli looked at him sideways. Very quietly—Joe had to strain forward to hear him—Pirelli said, "Robin called me yesterday. She said she's been trying to call you. She wants to undergo reincarnation surgery."

"So let her."

"She's broke."

"Then let her Gaeist clan or compound or whatever it is pay for it."

"They don't carry insurance. You know that."

"So let her stay in this life. It's not as wonderful as she probably thinks to be spread across forty centuries. It probably wouldn't let her evade as many responsibilities as she imagines."

"She has Alzheimer's, Joe."

It hit him between the eyes. In the brain, he thought inanely. In the cortex. In the memory. Robin. Robin with Alzheimer's.

"It's still in the very earliest stages. Carnie surgery would cure it."

"No . . . insurance for that, either?"

"No. I told her," Pirelli said carefully, not looking at Joe, "that I'd help with what I could. I know neither of us has much—I spend it on toys and you work *pro bono* or for peanuts. But Robin has even less. Now. She left the Gaeists, or they kicked her out—it's not clear. And I told her I'd tell you all this."

"So you have. You have. Robin can . . . can . . ." Joe wasn't sure what he was going to say next. Before he could find out, the open computer on the bench between him and Pirelli started to shriek.

The noise it made was deafening: not loud but high, a thin wail at a pitch that made Joe's ears hurt. Pirelli lunged forward and cut the power. The intertwined Hofstader models vanished. The screen, however, drawing on some unsuspected auxiliary, stayed lit, displaying compass coordinates and an elevation reading.

"Up there," Pirelli said, pointing. "Fourth floor of your building, eastern end. Someone trying a broad-band field siphon of open data. Who?"

Joe stared at the Institute, trying to remember who was on the fourth floor, his mind a blank. Then it came. "Bill Prokop?"

"Who is he?"

"Journalist. And crazy. Did he get anything?"

"Not from *this* whirligig," Pirelli said, patting the computer. "But a better question is why would he want it? For a story? For who, and on what?"

"I don't think it's for a story. He's here on his own, mostly, trying to prove he was Armand Kyle."

"Was he?"

"No."

"Then why would—"

"I said he was crazy," Joe said shortly. He didn't want to talk about Prokop. Then, realizing how he'd sounded, he added grudgingly, "He thinks I know something about when he was Kyle."

"You?" Pirelli's mouth quirked; his dark eyes took on a look of sly amusement that made Joe want to hit him. "*You*, of all people—an inside source on shadowy fag Armand Kyle? With your stands on subduing sex for the public good and playing everything straight, strictly by law?"

Joe ignored him. The kidding was supposed to soften the news about Robin—humorous insult as distraction. It didn't work. All his life people—women especially—had been telling Joe he had no sense of humor. After a moment Pirelli saw that it didn't work; he returned to business. Joe saw that Pirelli's mood had lifted: Defeating Prokop's sophisticated equipment with his own sophisticated equipment had pleased him.

"So why didn't Prokop's attempted siphon bring an electronics security team dashing out from the Institute?"

"It's very selective security," Joe said dryly, thinking of Colin Cadavy and Angel Whittaker. Of Caroline. Of Catherine, one small point somewhere on a purple Hofstader model. Of Robin. Robin, with Alzheimer's . . .

Pirelli said, "Sholomeis and his medical team promised an interim report tomorrow on the slow virus testing results. When I get it, I'll call you right away."

"Thanks."

"The report should show whether or not their serum can identify the presence of the virus in the brain."

"Yes," Joe said. His head hurt—did Pirelli even realize how much staggering data he had just dumped out in a pile of purple and orange light? Maybe he did; he sat watching Joe quietly, his round body quiet on the stone bench. Behind him small waves rose on the lake as the wind picked up. Joe looked out over the water. It seemed to him that he could still see the intertwined Hofstader diagrams, dense purple ropes inside shifting orange folds, glowing with light, mathematical consequences of choices and decisions, making no sense. Glowing with light . . .

"Jeff," he said. At his tone, something moved behind Pirelli's eyes.

"Yeah?"

"Those models . . ."

"Spit it out, Joey."

Nobody but Pirelli ever called him "Joey." Joey McLareni, honorary Wop. Joey and Guiseppi and Robin. "Those models—both of them had one glowing spot of light at the end, at the only place you said the mathematics intersected perfectly."

"Yes."

"What is that intersection? Those two spots?"

Pirelli shifted his weight on the hard bench. "As far as we can tell, they're Robert Anthony Brekke."

12 <u>ROBBIE</u>

Robbie stripped off his shirt and let the mountain air of the Wind River Range flow over his sweaty skin. Immediately hordes of tiny black insects attacked his back and shoulders. Cursing, he put the shirt back on, wiped his forehead, and stared up at the ledge of gray rock directly above him.

It was the wrong ledge. The wrong direction, the wrong jumble of boulders and pine, maybe the wrong fucking *mountain*.

It had taken him twenty minutes of hard climbing to reach the ledge, which was a narrow shelf jutting southwest along the bottom of a cliff face above a small flat plateau. He had left the aircar on the plateau, parked among a fall of olive-yellow leaves he couldn't name. But, then, he couldn't name anything here: not the trees, not the mountains, not the steep cold streams, not the insects that bit unmercifully every time he stopped moving long enough to catch his breath.

He had been looking since morning, so sure of what he was looking for, so convinced he would recognize from the air the path Mallie Callahan and Johnny Lee Benson had taken from the Sweetwater River into the mountains. A second river, leading to a stream, followed upward until there was a clear view of a huge bare rock face in the middle distance on the left and a closer mountain on the right. Up the broken folds of the mountain, to a small plateau with a rock ledge slanting back southwest. Climb to the ledge, follow its twists backward until it abruptly disappeared between two huge boulders with barely enough room to squeeze between them, boulders that led to a narrow downward slanting pocket ending in the low, hidden entrance to the cave.

But now there were so many plateaus, wooded and un-wooded; so many twisting ledges; so many double sets of immense boulders. Huge outcroppings of stone, cold abrupt waterfalls six inches across, massive wooded ridges filled with all these trees he couldn't name. None of it matched Mallie's memory. Time and time again he had looked down from the air, sure he'd found it, and set down the car with the double vision of the place filming his mind: his view, and Mallie's. But then landmarks that from the air had seemed hard and clear changed as he started yet another long climb on the ground. A shimmer lay over each deserted, silent ledge, a film of memory that shifted and folded until Robbie was no longer sure this was the place, was no longer sure of anything at all, except that he wanted to scream just to add some noise to the empty, luminous air.

He started the climb back from the ledge, the wrong ledge, to where the car was parked. His head hurt. His shoulders ached, his leg muscles groaned. He dragged himself into the aircar, lifted it, scanned another section of terrain until he saw beneath him another quicksilver stream leave the river, another plateau fifteen minutes later, another ledge.

What if the right stream no longer existed after a hundred and forty years? What if the place it joined the river was invisible from the air under blankets of treetops? What if—

Robbie set the car down on another level plateau, this one a bare stretch of rubble from some minor landslide above, the level space fringed with pine like a green tonsure. Under the trees the light already held the blue shadows of evening. The lighter blue paint of the aircar, so shiny at the airport this morning, was pitted by small stones, tattooed with wet leaves. Grit clogged the chrome grillwork. The fuel monitor showed two-thirds empty.

From the barren clearing Robbie climbed toward the ledge. On his other side the distant large rock face began to glow in the long slanting sun. He didn't think it was pretty; he didn't think anything out here in this world-forsaken place was pretty. His shadow shifted before him, a dark beacon. To his left all the leaves on a clump of tall thin trees shuddered and shook with every slight breeze, palsied and dim. Below him the mountain fell away in jumbled, recessed folds. He climbed faster, breathing hard.

The wind picked up. *Paul*, it whispered to him. *Paul*. Robbie shook his head, but that only made him more light-headed, made the throbbing in his head worse.

This time he really thought he had found it. At the top of the incline the ledge turned abruptly, and a narrow, rubble-strewn passage twisted between boulders. The sound of his heartbeat thudded loud in his ears. Behind his eyelids a sudden light exploded, such a frightening and unexpected light that he sagged against the nearest boulder and clutched with one hand at the rough gray granite. Then the light passed and he pushed on between the boulders—to a blank wall of rock.

Disappointment seized him. It felt like an actual seizure: a convulsion in his brain that left him weak and panting. He leaned against the wall that was not a cave, was not *the* cave, for support. Stone scraped his cheek, leaving a thin smear of blood.

Paul.

Robbie straightened. Above, very high in the translucent air, a large bird circled lazily. He didn't know what kind of bird it was; birds had never interested him. He knew that the voice must be coming from inside his head and not from the bird, but it was to the bird that he shouted out loud. "I don't know any fucking Paul!"

The words echoed off all the cliffs, all the bare stone:
PAUULL . . . Pauulll . . . Paul . . .

Perversely, both shouting and echoes made him feel better.
He pulled his weary body together, squeezed back through the
rocky passage, and began the descent to the car.

By the time he reached it, the sky had begun to color with
sunset. Long ribbons of pink stretched above the purple mountains. The air around him turned clear and gold, fragrant with
pine and with what seemed to him the smell of light itself. But
light had no smell—did it? When had he ever smelled air this
oppressively pure? God, his head hurt.

At the very edge of a long pink ribbon in the sky, an aircar
appeared.

Robbie stood with one hand on the door of his own car,
watching. The other car appeared black, silhouetted against
the light. As he watched, it disappeared behind a high ridge.
A sudden flash of previous life memory came to him: something
black silhouetted against the moon. A bat? A plane? Or just a
crude drawing of a witch like children used to make at Halloween? He couldn't remember. He could see the black silhouette against the moon but the memory drifted free of a life,
a memory he had for a second time without ever having had it
for a first. But carnie memory wasn't supposed to work like that.
They had told him. They had promised him. They had *said*.

Robbie shook his head as hard as he could. Bright flashes of
light, painful as electric shocks, darted across the inside of his
eyelids. He cried out, crumpled into the aircar, and slumped
against the seat.

The black car reappeared from behind the far end of the
ridge. Methodically it crisscrossed the land between that ridge
and the next. Searching. For him.

Hatton. There were no other possibilities. Robbie had
expected Hatton to trace the aircar rental at Rawlins; he had
had to use his own ID and the credit numbers because the

rental outfit had a retina scan—but how the hell had Hatton known where he had flown since this morning? The aircar must leave electronic traces Robbie hadn't known about, some kind of homing signal or checkpoint system. And Hatton must have alerted goons in Denver or Cheyenne or even in Rawlins itself—all of which said a lot more about the extensiveness of Hatton's connections than Robbie had suspected.

Perversely, this heartened him. He straightened in the driver's seat and pushed away the ribbons of light snaking across his brain. Hatton was good, Hatton was connected, Hatton was *major*. And Hatton was chasing *him*.

Robbie laughed softly. Immediately the flashes of light started again behind his eyes, carrying memories with no lives attached to them: the swoop of a parrot through emerald trees, a sealed black metal box, an old woman on her knees pounding cloth on rocks beside a river, a man throwing a net over darting silver fish. None of them made sense. Robbie grunted with the effort of ignoring them and tried to think.

Hatton's car couldn't be receiving signals directly from his, or they wouldn't be searching so carefully for him. His trail must be somehow relayed back to a central datanet and then bought or pirated by Hatton's wizards. If the aircar emitted a homing signal, it probably needed reasonable elevation to be picked up. If, on the other hand, the car would register by just passing within a set radius of a checkpoint, then keeping to the fairly deserted areas north of the heavily farmed Sweetwater Basin and east of the tourist areas near Green River would offer the best chance of avoiding any checkpoint. So if he pulled the aircar under the nearby trees and waited for dark, he could make a low flight between the ridges to a motel somewhere north of the Sweetwater, along the deserted hill highways.

The black car gave up an hour later, lifting to a high elevation and racing due south. Robbie waited a half hour longer. As soon as the sun had set, the air had begun to chill, but he didn't turn on the heater, partly to conserve fuel and partly for the sake of the cold itself. It cleared his head of the images. A little.

A black Labrador puppy with a red bow around its neck. A sealed black metal box. A sundial, the carved stone numerals so old they were nearly invisible in the strong sunlight. A tent crowded with goats. Silver tankards on a polished sideboard—

The tankards were George III. And they belonged to . . . to . . .

Shit. What was wrong with his head? He couldn't slip now, not with Hatton's goons out there and Mallie's fortune in a cave somewhere around here, waiting for him. And Caroline would be so impressed—

Caroline? Who did he know named Caroline?

Caroline Herschel, Carolina Calarco, Caroline of Brunswick-Wolfenbuttell, Carolyn Thompson, Caroline Matilda, Caroline Spurgeon, Caroline Chin—

Robbie backed the aircar from under the trees. Sweating in the cold air, he lifted to sixty feet and activated the terrain radar. No lights; there were too many ways they could be picked up. Staring at the screen that told him what was below him and what was ahead of him, he began the careful, frustratingly slow flight through the ridges and mountains and hogbacks, over the crevasses and unseen lakes, southeast in the darkness.

It was nearly midnight when he reached a highway, a thin ribbon of hard smoothness on his radar screen. One set of headlights sped along it. Robbie, his eyes burning and all the muscles in his shoulders and back aching, increased his speed to follow the groundcar. He stayed a hundred yards behind and twenty above, running blind. The highway twisted and raced on the screen.

Eventually he found what he was almost too tired to recognize: a lonely cluster of strung-out lights centered with a neon glow. Not even a holo, just old-fashioned neon. Chunks of higher darkness stood to the west: woods.

He set the car down on the far side of the fringe of woods, well away from the highway, inched it under the trees, and locked it. Robbie's flashlight was powerful, but even so the silent blackness of the woods unnerved him. He felt something soft squish under his left foot and made the decision not to swing the light down and look. Smells rose around him, smells he never found in the city, disorienting him further: damp leaves and living pine and the rich, sweet smell of decay. Once he tripped, sprawling headlong over a small log so rotted that its collapse under him was completely silent. He reached the motel with relief.

The office was a single peeling room furnished with a counter, a sagging armchair missing one arm, and an ancient terminal like a grimy plastic box. A faded Indian blanket hung across a doorway behind the counter, which held only a bell. Robbie rang.

A young woman with long black braids pushed the blanket aside with one hand. She wore jeans, a loose shirt, and neither makeup nor headband. Her face was completely without expression.

"A room, please," Robbie said. "My car broke down on the highway. And I'd like to pay in advance."

The woman studied him and said nothing.

"How much?" Robbie said too loudly. He was having trouble with the blanket on the wall. The faded patterns stirred too much.

"Seventy-five," the blanket said, or the woman. Robbie fumbled with his wallet. A stained book appeared in front of him: a register. His name. She wanted him to sign it. He did.

"You want me to call a tow truck?"

Robbie looked at her. The blanket receded, approached, receded again, trying to tell him something.

"For the car," she said.

"Oh. No. Yes. In the morning."

"Okay by me. You didn't sign in your credit ID number."

"I gave you cash."

"Against damages."

"I never used it in Liberia," Robbie said, to either the woman or the blanket, and waited.

She shrugged. "Okay by me. I'm supposed to ask, I asked. Room four, out the door to the right."

He felt her watching him as he turned to leave, felt there was something else he was supposed to say or notice or do, but he couldn't think what. Before he could get the door closed she called, "Mr. Winter?" He closed the door. The cold outside air washed through his head like water.

She followed him outside. "Sir? Did you want to leave a wake-up call?"

"Me? No. Wait—yes. For dawn."

"Okay by me. Good night, Mr. Winter."

The room was as bare and faded as the office. Robbie lay down on the bed without undressing. The images started again on the insides of his eyelids, so bright he rolled facedown and flailed his arms in pain, images somehow pushing to get out: a rice field at the edge of a wide yellow river; red candles on a white altar cloth; a goatskin wine bag heavy and cool in his hands in the noonday sun. In *whose* hands? His. Robbie's. Yes? No.

He staggered off the bed and into the bathroom and poured himself a glass of water. The water tasted cold and clean. At the first gulp, the glass slipped from his hand and shattered on the floor. Robbie grabbed the edge of the sink, eased his body backward to sit on the toilet lid, and felt himself begin to shake. Then he was watching himself shake, watching the shards of broken glass on the tile floor, watching Mallie Callahan and Johnny Lee Benson on the banks of the Sweetwater. At the first sip of water it had all come back, he couldn't stop it from coming back to flood his mind, and

he watched from outside his mind while Johnny Lee ended
the world.

"Indians. Looky there."

Mallie looked. It was an effort; his head still hurt even
though he was pretty sure it wasn't his head that had been hit
in the explosion. His head had become very light and then very
heavy again, so that it had seemed to float off his body and travel
alongside his and Johnny Lee's horses. All day it had been
doing that. Now, cut off from the sight of the river by the thick
clump of willows where he and Johnny Lee lay, his head had
returned to his shoulders. It wanted to sleep.

"*Look*, damn you!" Johnny Lee said. "Be good for something, damn it!"

Mallie looked. He must have looked a long time because at
first all he saw was some ponies at a great distance. Then later
there was a camp near the ponies, and later still a woman
bending over a fire and another by the water and an old man.
It must be a real camp. The Indian woman on the railroad
platform must have made it, from the two bits the white woman
gave her for looking at the baby. There was a baby here, in a
blanket, lying on the ground. Cooking smells rode the air.

"If you don't stay awake," Johnny Lee said tonelessly. "I'll
. . . you ain't that bad off anyway. I make it two old men, two
women, and the kids. You?"

Mallie didn't make it anything. He wanted to say that he
had never seen an Indian at all before he and Johnny Lee rode
the cars from St. Louis, but he couldn't find the words. Johnny
Lee was looking at him so hard it seemed he had to say
something. In their days of travel Johnny Lee's face had become so black with grime he looked like a nigger. They had had
niggers near St. Louis, Mallie thought, and felt a little better.
He knew something, at least. Johnny Lee was still waiting for
him to say something. Mallie said. "Did we get any money in
that explosion, Johnny Lee?"

There was a little silence before Johnny Lee answered. His hand rested on his saddlebag. "No."

Mallie nodded. "Sometimes I can't feel my head. It comes off."

Johnny Lee stared out at the Indians.

"Did we go to see the elephant again, Johnny Lee?"

"Goddamn it to hell," Johnny Lee said softly. He crouched in the willows with his right hand caressing the butt of his gun. Mallie's eyes got stuck on the caress: two passes of Johnny Lee's filthy thumb, then a tightening of the whole hand, then the thumb again. Over and over.

"They got food," Johnny Lee said. "Smell it."

Mallie did, but it wasn't like a real smell, it was more like someone was telling him about a smell. He suddenly heard his father's voice *dog smells like a dungheap something wrong with the bitch take her out and shoot her*. He said, "Do they know we're here?"

"Course they know. Indians always know." He spat to one side, and his voice changed. "I can take 'em."

"Take them?"

"Yeah."

"Why? We came from St. Louis." This sounded so reasonable to Mallie that he repeated it. "We came from St. Louis."

Johnny Lee turned his head to gaze at Mallie. At the first touch of that look, flat light eyes in the blackened face, Mallie knew that Johnny Lee hated him. Instantaneous grief flooded him—not surprise but grief, so deep Mallie thought he would drown in it. Johnny Lee hated him, he had no idea why, and it didn't matter why. It only mattered that he did. Johnny Lee—Johnny Lee!—hated him.

"You're a whining coward, you know that, Mallie?"

The detached head answered for him. "Yes."

"Well, I ain't! You hear me—I ain't!" Johnny Lee shouted it. The Indians by the fire disappeared, Mallie couldn't quite tell where. What did he know about Indians—he came from St.

Louis. He tried to repeat this a third time but the detached head wouldn't talk, and anyway Johnny Lee couldn't hear it because he was shouting.

"I ain't no coward and I ain't no dumb kid! I'm prob'ly gonna die tomorrow and so are you, we barely got away from that marshal today, he's close behind—but I ain't no coward like you! I'm, I'm—"

Incredibly, it looked as if Johnny Lee were going to cry. Mallie's hand groped for Johnny Lee's where it rested on the saddlebag. Johnny Lee knocked it aside and hit Mallie in the mouth. Blood spurted across his tongue. Johnny Lee made a horrible noise deep in his throat and raised his gun.

It turned out the Indians hadn't quite disappeared after all because there they were, a feeble ancient brave falling sideways while another raised a rifle to his shoulder. And then Johnny Lee made the throat noise again and went on firing, bolted from the willows and went on firing, charged down the slope firing. Mallie stumbled after him, shouting. By the time he reached the camp the old men and two women lay dead, and Johnny Lee was clicking the empty chambers of both guns over and over in a little metallic song.

One squaw wasn't dead. She lay at Mallie's feet, blood gurgling from a hole in her throat, her eyes on Mallie's face. Vomit rose in him and he started to cry. Before he knew it, he had drawn his gun and fired at her chest. She bucked, twitched, and settled, and Mallie staggered away and choked down his vomit.

The baby wailed. Johnny Lee grabbed it up and crushed in its skull with the butt of his empty gun.

Mallie, swaying on his feet, watched unbelieving. Johnny Lee couldn't be doing that. He couldn't. Therefore he wasn't. The detached head knew that very clearly, knew that none of this was happening because it couldn't be, and so Mallie knew it too and raised his gun and fired twice at Johnny Lee's heart.

Afterward there was a black period. Then a light one,

blindingly bright. It was midday and he was on Johnny Lee's horse, climbing into the mountains of the Wind River Range, and he had never seen anything so clearly in his life. Everything was so sharp it pierced his brain like separate, shining needles: the heavy drag of the saddlebags behind his knees, the smell of pine and sun, the silver thread of stream leading to the incline and the ledge and the boulders and the passage and the cave, all of it so clear and filled with light that Mallie knew his brain would never forget it, not any of it, as long as he lived, forever.

Robbie sat on the toilet lid until he could make himself stop shaking, muscle by muscle. Picking his way over broken glass, he went into the bedroom. The phone, a separate old-fashioned unit, looked naked without a terminal. He punched slowly and carefully. An electronic voice answered:

"You have reached the Institute For Previous Life Access Surgery in Rochester, New York. The Institute does not accept collect calls. We are sorry." *Click.*

He punched again, the credit code number rising unbidden in his mind.

"Institute For Previous Life Access Surgery." The shrill voice of the night receptionist. What time was it in Rochester? He couldn't remember.

"Hello? Hello?"

"Caroline Bohentin, please. She's a client."

"Is this an emergency? It's nearly three in the morning, sir."

"An emergency. Yes."

"Who is calling, please."

"Paul Winter."

"Just a moment, please."

Robbie waited. The room began to click slowly, a little metallic song.

"I'm sorry, we have no record of a Paul Winter on Ms.

Bohentin's authorized call list. In addition, Ms. Bohentin is not here at the moment. I'm sorry, sir. Good-bye."

"Wait!" Robbie cried. "Where did she go? This is her brother. I'm not on the list because she thought I was still on Luna Station, but there's a family emergency involving her father. Colin Cadavy."

"Colin *Cadavy*? Oh, I . . . you didn't hear, then!"

"Hear what? I've been away, away on . . ." He couldn't remember what he had told her.

"I'm sorry to have to tell you this, Mr. Winter," the voice said sympathetically, "but Ms. Bohentin has left for the funeral of her daughter."

"Catherine?"

"I'm so sorry. Can I take a message? Or would you like shielded terminal access to leave her one yourself? Or could I—"

Robbie hung up. He punched the phone again: credit code, call name and city, number search request.

"Meadows Home. Nurse Darrow speaking."

"Caroline Bohentin, please. She's there for her daughter Catherine's death. It's an emergency. This is Paul Winter."

"Just a moment please, Mr. Winter."

It was a long moment. The room stopped clicking. In the corner there had appeared a holo of a long alloy table, like those used in medical labs, centered with a sealed black metal box. Robbie stared at it while Caroline came to the phone.

"Who is this? Who are you?"

"It's Paul Winter, Caroline. Listen—I'm in trouble." He was surprised to hear his own voice wracked with emotion; now why was that happening?

"*Robbie?* Is that you?"

"Yes."

"My God—what's wrong? Where are you?"

"They're dead, Caroline. Johnny Lee Benson and Armand both. I killed them."

He heard her catch her breath. It made him remember; he blurted out, "And your daughter, too. Oh, God, I'm sorry, Caroline. I know you loved her."

"Robbie . . . *Robbie* . . ."

"I loved Armand, too."

"Are you doing blues, Robbie? Or psychos? Do you have any brainies to bring you down?"

"Nothing. I'm so sorry about Catherine, love."

"I—where are you? Why did you say your name was Paul Winter?"

"He was there," Robbie said. "At the Sweetwater. Watching. But it was too late."

"Where are you?"

"Wyoming."

"Why?"

"Money. From a past life," Robbie said, and his head felt a little clearer. Yes, of course. The holo in the corner, he saw, had disappeared.

"And you're in trouble—"

"Yes. No. No, I—" He couldn't remember what he had been going to say, or why he had called her.

"Robbie, listen to me. Listen." Caroline spoke slowly and carefully now. Despite himself, it made Robbie grin. He was feeling more like himself every minute.

"You sound like you're talking to a child, love."

She made a strangled, despairing sound he didn't understand. But her voice stayed slow and clear. "You said you're in trouble. What can I do?"

"Nothing. I'm not in trouble." Had he really said that? Why?

"Robbie—how did you find me?"

"I called the Institute and said I was your brother. They told me you were away for Catherine's funeral. So I called her Home."

"But—they wouldn't have given you the name of the Home. Even if you did say you were my brother. No one there even knows the name of the Home, except for Patrick Shahid. And Joe. Did you talk to Joe?"

"No. I—no." He felt himself getting confused again.

"Then how did you know where to call me? Robbie?"

The confusion came closer, shot with flashes of light. Robbie said quickly, "Take care, Caroline. I'm really sorry about Catherine."

"No, don't hang up! Robbie? Robbie!"

He punched the call closed, willing the confusion and light to go away. They did. He was all right.

He was all right, and utterly exhausted.

He crawled into the bed and pulled the blankets up to his chin. He tried not to think, about anything. But just before he slept, an image came to him strongly: the woman with the black braids in the motel office. He saw her face clearly and realized, for the first time, that she must be at least part Indian; realized, more significantly, that she was really beautiful; realized, most significantly of all, that he had not even noticed.

13 CAROLINE

Caroline sat still and dry-eyed through the short funeral service for Catherine. The chapel of the Meadows Home had none of the grace of the Institute chapel. Neutral pine-paneled walls, electric lighting, featureless pews. Catherine's ashes rested in a rose-colored alloy box on the altar—Caroline supposed it was an altar; in its quest for ecumenicism, it might have been a restaurant table. Catherine's father sat in the pew ahead of her, his head bent. Caroline sat trying to remember her daughter as an infant, a toddler; she could not.

The only thoughts that would come concerned the immediate moment: This pew is hard. Charles is beginning to go bald at the back. The chaplain's voice is more careful than even Patrick Shahid's. The air smells of rain. It was, she thought wearily, a kind of emotional Korsakov's syndrome: all reactions invented at the moment, to the moment, the real past lost.

" 'As for man, his days are as grass,' " the chaplain read. " 'As a flower of the field, so he flourisheth. For the wind passeth over it, and it is gone . . .' " A woman Caroline didn't know began to cry soundlessly. She must be a nurse, an aide, someone who had taken care of Catherine. But it wasn't Catherine that had made her cry, Caroline thought; it was the beauty of the King James language, the heartbreaking dignity of words. The woman, whoever she was, obviously hadn't grown up with enough words, enough winds, enough flowers that flourisheth nightly at eight, matinees twice weekly. Shakespeare. Anouilh. Vaessen. The woman had missed her inoculation. She wasn't immune.

He came in halfway through the service. Caroline knew the moment; she heard it in the here-comes-a-celebrity-don't-turn-your-head-now-though murmurs. A memory did surface, then: herself at fifteen, choking with laughter, Colin's voice with its lilting cadences: "Why don't they just bloody well *stare*. God preserve us from furtive good breeding."

But she couldn't remember Catherine. Try as she would, stony in her solitary pew, the living memories of her dead daughter would not come.

" 'To every thing there is a season, and a time for every purpose under the heaven: A time to be born and a time to die . . . ' " *Bloody hell*, Caroline thought. What did this mild, inoffensive minister know of time, or birth, or death, or what those meant now, in this age of plazzing and carnies and plague? Time itself had changed, had mutated past the two-thousand-year-old words of comfort that probably had never been much comfort in the first place. Was it a comfort to know you would have a time to die? Was it a comfort to know you wouldn't? Was it a comfort to know you would both die and be born again from the over-memory but wouldn't remember either one?

She should not have allowed this religious service at all. But Charles had wanted it, a Charles who asked with such painful humbleness—from *Charles*, the human volcano, exploding at the slightest opposition—that she had agreed. But she could not sit here, she could not, with her lifeless memories of Catherine and with Charles bent in the seat ahead and Colin somewhere behind undoubtedly shedding perfectly shaped actor's tears and this simpleminded vestigial mouthpiece for a concept of time as dead as Catherine. She could not sit here a moment longer, if she did she would shriek or yell or tear her hair—

—A sudden memory of women in a circle, herself among them, wailing beside a gray-green river, above a young bronzed warrior decked with flowers.

" 'A time to get, and a time to lose—' "

Caroline groped for her purse. Under the tissues and data-remote and makeup her hand closed on the blue-glazed porcelain box Shahid had given her. She drew it onto her lap and held it tightly, her eyes closed, her thumb circling over the glassy surface. Linyi. Tsemo. The sound of the flute and the courtyard filled with light, with peace, with her children's laughter—

The memories would not come.

Caroline's eyes jerked open. She couldn't remember that perfect, tranquil life, she couldn't remember—or rather, she could, but the memories were detached, cold, secondhand. She couldn't *feel* it. She tried again, her hand tightening so hard on the porcelain that the cover slipped off the box and clattered to the floor. Charles half turned in his pew, turned back. His cheeks were wet.

Gone. The memories of her one perfect life, the one time of serenity. Gone. Like those of Catherine, those of her baby. Linyi, the flute, the courtyard . . . It had all happened to someone else, long ago, in another country. And they all were dead.

" 'All go unto one place; all are of the dust, and all turn to dust again . . .' "

Gone.

"Oh, fuck. Fuck, fuck, fuck," Caroline said softly, but not softly enough. Charles's shoulders stiffened in shock, then again in fury.

Caroline placed the porcelain box back in her purse. She left the cover lying on the floor. In front of her the ugly altar with its sealed rose-colored box blurred, and in the blur of tears the rose box softened around the edges and spread, soft as dust, large enough to stretch to the end of her vision and shroud it completely.

On the sidewalk outside the chapel, Colin was the first one to reach her. He took both her hands in his. "Callie. Callie . . ."

Caroline looked through him. Sun shone on the scrubbed stone walks, the late-summer marigolds and chrysanthemums bordering the Home cottages. A few of the maples had begun to turn color on the sides facing the sun.

Colin said sonorously, "There isn't any loss like that of a child."

"How would *you* know?"

He didn't drop her hands. "Who should know better?"

Caroline pulled away. *All gone.* "What's that supposed to mean—that you've lost *me*? Well, you're right. You have. But I'll be damned if I'll feel guilty about it at my daughter's funeral."

"Callie, Callie—I don't want you to feel guilty. I've never wanted that. I want to help. Please—let me help."

"Very nice, Colin. But don't let your voice break quite so much in the middle."

He was silent so long that people who had begun to approach her and turned away at the sound of angry words between father and daughter began to approach again. Before anyone could actually reach them, he said softly, "You're not ever going to let me help you, are you? With anything. That would be too much forgiveness."

"Oh, God, spare me the Act III curtain lines."

His face did something complicated. Caroline felt a hand jerk her shoulder; Charles turned her roughly to face him. At the sight of his red eyes, of the deep lines from his nose to his chin, Caroline said softly, "Charles—I'm sorry I spoiled your funeral, Charles."

Fury leapt into his eyes; he thought she was mocking him. Whereas Colin, whom she *was* mocking, stood looking at her with such gentle understanding that she wanted to hit him, wanted to snarl and claw and bite. *All gone*.

Charles said through closed teeth, "I want Catherine's ashes. To keep."

"Yes."

" 'Yes'? Just like that? You'll give them to me?"

"Yes."

"Why?"

Something broke. Caroline reached out one last time for Linyi, knowing it was one last time . . . the courtyard, the flute, the children's laughter . . . It was gone. Cold. Dead.

"Because that isn't Catherine. It hasn't been Catherine for years. Not without her memory, her mind—take the ashes, Charles. I don't want them. Colin, let go of me!"

"Callie—let me help . . ."

She started walking away from the chapel, her heels pounding on the stone walk. Jason saw her coming and opened the door of the aircar. Footsteps sounded behind her, but she didn't turn. Just as she reached the car, Patrick Shahid slipped his arm around her shoulders. He had to reach up to do so; Caroline leaned her cheek against the top of his head. Jason turned courteously away.

"I didn't see you there, Patrick," she whispered.

"I came in late and sat in the back."

"They're gone."

"What are, Caroline?"

"The memories."

"Of what?"

"Past lives. And Catherine. They're there, but I can't reach them."

Shahid drew her into the car. To Jason he said, "Come back in ten minutes." Jason nodded and disappeared; Caroline realized for the first time that somewhere in his unknown life in

Pakistan, Shahid must have been used to servants, used to giving orders. That natural tone had to be learned early, or it was always strained.

He said, "What do you mean, you can't reach the memories?"

"They feel like they happened to someone else. They're *cold*, Patrick. They're gone."

"You mean they are gone as an escape for you." She didn't answer. "But they should never have been that in the first place, you know, Caroline. It was only your need that made memory an escape."

"And what the hell am I supposed to do with this stupid so-called need now?"

He didn't answer her directly. "Where are you going in the aircar?"

"I don't know. Back to the Institute, I guess."

Shahid looked at her black dress and headband. "Where are your bags?"

"Here. At the Home guest house. I was supposed to stay one more night. You can't have the surgery done because you are Catholic, can you? Because the Pope has forbidden it."

Shahid stared straight ahead. "There is but one rebirth, and that in Christ."

"Oh, Patrick. Oh, bloody hell. You're the one who wants it so bad you can taste it."

Shahid didn't answer. Through the car window Caroline saw Jason intercepting anyone who tried to approach the aircar, politely turning them back. Conscientious, efficient. Caroline lit a cigarette. For a few minutes she smoked in silence.

"You may as well stay here and tend to Catherine's things," Shahid said. "I have a seat on an airbus back to the Institute."

Caroline extended her arm toward the back of the front seat; a flexible chute grew toward it, sucked in her cigarette, and began to clean the air. The smoke had suddenly refused to go down her lungs any longer. It felt thick, a solid and slimy grayness stuck in her throat. "All right."

"Caroline," Shahid said so gently she had to turn toward him to hear, "it would help if you cried."

"No," Caroline said. "Do you know what happens when I cry? I talk. I spew out the most incredible garbage—tearful justifications and melodramatic howls against heaven and grandiose plans to redeem my life—and then after I'm done inventing all that rot I start laughing and can't stop. And I just don't have the energy for it, Patrick. I don't."

Shahid put his hand over hers. "You need somewhere to put the energy you do have, Caroline."

Caroline didn't answer. It didn't seem to her that Shahid knew any more about how to do that than she did, or what was he doing agonizing over a data anomaly, trying to elevate it to divinity? She wanted to ask him about what he had said in the Institute chapel, about what it meant to him, but she was too worn out with questions. She tried to picture Catherine, but every image she made seemed flat, a photograph of a child, lacking even the three-dimensional roundness of a holo. Through the window she saw Jason talking with her father, keeping him away, both of their lips moving soundlessly on the other side of the bulletproof glass.

That night the phone knocked her out of a fitful sleep. She groped for it in the unfamiliar darkness of the guest cottage at the Meadows Home.

"Ms. Bohentin? I'm sorry to wake you. You have an emergency call. One moment, please."

"What— Who is this? Who are you?"

"It's Paul Winter, Caroline. Listen, I'm in trouble."

Paul Winter? She sat fuddled with sleep on the edge of the bed, unable at first to place the voice. "*Robbie?* Is that you?"

"Yes."

"My God—what's wrong? Where are you?"

"They're dead, Caroline. Johnny Lee Benson and Armand both. I killed them."

Paul Winter. Armand. She saw Bill Prokop's desperate face, the murder pictures he had forced on her by the flower bed, and all at once what Robbie was saying hit her. His voice added, "And your daughter, too. Oh, God, I'm sorry, Caroline. I know you loved her."

When she could get words out, she said, "Robbie . . . Robbie . . . "

"I loved Armand, too."

"Are you doing blues, Robbie? Or psychos? Do you have any brainies to bring you down?"

"Nothing. I'm just so sorry about Catherine, love."

Now the voice subtly wasn't his. Caroline, her hand still on the phone, squeezed her eyes shut. "I—where are you? Why did you say your name was Paul Winter?"

"He was there. At the Sweetwater. Watching. But it was too late."

None of that made any sense. Robbie's voice slipped a few notes lower and slurred slightly, making the words even harder to understand. *Sweetwater?* She heard his panic, his disorientation, his clutching out for her in the dark—

—and the memory was there, strong and vivid and as immediate as anything in the room, more immediate, *real.* Timmy, curled against her in the bed, his small hand clutching his pillowcase, his voice slurred with earache and sleepiness. Timmy. The sound of his congested breathing, the sturdiness of the small back under her hand. Real. Alive.

She said, "Where are you?"

"Wyoming."

"Why?"

"Money. From a past life." The voice cleared, steadied. "And you're in trouble—"

"Yes. No. No, I—"

"Robbie, listen to me. Listen." She spoke slowly and carefully: to Timmy, to Catherine.

He caught it. "You sound like you're talking to a child, love," he said, and she heard the difference in his tone immediately: clearer, stronger. She was losing him.

Quickly she said, "You said you're in trouble. What can I do?"

"Nothing. I'm not in trouble."

She was losing him. "Robbie—how did you find me?"

"I called the Institute and said I was your brother. They told me you were away for Catherine's funeral. So I called her Home."

"But—they wouldn't have given you the name of the Home. Even if you did say you were my brother. No one there even knows the name of the Home, except for Patrick Shahid. And Joe. Did you talk to Joe?"

"No. I—no." She heard his confusion returning, but she had to keep him talking, had to keep him on the line until he told her where he was. Timmy. Catherine.

"Then how did you know where to call me? Robbie?"

"Take care. Caroline. I'm really sorry about Catherine."

"No, don't hang up! Robbie? Robbie!" The line clicked.

Caroline sat on the edge of the bed, thinking furiously. She groped for the light and punched in Joe McLaren's direct line at the Institute. The terminal clock glowed yellow: 3:13 A.M. Joe answered on the second ring. "McLaren."

"Joe—it's Caroline. In Albany. I need your help."

"What is it, Caroline?" There was something complex in his voice, but no trace of sleepiness.

"I just got a call from—someone very important to me. He's in trouble. But we got cut off and I know he won't call back. I need to know exactly where he is. You're a lawyer, you're part of that Blue-Ribbon Presidential Commission, you must know people who either have access to the phone net or can break into it. Fast, I mean. I need to have the number and exact location now."

He was silent too long. "That's not legal, Caroline."

"But you can do it?"

"It's Robbie Brekke, isn't it?"

"Does it matter who it is? I'm asking you, as a friend."

"As a *friend?*" His voice scaled upward. "Knowing what I think about law, knowing what it could cost my professional reputation to break it? As a friend?" Caroline sat, willing herself to wait. She wanted to call him a prig, a Boy Scout, a goddamn niggler interested only in protecting himself. But she forced herself to wait; her best chance was Joe himself. She could sense him, two hundred miles away, struggling for control of himself.

"I'm sorry I shouted at you, Caroline. It's been quite a day. My secretary, Angel—never mind. And you went today to Catherine's—I'm sorry."

"Shout at me if you want, but help me. Robbie was my child, too, just as much as Catherine was."

She heard his quick indrawn breath, ragged, as if he had been breathing hard.

"He was, Joe. You can't deny it."

"You can't do it that way, Caroline," he said, more gently even than she had hoped. "That was another life."

"He's alive in this one. And he needs me."

"I'm sorry, Caroline."

"Joe—*listen.* He's in real trouble. Something about his past lives isn't working right. He remembers being Paul Winter"— she didn't even slow down for his reaction— "and it's affecting his brain. I don't know how. But he needs me!"

"He needs Shahid, or Armstrong. Have you—"

"They couldn't find out where he is, and you can!"

"I'm sorry. I can't help you."

"You mean you won't!"

"I can't."

"This isn't some abstract on choice and inventing the self, Joe, this is a real live human being! My son!"

"I'm sorry."

Caroline cut off the call. She forced herself to go into the bathroom, wash her face, brush her teeth. She would give him twenty minutes—and then who? Charles? He might be able to do it through political connections, but he never would. A friend? There were none with that kind of datanet connections, or at any rate none who would help her. Over the past years she had not paid much attention to friends. They belonged to a discarded past, a past in which Catherine had talked, learned, laughed, lived . . .

Caroline dressed in jeans and a warm sweater and packed her bag. Twenty minutes later the phone rang.

"Caroline? Take down these numbers, they're phone and air coordinates." Joe's voice giving the numbers was tight and clipped. "He's in the township of Sanderton, there's no actual town, in Wyoming. Near the Wind River Mountains. At the Rock End Motel."

Her own handwriting looked jagged, unfamiliar. She started to thank him, but he cut her off. "How did Brekke know where you were? Did you talk to him after he left the Institute two days ago and before you heard about Catherine?"

"No. He called the Institute and they told him I'd left for the—for Catherine's Home. But I don't know how he even knew what city it was in. Why?"

"Is that the truth, Caroline?"

"Yes!"

"Then you don't know how he got the credit number he used to call you from Wyoming?"

"Got it? What do you mean? Wasn't it his?"

"No."

"Whose was it?" *Paul Winter's*, she thought. But, no—Paul Winter was long dead, his number inactive. "Whose?"

Joe said, "Mine."

She struggled to make sense of this. "You didn't give it to him?"

"Of course not."

"He steals."

"But not my credit number. I'm not that careless, and he's not that good. And if he's working for somebody that good, I'm too petty to bother with."

"Then how—"

"It won't do you any good to call him now, Caroline. We tried. The line's dead. Not just inactive—*dead*. He either disconnected or cut the line. And the motel desk doesn't answer."

" 'We'? Who's 'we'? Who did you tell about Robbie!"

"I gave you the phone number in case he decides to re-connect the line. So you can keep trying."

His tone made her wince. She said, humbly and with resentment, "Thank you, Joe. I do know what this must be costing you . . ."

"You don't know what anything costs," Joe said, and broke the call.

Caroline pressed both hands to her forehead. A moment later she had turned on the wall terminal, paid for full library access, and was scanning maps. Sanderton, Wyoming, had a reported population of thirty-two. The closest airport was Lander. She punched in the charter airline Colin had always used and entered her credit data.

How had Robbie gotten Joe's?

It didn't matter. Why should it? Whatever Robbie was, he was solid and alive, as Catherine was not. *The past is dead*, Joe and Patrick had both said to her in their different voices: Joe's cold reason that left him the most alone person she had ever seen, Shahid's tortured longing for a God he could see nowhere else. And both had been right, both had been wrong. Catherine was dead to her, Linyi and her children were dead to her, even

Timmy asleep with his small earache had been dead since June, 1976. But something of the past had been left to her. Robbie, linked by memory to Timmy and so to her, was alive, and in trouble, and in need of her help.

Where did the bonds of maternity end? All children grew up, changed, became somebody else. Parents who trembled that they might lose a gap-toothed toddler to some terrible accident ended up losing him anyway, always, to time. The toddlers died, after all, and what was left was a bond with another adult, who had once been the beloved child. Did it really make so much difference whether that child—flesh of one's flesh, bone of one's bone—had existed twenty years ago, or fifty-five? Did it matter whether the intense maternal love—*this is my child, whom I would die for*—was forged one lifetime ago, or three? Emotional time was more flexible than she had ever dreamed.

The terminal responded two minutes after she had typed, "Urgent—will pay three times top priority rates." A human voice, not a computer, even at three-thirty in the morning; a respectful human face, even at full-color transmission rates. Caroline chartered a plane and pilot, an aircar to be flown in from Rawlins, and a driver who knew the terrain in Wyoming.

14 JOE

       The phone had rung the first time at 2 A.M. Joe, startled out of fitful sleep, had thought first of Caroline, then of Pirelli, then of Robin. If Caroline was calling him from Albany, maybe needing to talk in that long night between the day of the funeral and the day she could drive back . . . he fumbled for the light switch, the phone receiver. But, no, far more likely to be Pirelli, already overdue with the report on plague testing. Or a report on Robin . . . or, oh God, Robin herself, his number passed on by a self-righteous Pirelli . . .

It was Angel Whittaker.

The music was off in Angel's apartment. It was the first thing Joe noticed: that weird absence of sound, stranding Angel's handsome, ravaged face in silence as completely as a dolphin without water. Deep lines ran from the corners of Angel's nose to his grim mouth. He stared outward from the screen without blinking. *"Hola, compadre."*

Joe said quietly, "You're finally going to tell me what's wrong."

"Yeah." The young man glanced off-screen, then back. *Hunted*, Joe thought.

"Who's there with you Angel?"

"Nobody. But the cops will be, in about five minutes."

"Why? How do you know?"

"They phoned. Said not to run."

"They don't do that. Unless it's—"

"Yeah. A Special Custody Act."

Joe's mouth felt dry. The Special Custody Acts were relics from before the Caswell neo-Libertarian administration, when government had had more power, not less. Power designed and shaped toward specific ends which nobody, not even neo-Libertarians, had after all chosen to revoke. "Which Special Custody Act?"

"R-52," Angel said, but even before Angel answered, Joe knew. Things added up furiously in his head, words and evasions and clues he had seen but not put together. Had not wanted to put together.

"You've committed homosexual acts."

Anger flared in Angel's dark eyes. "Christ, listen to you! You make it sound like grand larceny or murder one! I *am* homosexual. That's who I *am*."

Joe said nothing. The Special Custody Acts came from a time when to be a male homosexual was to risk committing murder one, through ignorance if not defiance. In the 1990s, at the height of the first plague, the AIDS one, the zeal for public protection had not made fine distinctions.

"I need help," Angel said. His face wore a curious mixture of defiance, sullenness, and pleading.

"Of course," Joe said. "Tell the cops I'm your attorney of record, and that they have to talk to me. That will hold until we can find someone with experience in this area of defense. Then don't say a word, Angel. Not a word. I'll call the D.A. and see what she'll tell me about the charges—"

"No," Angel said. His mouth worked briefly, and he glanced down. His lashes made spiky shadows on his cheeks. "I don't want you to defend me."

"Then what—"

"I want you to make the charges go away."

It took a moment for Joe to realize what he was saying.

"You got real powerful friends," Angel said. He leaned forward, into the screen; Joe shifted backward. "Even if you choose to practice in this low-rent place, *pro bono*, even if you only got on the Plague Commission through Pirelli—you go to meetings at the White House! Your friend Esterhazy is going to be tapped for Justice, everybody knows it, Pat Gocek is a federal judge, even your crazy *compadre* Pirelli has pull—"

"My God, Angel—"

"The kind of pull my kind never gets!" Angel shouted. "They want to law us out of existence, you know it as well as I do, I don't have any fucking AIDS virus and you know it!"

"I know it," Joe said as calmly as he could manage.

"It's homophobia, pure and simple, nothing fucking else. Find a cure, eliminate AIDS, but keep the laws on the books for how good they are in exterminating us—"

"The laws stayed because nobody ever changed them," Joe said. His hand shook, only one hand, which made no sense. "And because there are CDC statistics showing that other mutated viruses have started their spread with the gay population." *Including the plague.* But that was new, classified information from Pirelli's file, as uncertain in statistical significance as it was horrible in implications.

"Bullshit!" Angel screamed. "Joe, listen, I need you, man, they're going to lock me up in some dark hole for life, I need your help! You've got to help me! You've got to get the charges erased!"

Angel's fear was palpable, heating the screen like fever. Joe wanted to close his eyes, to blank the terminal. "I can't."

"You've got to! You've got to, man! You've got to get the charges deleted!"

"I *can't*."

"You mean you won't," Angel said. "I know goddamn well you *can*, Counselor."

Joe said evenly, "That's right, then. I won't. I'll do everything I can to help your defense, Angel, you're entitled under law to the best defense the system can—"

"Don't bother," Angel said. His hysteria vanished. He stared out at Joe from the screen, his eyes flat and black and shiny as a bird's. "You won't help because you don't want to. Because you believe in the goddamn law. Because you think it *is* a crime to fuck another man."

"I think it's a crime because the Congress of the United States made it one, for good and sufficient reason," Joe said, knowing how he sounded, unable to stop. "For the common good. And without law—" He stopped. There was no use explaining; it was an obscenity to even try, given what Angel faced. A small fierce flame of anger ignited in him, that people's choices should be able to make an obscenity out of necessary law.

"Wipe your hard drive with it, Counselor," Angel said harshly. "I know you. You don't just think it's a crime. You sit there with your safe gringo education and your government-approved maleness and your nice Catholic boy guilt and you think who I love is a fucking *sin.*"

Pounding started off screen. Angel turned his head toward the sound. In a voice Joe had never heard before, shrill and thin with fear, he said, "Oh, God—"

"Angel . . . Angel!" The screen went dead.

Joe called back instantly. He could talk to the cops, make sure they read Angel his rights, impress them with legal jargon . . . the terminal said cheerfully, "We're sorry—your call cannot go through. The terminal at the other end of your call has been manually disconnected. We're sorry—your call cannot—"

Joe sat still a long moment, thinking. He drank a glass of water from the bedside table and then called a Washington number, the best attorney he could think of with Special Custody Acts experience. The lawyer listened intently and

promised, despite the hour, to go down to the station immediately. He warned Joe not to expect too much. "Nobody," he
said grimly, "has ever beaten an R-52 since 1993. Maybe it's
about time somebody did."

Joe didn't answer. There was no way he could say to Angel's
lawyer that maybe nobody should.

He lay in the darkness, tossing and turning, unable to sleep.
Images kept coming to him: Robin when they had first been
married. Pirelli when they had been kids in Pittsburgh. Caroline in the blue dress. Angel, in jail. In a cramped filthy cell,
in an unwatched recreation area with an R-52 conviction plas-
tered to him. None of the images seemed connected, except in
their power to knot his stomach. The only thing he felt grateful
for, lying in the thick, cold black air, was that no memories
came from past lives as well.

Finally he got up from bed, drank another glass of water,
answered the phone to Caroline's frantic call, begging him to
use his influence to break the law to get her Robbie Brekke's
number in Wyoming.

Joe sat in the Institute dining room, eating a meal somewhere between breakfast and lunch, a salad with a creamy
real-cucumber dressing he barely tasted. Three other Institute
clients sat, each singly, around the room, having coffee or a
sandwich; Joe recognized none of them. New surgical clients,
arrived in time for tonight's orientation reception. Armstrong,
Park, the holo of a giant brain crawling with light. Sandy Ochs,
who had disappeared as swiftly and cleanly as a scalpel cut. The
three new patients all glanced furtively at Joe's face; each
looked away, frowning.

Jeff Pirelli walked through the dining room's antique double doors draped with filmy white silk. Joe held a forkful of
lettuce and green pepper suspended halfway to his mouth and
stared; Pirelli had been here only yesterday and had not told
him he was coming again this morning. Pirelli's round face

looked haggard. He needed a shave, stubble dotted his chin like fly specks on suet. Even when he sat down at the table he didn't smile.

"God, I hate flying in the early morning."

Joe put the forkful of lettuce back into the bowl. "I said I'm not going, Jeff."

"Skipton says you are."

"You took this to the *Vice President*?"

"He's the nominal head of the Plague Commission, remember? Just because he doesn't do anything for it doesn't mean we don't keep him informed. We tell him, he tells Caswell."

Joe buttered a cracker he didn't want. "There's nothing to inform anyone about. At least not where I'm concerned personally."

"There's plenty. You know Brekke, and Brekke is some sort of key. He and his Paul Winter past. Plugging that into the data scans has done unbelievable things to the math, Joey. The plague started, somehow, around Winter. It all points to that crazy bastard Armand Kyle. When his home lab was trashed, the night of the murder—that was already speculation for years, you know that. Only now it appears that something else got started that night, too, something nobody suspected, and Brekke is the key."

"So go get Brekke yourself. You don't need me. Why aren't there agents picking him up right this minute in Wyoming? You know where he is."

"Agents are. But I need you there, too. Skipton is leary about this—it's just too weird for him—"

"It's just too weird for me!" Joe burst out, and regretted it instantly. Pirelli regarded him calmly. "There's something else you're not telling me, Jeff. You could take other people who know Brekke, experts . . . Dr. Shahid, Dr. Armstrong . . ."

"Skipton says you go."

"You told Skipton what to say, and you know it. You filled him full of mathematical double-talk and impressive colored holos of mathematical models and pretty soon he gave up just to avoid the one-thousand-thousandth chance that the sun will go nova if he doesn't listen to you. He's half a Gaeist anyway; go with the flow, and at that moment the flow was you. But I don't want any part of this, Jeff. Reincarnation surgery and the plague have nothing to do with each other."

Pirelli said, "We have the results from the initial preplague testing."

Joe's gaze snapped to Pirelli's. "What did you find out?"

"We found out who has the slow virus present in the hippocampus in its preactive phase."

"Who does?"

"Everybody."

"*What?*"

"Everybody has the virus in the brain already. All the randomly chosen volunteers, all the medical staff, everyone on the Commission who the medical team could get to hold still and be tested. They went a little crazy. And even crazier when it turned out everybody has it: Sholomeis, Esterhazy, Donatelli, Bevington, Lin, Kushall. Me."

Joe stared at him. "You mean, everyone is going to get the plague? Everyone alive?"

"No. It doesn't seem to work like that. Only some people get it. Everyone has the seed, but only in some people does it ripen. Like the parable of wheat seeds falling on stone, on water, on fertile soil. Some brains are a fertile environment for the plague virus and some are not."

Words were having trouble getting past Joe's throat. "Which are which?"

"We don't know. All we have is what we know from the statistics: Nobody who has ever had, or ever will have, carnie surgery has developed plague. So you're going to Wyoming with me to talk to Paul Winter Brekke."

Joe sat still, trying to absorb the enormity of what Pirelli had said. Everybody carried the hippocampal slow virus . . .

everybody . . . "Jeff—having the surgery might well make the brain a less fertile environment for plague. I accept that as a medical possibility, if Sholomeis's team says it is. But this bullshit about nobody getting plague now because they'll make a decision in the future to have surgery—no. *No*. Decisions don't work that way, *choice* doesn't work that way—"

"You're shouting at me," Pirelli said coldly, and Joe realized that he was. The other lone diners stared at him open-mouthed. Three men stood at the dining-room doors; Joe was aware of them only vaguely. He felt choked with anger he didn't understand. Pirelli stood up.

"You're coming with me to Wyoming. You're still a member of the Commission."

"I resign."

Pirelli moved his hand, and the three men walked into the room. They were U.S. marshals.

No one said anything.

Joe crumpled his napkin, put it on the table, and stood up. His knees shook, which made him angrier. He locked them and said as calmly as he could, "What is your authority?"

"Special Custody Act R-52."

"For *me?*"

"The only one we could get that fast. And it applies—Paul Winter was a homosexual. You associate with Robbie Brekke. No, of course you're not committing acts against the law. But I didn't think you'd come of your own free will. And I was right."

"You know a Special Custody Act will finish me in Washington." He thought of Angel, arrested at the same time, his secretary . . .

"Only if I have to use it. So come voluntarily with me to Wyoming, Joe."

Joe looked at Pirelli. For a flash of time he had a memory so vivid, so intense, he couldn't place it and thought it was from a past life of unusual power. Then he had it: Pirelli as a kid, crouched over his keyboard like a guerrilla over a gun mount, grinning insanely as he moved around supplies, people, weapons in an electronic war game against a teenage team from Jamestown: *We got 'em! We got the bastards cornered . . .* In one swift motion Joe stood up and hit Pirelli in the mouth.

The fat man staggered backward against one of the marshals. The other two sprang forward and grabbed Joe's arms hard. Pirelli struggled to right himself and waved them off, looking at Joe with disbelief that gradually changed to something harder but not, Joe thought with a kind of dull surprise, any colder. Pirelli reached for Joe's discarded napkin to wipe away a thin trickle of blood from one corner of his mouth.

"Jeff . . . *I'm sorry.*"

Pirelli smiled thinly, rubbing his jaw. "Good. Nobody gets sorrier than you always did. You'll get so goddamn sorry you'll lash yourself into a frenzy of self-abasement, and then you'll cooperate just to atone. Ah, Joey, you should have stayed a Catholic."

Joe stared straight ahead. Pirelli led the way from the dining room to an aircar waiting at the front driveway. Pirelli and one marshal, who drove, sat in front. Joe was squeezed in the back between the other two marshals, both huge men. A rare unbidden memory came to him: riding three abreast in a troika between two heavy bodies smelling of sweat and dirty fur across a barren tundra. Snow on his eyelids, winds whipping across his bare cheeks.

Pirelli half turned in his seat. "We'll take a government plane at the airport, then another car. Agents should already have Brekke. I hope. They'll report in soon."

Joe said, just as if it were an answer, "Individual decisions are not caused retroactively by totally unrelated circumstances."

"Right," Pirelli said; it seemed Joe had finally made him angry. "And no cell in my body influences any other."

"I am not a cell, Pirelli. *I am not a cell.*"

"Right again. You're not connected to anything else. And by the way, Robin sends her regards. Angel does, too."

The aircar lifted. Just before it turned to fly south toward the Rochester airport, Joe glanced across the bulk of a U.S. marshal to see Bill Prokop, half-dressed, running from the Institute toward the lifting car. In one hand he waved a portable terminal, in the other his shirt; his face was twisted with desperation as he called something absorbed by the window glass. Then the car turned and sped away, and Prokop was lost to view.

15 ROBBIE

Robbie woke feeling wonderful. Sweet morning air streamed in the window, smelling of pine. Through a crack in the drawn curtains, pale gray light suffused the room. All the confusion had left Robbie's head. He had no dreams. He sprang out of bed, enjoying the satisfying *whomp!* of his feet striking the floor.

A memory came to him: waking under steamy palms, soaked in dread and sweat, small insects working at his flesh like fine-bit drills. Where? Liberia. So it had been *this* life, not another. The realization made him laugh out loud.

The motel room, like the front office the night before, was bare, shabby, and clean. Bed with scarred headboard, green army blankets, green-painted dresser with one drawer chipped at the corner. A bedside table held the lamp and old-fashioned, off-line phone, its cord pulled from the wall. The single chair was dotted with cigarette burns. Under Robbie's feet the cracked vinyl floor was cold, even though he had slept in his socks. Whistling, he padded into the bathroom.

The broken glass all over the floor brought him up short for a moment, but he stepped carefully over it into the shower. Twenty minutes later he slid into the seat of the aircar, wet leaves from the woods still clinging to his shoes. He scuffed the leaves off onto the car's gray carpet—clean yesterday morning, filthy now—and carefully backed the car from its hiding place under the trees. It lifted silently. He flew just ten or fifteen feet above the ground, completely on manual, dividing his gaze between the terrain below and the screen graphics that let him retrace exactly his route of the night before.

Nothing seemed hard to do. He watched for the black aircar; it didn't appear. He watched inside his head; nothing unwelcome appeared there, either. The memories that had fought inside him yesterday—Mallie's memories, Paul Winter's, Robbie Brekke's—lay still.

Whatever that craziness had been, it was over. Today was the day he got rich. Today was the breakthrough, the main run, the deserved reward. Today was the big one.

"God bless 'em all, Hatton and Paul, beautiful Caroline tooooo," Robbie sang, off-key and not caring, keeping time with one foot on the leaf-sodden floor.

"God bless 'em all, They're what I call The ticket to do what I do."

No—"My ticket right out of this zoo."

No—"My reason to fuck them aaa-new!"

But he never had gotten the chance to fuck Caroline. Too bad. Pretty, rich, intelligent, rich, warm-hearted, rich . . . but too complicated. Now that he had time to think about it at a distance of two thousand miles, *way* too complicated. And too vulnerable. Her daughter, her father . . . sooner or later there would have been bonds he was far better off without. And he and Caroline could remain friends. And after he reached the money in the cave—not the gold, that was paltry, but the diamond, all eleven gorgeous carats of it—and took off for Africa or England or South America—money went far in South America if you stayed away from the war, farther still if you didn't. There would be other women as desirable as Caroline. Or almost, anyway.

The ground beneath the aircar grew wilder, forcing Robbie to lift it higher. He had a clear picture of the area he had searched yesterday, or at least until the end of yesterday when things had gotten so confusing. Now he leaned out the window to study the terrain below, chose a ridge with a logical approach for Mallie's horse, and set the aircar down below the first of the incline, ledge, rock-face combinations that matched his memory.

On the third try, he found it.

The air was completely still. Hiking up the incline, Robbie noticed first the preternatural quiet. No breeze. No small animal stirring in the grass. No distant splash of water. The silence was more like the desert than the mountains, he thought, heavy and clear, like the weight of crystal. Sometimes that happened just before an earthquake—Christ, an earthquake out here, with him scrambling between boulders and the aircar damaged beyond flying . . . Then the memory came, sharp as a bayonet: Mallie, seeing this same place, sight tuned to a painful pitch by what fever was doing to his brain, hearing nothing. *This same place*. Robbie forgot the silence and began to run, struggling up the incline, panting, grinning.

In 140 years more rocks had slid down the cliff face. The pattern of trees had altered: tall pine where there had been only grass, cedar saplings growing from the decay of what he remembered as a thick copse. It seemed to Robbie that the very colors of the place had changed, intensifying to an eye-piercing purity, although even in his excitement this didn't seem likely.

He struggled up the incline to the ledge above and followed it along the face of uneven, striated stone. Fallen rocks and rubble littered his way. At the eastern end the ledge ended in a rockfall; at the western end it turned abruptly, narrowed, and angled slightly downward. After about twenty feet this hidden rough ravine, squeezed here into a passage of little more than a foot by two huge boulders, once again began to climb. It folded in on itself and became a maze of granite outcroppings, sloping cliff faces, and hidden caves.

Some of the caves were little more than shallow indenta-

tions in the rock. Others looked deep and dark, and Robbie
could hear in them the distant murmur of subterranean
streams. It was not as hard as he had expected to locate the one
he wanted, despite its obscure entrance; Mallie Callahan had
not had the strength for careful choosing. The entrance was
only about eighteen inches high, a low slit covered by brush.
Robbie cut the brush away, turned on his powerful flashlight,
and lay flat on his belly. He peered inside.

A foot in, the cave abruptly widened and rose to the size of
his room at the Rock End Motel. It smelled damp, but not of
either carrion or the musty dung of living animal inhabitants.
Robbie crawled inside. Moving forward, he nearly stumbled;
the floor of striated rock was not as even as it looked, rising and
falling like ancient frozen waves. Robbie's heart pounded in his
ears. He stood upright and swept the beam of his flashlight
around the walls. To his left a part of the ceiling had fallen in
jagged piles that did not match his memory. To his right a
skeleton sat leaning against the smooth backward slope of the
intact wall.

Robbie looked at himself.

The bones had all survived, although they had fallen into a
disordered heap, probably from the same shifting of rock that
had caused the ceiling collapse. Only the long thigh and leg
bones lay undisturbed, stretched out neatly in a sitting position, the end of each tibia hidden inside rotting leather boots.
Mixed with the rest of the white bones were remnants of a
heavy jacket. The cotton cloth of pants and shirt was all gone,
although bits of red bandana dotted the ground, incongruously
cheerful. Least touched by time were the saddlebags, the big
gun covered with rust, and the skull itself, grinning at Robbie
from the top of his collapsed skeleton.

He reached out one finger and touched the empty eye
socket. At his touch, the heap of bones shifted and settled,
rattling dryly.

Robbie Callahan. Mallie Brekke.

He knelt on the stone floor and picked up the gun. Rust flaked off in chunks. He opened it, feeling how much heavier the six-gun was than the plastic gun he had carried in Liberia, how much clumsier. The six-pocketed chamber held two bullets. He had fired two into Johnny Lee Benson on the banks of the Sweetwater, one into the squaw. Now he lifted the skull and shone his flashlight directly into the pile of bones beneath it. The bullet was there, close to the wall, flattened on one side. So it hadn't after all been the rock slide that had made the sitting skeleton slump over and collapse.

A sudden heaviness pressed down on Robbie. He felt it as distinctly as if the weight had been rocks: a relentless slow push at the back of his skull, like a glacier trying to force its way in. Or out. He put both hands to his head. But in a moment the pressure vanished and he took his hands away, shuddering the whole length of his body.

The leather saddlebags were stiff and green with age, heavier than he had expected. Everything here seemed heavy: the gun, the bags, the metal clasp that refused to yield. He forced it and tipped the bags upside down. Money spilled out, packets of bills primly tied with string, along with several bars of gold. And the diamond necklace.

The flawless eleven-carat stone hung from a gold chain, flanked with clusters of rubies and emeralds. The necklace was gaudy, as gaudy as the woman it must have been intended for as it traveled by mail coach to San Francisco because the best protection was invisibility, and no one would try to snatch what they had no heavily armored reason to suppose was there. No one but Johnny Lee Benson, stumbling onto a genuine fortune only as he stumbled out of life.

Robbie rubbed the diamond free of dust and grit. It was the only thing in the cave that looked brand-new, untouched by time. Without counting the money, he packed it and the gold bars back into the saddlebags, stood, and started for the cave entrance, a spot of dull light on the black floor. Just before he knelt to crawl through, he turned and went back for the skull. It felt cold and powdery under his fingers, like marbleized moth wings.

With the skull in one hand and the saddlebags and flashlight in the other, Robbie crawled into the sunlight. The moment he stood, blinking, the pressure pushed again at the back of his head.

This time it was so palpable he lurched forward, as if shoved from behind, thrown off balance. He saved himself from falling only by dropping the saddlebags and flashlight and clawing at the rock face beside him. One of his fingernails tore. When after a minute the pressure vanished, it left him weak and shaky. He leaned against the cliff, breathing hard.

Something had tried to push into his brain.

But that was ridiculous. Robbie shook his head vigorously and knelt to retrieve the saddlebags. In his other hand he still gripped the skull. Why hadn't he dropped that instead? He didn't know.

He climbed down from the ledge slowly, shocked that the sun was already so far up the sky. It seemed to him he had only been in the cave a few minutes, but his watch said nearly noon. Uneasy, he skittered over the fallen rocks, balancing himself between saddlebags and skull, until he reached the bottom of the incline where rock gave way to moss, old pine needles, and tough spiky grasses.

He had just reached the aircar when the pressure struck again for the third time—this time *inside* his head, pushing to get out. Robbie cried out and dropped both saddlebags and skull. He sank to his knees, and so the first he saw of Hatton's men was the knees of their black jeans as they rushed him.

"Armand!" Robbie screamed. "Armand!" But when he was kicked to the ground there were pine needles under his hands, not the marble of the terrace yellow under slanting light from the French doors. How had pine needles gotten onto the terrace? Johnny Lee wouldn't let them into the cave, they might catch on fire, and they couldn't have a fire until they were at least safe beyond the Sweetwater—

"He don't even *fight*," a voice said in disgust. A scuffed brown hiking boot slammed into his right side. A rib broke and knifed into him; the piercing pain jerked his body along the ground. Paul screamed, a single high, clear note. There were too many of them, he couldn't get away, couldn't get to Armand—

"Yells like a girl," a voice said. Hands yanked him off the terrace and held him, and a fist slammed into his solar plexis. He doubled over, gasping. As he went over the fist caught him on the jaw. Blood spurted into his mouth. They were going to kill him, like he had killed Johnny Lee—

A second kick caught him on the right shoulder. Blackness moved over him like lava, like burning, like the nausea he couldn't hold back. His head hurt too much to even turn; he puked, vomit mixed with long ropes of blood, over his own face.

"Enough. Let's go. Grab them bags."

Boots moved away from him, past the light from the French doors farther down the Sweetwater. He curled into a ball, lungs tearing for breath, mewling at the pain of even the smallest movement. Vomit dripped onto the pine needles. But he couldn't faint now, he had to bury Johnny Lee's body, only there was no time for that because he had to get to Armand in the library, they might have hurt Armand too—

He forced himself to sit. At first the motion stabbed his broken rib inside the right side of his chest so hard he thought he *would* faint. But then the same motion must have shifted something inside his body; the pain lessened a little and he could breathe again. Wrapping his left arm tightly around his torso, he staggered to his feet, then toward the aircar.

Blackness swept from his jaw to his temples, receded, attacked again. They had broken the hall lamps, the expensive antique Tiffany glass Armand had bought in England. Now it was so dim he could barely find the library. But Armand wasn't in the library, he remembered, he had gone to the lab to work, the lab he had built at home and equipped with smuggled equipment from USC so he and Paul could have more time together. "We remember! We remember!" they had screamed, and he would goddamn give them something to remember—oh God, it was too dim to find the aircar.

But he did find it, crawling the last few feet on his knees and right hand, the left still wrapped around his ribs. *They're animals*, Johnny Lee had said, but he had killed them, even the baby, and the wages of sin is death. His father said. The Bible said. Then let them die of AIDS, the thing they accused Armand of, the thing they killed him for, the thing they swore to remember—let them die, rot without the cure Armand was working to bring them, let the whole damn world rot and die that would murder Armand, his love—

He had to keep going to reach Armand.

In the aircar he collapsed but did not lose consciousness. He started the car. Armand needed him; Armand lay bloody beside the Sweetwater. He got the car into the air, got it set on automatic retrace. It rolled and swayed beneath him but Johnny Lee had said it was a good horse and he clung to the pommel, his head floating along beside him. It wasn't that much farther to the lab, only down the hall and through the library, he could make it. He could. The cave was just ahead.

Then suddenly the aircar was filled with other people, people he didn't even know. Who were they all? A ragged peddler with hooded eyes, a Chinese in yellow silk and long pigtail, a man in furs—what the hell was this? All of them were looking at him. Beside him, in the other bucket seat, was a teenager dressed in a blue suit and mortarboard, one elbow jaunty on the open window, smiling over a can of beer. Robbie closed his eyes. The aircar hit a brief updraft and bucked, the retrace program reaching for the same elevation as this morning. Robbie opened his eyes. The people were gone. It wasn't until then that he remembered all of them, remembered being all of them.

He whimpered and raised one arm, and his broken rib shifted a second time and stabbed him. He again wrapped the other arm around it and tried to breathe shallowly, tried to manage the pain, tried to keep on top of it until he could reach Armand. Until he could get to the lab and crawl through the low hidden entrance to the cool, dry cave behind.

He dropped the aircar directly in front of the cave entrance. The lab key was still in his pocket from the morning. It took him six tries to get it to open the door; he kept slumping forward, against the wood. Finally he turned the key, fell, and crawled forward into the room.

"Mr. Brekke," someone said above him, "you are under arrest under Special Custody Act R-52. You have the right to remain silent—"

He tried to close the door behind him to lock it; they could come back, could kill him as well as Armand this time. But one of them was already there, bending over him—the least they could do was give him some fucking time alone with Armand's body, Armand's beloved body, bloody and mutilated, as he would now be forced to picture it for the rest of his life.

"—medical help immediately, hang on—"

He crawled across the floor. Toward the lab, toward Armand, toward Johnny Lee Benson, toward the sealed black metal box on the lab table from which he would fucking well give those gay-killers something to remember Armand by forever—

The pressure started again then at the back of his skull, in anguish and confusion of birth equal to his own of loss, and they crawled forward together.

16 CAROLINE

Halfway to Wyoming, watching the monotonous robot-tended fields tear by below the small chartered plane, Caroline leaned her forehead against the window. It felt cold. By raising her eyelids she could see a close-up, distorted view of her own face in the polarized plastic, looking like nothing human. Not like Catherine, Robbie, Linyi's children Shujen and Piao, Timmy . . .

"Women are crazy," she said aloud. From the seat beside her the pilot, a woman in her fifties with hair the same metal gray as her aircraft, glanced at her suspiciously.

"How long till Wyoming?" Caroline asked, wanting to make the woman say something, anything.

"Two more hours."

"Do you have children, Ms. Cary?"

"No," the pilot said, looking with pointed concentration at her screens.

"Neither do I," Caroline said.

She looked again out the window, her forehead against the plastic. This time it triggered a memory: herself as a small girl in a blue dress, pressing her face against a glass window, waiting for Papa to come home from taking the wood down the river to Wellington. She was Victoria Jane. She was waiting for Papa because he had promised to bring her a doll from Wellington, if it had come yet on the sailing ship from England, a doll with blue eyes and yellow hair like the Princess Alice. But only if she was good for Mama while he was gone. She was ten years old. A child.

"God damn it all to hell," Caroline said softly, into the glass/plastic. The pilot stared straight ahead. Caroline grinned sourly. *A crazy lady for sure, you're right, don't get too close it might be catching. Why not? Plague is, why not insanity? All of us in here caught it, all of us are split-brain gone, mothers and children, mothers of children, children who become mothers, mothers who are children of their children's children . . .* the generational dance gone Blues and Psycho courtesy of carnie surgery, change your partners, do-si-die.

The plane banked hard to the left. Caroline rolled with it, then looked out the window. There was nothing to see. On the control board, a buzzer began to shrill.

"What's wrong?"

"Detour. Radioactive ash dump. Can't fly over that stuff."

The buzzer wailed. Caroline tried to remember what she'd read about radioactive ash dumps. "Is it dangerous to fly this close?"

The pilot shrugged. "They say not."

"Who says not?"

"Government. And the Gaeists. *They* say a radioactive dump this close to Des Moines is a good thing."

"Why?"

The pilot threw her a look without answering.

"So you're not a Gaeist," Caroline said. "Do you think they're all crazy?"

The woman waited a long time before answering—as long, Caroline thought, as she could, before she had to. Triple rates, donchaknow. "I don't know if they're crazy, and I don't care. The world runs like it runs. What does it matter if the earth is trying to do it or not trying to do it? It runs like it runs."

"Thank you," Caroline said dryly, and the woman scowled.

She was a good pilot; the plane set down at Lander without a bump and twenty minutes early. Caroline paid the triple rates plus a tip that made the woman blink. The driver of the aircar she had reserved from Rochester stood waiting for her, a dark still Hispanic face above a ridiculously theatrical black-and-silver uniform.

"Dr. Jeeves, I presume?" Caroline said. The man looked puzzled. Well, of course he did—she was behaving like a lunatic, was revved up right to the edge. She could feel it in herself, the half-terrifying and half-delicious panic, like stage-fright. Or love.

The driver said gravely, with dignity, "My name is Cristobal Ramos, ma'am."

"I need to go to the Rock End Motel, in Sanderton—only there isn't a town of Sanderton, only a township—" She heard herself babbling, and tried to take hold of her words. "It's on Highway—look, here're the air coordinates. How long will it take?"

"Half an hour," Ramos said.

"Really? I'm impressed."

Ramos suddenly grinned, a wide flash of teeth that completely changed his severe face. Made him a different person, Caroline thought, and felt the sudden urge to giggle. *How many different people are* you, *Cristobal? Match you!* But no, not here, not now, please no laughter or hysteria here and now.

In the aircar, incredibly, she fell asleep. She woke to Ramos's hand gently shaking her shoulder, his grave face very smooth in harsh sunlight. "Ma'am. Ma'am. The Rock End Motel."

A slim woman with long black braids stood leaning against the doorjamb of the front office. Blinking, Caroline climbed from the car. The motel sat between the empty highway and a small woods growing along what Caroline guessed to be a creek. Magnificent mountains rose on all sides. The ten motel units were all alike: peeling green paint, weeds sprouting along the cement walls, a huge, old-fashioned neon sign, now inert, on the roof. In front of the farthest unit were parked two aircars, one of them official-looking and black, the other coated with grit, the grille choked with dried leaves. Caroline's heart jumped.

She said to the woman, "I'm looking for someone who stayed here last night and might still be here. My brother. His name is Robert Brekke."

The woman shook her head. Her eyes were wary.

"Sometimes he goes by the name of Paul Winter."

The woman's face did not change. She and Caroline gazed at each other.

"If he owes a bill or something—I'll be glad to pay it."

"Number four," the woman said so softly that Caroline had to lean forward to hear her, "but the agent, he is in there too."

"Agent?"

"FBI."

Caroline stared. She ran toward number four and yanked open the door. "Turn right out again, miss, and close the door," said a man in a dark suit standing quietly just inside the door. Caroline ignored him.

At the far end of the room Robbie stood holding a piece of silvered glass under his chin. From the way he held it— loose-bodied, his left arm wrapped around his right side and his legs slack—she couldn't tell if the jagged edge rested so close to his chin deliberately, or by accident. His face was swollen and bloody, the eyes reduced to unreadable slits. The room had been trashed: mattress thrown from the bed, its fitted sheet still clinging at the corners; bureau overturned; lamp smashed; thin curtains clawed from their flimsy rod. In the uncurtained sunlight the shards of mirror that were scattered over the floor glittered like diamonds.

"Armand is dead," Robbie said. Caroline, her hand to her

mouth, recognized his tone: the temporary calm of perfect despair. She couldn't tell whether Robbie was capable of recognizing her. "They killed him. Because of me."

She took a step toward him. He moved slightly; light ricocheted off the piece of mirror. The agent moved to put a hand on her arm and then withdrew it, watching them both.

"I killed Johnny Lee," he said in that same toneless voice. "By the Sweetwater."

She had to say something. "I know."

"No. You weren't there, Caroline."

So he recognized her. Relief washed over her. Before she could answer, he said, "Only Joe knows. Ask him. He was there. He was always there."

"Robbie," she whispered, "give me the mirror. You're hurt, darling. Give me the glass."

He walked toward her. She had a sudden flash of nestling against him on the floor of her room at the Institute, his back to the bed, and feeling the comforting power in his long body . . . He handed her the jagged glass.

The edge cut the heel of her thumb. She turned to lay the glass down on the side of the upturned bureau. Out of the corner of her eye she saw the FBI man pull handcuffs from the pocket of his suit.

"No!" she said. "Can't you see he's hurt a rib?"

The man clicked the cuff onto Robbie's right hand only, holding the empty cuff in his own hand. Robbie didn't even seem to notice this was happening. He said to Caroline, "Joe's here."

"No," she said soothingly, "he isn't. Sit down, Robbie, in this chair . . ." The door opened and a heavy, balding man burst through. Joe McLaren followed.

The agent said, "He's been hurt, Dr. Pirelli. And he's babbling. He needs that med team."

"Outside," the heavy man said, "but keep them there until I call. Thanks, Forster. Wait outside, please."

The agent hesitated, looking doubtfully from Robbie to Caroline. He left. Caroline, dazed, led Robbie to sit in the ugly green chair. How had he known Joe was here? And why *was* Joe here?

"Robert Brekke," said the man called Pirelli, more gently than Caroline would have expected. Robbie ignored him.

"Paul Winter," Pirelli said.

Robbie's face lost his calm. He snarled and tried to jump up from the chair. His right side jerked and he fell back clutching it, his face clenched with pain. "You're too late! All of you! I destroyed it, the whole lab, the mice are loose—it's too late! 'We remember,' they said, I'll fucking well give them something to remember . . ."

"Who?" Pirelli said reasonably. "Give who something to remember, Winter?"

"The bastards who killed . . . killed Armand." He started to cry. Caroline looked away. It was horrible, and she was horrible for wanting to leave him, to just not hear it. The pictures Prokop had shown her of the Kyle lab the night of the mutilation rose in her mind, as powerful as if she had been there.

Pirelli said, "What did they say? No, don't touch him, Ms. Bohentin. Joe, just stand on his other side here in case he tries to get up again. Now, Paul—" Pirelli squatted down in front of Robbie's chair. Caroline watched the light move over the top of his bald head. "Paul, what did the killers say? What did they say?"

Pirelli's reasonable tone seemed to have calmed Robbie. He answered mechanically, fumbling a little at the words, as if they slid in and out of his grasp. "They said . . . 'We remember. A fucking cure doesn't make us forget. We remember AIDS and you asshole stuffers who caused it and'—only that was before, in the letters."

"In the death threats," Pirelli said.

"Yes. In the mail. To Armand, to me. And I said, 'Oh, forget it, love, they're just dicks—' " His voice broke.

Pirelli kept on with the calm, reasonable tone. "And that night they came and beat you and you found Armand dead in the lab, didn't you?"

"Johnny Lee Benson killed six Indians at the Sweetwater. He bashed in a baby's skull. I shot him."

Pirelli frowned; Caroline could just see the movement of the lower part of his face over the rim of his pink skull. She looked up and saw Joe's eyes suddenly wide and frightened. He backed slowly away until he reached the closed door and put one hand on the doorjamb, as if to steady himself.

Pirelli didn't seem to notice Joe. He said to Robbie, "What did Armand have in the lab? What had he told you was in there, Paul?"

"The viruses. And the mice. They ran all around the blood, getting away from it, running in circles until they found the door . . . in circles . . ." Now Robbie's voice had become high and light. A child's voice, some child who had once seen mice too, the memory jumbled with the murder, the mutilation, Armand Kyle's lab mice, which Caroline could not remember seeing in any of Prokop's horrible pictures.

"What were the mice for?" Pirelli said. "What was Armand doing with them? The university thought he was working on human immunity resplices, but not at home. In the guarded labs at the university. Was he?"

"No."

"What were the mice for?"

"Memories. Of mazes and cheese. Around and around and around . . . Armand wanted them to remember better. Long-term memory, short-term stimulation . . . He smuggled things home from the college. Slow viruses. For the memories of mice."

"And Armand's experiments weren't—"

"*Memory*," Robbie said suddenly, viciously, in a different voice. "I'll give them memories they won't forget! I'll give the whole fucking world memories they won't forget, the whole fucking world of gay bashers that won't leave us alone, won't— I'll give them the memories they deserve, of rats and viruses, of . . . of . . ." He put his head in his hands. The handcuff dangled from one wrist. By the door, Joe made a sudden sound. Caroline didn't look at him. She stood very still, her eyes on the top of Pirelli's head, all at once understanding.

Robbie had caused the plague.

She backed away until the wall stopped her. The rough stucco pulled unevenly at her sweater. Pirelli leaned forward and took Robbie's hands away from his face. Caroline saw Pirelli's face straight on; from its expression something had changed on Robbie's, something Caroline, against the wall, couldn't see. She didn't want to see, didn't want to hear. Robbie had caused the plague. That had killed Catherine.

"Brekke!" Pirelli said at the same moment that Robbie spoke in a high, unpleasant whine, "I only left them for a moment, Your Excellency, how was I to believe they would run off like that, I left them working hard at their little tasks—"

"Who was, Brekke?" Pirelli asked.

Robbie ignored him. His voice deepened and he raised his right arm, cuff dangling. "There. By the big rock on the river. Three days ago." He lowered his arm. "You remember."

Pirelli shook his head. But Robbie wasn't looking at Pirelli; he looked past the squatting man toward the doorway, at Joe. Caroline forced herself to look at Joe.

"I won't!" Robbie suddenly shouted in the petulant voice of a child. Without rising from the chair, he stamped one foot. "I won't! And you can't make me, Father!"

Joe still stood with one hand braced against the doorjamb. His eyes stared from a slack face. Caroline recognized the look: clarity-within-unfocusedness, the look she had been seeing for weeks on faces in the Institute. On her own face in the mirror. Joe was remembering.

"In the name of the Father, the Son, and the Holy Spirit," Robbie said pleasantly. "Come, my son, let us walk in the garden."

Everything. Everything Robbie said, everyone he remembered being, triggered a memory in Joe. From the mention of the Sweetwater on. But that wasn't possible, that couldn't be—

Pirelli straightened. "What's he doing? Are those other lives of his he's talking about?"

"Yes," Caroline whispered.

"Does he think he still *is* those people?"

"I don't know. It's not . . . supposed to work that way."

"I saw you that day," Robbie said sonorously, "in the legion of Flavius son of Decimus, although you did not see me."

And in a different voice, "I did *not* kill her—I did not! O Queen of Heaven . . ."

And, after a long pause, "Leave the duck sauce alone. I never loved you."

"Christ on a ramchip," Pirelli said softly. Caroline shuddered. Robbie's words started to come faster, with less change in his voice, spilling out desperately in an unstoppable torrent. She thought of Mr. Holiworth, the Korsakov's patient at Catherine's Home who had changed identity every few minutes. But this was worse, was unbearable, was Robbie.

"Buy a new red paper dress for the god for the New Year—"

"Did you see it, Goro? A dolphin!"

"Here I stand. I can do no other. God help me. Amen."

"The best thing for Timmy's earache, Mrs. Hendrickson, is probably to—"

"*Wait*," Caroline said, "that's not his past life, it's *mine*—" The room spun around her, swirling furniture and shards of broken glass.

Pirelli said swiftly, "Then he was in it, too. He was the doctor."

"He was *not*."

"—put a little warm mineral water in his ear until the pain passes," Robbie finished.

"Start the fire, Yuri. It gets cold."

"*Sic semper tyrannis!* The South is avenged!"

"Six pounds! Hell, no, *my* baby was sixteen pounds, it felt like shitting a pumpkin!" He laughed, a high feminine laugh.

"No," Caroline forced herself to say to Pirelli. "*No.* Past lives never change sex, it's one of the unexplained constants—"

"Not all of those are his past lives," Pirelli said grimly. "He was never John Wilkes Booth. We know who was. This is something else, something different going on—Joe?" But Caroline saw that Joe still stood frozen by the doorway, staring at Robbie with that look Pirelli—or anyone else who had never become a carnie—would not recognize.

"The cursed horse threw a shoe, they are right behind me!"

"I had a new gown made special, my dear, with sleeves of blue velvet slashed with silver, and a skirt of blue velvet over scarlet silk."

"Water is best. But gold shines like fire blazing in the night, supreme of lordly wealth."

"You're willing to let Angel Whittaker rot."

The voice was once more Robbie's own. The shock was enormous—like seeing a dead man rise, Caroline thought, turning what should have been a relief into a monstrosity. Robbie spoke directly to Joe. "You'll let him rot. And Robin too."

Joe, ashen, whispered, "You can't know that."

"Callie," Robbie said, twisting in his chair, "I never meant to, that night. You made me. You know you did. If we hadn't both been doing Blues and Psychos, it never would have—my own daughter—God, Callie, I only want to help!"

Even the voice was close to Colin's.

But the next second the voice was different again, high and light: "Listen, Anna—that was a nightingale. Did you hear it?"

"Bring water jars to the temple."

"Daily I find it more difficult to live up to my blue china."

"*I am Robert Anthony Brekke.*"

Shakily Robbie stood, one hand on the battered arm of the chair, his body still twisted so the swollen blue eyes met Caroline's. They pleaded with her. "Caroline, I am Rob . . . Robbie Br . . ."

He staggered. Pirelli got one arm around his waist, lowered him back to the chair. The right side of Robbie's body spasmed in pain. "Jefferson Pirelli, you are hereby sentenced to three months incarceration for data piracy, sentence to be suspended in light of your juvenile status and previous clean record. You are remanded to the custody of your mother. Listen up, son, and listen well—"

Pirelli straightened slowly, his florid face gone the color of parchment.

"I am Robbie Brekke . . . I am . . ."

"The King's mistress wore—it is scarcely credible!—the jewels that belonged to the Queen—"

"Robert Anth . . . Anthon . . . Robert . . ."

Pirelli said to Joe, "Call the med team." Joe, glassy-eyed, didn't move. Caroline lurched around him and out the door, followed by a shout from Robbie, "There they are! Get the lines—"

Two men waited with the FBI agent by yet a third aircar. Caroline waved them in; she was suddenly breathing so hard she couldn't speak. A little way off a knot of people had gathered, staring silently. Caroline had thought she would stay out here, away from the motel room, away from what Robbie had become—a man with the aggressive stance of a reporter started toward her. "Miss—" She went back inside.

The medical team was trying to lay Robbie onto a stretcher. He fought feebly, tears scalding his battered face, talking the whole time, jumping from dead life to dead life . . . but no, they weren't all dead, he had said to her in Colin's words . . . *Colin's* . . .

"Be careful," Pirelli said. "Give him a stun strip, I want him out cold—*no, wait, don't.*"

"I am trying to come out," Robbie said in a voice unlike the others—this was Robbie's own voice, and yet it was not. It was Robbie's voice the way it might have been, maybe, if he had just woken up rich, or the biggest winner of all time.

"I am trying to get out," the voice said again.

"Get out," Pirelli said harshly to the med team. "You, too!" he snapped at Caroline. They went; she did not.

"I am Robert . . . Rob . . . I am trying to get out."

"Yes," Pirelli said, "you are. Who are you?"

Robbie didn't answer.

The sudden silence, after the wild flow of tortured, dizzying words, seemed monstrous. Caroline took a step forward. Robbie's gaze had been on Pirelli's face, but at her tentative motion it shifted to her. Caroline stopped dead. Pirelli, the only one who seemed to have any idea what was happening, grabbed her by the elbow and pulled her toward the stretcher on the floor, not gently. The air seemed to her to have thickened, so that she moved through it as through something transparent but viscous. *Too many people. Too many ghosts.* She shook off Pirelli's hand and knelt on the floor beside Robbie's stretcher.

"Robbie—what's happening? Who are you?"

He smiled at her. Caroline's heart clutched; the smile in the raw pulpy face, in the blue eyes, was the joyous and trusting smile of a very young child, overlaid with something else equally young but not at all childlike. His hand tried to hold the fabric of her jeans. His right side spasmed in pain. "Mommy."

Then it was gone. He began to babble again, whole sentences mixed with fragments and then just names, on and on, more and more incoherent. This time even Caroline knew that not all the lives spewing out were his; they were bits and pieces of the over-memory, of all the lives that had ever been, in a current so strong it swept Robbie away and made him no more than a conduit, a channel. The past spilled out, incoherent and without control, jerking Robbie's broken body around the shattered rib until even Pirelli could not stand it and cut off the flow of data, calling in the med team who pressed the sedative-laden stun strip to Robbie's neck and knocked him out cold.

"I want some answers," Caroline said.

Pirelli looked at her wearily. He hadn't wanted either her or Joe admitted to Robbie's small hospital room in whatever small town this was—her aircar had followed the ambulance car, carrying her and Joe in utter silence. Pirelli had gone with Robbie, and at the tiny hospital the volunteer receptionist, an ancient lady bewildered by the idea of an FBI guard in her quiet domain, had tried to prevent Caroline from getting into the elevator. Caroline had simply shoved past her, and outside the door to Robbie's room she had stood in the corridor in front of the guards and started to scream at the top of her voice for the press. Pirelli, looking annoyed, had said, "Press? *Here?*" and had let her in.

Robbie lay quietly asleep, his ribs taped and his face washed clean of blood and embedded grit. In sleep his face looked younger than she had ever seen it. Joe sat on a puce-colored chair in a corner of the room, his face rigid with the same stunned refusal it had worn in the aircar. Pirelli sat at a make-shift desk made of Robbie's hospital table, the narrow space crowded with a computer plugged to an expensive telecommunications system. The computer screen was dark; Pirelli had finished whatever he was doing, with whomever in some other place he had been doing it. Washington, she guessed. The hospital wall terminal, a very simple model, remained un-folded against the wall.

Caroline stood close to Robbie's bed and glared at Pirelli, who answered with a faint unwilling smile and handed her a Styrofoam cup of cooling coffee. Oily concentric rings spread out over the surface, making Caroline suddenly dizzy; she knew better than anyone that she was running on bravado and nerves, and how easily both could dissolve. She refused the coffee.

"It was the plague," Pirelli said, "that started it."

"You know this," Joe said wearily.

"Of course I don't know it—how the fuck can I *know* anything? The data's still evolving."

"Christ," Joe said, "the Gaea theory of math. Save us all."

Startled despite herself, Caroline looked away from Robbie's face. "Gaea?"

"Not as we know it," Pirelli said. "Not the earth regulating itself for life. But self-regulation, anyways. Of . . . something."

Joe stood up abruptly and opened the door. One of the guards half turned to look at him. Joe repeated, "Christ," and went to stare out the room's single window.

Caroline said slowly, "The over-memory. That's what you mean. Regulating itself. Trying to . . . repair itself. Because the plague is destroying its normal flow of memories from human lives. First AIDS, ruining the even, steady doubling of the world's population, then the plague, further polluting the . . . the memory-sphere . . ."

Joe snapped, "It's not sentient! For God's sake, Caroline, listen to yourself—the over-memory is not sentient!"

"Neither is the earth," Pirelli said in a tone completely different from his previous anger.

Caroline felt dizzy. She set down the Styrofoam cup. "You're saying the over-memory adjusts itself like . . . like"— what had all those pamphlets said? They seemed to have been read by someone else, long ago—"like sea animals increased the manufacture of ammonia when rain got too acid? Like that? AIDS and the memory plague together make a shortage of racial memories from one source, and so the over-memory just makes more? *How?*"

"It doesn't make more memories," Pirelli said. "It makes

more links between memories. Increased connections. More . . . neural paths, if you will. To keep complexity on the same growth curve."

By the window, Joe snorted. Caroline glanced at his rigid back; she hadn't known a snort could convey such pain.

"I don't understand," Caroline said, a moment before understanding came. "You mean carnies. You mean it's using us, our reaching for past memories, to keep the racial biosphere complex enough to . . . it can't do that!"

"Why not?" Pirelli said. The discussion of probabilities seemed to have calmed him; he even smiled, faintly. "Methane in the farts of ruminant animals helps keep the oxygen level suitable for life. Why couldn't the over-memory use what it has to, what it needs—"

Caroline heard her own voice wobble. "Joe?"

"Leave me out of this."

She turned back to Pirelli. She had the feeling that if she put out her hand it would go through him, through the computer, through the wall. "But why *Robbie*? What was 'trying to come out'? That's what you said—"

All the tenseness returned to Pirelli's round body. "That's what *he* said."

"But why him? Why my Robbie? And *what is it?*"

Pirelli stared at her, blinked once.

Caroline suddenly remembered. "Patrick said . . ."

"Who's Patrick?"

"Father Shahid." Pirelli's eyes brightened with interest. "He said . . . he's been dBasing carnie data. He said it was . . . was God."

"Out of just the carnie data he said that? Christ on a ramchip. But no, it's not God. It's . . . the racial memory biosphere. The next step in evolution—but not necessarily ours. An over-memory Gaea, giving birth to self-regulating changes."

From somewhere—nowhere she could name, then or ever—Caroline said slowly, "Or being given birth to."

Joe turned from the window. Before Caroline could look at his face, Robbie stirred.

It started slow. She felt it first in her bones, even though it couldn't have started there: a weak helpless tingle, like infant electricity. It rose slowly, spreading out through her body and then through the charged air in the room, a wordless invisible bath of sensation that thickened on the air like a palpable shiver of déjà vu. "Someone's walking on your grave," her grandmother used to say when that same shiver came. Or sometimes, "An angel just spoke your name." But this was all names, all graves. A field carrying as much coded complexity as any global datanet, any pattern of microorganism production in the blood-salt ocean, any coded DNA carrying the potential for life. Caroline felt it in her synapses, in the bundles of cords in her spine. In that field she stood paralyzed, staring at Pirelli and Joe, seeing that they too felt the data field and that they too could not read it. It was another sort of electronic net—information-rich, pulsing with intent—and they stood with stylus and clay tablet.

Sorrow rose in Caroline. She thought at first that it was her own—for Catherine, for Robbie—but quickly recognized that it was not. The sorrow had a weird quality of impersonality, like a sepia photograph of a tragedy from another century. Yet it was real. It brimmed in her brain, wordless sorrow for an unimaginable loss, until it reached the saturation of her brain and overflowed. That was how it felt to her: That she could actually feel sorrow spill over the top of her head, real as water, flowing among the four human minds in the room. Then the sensation sank as rapidly as it had risen, draining back through her skull so that all that remained was a prickling at the base of her neck that might have been nothing more than ordinary fear.

Where the whole field had drained was back into Robbie.

Joe's face was ashen. He looked as if he might fall over. Unthinking, Caroline went to him and put a hand under his elbow. His body trembled.

Pirelli whispered, "That was the racial memory. Giving up."

Joe trembled again. Caroline cried, "Giving up *what*?"

"The chance to . . . to get out."

"Of *what*?"

"Of the dead past. Of . . . passive regulation, as opposed to active. Of limbo."

"No," Caroline said, "*no*," and was suddenly furious. She seized the fury eagerly, hanging onto it with both hands, screaming at Pirelli in scorn and disgust. "You're not even making sense! Listen to yourself—'dead past,' 'passive regulation,' 'limbo'—Christ what a mishmash! Mysticism and engineering and religion and—you're no scientist, you're a witch doctor! And Robbie . . ."

She ran down as rapidly as she had begun. Her hands rose slowly, palms up, in appeal; Caroline stared at the pink flesh as if the hands belonged to someone else. On the bed, Robbie moaned. Caroline moved toward him and he turned to look at her without recognition.

"Robbie—"

"Armand," he whispered softly. "Johnny Lee."

"That's all done now," she managed. "All over."

"I'll give them something to fucking remember," he said, without rancor, in the same soft, tired voice.

"Rob—"

"Don't go out tonight, Johnny Lee—stay here. We'll go see the elephant." Caroline had to bend close to even hear him.

Pirelli said, "Brekke, if you can hear me—"

"The porcelain is finished, Master."

Joe flinched.

Robbie closed his eyes, opened them again. The quiet empty voice never changed. "Every sacrifice of mere pleasure, sir, you will always find me ready to make to your convenience."

Caroline knelt by the bed and put her arms around him.
"Bring in the goats from the pasture now."

"The screen door needs mending."

"Nikos, watch out for their left flank above all."

Pirelli said softly, "Jesus, Mary, and Joseph."

"Sedate him," Caroline ordered. "Make it stop! Can't you see he's trapped?"

"But only in his own lives," Pirelli said. "Those are all *his*."

"Armand, let's go away this weekend, just the two of us."

"The piece of land beside the city wall is mine; I bought it for three pieces of silver."

"Mommy, my ear hurts."

Caroline moaned. Pirelli opened the door and motioned down the hallway; a moment later the same medic appeared with a stun strip. Pirelli gestured for him to wait.

Caroline begged, "For God's sake—"

"Wait. Just a minute. I want to be sure—"

"Sure!" She could have clawed his eyes out, could have torn the small fat man limb to limb. She was going to, was springing up—but instead she was holding Robbie, his body quiet and thin in her arms while his tired voice went on and on, through life after jumbled life, while she stretched her arms around the crowded emptiness Robbie had become and watched Joe's face show memory after memory triggered by Robbie's words. All of them. Every one.

Finally even Pirelli had had enough and the medic pressed the stun strip to Robbie's neck. His blue eyes closed and the endless splinters of dead lives stopped coming. Caroline staggered to her feet.

"He's trapped. He's trapped in some sort of—sort of time loop! *Why?*"

Pirelli shook his head. Caroline sat at the edge of the bed and put a hand on Robbie's forehead. It felt cool. "Forever? Not able to have a present, stuck in memory, trapped in there in the past—forever?"

"I don't know," Pirelli said. "I'm not a doctor."

"You mean it might have cut off Robbie's present, that thing—for good? Just like another version of the plague?"

"Survival. Its own. Brekke is some kind of nexus, a nerve center . . . he can't help that any more than an individual cell of your body can help being the first cell transformed by a cancer."

For the first time in fifteen minutes, Joe spoke. "Anthropomorphism."

Pirelli said, "Data."

The two men looked at each other like gunfighters. Clouds shifted and sunlight streamed through the window in dusty slanting lines like bars. Pirelli said, half question and half challenge, "You aren't even looking at how big this is. What it fucking *means*."

"I don't have to," Joe said so bitterly that Caroline looked up, her hand still on Robbie's forehead. "*You* will."

"Angel," Pirelli said, "Robin. You're in no position to make accusations of global-mindedness at the expense of the individual."

Joe turned away. Caroline suddenly remembered Joe's face during both of Robbie's long strings of disconnected bits of other lives: wide-eyed, shocked, remembering. *Remembering*. ". . . no more than an individual cell can help being the first cell transformed by a cancer."

Or the second.

Joe said to the medic, very low, "What will happen to Brekke?"

"There's nothing more I can do to help him," the man said. "An FBI brainwashing specialist is on the way from Washington."

Caroline tightened her hand. Robbie's cool, slack skin did

not respond. He might have been Timmy, the earache pain broken, asleep at last. Safe. For the moment anyway, safe from memory—his, hers, theirs, everybody's. But he wouldn't stay safe. Not from a racial mnemonic Gaea struggling to regulate its own existence as much—or as little—as did the earth itself. Not from the collective global striving of all of them—everyone, every single last brief life that had ever walked or crawled or squirmed in human form—to survive. She couldn't save Robbie from his memories, no matter how much she wanted to, in order to serve hers. He would stay trapped by a neural Gaea too impersonal to let its complex biosphere be destroyed and too self-serving to destroy Robbie, the intended nexus of its evolution to whatever came next . . . Robbie would stay trapped there, between birth and neural death, light and darkness, until Gaea readjusted itself. Because the overall pattern was what counted, the overall history, the racial evolution, not the individual life with its stupidities and failures and tiny brief pathetic loves and hatreds and carings that seemed so monumental but were utterly unimportant without the constant invention and redemption of memory—

"*No*," Caroline said.

The medic looked at her with a faintly wounded professional pride. He was a thin, rangy man with a thick mustache. In Caroline's mind a memory came. Out of this life. Out of the storehouse, out of the treasury, out of the otherness of one's own self . . . for God's sake, Caroline, delete the scenery chewing.

"I'm afraid not, ma'am," the medic said distantly. "There's nothing more anyone, not just *me*, could do to help him right now."

She put her other hand on Robbie's shoulder. He moved a little, drawing his arms toward his knees, like a child.

"Yes," Caroline said. "There is."

Pirelli looked sharply. In the distance a siren began to wail: probably the brainwashing specialist. And maybe it would be all right. Maybe Pirelli with his global-mindedness—another Gaea himself, she thought—would be wrong. Maybe the lock on Robbie's memory would break by itself, maybe he would wake up all right tomorrow or next week or next month, maybe no one would have to invent anything to do about this . . .

She suddenly remembered, sharp and clear, the night Catherine had been born. Charles was not there; he had stormed out of the house after one of their senseless fights, she didn't know where. The baby had not been due for another three weeks. Labor started unexpectedly hard and not in her swollen belly, where she had expected it, but in the small of her back, an intense grinding pain that had made her think she was going to break in two at the waist. Panicked, not able to think, she had called Colin. He appeared in velvet hose and doublet and full makeup for Falstaff; he had received her message backstage between Acts II and III and simply strode out of the theater. "You can't do that!" she cried: scandalized, angry, grateful, in pain. "I can do anything I have the ingenuity to invent," he said, "and so can you, Callie." "Bullshit," she had gasped, doubled over. Fifteen excruciating hours later Catherine had been born: red, wrinkled, bloody, squalling, perfect.

And until this very moment Caroline had not remembered any of it.

The siren outside rose in a Doppler crescendo, then cut off sharply. Voices sounded below the window. Pirelli and the medic went into the corridor to meet the men from Washington. Over Robbie's sleeping form Caroline and Joe looked at each other. Then the room was full of people, machines were being wheeled in on metal dollies, the words "classified" and "virus" and "the Vice President" sounded all around her, until someone grasped her firmly by the elbow and led her out of the room, away from where Robbie lay peacefully asleep, flushed on his pillow with his blond hair tumbling over the sides of his cheeks where stubble had sprouted since the last time he had shaved.

EPILOGUE

JUNE, 2023

June of 2023 turned unexpectedly cold, confounding environmentalists predicting another greenhouse effect. Caroline raised the window of her aircar, suspended in traffic over midtown Manhattan. Too much traffic—she still hadn't gotten used to the exponential increase in aircars during the months she had spent away from New York. In a year, Manhattan had changed.

Everything had changed. Nothing had changed.

But the street below looked as it always did twenty minutes before curtain during the theater season: congested, noisy, garish with holograms, alive with people jamming up against each other to arrive at an off-Broadway production thirty seconds earlier. Not that she could claim to be any better . . . She adjusted the diamond necklace at her throat, and then grinned as the bodyguard seated opposite leaned forward for a closer look at the clasp. Cassidy, she remembered: His name was Cassidy. He was good. He would have to be; it was the height of stupidity to wear diamonds where she was going, and Cassidy knew it, and she knew it, and she was going to wear them anyway. *I would,* she thought, *wear peacock feathers and beetle carapaces if it would help make this theater opening a gala occasion.*

Please, let it be an occasion.

God, she was nervous.

"Do you like theater, Mr. Cassidy?"

"Not at all." He went on studying the clasp on her dia-monds.

"Caroline—TV item," said the screen set into the back of Jason's seat. "Would you like it taped or in real time?"

"Real time," Caroline said. She had added the screen to the car a few months ago; like the one in her apartment, it was programmed to scan the major newsnets and notify her only when a story contained key words or names. Caroline leaned forward. The screen flashed into two-dimensional color: a fakely homey talk-show studio, decorated in this year's ragingly fashionable colors, pink and gray. The hostess pretending to be an anchorwoman radiated restrained joy. "—cials at the Atlanta Centers for Disease Control have released the latest data on the national plague inoculation program. Sixty-five percent of the population has currently received the updated vaccination, with less than .001 per-cent reporting any of the side effects that had so troubled the earlier version of the vaccine. Presidential Commission Chief Jefferson Pirelli had this to say:"

The screen suddenly widened to include Pirelli. He looked thinner, and he had lost even more hair. He wore a sleek gray suit with a headband patterned with what appeared to be purple circuit boards, and sat in his studio chair as if his hands were ready to spring onto a keyboard. "Preliminary data scans indicate that although sixty-five percent of the population has been inoculated, we've reached over ninety percent of those at greatest risk of contacting plague."

"Dr. Pirelli, how do you determine just who is at risk? I'm sure a number of us have never really understood that," the hostess said brightly. She sat with her body held slightly to one side, away from Pirelli, as if afraid her skirt might brush him. Caroline imagined their pre-air conversation in the green room. *Data.*

Pirelli said, "We determine who is at risk by complex mathematical models."

"And you were instrumental, I believe, in formulating those models in your work as a data scanner."

"No," Pirelli said. "The people who were instrumental in formulating the models were the anonymous victims of brain disease that the Commission studied."

"Victims of plague, you mean," the hostess said solemnly.

"Not necessarily," Pirelli said quietly, and Caroline switched the system back to silent record. For a long moment she sat silent. *Not necessarily*.

The aircar landed on the theater roof, one of dozens of flying metal bullets sweeping out of the sky. A sudden memory came to Caroline: geese flying so low overhead she felt she could touch them from where she lay on her back in the marsh grass, her brown arm a slash across the warm gray sky . . .

She pushed the memory away. It was only the past.

"Jason, are we late?"

"You'll be there in time for a drink in the lobby."

Caroline smiled at the thought that this particular lobby would offer drinks.

It didn't, of course. Patrick Shahid, dressed in a severe black suit, met her just inside the theater door, which was the original loading dock hydraulic plate refitted for computer operation. The lobby was avant garde junk-tech, with bulky antiques half cemented into the walls in patterns presumably significant to someone: a gas-powered lawn-mower chassis, stripped; several ancient green display screens; a waffle iron; a separate-unit VCR, trailing power cords toward the ceiling. Caroline looked fondly at the amazing ugliness, at the old-fashioned paper poster deliberately tacked above the standard electronic playbill, at the theater patrons, mostly young, in jeans or casual synthetic leathers. None appeared to pay the slightest attention to a woman wearing silk and diamonds and followed by a bodyguard.

"I forget how much I love New York," she said to Shahid. "How are you, Patrick?"

He smiled; tight small lines pulled at the corners of his eyes and mouth. "I see from looking at you that you love New York."

She touched her headband, set with the diamond match to her necklace. "Too much?"

"Not for this occasion."

"That's what I thought." She tried to smile again, but her lips felt stiff. Shahid was thinner, his smooth calmness gone jagged underneath, fierce. Caroline saw that whatever it was, he was going to talk about it with her, was going to involve her in it, whether she wanted to hear it or not. But not yet. Not until after this performance, after this . . .

She said abruptly, "He's ready?"

"He was yesterday."

The lobby lights flickered and blinked. They stood in line to punch the playbill for a program; it whirred softly as it printed out the number requested. Caroline clutched it hard, and the crowd jostled them into the theater, Cassidy so close behind she could feel his breath on her neck. The seats were unadjustable plastic and winfoam: very cheap, very uncomfortable, very correct for a theater disdaining middle-class amenities. Caroline fingered the shaped winfoam arms. There still was no engineered microbe that would eat winfoam trash.

The curtain, a magnetic field, shimmered and dissolved. An electronic voice intoned solemnly: "Two Greek plays. One: Aeschylus: *Prometheus Bound*." The word "Bound," repeated, fading away in tinny manufactured echoes, the last of which was inadvertently distorted by the sound system to a rising whine. "Oh, Lord," Caroline said. "Amateur time."

Shahid smiled in the gloom. "You knew how it would be."

She knew. It was a New York cycle, as inevitable as the harbor tides: When Broadway went light with frothy musicals, experimental theater did soul-searching explorations of suicide. When Broadway did revivals, the experimentals did avant garde. This year Broadway had three smash technological satires, witty biting plays about data piracy, marital clones, and synth-protein chefs, and on this same street two other small houses were playing *Tartuffe* and *Medea*, probably both in productions as earnest and stodge as this one promised to be. She knew. But she was stung anyway; she had hoped for something better, for him.

Four actors entered stage left, which was furnished solely with a black boulder fitted with iron rings. Hephaestus, Force, and Power looked as if they needed every bit of concentration to keep from glancing out across the footlights. They wore stiff togas and headbands. Between them Force and Power dragged Robbie Brekke, dressed in rags, his head so far down that Caroline could not see his face.

Power began: "To this far region of the earth, this pathless wilderness of Scythia, at last we are come . . ." Scythia sounded about as far away as Brooklyn. Hephaestus was no better; Force was worse. Caroline let go of Shahid's hands and gripped her own together on her lap. A whole play of this, with the main character spending the entire time chained motionless to a rock . . . it was impossible. The theater would empty in twenty minutes. It was a mistake . . . a woman in the row in front of her twisted impatiently.

"Caroline," Shahid whispered, "are you all right?" His whispering disturbed nothing; half the audience was still rustling and murmuring.

"In the row ahead of us—to my right, with the scarlet headband—that's Antonia Trego."

Shahid had clearly never heard of Antonia Trego. Caroline shrugged and turned back to the stage. Power and Force shackled Prometheus to the rock as if mooring a small boat. Who had invited Antonia? New York's hottest director didn't spend Saturday night attending poor openings. But she already knew who had invited Antonia. Her throat thickened.

On stage Hephaestus recited. "Let us go; now the clinging

web binds all his limbs." He flung out one arm, posed, and strode off stage. Force and Power trailed meekly after. Somewhere behind Caroline, someone snickered. The stage lights dimmed, and a too-obvious spotlight picked out Robbie.

He raised his head. Caroline knew that Prometheus's first speech was one of those chanted invocations of nature that made pastoral plays so perfectly irrelevant to twenty-first-century New York:

> "O air divine, and O swift-winged winds!
> Ye river fountains, and thou myriad-twinkling
> Laughter of ocean waves! O mother earth!
> And thou, O all-discerning orb o' the sun!"

It didn't sound irrelevant. Prometheus spoke with deceptive lightness, with calm undercut by splintering pain. The air divine and mother earth were there, solid and eternal, but he expected no comfort from them.

> "Behold, with what dread torments
> I through the slow-revolving
> Ages of time must wrestle—"

Sarcasm now, pitiful words refusing even the luxury of self-pity. And yet the disturbing lightness was there as well, holding in check something terrifying and too deep to face . . . *the slow-revolving ages of time must wrestle* . . . No, Caroline thought, he didn't know what he was saying, that was the whole point, he *couldn't* know . . .

She saw Antonia Trego lean abruptly forward.

> "Yet what is this I say? All future things
> I see unerring, nor shall any chance
> Of evil overtake me unaware—"

Shahid raised one hand, let it drop. Robbie's voice, Caroline thought numbly, was lighter than her father's, with less resonance. He did not project as well. But his voice was strong and clear, and it carried something she had never heard before, and couldn't at first identify. Then it came to her: utter conviction. Robbie's voice lacked that slight shift in pitch of words contrary to truth, a shift detectable both by electronic wavelength scanner and by aphasiacs who had lost all sense of words but not of vocal color. Every actor Caroline had ever heard, no matter how good, spoke at least some words with that faint undercolor of lies. Until now.

She strained to listen, sure she must be mistaken, too disoriented to be sure of anything at all.

> "Silent I cannot keep, I cannot tongue
> These strange calamities . . ."

Every phrase held a double meaning. The motel room in Wyoming rose before her: slashed curtains, overturned bureau, floor covered with glass. But Robbie could not possibly be drawing on the motel room for this performance—*silent I cannot keep*—he would never remember that room again. That was the whole point of what had been done to him. *All future things I see unerring . . .* Caroline shook her head. The future was there, in his words: the future, the past, the present, just beyond the reach of the spotlight, heavy crowding presences she could feel in every line of his chained body. Waiting.

It was not just her, not just what she remembered of the Rock End Motel and the Wyoming hospital. Almost wildly, Caroline looked around. The rest of the audience saw it, too. They sat hushed, rapt, hanging on words two and a half millennia old, on the pain of a story from the start of mythological time, on Robbie's voice rising and falling. No one moved. No one, it seemed to Caroline, breathed. She looked at the stage, and listened, and forgot the rest of the audience.

The entrance of the Chorus ruined it. Dressed in togas, seashells, and purple flowers, they shuffled across the stage in a hologram of a winged car, the clumsiest holo Caroline had ever seen. "Fear nothing," they told Prometheus in the tones of third-grade teachers assigning math. All around Caroline people jerked awake, blinked, looked at each other. Robbie couldn't carry the play alone. The Chorus stood so close to him that their hologram overlapped Prometheus's rock, giving it the appearance of having sprouted a left wing. Prometheus answered with grace and force, but his speeches were short and alternated with theirs. Caroline watched with disbelief; it was like craning one's neck at a tennis match between three cripples and a balletic flamethrower. The women grew even worse, stumbling over their lines, fumbling on their clay court in the face of Robbie's sheer heat.

He couldn't recapture the play until the end. Everyone else was too terrible. But even so, isolated lines pierced Caroline:

"Through me mankind ceased to foresee death . . .
Blind hopes I made to dwell in them."

Beside her, Shahid moved suddenly on his hard seat.

"Better for you not to know than to know.
It is not churlishness; I am loathe to bruise
your heart."

Loathe to bruise your heart. Caroline saw again her room at the Institute after Colin had just left it, Robbie's hand gentle under her elbow, his body firm against hers as he held her while they both sat on the floor and she fumbled with Catherine's letter in her right hand. *Better for you not to know than to know* . . .

"Do you want to leave?" Shahid whispered to her.

"No. No, I don't."

Loathe to bruise your heart. From the corner of her eye, she saw Joe McLaren.

He sat at the far right, against the cinder-block wall, in the second row. Even in the half light from the stage and in half profile, she recognized him by the aggressive way he sat: shoulders rolled forward, chin raised. A fighter's stance. His hair had grown longer over the last year. He sat alone, empty seats around him like a demilitarized zone.

"Speak, tell us all," someone said on stage. "To the sick it is sweet to know betimes what awaits them of pain."

Bullshit, Caroline thought. She looked away from Joe, at the stage. At first it was just a blur, colored around the edges where stage lights met the darkness, but then Robbie began to speak.

In contrast to the complex force of his previous speeches, he spoke simply, detailing terrible torments in a voice so natural the torments too seemed natural, inevitable, and thus even more cruel. The theater fell completely silent. Robbie had four long speeches, and throughout each there was no stage, no actors, no shabby theater: only Prometheus, foretelling things to come from his chains, a channel to a future he would never see. When lightning and thunder finally engulfed him, cheap holographic effects that broke the net of words, the audience blinked, and stirred, and looked at one another for a moment without recognition.

Caroline stumbled to her feet before the applause broke or the house lights came up. She made her way up the dark aisle to the empty lobby, waved Cassidy away, and leaned against a section of wall embedded with antique toasters like slitted barnacles. She tried to breathe evenly. In, one two three, out, one two three . . . the theater door opened on a wave of applause. She expected Patrick Shahid, but it was Joe.

"Are you all right?"

Caroline laughed weakly. "People keep asking me that. Yes. No. Of course I am. How are you, Joe?"

"Fine," he said. He didn't smile. Up close, she could see the changes in him.

"You're thinner."

"You're not."

"Still not one for compliments, are you?" Caroline said.

"Watching Robbie, you looked more beautiful than I've ever seen you. Or anyone."

She was surprised and amused. "I take it back. And you look very tan for New York in June. And what a stupid conversation this is."

He finally smiled. "I've been in California the last three months."

"Business? Pleasure?"

"Neither. My ex-wife needed help. And an old business associate of mine lives out there, too. Angel Whittaker."

"So you were visiting."

"Yes." For a moment his face showed strain, then it folded quietly into an expression new to him, some variety of calm Caroline couldn't dBase but found she liked. The theater doors opened and the first few people came out. Behind them still sounded scattered applause. Joe looked directly at her. "You arranged this play for Robbie, didn't you? Through your father."

Before Caroline could answer, Antonia Trego pushed through the crowd and laid a long, bony hand on her arm. The director's sharp black eyes, heavily made up in a face defiantly left to age at its natural rate, glittered.

"Caroline, how lovely to see you. Nobody told me you were in New York. You look wonderful, darling. And now that that's out of the way, are you going to tell me where Colin found this talented young protégé of his?"

"Hello, Antonia. This is Joe McLaren. Joe, Antonia Trego. I wish I could tell you, Antonia, but Colin didn't tell *me*. You know how Colin is."

Antonia tilted back her head and studied Caroline shrewdly. "I do. And so, I gather, do you. Again."

Caroline smiled without answering. Antonia Trego said, "I'm glad to hear it. One's family is simply not replaceable, no? And Colin is always so eager to help. At any rate, this young man, this 'Robbie Brekke'—terrible name—is very good. Quite extraordinary, in fact. There are rumors, of course. That he has had some kind of experimental brain operation. That it left him simpleminded.'

"I haven't heard any rumors."

"You are quite sure."

"Yes. Sorry."

"Do you know young Brekke?"

"No," Caroline said. She felt Joe's eyes on her. "We've never met."

"Ah," Antonia said, spreading both hands wide in wry defeat. Her gaze never left Caroline's face. "Well, then. There you have it. I must go; the young man's agent is trying most earnestly to waylay me, and I shall of course let her. Nice to have met you, Mr. McRalen. Caroline, give my love to Colin."

When she had gone, Joe said, "Are you going backstage?"

Caroline stared at him dumbly. She thought he would, must, know that she was not going to do that. Behind them, Cassidy waited patiently.

"You haven't seen him," Joe said slowly. "Not since the operation—have you? I thought . . ." He didn't say what he had thought. "You arranged all this for him, but you haven't seen him."

"All I arranged was an audition. Robbie did the rest himself. How often do you . . . see him?"

"Every time I've been in New York."

"You? Why?"

Joe smiled. "You mean, why me, when I ducked every connection with him I could for as long as I could? That is what you mean, isn't it? Come on with me, Caroline. Come back-stage."

"I'm here with Patrick Shahid, he wants to talk to me . . ."

"He'll wait. I saw him. He looks prepared to wait days to talk to you, if he has to."

Caroline nodded, meaning that *was* how Shahid looked, but Joe took the nod to mean that she would go backstage. He led the way. At the dressing room—ROBBIE BREKKE handprinted on white cardboard taped to the scarred and rickety door—Caroline groped for Joe's hand. He gave it immediately; his fingers felt warm and firm. At the first knock, Robbie himself opened the door.

"Joe! Come in!"

Still in makeup and his cheap costume, Robbie stood aside to let them pass, giving Caroline a friendly, impersonal smile.

Joe said, "This is Caroline Bohentin."

"Hello," Robbie said, holding out his hand. "I'm Robbie Brekke."

She felt herself taking his fingers with her free hand, the other tightening on Joe's, and had a sudden detached picture of the three of them, as if taken from a great height. Linked.

"It's nice to meet you, Caroline."

Joe said, "We enjoyed your performance."

The blue eyes sparkled. Caroline, mute, saw their vitality and unself-conscious pleasure. And behind the pleasure, the new flatness. The something missing. Gone. Taken away. What was it? Not intelligence, not charm.

"Thank you," Robbie said. "I was glad to get the part. Do you see a lot of theater, Caroline?"

She nodded, unable to speak. Robbie waited politely; when she said nothing more, he turned back to Joe. "Thanks for the book. It helps a lot."

"You're welcome."

"Joe made me a book," Robbie said to Caroline. "With pictures of people I know. If I haven't seen them for a few weeks, I forget them. I don't know if Joe told you that I have Korsakov's syndrome?"

Caroline shook her head.

"Yes," Robbie said. "A mild form. I can remember things for a few weeks before they fade. It doesn't affect my acting, of course, because I go over my lines every day. But I forget people and events." He smiled at her, his blue eyes serene. "It's not a big problem, really. I'm used to it. I was born with it."

A sound formed again in Caroline's throat. The dressing-room door opened and more people crowded in, all talking at once. She couldn't distinguish the words, none of them made any sense. Then she was being pulled through the lobby, Patrick Shahid was still there, she was out on the street, was walking into a bar between the two men.

The mist lifted. "Joe—I have my aircar. Where's Jason? And the bodyguard?"

Shahid said, "You dismissed them."

"I did?" She felt her neck; the diamond necklace was gone.

"You gave them your jewelry to take home. Sit down here, Caroline. You too, Joe. It's quiet here." The bar was ringed with cubicles draped in red velvet and linked by pretentious wooden walkways laid over red sand. She sank down next to Shahid, across the tiny table from Joe.

Joe said, "It's all right, Caroline. The first time I talked to him, I felt the same."

"He's like . . . a picture. Two-dimensional, shrunk down from three. Brilliant paint, clever perspective, tone and balance and all those good things, but it still feels flat when you touch it . . ."

Joe didn't deny it. "The only alternative was to leave him the way he was in Wyoming. He stayed that way for three months, you know, every time they brought him out of sedation."

"In Pirelli's 'memory loop.' "

"In his own memory loop. Caroline, don't cry."

"I'm not."

"All right, you're not." Joe let go of her hand. After a moment he added, "I think the induced Korsakov's is why he's such a good actor. The part is so real to him, so vivid, because nothing else is very real. Only what identities he invents in his head, and he doesn't invent as well as Aeschylus. So he takes that. Tonight he *was* Prometheus."

Shahid said, "And who are you tonight, Joe? Who are you every night? A lawyer still?" His voice was low and intense; surprised, Caroline turned her head to see his face. Shahid gazed hungrily across the table at Joe, his dark eyes like lasers

Joe said quietly, "I resigned from McLaren and Geisler nine months ago, except for a few cases that have personal meaning, such as defending a friend from a Special Custody Act charge that—now I'm with the Environmental Protection Agency. They revived it, you know, despite the Caswell administration's opposition, because of the microbe mess in Boston Harbor." His face darkened. "The engineered microbes they put in there to eat the pollution have mutated into something that attacks the alloys the pier pilings are made of—it's a mess. And it's *important*. It's just a forerunner of what we can expect unless the whole Gaeist movement is stopped cold."

"That will be impossible," Shahid said.

Joe scowled. "Why?"

"You will not stop the Gaeists. Not in the way you mean."

"Why not?"

"Who do you think the Gaeists are?"

"A self-serving political movement capable of destroying the ecology of the entire planet."

"Just so," Shahid said softly. "And what else?"

"And nothing else."

"I think you know better. They will succeed."

"No," Joe said, biting off each word, "they will not."

The two men stared fiercely at each other. Caroline

thought, *I'm missing something here*. The waiter brought their drinks, glanced at Shahid's face, and backed out of the cubicle, eyes averted. Caroline looked at Shahid. A cold prickling started at the base of her lungs.

Shahid said, " 'And the third part of the creatures which were in the sea and had life died; and the third part of the—' "

"Bullshit," Joe said, loudly.

"You recognize it."

"I was Catholic. But you already know that."

"What are you now?"

"Stop asking me that."

"All right—what were you then? Were you Armand Kyle in your previous life?"

None of them moved. Caroline was once again standing in the motel room in Wyoming, watching Robbie spout a jumble of dead lives, names, and disconnected requests and pleadings and orders, all of which Joe recognized. Every single one. But she, Caroline, had not asked him. Whatever the link between Robbie and Joe through every previous life, she would not have asked Joe about it. The past, she now knew, was an enormous weight, the weight of the entire earth, and there was no Atlas for hire.

But Shahid, Jesuit, was inexorable. "You haven't answered me, Joe. Were you Armand Kyle?"

Caroline said swiftly, "You don't have to answer that, Joe."

"I don't intend to."

Shahid said, "The datanet—"

"I never use the carnie net. I'm only entered three times, all early in my stay at the Institute."

"Bill Prokop—"

"—gave up months ago. No data on any net, anywhere. Poor sad bastard. Another victim of technological laissez-faire."

"Jeff Pirelli—"

"—is a friend."

"Did you tell him?"

"I have told him nothing. Which is what I've told you."

"But he guesses," Shahid said.

"Guessing is his profession."

"Then in your case he's not pursuing it?"

"There's nothing to pursue."

"Ah," Shahid said.

Caroline said, "For God's sake, Patrick, let it go!"

"I can't," Shahid said quietly. "He is the Christ."

Joe threw up a short bark of laughter.

"Not literally, of course," Shahid said. Suddenly, shockingly, he smiled, the old contained secret smile. "Despite what I quoted from Revelations. You don't by any chance recall being Jesus of Nazareth, Joe?"

"No."

"I didn't suppose so. It's not necessary."

Caroline said, "Patrick—you're not making sense."

"No, you're not," Joe said. He seemed to have regained his calm. He looked at Shahid with amusement. No, more than amusement, Caroline thought. With something that—in anyone else—she would have dBased as pity.

Shahid said intently, "You have not even thought about what has happened. Neither of you. You have had your multiple sclerosis cured, you have learned to handle your own memories, you have solved the problem of Robbie Brekke, and so you think the personal is all there is. The personal is *nothing.*"

"I don't accept that any longer," Joe said, and Caroline caught his phrasing.

"Yes, you do," Shahid said. "Dimly, but yes, you do accept that the personal is minor or you would not be pouring your energy into the fight against the Gaeists to save the ecology of the planet. But that too is minor. It's not really the battle you're fighting. The battle is larger, so much larger, and you won't even look at it. But you, Joe McLaren, aren't going to have any choice."

"Rot," Joe said again.

"You and Robbie Brekke. Linked over and over again. And Robbie was the first sacrifice. The first. A voice in the wilderness, leading the way—"

Joe laughed. "Robbie Brekke as John the Baptist? *Brekke?* Come on, Shahid, restrain that overheated Catholic imagination of yours."

"I've left the Church."

Caroline drew in a sharp breath. Shahid lay both hands flat on the table, palms down, his eyes still on Joe. "Three weeks ago I entered the Institute for Previous Life Access Surgery in Boston. I'm only in New York this weekend to tell Caroline. I didn't expect you to be with her; I didn't plan on seeking you myself until I finish at the Institute. Not until I can be of some use to you in the battle."

"Waiter!" Joe called. "Check!"

"Patrick," Caroline said, "you haven't even had time to learn to handle your own memories. You of all people know you shouldn't be here yet, you need more time—" She stopped. Shahid looked down at his spread hands. She couldn't see his eyes.

Finally he looked up. "I haven't had any memories yet. But that's not important. Joe, you're the one who has to listen to your memories. And to me. I know you already know much of this from your friend Pirelli. Yes, I researched him. I researched everything. That's what we Jesuits learn to do.

"The racial memory is evolving. It is evolving to do what the biosphere Gaea already does: protect life on the planet. Gaea manipulates a sea reef here, methane output there—why? To keep earth viable for life. It uses whatever is there to correct imbalances in the biosphere so life may evolve. And just the same—*just the same*—the over-memory manipulates people into reincarnation surgery. Robbie Brekke here, Joe McLaren there—people who would never choose such surgery on their own. Why? To protect its own life, its own evolution, threatened by a worldwide memory plague and a falling birth rate. To correct imbalances. To fight for the survival of its part of life on the planet.

"Do you see yet? Gaea and the over-memory, taken together, are fighting to save the human race by transforming it into something better. To *save* us, despite ourselves. To redeem us."

Caroline said, "Oh, no, Patrick, you're not thinking that Gaea and the over-memory . . ."

"If their purpose is salvation and redemption, what else would you call it but God?"

Joe said, more gently than Caroline would have expected, "Why not call it evolution? Why try to fit it to some preset irrational mold? I'm sorry, Shahid, but this just doesn't interest me." He stood in the narrow space between the table and the velvet curtains. Shahid let go of Caroline's hand, reached for Joe's wrist, and wrapped his hand around it. Joe looked down at the wrist expressionlessly. To Caroline, Shahid's fingers looked small and skinny.

"The Gaeists are opposing evolution itself," Shahid said quietly. "They don't know it, most of them, as individuals. They think the planet can handle anything, or they think they follow a warm sentimental Mother Goddess. But you are right, Joe, about the pollution, the destruction, the danger they present to life itself, forever. Satan takes many wayward forms, especially in the time of the end."

"So does man," Joe said. "Thanks for the drink. Sorry I'm not interested in being the next Redeemer."

"Neither was Christ at one point," Shahid said calmly. "But the battle will come. It will start to happen soon. People who have had surgery and think they've now mastered the past, people like you, will start to feel it, the new form of life growing strong enough to save us all from planetary destruction. Like Robbie Brekke. And some of them will be lost, as some foot soldiers always are. But not all. Some will survive the transformation, and the new force will emerge, led by someone close to the source, the start, the beginning—"

"But not me," Joe said with complete conviction. He unwrapped Shahid's fingers from his wrist. "Caroline, are you coming?"

Caroline looked up at Joe. He held out his hand and something stirred in her, not a memory. But how could she leave Patrick? She glanced helplessly at Shahid.

He was *smiling*.

"Go on, Caroline," he said softly, reasonably. "I'm fine. Go after him."

"Are you sure? I—"

"I'm sure."

Caroline leaned forward to kiss Shahid on the cheek; he surprised her by kissing her back, a kiss as light and dry as paper. "I'll call you in the morning," she said. He nodded.

She put her hand in Joe's.

Shahid finished his drink slowly. When he left, it was midnight. Broadway was hysterical holographic chaos: whole building fronts changing every thirty seconds, words swooping through the air in electronic arcs, bars and HOLO DANCERS! and flower shops and Korean restaurants and LATEST DATA! and Arab jewelry souks and Colombian chocolates and BRAINIES! NEW! IMPROVED! STRONG!

He walked toward Times Square. The renovation had been finished only a year ago, and then the Square had been permanently closed to all but foot traffic. People jammed the huge lighted space, even at this hour, strolling and eating and laughing and arguing and stealing. Aircars flew overhead, the surviving pigeons fluttered below. Halfway to his hotel, the brandnew Ricoh Plaza, a bright globe of light exploded four feet in front of Shahid. The white light turned into a holographic figure: a woman in white, ten feet tall, kneeling with her arms full of blue-green roses, pink ocean diatoms, and a single hypodermic needle. The resolution was remarkable. The woman's upturned face smiled radiantly: the Gaeist movement's thankful advertisement for the memory-plague vaccine. Which they considered to have been produced as just one more instance of biosphere regulation that just happened to use the agency of human minds. Within ten seconds, the holo had vanished.

Shahid's room overlooked Times Square. He set the window for maximum opacity and knelt by the bed. A childhood habit, then an aid to concentration, and, when he was a teenager, an obdurate denial of secular comfort embraced by an Order Loyola had meant to burn with ascetic passion. In seminary, knowing his kneeling to be a defiance more showy than substantial, he had stopped it. That had taught him the substantive power of outward show.

That Joe McLaren should deny the role chosen for him, Shahid thought, mattered nothing. It was not, after all, given to humankind to do the choosing. Joe's arrogance, the common arrogance of the atheist, was immaterial. His, Shahid's, was not.

He wanted to be part of the coming great apocalyptic battle. For that, he had left the Church that had shown him the battle was possible. In that, he stood condemned of arrogance.

He wanted to be mentor, guide, to what Joe would become. Disciple, yes—that, too, when the time came. But first of all, mentor, the one who knew more. In that, he stood condemned of arrogance.

He wanted to be right about what would happen: right not with the knowledge of faith, that must always make a leap across darkness, but right with the data-supported certainty of intellectual science. From that desire, he would not even consider the secular reading of events that Joe himself had offered.

There must be more than evolution, more than humankind alone, at stake for the battle to be large enough—showy enough—for Patrick Martin Shahid. Did there exist any greater arrogance than that?

Yes. He wanted to be Joe.

Shahid put his face in his hands. Jealousy petty enough to wound his arrogance, arrogance deep enough to drown him. Where were the memories? Three weeks since his surgery and nothing recalled, nothing remembered. For this he had broken his vows, broken with Rome . . . for this path that had led him nowhere, to nothing. Nothing but the arrogance of his own mind, the nothingness of his own being. A deserved nothingness, because he had relied on his own superior reasoning about the future of the whole world, relied on his faith that because of his superior reasoning and vision, the over-memory would use him. Relied on his own arrogance. You could not be used by a great power if you did not surrender your own.

Where were the memories?

Wearily, Shahid rose from his knees. He could not pray. Since the surgery, he had been unable to pray. That was the worst.

He returned to the window and changed its setting back to transparent. Seventeen floors below, Times Square seethed with nocturnal humanity. This far up, individual identities blurred. The square might have been in Karachi, destroyed in the last revolution, when he had fled Pakistan. It might have been in Brasilia, in Paris, in Tokyo, in St. Louis . . .

He stood in a square in St. Louis, holding a pair of gold crescent earrings, staring at that damn fool kid Mallie Callahan who had actually moll-buzzed them on a trolley . . .

Shahid gasped. He put one hand against the window. Below, people surged in waves of color.

He opened the bedroom door, tiptoed into the darkness, saw in the rectangle of light from the hallway that Janet had

fallen asleep holding Timmy. The little boy must have had
another of those darn earaches . . .

In Times Square the waves of color blurred and rocked,
pitching him forward against the window.

He held the dying man tight on the cot in the volunteer
shelter and whispered, "It's all right, Paul, I'm glad you told
me, I don't care who you were or what happened, it's all
right . . ."

Below, the colors steadied and once more separated themselves into individual people. Separate people, each with a
past, an eternal life. People, not God.

Or were they? Arrogance, Revelation . . .

Shahid staggered to his feet, staring down at the people
scurrying across Times Square.

And the memories came.